THE MEMORY OF EVA RYKER

THE MEMORY OF EVA RYKER

DONALD A. STANWOOD

Coward, McCann and Geoghegan, Inc.
New York

For permission to quote from copyrighted material the author wishes to thank the following:
Screen Gems-EMI Music, Inc., for a line from "Surf City" by Brian Wilson and Jan Berry. Copyright © 1963 Screen Gems-EMI Music, Inc. Used by permission. All rights reserved.

SBN: 698–10876–0

Library of Congress Cataloging in Publication Data

Stanwood, Donald A
    The memory of Eva Ryker.

    1. Titanic (Steamship)—Fiction. I. Title.
PZ4.S79344Me [PS3569.T3343] 813′.5′4 77–23897

PRINTED IN THE UNITED STATES OF AMERICA

To
Pat Kubis
Lawrence Watkin
John Schwarz
and especially to
Viege Traub

PART I

The Pieces

1

November 30, 1941

My first meeting with Martha Klein was nearly fatal for both of us.

I was herding my patrol car up over the Pali Highway, not paying much attention to the road. Clouds had grumbled at me all the way up the Nuuanu Valley, but once I passed the Pali Lookout, they gave up without a fight. It looked like a regular tourist-poster morning.

Jimmy Wong, the HPD dispatcher, had made me the same promise at five A.M., when I arrived at Headquarters. "Beautiful day, kid."

I stopped at his desk and blinked at the charcoal sky beyond the windows. "Yeah, Sarge."

"Say, how's Louise coming along?"

"Eight months, eleven days."

"You make that kid of yours sound like a time bomb."

"It is."

He laughed. "Norm, how'd you like to get away from the Honolulu traffic? Get a little sunshine and fresh air."

"Some sort of scut work, no doubt."

Wong grinned breezily. "I just thought you might like to drive over to Laie. The Mormons had their big hukilau last

7

night and . . . well, somebody—kids probably—raised some hell around the Tabernacle. Broken windows, some four-letter words on the walls. Nobody saw anything, but the Church is pretty upset and the Captain promised we'd send somebody over."

I adjusted the brim of my cap. "It's fifty miles to Laie and back."

"So? You're not going by taxi. God knows we won't need you downtown. You know what Sundays are like." His grin grew stale around the edges. "Besides, maybe the Mormons will put in a good word for you. I've never seen you miss a chance to suckle up to the Captain."

"What's the matter, Sarge? On the rag again?"

Wong pretended not to have heard. "Don't get me wrong, Norm. Nobody wants to be a patrolman forever. Much less you college kids . . . "

"What a crock," I snorted. "Five months on the force and you've got me running for governor."

"Please, Norm. No bullshit," he said cheerfully. "I caught that lean and hungry look the first day you walked through that door. And, every day since then, your ribs have been getting skinnier."

His words sulked in a corner of my skull as I eased the car down the S-bends snaking toward Kaneohe Bay. Giving up their retreat, the clouds brooded and poured. I swore and fiddled with the wipers as the Chevy swerved around the cliff face.

She came out of nowhere, congealing from the rain. Waving her arms right in my path.

I tromped the pedal to the floor. The woman screamed even louder than the brakes, her body flashing past the flanks of the car.

Rubber burned and rock chips flew as I leaned against the side window, watching the road wheel in circles beyond my windshield.

What was it the books said about turning *into* a skid?

My hands scrambled on the spinning spokes and the car cartwheeled to a long sliding stop.

Hands clenched on the wheel, I peered stupidly through the windshield. The hood ornament pointed at rolling gray clouds. I glanced out the side windows and was reassured to find myself still on solid ground.

With the care of a jeweler cutting a diamond, I shifted into reverse and gave it some gas. The rear tires chirped, then gained confidence, and hauled the Chevy back to even footing on the highway.

Yanking the emergency brake, my ears filled with the drumming of raindrops on the hood. And a different sort of tapping on the right window.

For a second I'd forgotten her. She pounded on the glass, pointing at the door latch.

"Jesus Christ, ma'am!" I said, flipping the handle. "What's the matter? You could have . . . "

My words stopped as she leaned toward me and I got a good look at her face. I'd never seen such terror in anyone's eyes.

"My husband!" She cried, fighting for breath. "Down the road! I tried . . . I tried to stop . . . "

"Get in." I waved her to silence and pushed open the door. "How far?"

She settled in the seat, gazing blankly at me. "Uh . . . I was running . . . no one came . . . "

"How far down the road!"

" . . . God, I . . . "

"Never mind." I slammed the door and floored the Chevy around the next bend in the highway.

The siren moaned to life as I took the corners with tires screeching. The clouds were playing possum again, but the road remained spit-slick.

Still no signs of an accident. I sneaked a second glance at the woman.

Early fifties. Unpleasingly plump. Mousy brown-blonde. Blue eyes and tears running in pink streaks over rouged cheeks. The best thing I could do for her was to keep my eyes on the road.

I spotted the wreck. Skid marks careened across the highway to a '35 Ford canted by the cliff side. Through the cracked windshield I could see a crumpled form behind the wheel.

The woman bolted upright at the sight of the car. "I ran as fast as I could! Running for help . . . I knew he needed a doctor . . . he looked . . . "

He was. I was glad I made her stay behind.

The deceased was in his late fifties or early sixties. I leaned through the side window, feeling his throat for a pulse. His flesh was already cooling to my touch.

The windshield cracks matched the egg shell fissures on his forehead. His skull looked as pulpy and unformed as an infant's. Through the blood the eyes stared in bland surprise.

I clamped my teeth shut against the vomit rising in my throat and walked back to the car.

She looked up at me for the verdict. But I didn't feel like playing a I-Don't-Know-How-To-Tell-You-This scene. Instead, I reached for the radio mike and gave Central Dispatch the story.

The radio rattled its reply: "Roger, Car 48. We'll send an ambulance and tow truck. Lieutenant Galbraith is coming up, too."

"Okay. I'll stay with Mrs. . . . uh . . . "

" . . . Klein," the woman mumbled without expression. "Martha Klein."

I repeated her words into the mike.

"Roger, Car 48. Out."

The radio's crackling stopped, the silence forcing me to face her.

"I'm . . . I'm very sorry, Mrs. Klein. Sometimes . . . you can't . . . "

"Yes, Officer, I know."

"The ambulance should be here soon. I hope you don't mind . . . "

"No. I don't mind."

"There are some questions I need to ask."

Mrs. Klein didn't reply.

"Are you a resident of Hawaii?" I said.

She stared at the body across the highway.

"Mrs. Klein, I know how you feel . . . "

"Do you?" The eyes were cool and dead, as if shock had burned them out. "My husband's been murdered and you know how I feel."

The word rolled around in my mouth before I actually spoke. "Murdered."

She nodded.

"Mrs. Klein, you're very upset . . . "

"Officer . . . "

" . . . Hall."

" . . . I'm stating a fact. Someone killed my husband. Poisoned him."

"Who?"

Her jaw grew stubborn with the silence. "I don't know."

I wondered if it was too late to head for Laie and the Mormons. "All right, Mrs. Klein. Tell me what happened this morning."

"We're from St. Petersburg, Albert and me. Florida. We checked in yesterday at the Moana. Anyway, after breakfast Al and I rented that car and headed up the highway. We passed the Pali. He figured we'd drive on for a bit.

"We were rounding a curve a mile or so back when Al said he didn't feel so good. I told him it was probably just indigestion. He said maybe so.

"Al worried me. He looked kind of pale. And he was sweating. I said maybe he should pull over.

"He told me not to act foolish, then he let out a little scream, sort of, and bent over the wheel. His foot jammed on the gas. The car weaved from side to side. His face was so pale. Like ice. His fingers clung to the wheel."

Her head shook. "I tried to pull him loose. His arms were like iron.

"He fell over on his side . . . throwing up. Over and over. Clawing at his throat. The car went off the road, into the ditch . . . " Her voice trailed off.

"Mrs. Klein?"

"That's all I know." She turned her back to me. "I ran and found you. But it was too late."

I didn't say anything. A meadowlark trilled gaily in a near-by tree.

"Mrs. Klein, did your husband have any heart trouble? Fainting spells?"

"No! Al was always healthy."

"But he wasn't a young man any longer, was he?"

"No, I suppose not." She glared at me in the resentful way older people reserve for the young. "But do you think I don't know my own husband? You have no idea what we've been through together. We were newlyweds on the *Titanic*. Two kids, twenty and eighteen. I refused a place in the boats when everyone knew the ship was gone. We jumped over-board and were picked up in separate boats. Hour after hour, not knowing if my husband was alive or dead . . . " Her lips bit down on the words. "Officer Hall, my husband did not have 'heart trouble.' He was murdered!"

"Why?"

Her voice was mechanical. "All I know is that something was worrying him. He received strange phone calls just be-fore we left. He was always moving the telephone into the other room, away from me. I started answering first, but they hung up."

The whole thing sounded rather lurid, but I kept quiet as she searched her memory.

"A few days later I saw a man standing across from our apartment building. He didn't move. The only time he left for long periods was when Al left the house on errands."

"Could you describe him?"

"Dark. And tall . . . " One hand tightened its grip around the armrest. "I don't know. Maybe later . . . "

I nodded. "By the way, why did you come to Hawaii?"

"It was Al's idea. He was almost frantic about getting away. We took the Pan Am Clipper. This was only our first stop." She couldn't keep a little of the world-traveler tone from her voice. "We were taking a Pacific tour. Samoa, Tahiti, the Phil-ippines . . . "

I listened carefully and decided she was serious. "Mrs. Klein, don't you read the papers?"

"Why no, not very often." Her voice was calm and uninterested. "Whatever are you talking about?"

This wasn't the moment for a crash course in world politics. "Never mind. Did your husband act any different when you were away from St. Petersburg?"

"He seemed . . . relieved, sort of. I forgot about the phone calls and strange men."

"Until now."

"You've got to find them, Officer!"

" 'Them?' "

"The people who killed my husband. Poisoned him."

This had gone far enough. "Now, Mrs. Klein . . . "

The tearful eyes locked with mine. "You've got to believe me!"

"No." I shook my head. "I'm sorry, but I need more than your faith. Two months ago a very kind, earnest woman came into Headquarters and demanded we set up a twenty-four hour watch to protect her pet poodle from the Chinese Tong. Ever since, I've been damn wary of heartfelt pleas."

Her fingers reached around my wrist. "I'm sorry if I sound like a . . . a crackpot. But my husband is dead. He was not sick. Everything I've told you is the truth."

I didn't answer her at first, and in the silence we heard the sirens. We both sat and listened.

"You'll have to stay in Honolulu for a few days," I finally said. "There'll be questions to answer."

Mrs. Klein looked ready for burial herself. "Oh Lord, not now. Maybe tonight? I'm very tired."

"All right. We'll send someone to your hotel later. I guess you'll want to be alone to think things out. There'll be details to arrange."

Martha Klein nodded, not listening.

The sirens grew frantic as the ambulance, tow truck, and unmarked patrol car swung into view and braked on the soft shoulder. The noise drooped to a growl as I pulled away from her grasp.

"Excuse me," I said, stepping into the sunlight.

Two white-coated men wrangled with a gleaming stretcher and ambled to the Ford.

Lieutenant Galbraith walked from the car to meet me. He was tall and rumpled and looked as old as the morning was new.

"Morning, Norman. How's the woman?"

"Holding up pretty fair, sir." Then I thought again. "Actually, she's sort of rattled. She wonders if we could wait until tonight to get a statement."

"Hell, yes." His shoulders shrugged thinly beneath the plaid jacket. "You're taking her to the hotel?"

"Yes, sir."

Galbraith started for the wreck, then looked over his shoulder. "Did she say much?"

Martha Klein watched the men load her husband on the stretcher. Her face was turned from me.

"No, sir," I answered. "Nothing useful."

2

Nearly twelve hours later I was patroling Kapiolani Boulevard, piddling away the final minutes of my ungodly long shift. I wheeled the Chevy right at Kalakaua Avenue, heading for the beach. The sunset reflected in red ragged streaks across the black hood. It was the time of evening when you can't decide whether or not to switch on your headlights. I switched mine on, hoping to set an example.

The radio cut in on my thoughts. "Calling Car 48."

I reached for the mike. "Car 48 here."

"Got one last job for you, Norman," said Sergeant Wong. "Galbraith wants that statement from Mrs. Klein. She's waiting at the Moana. Room 307. Drop by and bring her in."

I swallowed my irritation. "Roger. Car 48 out."

The Moana's doorman looked distressed as I slid the patrol car under the main porte-cochère.

"No trouble, I hope." It wasn't a question.

"Nothing to worry about," I said over my shoulder.

The desk clerk had the same question as the doorman and I gave him the same answer. He looked unconvinced but kept quiet.

The third-floor hallway was completely deserted. Only

faint noises filtering from behind the doors hinted at human habitation. Gurgling water. Squeaking mattresses. Clattering dinner dishes.

I rapped on the door of 307. "Mrs. Klein, this is Patrolman Hall."

Inside, a dreamy chorus was working its way through "When You Wish Upon a Star."

I waited, then knocked again.

"Mrs. Klein?"

My hand twisted the knob. It wasn't locked. I pushed the door open.

"Mrs. Klein? It's Patrolman Hall. Are you there?"

Fading orange sunbeams peeked between the gap in the drapes.

The music came from a hulking Philco console. Its dial glowed feebly in the gloom. A group began playing "Song of the Islands." The electric guitars moaning from the radio's belly sounded like dying mattress springs.

I pulled back the curtains, exposing rumpled covers of an unmade bed. The sheets had a slept-in smell.

My hands groped for the bathroom switch. White tile glared under the light. The basin and tub were scrubbed and unused.

Back in the bedroom a tenor was singing something about the waiting palms of Waikiki. I reached for the phone on the end table. The receiver buzzed dully as I stared out the window. Waikiki Beach was rusty amber, a smattering of Tiki torches fluttering to life along its length.

"Main desk," a man said. "May I help you?"

"Yes, this is Patrolman Hall . . . "

" . . . Yes?" It was a Who-The-Hell-Are-You voice.

"I came by your desk a few minutes ago."

"Oh!" Alarm followed recognition. "Is anything wrong?"

"No, I don't think so. I was supposed to meet Martha Klein here. Has she gone out?"

"No, Officer, she hasn't checked out here, if that's what you mean."

"Okay. If she comes by in the next few minutes, tell her I'm waiting in her room."

"Yes, Officer, I certainly will."

To kill time, I began poking through drawers. No sign of cold cream, hair curlers, or any of the junk women collect wherever they spend the night.

I opened the heavy closet door, revealing three smart but worn suits. A Samsonite pullman sat neatly beneath the racks. Hooked to the inside closet door was a matching woman's dress carrier.

I glanced at my watch. Nearly six. If there was any justice in the world, I'd be home right now. I lit a cigarette, sat in a rattan chair and waited.

"Song of the Islands" mercifully quit. "This is radio KGMB." The voice had the assurance of Jehovah. "Coming up now, we have the voice of Bing Crosby singing 'Aloha Oe.'"

Ukeleles and strings swooned. *"Proudly swept the rain cloud by the cliff . . . "*

My cigarette burned down like a fuse as I scowled at the radio. The sky was blackening beyond the window and the lone light from the bathroom cast dingy silhouettes slanting across the carpet.

" . . . as on it glided through the trees . . . "

To hell with this. I went to the phone and dialed Headquarters.

"Central Dispatch. Sergeant Kroger speaking."

"This is Hall, Car 48. Is Sergeant Wong there?"

"He just went home, Norman. What happened to you? Your radio break down again?"

"No, sir. I was supposed to pick up Martha Klein, but she's not here. Did Sergeant Wong get his wires crossed?"

"It's news to me. Galbraith's been waiting for the last hour."

"Well, she didn't check out at the front desk." Casually, I looked around the room, then stopped still.

"Norman?" the receiver whispered. "Are you there?"

I ignored the voice. Something was wrong. A flicker of movement in the corner of my eye. Now it was gone. I turned back to the phone.

" . . . Uh, just a minute, sir. There's something I want to check out."

" . . . *still following with grief the Liko* . . . "

I examined every corner for a second glimpse of what I'd seen. The room yawned at my efforts.

Then I saw it. The dress carrier was swinging silently on its closet hook. Swinging where there was no breeze.

" . . . *one fond embrace* . . . "

Reaching behind me, I dropped the receiver. The little voice clicked to silence. Only the radio played.

" . . . *Thus sweet memories came back to me* . . . "

The carrier still moved. It looked bottom-heavy, like a half-full potato sack.

" . . . *bringing first remembrance of the past* . . . "

Walking to the closet, I grappled over my head for the pull cord. My shoes slapped wetly on the floor and my nose picked up a seawater smell.

" . . . *Dearest one, yes thou art mine own* . . . "

My fingers found the chain and yanked it.

" . . . *From thee true love shall ne'er depart.* . . . "

The bulb swung metronome-fast over my head. Clothes hanger shadows shifted back and forth, covering, then revealing a rusty blood puddle beneath my feet. A fresh spot spattered red on shiny black shoe leather. Another. And another. The stream came from the dress carrier's bottom.

" . . . *Aloha oe* . . . "

I tore at the carrier's zipper. The seam split in half.

Blood splashed through the gap and over my face. It covered my eyes.

" . . . *Aloha oe* . . . "

Fingers emerged from the bag and touched my shoulder. I grabbed blindly and clenched the wrist, which swung free in my hand.

" . . . *Eke-o-na-o-na-no-ho-i-ka-li-po.* . . . "

Another arm brushed my cheek. The weight forced me back. I clung to the dress carrier. It snapped off the hook, landing on me.

" . . . *A fond embrace* . . . "

Pushing off the floor, I felt slimy pulp underneath my palm. My tongue lolled around the inside of my mouth. I spit out a bile taste.

" . . . *before I* . . . "

Blood. Blinding me. Thick and dark between my lashes, gumming them shut.

My hands patted the wet carpet, stopping when I found a sphere about the weight of a medicine ball.

Cradling it in one arm, I wiped my eyes. Shiny blood spread over the carpet. A foot. But not mine. Attached to a leg.

It wasn't real. Some goddam nightmare. A monstrous practical joke!

" . . . *now depart* . . . "

What a gag! Just dye and arms and legs and rubber tripe you buy in a joke shop. One hell of a stunt!

" . . . *until we* . . . "

My face grew red and puffy with laughter and I held the ball to my chest. As my fingers ran over its surface, I felt a nose. And lips.

" . . . *meet again* . . . "

I pushed aside mousy brown curls. Two eyes glared through the red matted strands.

"That was Bing Crosby on KGMB," the voice said. "Now, for the six o'clock news . . . "

The six o'clock news. Six o'clock. The words circled around my head. Six o'clock. I should be home! Dinner's waiting.

The Philco was brisk and all-knowing. "Secretary of State Cordell Hull announced today . . . "

I'd never heard anything like the scream coming from my throat.

Flung across the room, the head hit the window, cracking the pane and rolling along the bed sheets.

The announcer cleared his throat. " . . . remains hopeful concerning the current negotiations with Japanese ambassadors Nomura and Kurusu. However . . . "

I ran. Leaving an open door. Trailing red footprints. Past the shut-up rooms. Ignoring the screaming and shouting behind me. Down the stairs. Tripping over steps. Through the lobby. Tearing from gaping faces and grabbing hands. Into the night. Dodging the red pulsing light and squawking radio of my patrol car. Stumbling through the black sand. Fleeing the following voices and footsteps. Away from the Force and my future.

Running from the salt-brine smell of blood.

From the Honolulu *Star-Bulletin*

December 6, 1941

HPD FINDS KLEIN POISON VICTIM

An autopsy by the Honolulu Police Department of Albert Klein, the late husband of murder victim Martha Klein, has revealed the cause of death as deliberate poisoning.

"Nicotine sulfate was the substance we found in Mr. Klein's bloodstream," explained Coroner Ralph Krumins in a joint press conference with Police Commissioner John Davis late Friday night. "It's a very rare poison that's difficult to detect if you're not looking for it."

Krumins explained that there were no recent marks or punctures on the body.

"We must assume that the poison was administered orally. It would have taken effect very quickly after swallowing. Fifteen minutes at most."

Commissioner Davis had harsh words for Patrolman Norman Hall, who first talked with Martha Klein after her husband's death and later discovered Mrs. Klein's body at the Moana Hotel. He termed Hall's fleeing from the murder scene as "cowardly."

"When we finally found Hall," Davis said, "he confessed that Martha Klein had claimed that her husband was murdered. His excuse was that Mrs. Klein was distraught and had no evidence to back up her accusations. Thus he refused to pass on Martha Klein's testimony either to Inspector Frank Galbraith, who was immediately at the accident site, or to any other superior officer."

Davis admitted that Hall found Martha Klein's body under "distressing circumstances," but condemned the fact that Hall panicked and left his car.

"He showed no inclination of reporting the murder to Headquarters. Hall just wandered the streets until another patrol car found him. I believe Hall acted in a shameful manner and will testify to that effect at the inquiry of his performance, which convenes Monday."

Davis added that Hall is to be suspended from all HPD duties pending the inquiry's findings.

Questioned at HPD Headquarters immediately following Commissioner Davis' announcement, Hall ignored the pleas of his legal counselor, Alex Nichols, to refuse comment.

"I'll be there to answer all questions the Board of Inquiry may put to me," the young patrolman stated. "I have nothing to hide. There's nothing I *can* hide. But, whatever the verdict, I intend to resign from the Force after the inquest."

The patrolman's father, Jerome Hall, a Honolulu importer, refused to speak with reporters, as did Hall's wife, Louise.

HPD investigators are still searching for witnesses and leads concerning the brutal November 30 murder of Martha Klein. Wanted for questioning is Catherine Maurois, a maid at the Moana Hotel who left on sick call the night of the slaying.

She was reported missing the following day by Claudine Maurois, her daughter.

According to Commissioner Davis, Mrs. Maurois is 49, a brunette, five foot five, and weighs approximately 155 pounds.

"We've filed no charges against Mrs. Maurois. We're interested only in questioning her. We welcome any information concerning her whereabouts."

Police investigators still offer few theories concerning Martha Klein's assailant.

"We do know some facts," Coroner Krumins explained. "Martha Klein was shot in the back with a small .25-caliber handgun. We found the slug during the autopsy. No one reported any shots, so it's likely that the gun had a silencer."

Krumins seemed less eager to speculate upon the grisly dismemberment and disembowlment of the body. "If it wasn't a psychopathic act, I don't know what is," he snapped. "Patrolman Hall could offer very little useful information, but when the lab technicians arrived, they found limbs and major internal organs scattered over the room. The remains were wrapped in a rubber sheet, then stuffed in a dress carrier. Even the head had been defaced beyond recognition. The only way we could positively identify Martha Klein was by her fingerprints, which matched those on her passport and other belongings."

Krumins stated that a man is a probable suspect, since such an act required great strength.

"However, hysteria can produce incredible physical energy," he said. "Even in a woman. We cannot overlook all possibilities."

3

January 8, 1962

Reprinted from the dust jacket of *The Death Watch Beetle*, courtesy of Random House. Copyright 1961.

Norman Hall was a twenty-year-old patrolman in the Honolulu Police Department when he witnessed the Japanese attack on Pearl Harbor. Four years later, as a sergeant in Patton's Third Army, he saw action from Bastogne to Berlin.

Remaining in Europe after the war, he became a stringer for Reuters and then UPI. His personal experiences in both the Pacific and Atlantic theaters of World War II provided the background for his first three novels. *The First Sunday in December,* dealing with Pearl Harbor and its aftermath, *Through the Shadow of Death,* an examination of GI's in the Third Army, and *From the Ashes*, with its background of postwar Germany, have sold more than 5,500,000 copies.

Hall's successes continued in the 1950s. *The Web He Wove,* concerned with a Supreme Court judge caught in a McCarthyite smear campaign, won the National Book Award and topped the bestseller list for seven months.

With the collaboration of his wife, Janice Steiner, Hall has written several popular nonfiction works, notably *Opening in Theaters and Drive-Ins Near You*, a survey of the American film industry, as well as successful biographies of D. W. Griffith, Field Marshall Montgomery, and Pierre Laval. Hall is a frequent contributor of fiction to *Playboy* and the *Saturday Evening Post*, and of nonfiction to *Life*, *Look*, the *New Yorker*, and *Punch*.

Hall has one son by a previous marriage. He and his wife live in the village of Fourqueux, just outside Paris.

Last night I dreamed about Martha Klein.

It doesn't happen very often. Not anymore. There was a time, during the Inquest, when sleep was a personal enemy I fought every night.

Of course, that was years ago. Between then and now is the War, a divorce, remarriage, and my work. All of which makes a pretty fair padding to absorb the jolt of old memories. But, once in a while, the nightmares still come back.

Lying face down in bed, I listened to my pulse slow to a normal idle. My hand patted the crumpled percale. Jan was up early.

Sleeping late is one of the pastimes my wife and I usually share. I turned on my side and burrowed my head in the pillow.

The phone rang and Jan's footsteps thumped across the living room floor in response. My ears caught the phrase "We'll be there" before she hung up.

The footsteps came my way. A fist nudged me in the ribs.

"Wake up."

"Go away. I gave at the office."

"Come on, Norman." She tabbed off the electric blanket. "Time to leave the womb."

"The last thing I need in the morning is paperback Freud." I snuggled into the covers. "By the way, where is 'there?'"

"Huh?"

"As in 'we'll be there.' On the phone."

"The Rotunde. We're meeting Geoffrey Proctor for lunch."

I braved one eye outside the border of the electric blanket and saw she wasn't kidding. Every time we meet a publisher Janice wears one of her no-bullshit tailored suits. The kind Adrian designed for Joan Crawford. Dark green this time.

"You win." I flopped out of bed and padded to the bathroom. "What's Geoffrey want?"

"An article from you, apparently. For *World* magazine."

"God forbid." Hot water steamed over my razor as I leaned into the mirror, counting the broken veins in my eyes.

Jan leaned against the door. "You want any breakfast?"

"Just coffee." I took a second look in the mirror. "A quiet prayer wouldn't hurt either."

She nodded in agreement and headed for the kitchen.

After showering, I rummaged through my closet. What suit? The black? God, no. Combined with Jan's outfit we'd look like embalmers. I compromised on the gray with the red tie.

I sat at the dining room table as Jan poured the coffee. "Well, how do I look?"

She threw out the paper filter from the Chemex decanter, then glanced over the kitchen counter. "Dissipated. A little decadent. Byronic darkness in the eyes. Like Papa or, no . . . I've got it!" She snapped her fingers. "Scott Fitzgerald in *Beloved Infidel.*"

"Jesus." I sipped the coffee and added more cream.

"Don't worry. Geoffrey likes the look of shaggy genius."

"I'll try to be suitably unruly." I finished the coffee and rinsed the cup. "You about ready?"

Jan headed for the bathroom. "In a minute."

'In a minute' turned out to be ten. She was still fiddling with her face as the Silver Wraith convertible crunched across the gravel forecourt and snoozed down the tree-lined road leading toward the Autoroute.

"Norman, either I am misreading your sleepy Oscar Levant expression . . ."

". . . Or?"

". . . You're looking very lukewarm over the prospect of going back to work."

"My dear, I will eat a fattening lunch and listen to Geoffrey Proctor's hard sell. And then we shall see. In the meantime, we play it cool and dumb . . ."

". . . 'an unappreciated fine art.' Yes, I know."

"And please remember." I glanced over my shoulder, then launched the Rolls up the Autoroute ramp. "We don't turn anything down until he's paid the check."

We arrived at the Rotunde by eleven-thirty, but Geoffrey had still beaten us to the draw. I spotted him at a window table as we waited for the concierge to seat the people ahead of us.

The dining room was packed with worshipers of the French belly religion. A waiter wove between the tables with a brandy-induced inferno perched on a silver platter. I couldn't quite identify the delicacy behind all the flames, but it looked something like the Golden Calf from *The Ten Commandments.*

Jan was amused by my expression. "Just like Mother used to make?"

"Yeah. I have a sudden urge for a cheeseburger and fries."

The concierge's distant smile changed to an eager grin when I pointed Geoffrey out. Yes, of course! Mr. Proctor told me to expect you. Right this way!

Geoffrey's antenna picked us up before we got to the table. He advanced on me with teeth smiling and hands outstretched.

"Jesus Christ, Norman! How long has it been?"

"Three years, Jeff. Good to see you." His palm was tight and dry. Geoffrey Proctor is silvery and tan, like those fiftyish men who age gracefully in *Esquire* ads.

I helped Jan in her chair and half-listened to her and Geoffrey's bright and brittle words of greeting.

"How's business?" I asked.

"Up and down." He made a stoic face. "*Sports Today* is

booming. So is *Woman* and *Motor Life*. *World* is in a bit of a rut, but we're going into some fantastic new picture and story ideas."

I heard the bell tinkle but I resisted any Pavlovian drooling. "And Proctor-World stock is up, too. I'm sure Old Charlie would be pleased."

"Dad never disapproved of profits."

"Yep. Occasionally nepotism bears fruit."

Turning to Jan, he made a hissing noise through his teeth. "And I thought it was *females* who are supposed to be castrators."

"You know Norman," she said. "Bitchy on an empty stomach."

He glanced at both of us. "We could go ahead and order, but I've got someone with me. He should be back from the gent's room in a minute. Name's Mike Rogers. A real sharp kid."

"One of your execs?" Jan asked.

"Wish he was." Geoffrey leaned forward and folded his hands on the table. "Norman, I have the article of a lifetime waiting for someone with your talent. Not that you need the money. I've seen the figures on *The Death Watch Beetle*. Fantastic! God knows where you get your ideas."

"Quite simple. All my books are wet dreams set to prose."

He blinked. "I believe it. I wish I could ejaculate so profitably."

I peered over Geoffrey's shoulder. "Your boy's arrived, I think."

He got up and made introductions. Mike Rogers was thirty-plus. Short, stocky, and energetic. Light brown, expertly cropped curly hair. Candid eyes. Open smile. An all-American face just starting its slow slide into middle age. A very likable package.

Rogers kept within his shell while Geoffrey talked pleasantries. De Gaulle and Paris traffic and Reeperbahn sex parlors and Liz and Dick at Torre Astura. Fortunately, Jan and I are adept at verbal handball. I knew he would eventually get to the point.

We ordered from menus the size of an auto windshield. I remember Geoffrey slicing meat when he decided to talk business.

"Norman, this April will mark the fiftieth anniversary of the sinking of the *Titanic*. *World* is going to do a special story for our April issue. I think you're the man to write it."

"*The Titanic*? You mean with the iceberg and Clifton Webb going down singing 'Nearer My God to Thee?'"

Rogers spoke up for the first time. "Actually, Mr. Hall, the ship's band played the Episcopal hymn 'Autumn' in those last minutes." He grinned apologetically at his own expertise.

Geoffrey eyed my dubious expression. "Doesn't the subject appeal?"

"I'm not sure. I don't know much about ships. Why don't you contact someone like . . . well, like Walter Lord, that man who wrote *A Night to Remember*?"

"We've decided on a new approach, Norman. New angles someone like you can provide."

"A rehash with zing, right?"

Geoffrey's cheeks puffed in exasperation. "Mike, you tell him. He wears me out."

Mike Rogers smiled disarmingly, scratching the back of his ear. No doubt he'd seen plenty of Gary Cooper movies. "Mr. Hall, other people also think you're the best man for the job."

"Really? Who else?"

"First, I should fully explain my presence here. I'm an attorney and special representative for Mr. William Ryker. Have you heard of him?"

I turned to Jan. She shook her head and I followed suit.

"No reason why you should, really. Mr. Ryker hasn't exactly been a headline maker in many years. But he has been and still is vitally involved in American business. Oil, insurance, railroads. Not as solvent now that the IRS has acquired teeth. But . . . very comfortable. Mr. Ryker is currently retired in Veyrier, near Geneva."

I was amused by his mixture of PR lingo and carefully manicured candor. "A beautiful place. I've been there."

Rogers took his dessert fork and began tracing arabesques on the tablecloth. "Although confined much of his time to an iron lung, at eighty-five he's still very active. And he has a personal interest in the *Titanic*." A solemn frown. "His wife sailed on the ship. She wasn't among the rescued."

Geoffrey patted his lips. "Mrs. Ryker's bodyguard and maid were lost, too. The only survivor was her daughter, Eva."

Jan reached for the last of her Mouton Rothschild. "Really? How old was she?"

Rogers cast an ambiguous look at Geoffrey. "Nine or ten. I don't remember exactly."

"Is she still alive?" I asked.

"Oh, yes." He leaned forward, elbows on the table. "I'm sure you can understand Mr. Ryker's strong interest in the *Titanic* tragedy."

It sounded a bit morbid to me. "In what ways does your Mr. Ryker express this hobby of his?"

Rogers' face flushed. I had fed him the perfect straight line. "As it happens, he has the resources to indulge this particular hobby. Along with the National Geographic Society and the Navy Department. Have you heard of the bathyscaph *Trieste* and its exploration of the Marianas Trench off the Philippines?"

"The deepest spot in the ocean, isn't it?"

"Over thirty-five thousand feet. Anyway, the Navy was so pleased with the success of the *Trieste* that it decided to build two sister ships, the *Marianas* and *Neptune*. They're being loaned to the Geographic Society, which is matching the funds provided by Mr. Ryker. He recently purchased an Italian-built oceanographic research ship, the *Savonarola*, which will serve as a surface and supply vessel for the two bathyscaphs on their first assignment off the Grand Banks of Newfoundland. Twelve thousand feet, which is a milk run really."

He spread both hands flat on the table. "You see, the *Marianas* and *Neptune* will be searching for the wreckage of the *Titanic*."

"You're kidding."

"Mr. Ryker seldom makes jokes as expensive as this one," Rogers primly said. "He wants to salvage any cargo that remains."

I felt Geoffrey's eyes on me, watching my reaction.

"All right," I said. "You've made your pitch and I *am* impressed." I turned to Rogers. "Exactly what does Ryker expect to find?"

He pulled judiciously at his face. "Well, Mr. Hall, first the wreckage has to be located. But whether the ship is still intact . . ." He threw up his hands. "We'll just have to see. The bathyscaphs are both equipped with remote manipulators—the experts call them 'Waldos'—for working under the extreme pressure with underwater lights, cameras, torches—that sort of thing. They can cut through the hull if necessary so that we can explore the interior. Of course, most anything the Waldos turn up will be of interest to the National Geographic people. And there may be objects of financial value, too. Art objects, jewelry. . . . The passengers of the *Titanic* were collectively worth over two hundred fifty million dollars."

Jan glanced at me over her wine glass and raised an eyebrow. I nodded.

Geoffrey intercepted our exchange. "It's settled then?"

"Yes," I said. "She's got me hooked."

" 'She?' "

"The *Titanic.* Or does a ship cease to be a 'she' after it sinks?"

Mike Rogers grinned, leaning back in his chair. "An interesting point to ponder. You'll have to ask Harold Masterson, the man in charge of the salvage operation. He's in Halifax now, and I'm certain you'll want to talk to him." He stretched his hand to me. "Welcome aboard, Mr. Hall. Mr. Ryker will be very pleased."

"Now that I'm on your payroll, you can afford to call me Norman."

"Don't be silly," Geoffrey said. "You're not Ryker's employee. Or even mine, strictly speaking. We want you to have

a free hand in the story. I know it'll be good. Just make sure
it's on time."

I shrugged agreement. "One thing. Jan will be doing a lot
of background research . . ."

". . . as well as all-around dirty work," she said.

". . . so I think she should share the by-line with me."

He made a face. "It's a little unusual . . ."

"It's been a standard arrangement in all our nonfiction."

"Okay. 'Janice Steiner and Norman Hall' it'll be."

"That's 'Norman and Jan.'"

"Naturally. What else?"

"Who's doing the photos?"

"Burke Sheffield."

"Good. But I want to take some myself."

"Show me any pictures and we'll try to work them in." He
glanced brightly at both of us. "Anything else?"

Jan straightened upright. "Money."

He groaned theatrically, as if she'd swiped one of his testi-
cles. "I've never understood you, Norman, letting your wife
deal in this nasty business."

"Women are less sentimental than men concerning money.
Just look at the world around you."

"Don't try to divert me with your flaky philosophizing. I've
heard all this before . . ."

He'd heard all this before. So had I. I listened with one
ear, nodding to the rhythms of the contract being hammered
out. The money would be enough. It was the article I worried about.

For some reason it reminded me of this morning's nightmare.

"Checkmate."

Orange flames from the fireplace cast flickering shadows
between my king and remaining pawns. I rubbed my chin.

"Yeah. Yeah, you're right."

Jan leaned back from the chessboard, her face sympathetic. "You've been somewhere else all night."

"I know." Massaging my neck, I sighed. "Maybe I need a drink."

"Coming up." She headed for the liquor chest, returning with a snifter of brandy, gold in the firelight as I took it from her hands. It forged a warm, biting path down my throat.

Jan sat next to me and waited.

"Do you know why I took this job?"

"The subject got to you, I guess." She studied my face. "That and Mike's pitch."

"Yes, he's very glib. It's not often that I enjoy being conned."

"Don't you think he and Geoffrey were being straight?"

"Mike is as honest as young men on the make usually are. Bullshit oozes from Geoffrey's every pore, but what else is new?"

I swigged down more brandy. "No, it's *my* motives that bother me. The *Titanic* means something . . . personal to me that Geoffrey and Mike couldn't know."

"I don't understand."

"It's not easy to explain. But I had a bad dream about the Kleins last night . . ."

"Oh, Norman." She held my hand. "That's the first one in months."

"Tonight I finally remembered. Martha Klein told me she and her husband were survivors of the *Titanic*." I stared into the flames. "Curious, don't you think?"

"I think twenty years is a very long time, Norman. The newspapers and police records of the Inquest are rotting with age. Some janitor could throw them away tomorrow." Her fingertips gently brushed the veins on the back of my hand. "I don't like to see you worry about something dead and gone."

"Isn't that what this whole story's about? An old man on his deathbed literally dredging up his past. A sea disaster that's ancient history in most people's minds. And two survivors who changed my entire life."

"An odd coincidence, I suppose."

"Too odd. More like fate, perhaps?"

"Rubbish, Norman. 'Fate' should be stricken from the dictionaries."

"Sorry. I know I make a poor mystic." I downed the last of the brandy. "In any case, the Kleins belong in the story."

"Not if you ask me!"

"Don't be a backseat writer. The first thing in the morning, call Mike to set up a meeting with Harold Masterson, the director of the salvage operation. I also want to talk to Old Man Ryker, but be delicate about that."

"And where will you be?"

"London. For a day or two. I'm going to visit Tom Bramel at the Yard. I want to see the FBI and HPD files on the Kleins. Maybe he knows what strings to pull."

4

January 9, 1962

London was cold and grubby on the morning of the ninth. I stood at the second-story window of Tom Bramel's office and watched shivering pigeons skidding on the sidewalks as I worked my way through a *Reader's Digest* condensation of the meeting with Geoffrey and Mike.

Upon my conclusion, the assistant commissioner settled back and suckled his Kaywoodie briar. The pipe is part of a tweedy ensemble that includes a wide graying mustache, frayed public school ties, and big-shouldered corduroy coats with elbow patches. To my envy and to his wife's unending terror, women have found the combination devastating.

Tom leaned against his desk after a long smoky sigh. "Norman, are you certain all this isn't the scenario for your latest potboiler?"

"Hardly. Within a few months you'll be reading the spread in *World*, which makes it as close to truth as we mortals can get."

"When's the salvage project due to be announced?"

"The *Savonarola* and the bathyscaphs are off Nova Scotia right now, scouring the site. They better turn something up

34

quick. With an operation this size, press leaks are only days away."

"Offhand, it sounds like a good way to whittle away a few million pounds." He patted down a stubborn cowlick. "But I've heard of this William Ryker and I suspect he has it to spare."

"No doubt. But my article is also going to deal with the *Titanic* survivors. That's where you can help me."

"I'll do anything I can, Norman. But I have no special access to information on survivors. Unless any of them had criminal records."

I sat facing him and hoped my eyes looked candid. "What I'm looking for are the facts of a certain case. Jan and I came across a couple named Martha and Albert Klein. They were Americans who spent their honeymoon in Europe and returned on the *Titanic*. Both were later victims of a rather sensational murder that made the headlines back in the States. I'd like to see the police records. Mainly the FBI files."

"When was this?"

"I don't remember exactly. Late thirties, early forties."

"Where?"

"The murder, you mean? The West Coast, I think."

"Did you try back issues of the papers?"

"That's where I came across the story. But I want specific information about who knew the Kleins. Names and addresses. The FBI files could give me a lead."

Tom took a pipe cleaner from his desk and ran it through his briar. "Well, Norman, I can try." He tossed the cleaner away and blew through the stem. "I have some friends in Washington. A twenty-year-old murder shouldn't be too hot. I can't imagine anyone fretting over me seeing the file." Patting his pockets for matches, he glanced up at me. "By the way, who did it?"

"Did what?" I said blankly.

"This murder of the century you're so keen on."

"Oh! No suspects were ever found. Not that I know of, anyway."

"Hm. Pulling the file on an unsolved case might stir up

some dust." His fingers gingerly stuffed tobacco in the bowl. "But I'll try to keep it unofficial and low-key."

"I don't want to get you in trouble, Tom."

"No trouble. A bother, maybe, but no trouble." He smiled and held up his hand. "Norman, stop looking contrite. I'll get your file. But it may take a few days. Maybe a week."

"Can you mail copies to me, Tom?"

"I suppose so."

"Fine." I stood up. "Thanks very much. I hope you're free for lunch."

"I *can* be." He got his secretary on the line. "Helen, Norman and I are off. If you need me, we'll be at . . ." His eyes raised to mine.

"Scott's," I said into the microphone.

Tom let go of the switch. "I hope you have reservations."

"One o'clock."

"Wonderful." He grabbed his coat and umbrella and ushered me out the side door. "I love being extravagant on your money."

We drove in Tom's comfortable and ugly black Morris sedan. His grin was slow and amused as he slid the car through the traffic past the Haymarket. "After we order, you must tell me exactly how you 'came across' this particular case. I've always been a great fan of your fiction."

I didn't respond to his needling, and his smile evaporated. "I'm sorry, Norman. I didn't mean to pry."

"It's all right. You've a right to an explanation." I reached for the door handle as we stopped at the restaurant's entrance. "And, as soon as you see the file, you'll get one."

Jan met me at Orly bearing both good and bad news.

"I will make it clean and merciful," she said, piloting the Rolls away from the airport congestion. "I talked with Mike and got a hold of Harold Masterson in Halifax. He'll expect you there for an interview in a couple of weeks."

"Two weeks? Christ, I'll be sniffing the footprints of every damn reporter between here and New York."

"Mike said he was sorry. Apparently Masterson is spending all his time aboard the *Savonarola* working with the bathy-scaphs."

I brooded as Jan drove the car off the Autoroute. "What did Mike have to say about Ryker?"

"No go, Norman. Ryker's just too sick to see anybody."

"Until when?"

"Mike couldn't say."

My hands tightened on the armrest. "You know I'll be flapping around with one wing until I can wrangle an interview. I wonder if Geoffrey could cut through all the crap."

"He's back in New York. I talked to him on the phone yesterday. He said he is adopting a laissez-faire policy toward your assignment."

"In other words, fish or cut bait."

"Something like that. By the way," she said casually, "I picked up a book or two for background. They should keep you occupied."

"Good God."

"Impressed, no?"

I crept behind my desk, afraid to disturb the mound of books, newspaper clippings, maps, charts, and photocopies. "Would you like to give me a guided tour?"

"You can start with the basics. That's Walter Lord's book . . ."

"That I've read."

". . . then there's *The Loss of the Titanic, The Truth about the Titanic,* and *Titanic and Other Ships,* which are all by survivors." Jan dug under the rubble. "Here we have *Home From the Sea* by Captain Rostron, who was skipper of the *Carpathia.*"

"The who?"

She looked pained. "The rescue ship, Norman. I thought you read *A Night to Remember .*"

"Years ago."

Gathering up the unbound pages, she separated them into two piles. "On your left," she pointed, "the Senate report on the sinking. The other is the inquiry by the British Board of

Trade. There you have feature stories from the Philadelphia *Evening Bulletin* and the Cedar Rapids *Gazette,* as well as *Liberty* and *Harper's* magazine. Some of those eyewitness accounts were written ten to twenty years after the sinking. You might spot an idea you could crib."

"'A point of departure,'" my dear. You know I never copy."

"Stealing from one may be copying. Stealing from a dozen different men is research."

"Maybe so, but I'll be damned if I can't do more than reheat someone's thirty-year-old work." I gestured at the desk. "What's the rest of this stuff?"

"Data on the construction of the ship from *Engineering* and *Scientific American.*"

"Okay. Any maps of the *Titantic*?"

She held it up for me. "Courtesy of the Steamship Historical Society of Staten Island."

I spread it flat on the floor and examined the maze of corridors and staterooms on my hands and knees. Finally I stood, running my fingers through my hair.

"Well, I might as well get started. Plan to stay home for the next few days."

Jan started to retreat, then spun and faced me, arms akimbo. "You're welcome, Norman."

I lifted my nose from the papers and blinked at her. The set of her jaw told me all I needed to know.

"I'm sorry, Janice. Thank you. Sometimes I can be slow on the uptake."

"Quite all right." Her mouth curled downward and she ceased looking pugnacious and became very desirable. "You're going to need a lot of my help. I wouldn't want you feeling too guilty." She leaned against the door. "You've bitten off quite a mouthful, Norman. Until I started this research, I didn't realize how big a bite it was."

"As long as you're speaking in culinary metaphors, how about getting me some lunch?"

"Sure. What do you want?"

"Nothing much." I morosely prodded the overflowing stack of papers. "It'll have to be small to fit in this room."

5

January 12, 1962

For the next two days I subsisted on coffee, tuna sandwiches, and the *Titanic*.

To be honest, I was no more qualified to write about ships than a snake would be to write about shoes. I needed this crash course before I could decide which way to jump.

I already knew, courtesy of Mike Rogers, that the passengers didn't go down singing "Nearer My God To Thee." Nor was the accident an "unforeseeable act of God"; the White Star Line, owner of the *Titanic*, believed in speed before safety, and Captain Smith obediently steered his ship full-bore into the midst of an ice field.

I also picked up glimpses of shipboard life that haunted me as no statistics could. Nouveau riche Americans with private railroad cars and caravans of trunks at the Southampton docks. Irish couples traveling steerage to excape the famine. First-class passengers casually strolling the decks, ogling the distress rockets flaring into the night.

But I saw very little about the Rykers. The body of Georgia Ferrell, Clair Ryker's maid, was eventually recovered by the *MacKay-Bennett*, a cable-laying ship, but neither Clair nor James Martin, her bodyguard, were ever found.

The press had a few words to say about young Eva Ryker being reunited with her father in New York. One clipping mentioned the girl as suffering a "horrendous emotional strain"—hardly a profound analysis—and quoted Mr. Ryker offering "thanks to the Almighty" for the safety of his daughter.

After two days of reading, I knew a hell of a lot about a ship but virtually nothing about the man who wanted to explore it.

I tried to get the littered papers into a rough order, then rose from my armchair and stretched the kinks from my back. One leg had gone to sleep and I limped painfully into the living room.

Jan had her feet up on the couch, listening to John Coltrane on the stereo.

"Have you had it for today?" she asked.

"I've had it period. Fini."

"Good. I thought your eyes were about to fall out of your skull."

"They may yet." I moved her legs and sat beside her. "What time is it, anyway?"

"Nearly three. Like a sandwich?"

"I'll make it." I headed for the kitchen. "You want one, too?"

"Anything but tuna. Liverwurst is fine."

"Okay. While you're waiting, call up Mike. Tell him I want to see him tomorrow morning."

"What about?"

"His employer. And his lack of accessibility."

Jan tucked the receiver under her chin, fumbling with the dial. "Shall I tell him that?"

"I think it can remain an unspoken understanding between us."

The Paris office of the Ryker Corporation is on the avenue d'Iéna.

A pretty brunette receptionist discreetly sniffed out my

identity and led me up a sweeping staircase to a solid and unlabeled oak door. Her name was Solange and she had
worked here for three years. No, she had never met Mr. Ryker. She tapped once at the door and politely motioned me
in.

Mike's office was slick with Danish modern and wrought
iron, which went strangely with the old-fashioned high windows of the room.

"Come in! Come in!" He grinned, pointing at a chair.
"Like a drink?"

"Not this early, thanks."

Settling behind the desk, he looked momentarily uncomfortable, as if he had been reading a book and couldn't find
his place. "I guess Jan told you about Masterson."

I nodded.

"Norm, I wish I could get you two together sooner, but
he's simply swamped right now." Rogers went to a wall map
of the world and jabbed his finger at a point off Nova Scotia.
"That's where the *Titanic* went down. Latitude forty-one degrees, six minutes North; longitude fifty degrees, fourteen
minutes West. Masterson is there supervising the dive of the
bathyscaphs. But he'll be glad to meet with you in Halifax."
Mike flipped through his desk calendar. "January twenty-
third, to be exact."

Mike must have read my opaque expression, for he unbent
a bit. "Norman, you'll have the opportunity to dig deep, and
we'll take the time to give you what you need."

Leaning forward, I spread my hands on the desk. "That's
just what I want to see you about."

His face was affable and expansive. "I'm listening."

"I want to talk with your boss, Mike. It's that simple."

"I wish it *were* that simple, Norm."

I'd heard those words and that tone of voice before. I was
ten and Dad was explaining where babies came from.

". . . Mr. Ryker's physician called me yesterday and said
he was definitely improving," Mike was saying. "But he's simply not well enough to see anyone right now."

"Have you heard from the doctor today?"

"No, but . . ."

"Mr. Ryker could do a lot of recovering in twenty-four hours. Why don't you call and find out?"

His head shook. "I don't think that's wise, Norm. Dr. Bertrand said he should be getting plenty of rest."

"Sound advice," I said flatly. "If I were eighty-five, I think I'd be getting a lot of rest, too."

"I can appreciate your point of view, Norm . . ."

"Really? Then I suppose you know that this story of mine isn't worth a damn unless I can talk with your Mr. Ryker. He has to supply the 'why' for the salvage operation. A cold business proposition? Idle curiosity? A senile obsession with the past? Readers will want to know. And Ryker is the only man with the answer."

Mike grinned uneasily. "You sound like a reporter from the *National Enquirer.*"

"Sorry, Mike, but the whole story is loaded with pulp. Strain it out and you won't have a hell of a lot left."

Mike rose from his chair, fumbling for a smoke. Once he found the pack of L&Ms, he offered me one.

"No thanks."

Lighting a cigarette, he dropped the match in the ashtray. He walked to the window and watched the traffic hooting down the avenue. Sucking half the cigarette into his lungs, he blew the smoke against the glass. His face tightened against the cloud of tar and nicotine. When he turned back to me, his eyes looked red and defenseless.

"Norm, I don't know what to tell you. I certainly can't place Mr. Ryker's health in jeopardy. You want a definite time for an interview and I just can't do it. Not without Dr. Bertrand's okay."

I decided to make it easy for him. "Mike, who is Mr. Ryker's business manager?"

His eyebrows raised. "I don't know exactly what you mean. I perform most of the administrative and legal work."

"But who makes the big decisions? You know, when to buy, when to sell, all of that."

He smiled at my simplification. "Why, Mr. Ryker, of course."

"Even now?"

"Yes. The Ryker Corporation is primarily a holding company for Mr. Ryker's assets. It's not like he was president of General Motors. The work involved isn't severe."

"Glad to hear it." I stood and reached for my coat. "Now all you have to do is wait until your boss has one of his lucid spells. Then, instead of pondering a new tax dodge, you simply say that a modest, hardworking reporter wants to talk with him."

His face clouded. "Norman . . ."

"Tell him I won't take any more time than I have to. All I want to know is his favorite color and his most embarrassing moment."

Mike's anger dissipated. With a short barking laugh he spread his hands. "I'll see what I can do."

"Fine," I said lightly, one hand on the doorknob. "Don't take too long."

Tom Bramel phoned early that same evening with news of the FBI file on its way by special delivery.

"Norman," he said quietly. "You should have told me about Honolulu."

Was the voice a little sullen? It was hard to tell over the phone.

"I wasn't trying to cover up, Tom. Just postponing the inevitable, I guess. I couldn't stomach going to your office, spilling my guts over some ghastly skeleton in my closet."

"An unusual choice of words, Norman." Tom's laugh was chill. "Were you speaking literally or figuratively?"

What I had said came back to me and I flinched. I suddenly felt the blood slapping under my feet as I groped through the closet of Room 307.

"Let's drop it, Tom." My fingers were tight around the receiver. "Would you like some searing psychological insight into my behavior? I've spent good money on analysis and I can offer you multiple choice between Freudian, Gestalt, and Behavioral versions."

"Shut up, Norman. Please. I didn't call to pass judgment.

Maybe it was less painful for you to lie to me, but it wasn't
necessary. All right?"

"Okay, Tom. Sorry."

He seemed relieved to hear the ragged edge leave my
voice. "I don't want you to be too disappointed over the file.
There's not much in it you don't already know. Neither the
police nor the FBI ever found any suspects. Their only lead
was Catherine Maurois, the maid at the Moana who vanished. She must have left the islands, but no one ever caught
up with her. By now she's been declared legally dead."

"I know the case is unsolved. I'm more interested in the
Klein background before they came to Hawaii. Martha Klein
told me she and her husband lived in St. Petersburg, Florida.
Any relatives? Neighbors? Friends?"

"Hang on." Papers softly rustled. "Here's something. After
the murders, the FBI talked to the neighbors of the Kleins, a
Fred and Mima Heinley."

"Wait a minute." I grabbed a pen and had Tom spell the
names, jotting them on a back cover of *Paris Match.* "What
did they have to say?"

"It couldn't have been anything useful, Norman. The FBI
agent on the case didn't even quote them in his summary."

"Does it give their address?"

"Their 1941 address. Not much use now, I wouldn't
think."

"Tom, I know it's a big favor to ask, but do you think you
could trace their current address?"

"Norman . . ."

"You've already got the file. A request for follow-up information wouldn't be suspicious . . ."

"Norman . . ."

"God knows you don't want Hoover and the Yard on your
tail, but . . ."

"Norman!"

"Yes, Tom?"

"Did it ever occur to you to try a phone book?"

Tom's idea was easier said than done.

Jan and I spent most of the following morning combing through libraries. The Bibliothèque Nationale was the logical starting point.

Phone directories? Yes, monsieur, this way. St. Petersburg, Florida? Silver pince-nez glinted blankly. A search and a shrug. Perhaps the Bibliothèque Mazarine, monsieur.

The Mazarine was another dry well. But we finally hit pay-dirt at the Bibliothèque Forney. The phone book was dated 1959, but it would have to do.

I spread the book flat on the table and scanned the H's. There it was: HEINLEY, FRED 2121 Gulf Blvd. West KL5-9421.

When we got home, Jan pointed at the phone. "You or me?"

I pondered for a moment. "Go ahead."

"What exactly am I going to say, Norman?"

"Ask them if they'll consent to an interview."

"I know that. When?"

"As soon as I can hop a plane."

She shook her hands unhopefully. "We'll give it a try. The poor people might be dead for all you know."

Jan is a pessimist. Mr. and Mrs. Heinley were alive and eager to meet a reporter from *World* magazine. Yes, Tuesday morning was fine. The Bahia-Belle Cabañas. Just check at the manager's office.

While Jan and I were pawing through phone books at the Bibliothèque Forney, the bathyscaph *Marianas* sighted the *Titanic*.

The story filled the tube Sunday night. Blotchy photos showed a few patches of crumbly metal peering out of the gloom. Interviews featured Captain James Nicholson and Commander Phillip Toffler of the *Marianas,* who testified that the ship was laying on its starboard side and was in amazingly good condition.

Mike Rogers then flashed on the screen, looking tan and scrubbed. He told the story of Mr. William Ryker and his wonderful salvage operation. Scientific treasure trove. Historical bonanza and so on.

Harold Masterson appeared, hesitantly offering words to a reporter's microphone. He was in his late fifties. Paunchy but tidy, with bulbous, kindly features.

Yes, he said, new pictures would immediately be released. Sweat glared on his forehead. Of course, reporters would be welcome aboard the *Savonarola* at the wreckage site. As a matter of fact, the popular novelist and journalist Norman Hall is currently working on a feature story on the *Titanic* and its rediscovery to be published by *World* magazine in April.

Jan looked pale as she turned from the television. "Norman, do you realize what this means?"

"Afraid so." I pointed at the phone. "Brace yourself."

The first call came through in twenty seconds. *Paris Match*. Then *Der Spiegel*. *Punch*. Manchester *Guardian*. AP and UPI and Reuters stringers. I sat by the phone for the next two hours.

Yes, that's right, I'm currently researching background material. Well, I guess I got the assignment because Geoffrey Proctor and William Ryker thought I'd do a good job. No, I don't think I should talk about my salary. Yes, there are many people I'm going to interview. Obviously, Mr. Ryker and his staff. No, I can't say who my other contacts are.

At least that's what I told most of them. One AP man kept bearing down on me like a used car salesman, and to get rid of him I mentioned that I was leaving Monday morning for an interview in St. Petersburg, Florida.

6

January 16, 1962

The Bahia-Belle Cabañas were on Treasure Island, across Boca Ciega Bay, connected with the main part of the city by a causeway. I crept along Gulf Boulevard West in my rented Buick until I spotted the sign.

Each of the twenty-four tidy little bungalows resembled miniaturized tract houses, assembled in a horseshoe facing the beach, like spare pieces from some giant Monopoly board.

The sand beyond the cabañas had the color and texture of newsprint. Modest waves lapped politely on the beach. My eyes ached from the glare of the Gulf stretching to the horizon.

A sign over one unit proclaimed OFFICE in flickering pink neon. Opening the screen door, I rang the bell perched on top of the receptionist's counter.

Behind the counter lay an open doorway, and I could hear someone making getting-up noises. I studied the fading Caribbean watercolors on the pale green walls, unraveling my tie in an effort to combat the superheated stuffiness of the room.

A woman finally appeared, surveying me with bulging

jumping-bean eyes. Thyroid, I thought, fighting to keep my eyes from widening in response.

"Yes? May I help you?" She was thin and very old, but her polite smile seemed to contain some genuine warmth. "I'm afraid we don't have any vacancies. Unless you have a reservation."

"Mrs. Heinley?"

She nodded and I introduced myself.

Pulling up the counter top, she waved me through the door into the back part of the cottage. "Fred!" she yelled. "He's here!"

Fred was fat and bald and immobilized in an overstuffed green armchair. The sports page from the *Independent* rested on his paunch.

"H'lo." He bent painfully forward to shake my hand. I decided illness rather than rudeness was the reason for him not standing up.

The living room was sauna-hot. Mima Heinley must've seen the sweat bubbling up from my forehead, for she bustled over to crack the windows.

Sunlight poured into the little room, catching the dust motes flying up from expensive beige hook rugs. She tilted the Venetian blinds at a quarter angle, filling the room with zebra stripes of light.

"Sit down! Sit down, Mr. Hall." She waved me into a pillowy sofa. "Would you like some coffee?"

"Yes, thanks."

"Cream?"

"Please. No sugar."

Cups rattled in the tiny kitchen tucked in a cubby hole to my left. Stern New England faces glared down from oval frames over Mr. Heinley's chair. Above my head was a brass platter the size of a bus tire engraved with English burghers who seemed to be enjoying a fox hunt-cum-orgy. A floor-to-ceiling bookcase filled the fourth wall.

Mr. Heinley mildly watched me. "How do you like St. Petersburg, Mr. Hall?"

"It makes me homesick. I grew up in weather much like this."

"Really? Here on the coast?"

"Honolulu."

"Were you born there?"

I nodded. "The Hall family dates back to the early missionaries. Not to mention any whalers or natives who sneaked into the family tree."

Mima Heinley tottered in with a silver tray she balanced like a cautious tightrope walker. She eased it down on the coffee table and passed me a cup.

The lips smiled. "Is it all right?"

"Yes, thanks."

Mrs. Heinley turned and made straight for her bookcase. From a middle shelf she pulled out a copy of *The Web He Wove.*

"Of all your books, Mr. Hall, I think that's my favorite."

"Thank you. I'm flattered."

"We also remembered your face." She pointed at the jacket.

"Not my favorite portrait, I'm afraid."

"We figured to meet you one day. Sooner or later."

I looked from one face to another. "Maybe I don't quite understand."

"Mr. Hall," Fred rumbled gravely, "Mima and I have known you for many years." He pointed a thumb at the ceiling. "Up in our attic are clippings from newspapers across the country about Al and Martha. Your pictures as a young man are scattered all through those articles. Mima and I have read just about everything you've written. We've felt a personal interest in your success."

I walked to the window to let in more fresh air. "You've got me at a disadvantage. If you don't want to talk, I'd understand."

The Heinleys didn't answer, waiting to see which way I would spring.

"Let me explain one thing. I'm not here simply because of my personal interest in the Kleins. They were survivors of the *Titanic.* Which makes them my business."

Fred raised his arms helplessly. "Where do you want to start?"

"Were you close?"

"We lived next door to them for nearly thirty years," Mima said. "You can't get much closer than that."

"Where? Here at the beach?"

"No! No!" He tilted his head away from the Gulf. "Across the bay, off Central Avenue. In two little apartments over the store Al and Martha owned."

"What sort of store?"

"Produce mostly. A few canned goods and fish."

A thought struck me. "Is that store still there?"

"The building is," he sniffed. "It's a liquor store now."

I glanced at my watch. "My car's outside. I understand there's a restaurant out Tampa-way called Los Novedades that's pretty fair."

Fred grinned at the understatement. "Just about the best on the Coast."

"If you two would like to get out, I thought we could drive there for lunch. And on the way back you can show me the old Klein store."

Mima cast a doubtful glance at her husband. "I'm not so sure, Mr. Hall. Fred hasn't been feeling too well."

"To hell with that!" He lifted himself up, grabbed his cane and plunged into the bedroom, yelling, "Mima! Where's my good jacket!"

"Hush up, Fred!" She scurried after him, sparing me a contrite glance over her shoulder. "Just give us a few minutes."

The home of Albert and Martha Klein was on a narrow side street twisting down from Central Avenue between the Coast Guard station and the yacht basin.

I parked the Buick across the street, rolled down the window and squinted up at the building.

"There's the place," Mima said ruefully. "We lived there over forty years. God help us."

The Anchor Cove Liquor-Mart occupied the ground floor. Standing guard at the counter by the door was a pink-faced bald man who resembled an immense overgrown infant. He punched the register, then passed a tiny paper sack across the counter to someone out of sight. A skinny little black kid swung open the screen door and padded down the sidewalk in his dusty bare feet, red licorice snaking from his mouth.

I grabbed my Nikon and crossed the street. At the side of the building feeble wooden stairs led to the second-floor apartments. The steps and bannister sweated with too many coats of paint laid over the years.

Under the stairs a snoozing marmalade Tom raised one eye, then yawned and swaggered my way. His purring flanks hugged my calves, telling me we were friends for life. The cat's hideaway was littered with empty Red Mountain jugs and no-deposit root beer bottles.

The door to the Kleins' apartment was mottled with stains and finger smudges. A baby howled from one of the rooms.

Two smallish windows faced the street. The window belonging to the Kleins' old place was curtained shut. Sunlight seeped through rips in the cotton fabric.

"Believe it or not," Fred said upon my return to the car, "it was a real nice place at one time."

"I believe you. No one sets out to build a slum." I settled behind the wheel. "When did the Kleins move in?"

"Late April, nineteen twelve."

"Right after the sinking."

"That's right," she said.

"Did they talk much about being on board the *Titanic?*"

"Not at first." Fred gazed up at the second-story windows. "But their names were on the survivors' list printed in all the papers, so it was only natural we should ask them about it. Al said he jumped overboard and was picked up in the water. Martha always said she left in the last boat."

Mima leaned forward. "You can understand how it was, Mr. Hall. They had obviously gone through hell, and we felt it merciful not to press them for details."

"Did the Kleins have much money when they moved here?"

"Some. They weren't broke. The store took off pretty quick and they made even more." He chuckled sadly. "I hate to think of all the times they helped Mima and me through a tight spot. Al gave me money for Mima's heart operation in twenty-three. Let us charge groceries after the Crash, when some of our neighbors were digging through garbage cans. We might be dead now if not for them."

I inspected the battered upstairs curtains. "I'd like to take a look up there."

"It wouldn't do you much good," Mima said. "The owner tore out old walls and put in new ones to sublet the place into smaller units. That's why we moved." She stared down at her hands folded on her lap. "Also, it didn't seem very . . . healthy to stay there after, you know, they were gone."

"I would've felt the same way. The only reason why I wanted to see inside was to, well . . ." My shoulders shrugged. "I'd like to get some idea of how the Kleins lived."

Mima's face brightened. "Maybe I can help you there. Al and Martha didn't have any next of kin, so we had to do something with their belongings. I kept some odds and ends. They're stored in our attic. I could let you have a look if you like."

The Heinleys' "attic" wasn't much larger than the inside of a pup tent. Fred and Mima held the ladder as I climbed up through their bedroom ceiling, shoving a flashlight into the darkness.

"It's the big cardboard box on the left!" Mima cried.

Years of dust cushioned the insides of the box like filthy gray cotton. Mima spread newspapers on the living room floor and passed me a towel.

Most peoples' attic fodder is pitifully scruffy, and the Kleins' hoard was no exception.

A milk glass bud vase. Wood shoe trees smelling of leather and mothballs. Odd Mah-Jongg pieces. A tarnished souvenir spoon from the 1933 Chicago World's Fair, with tiny letters on the handle proclaiming "Century of Progress." Rotting Zane Grey paperbacks. An art deco ashtray, its orange mosaic tile scarred with ancient cigarette butts.

I set the f-stop on my Nikon, bent over the relics and clicked off a few exposures.

Replanted in his easy chair, Fred wheezed from the dust. Mima tut-tutted in sympathy, cranking open the windows. Fresh ocean breezes quick-chilled the sweat simmering between my shoulder blades.

"Mrs. Heinley, do you have any photos of the Kleins?"

"I wish we did. One of my cousins gave us a Kodak on our first anniversary and we never ran more than two or three rolls through it."

"After living together all those years?"

"Mr. Hall," Fred grumbled. "Al and Martha were what you might call camera shy. Martha claimed she couldn't take a good picture and Al just didn't give a damn."

"It's a shame," Mima sighed. "You should have seen them, Mr. Hall, when they first came here. Fair and beautiful . . . just like those little wedding cake statues."

"I thought the groom on the cake was always dark."

"Maybe." She smiled sheepishly. "But you know what I mean."

"Yes, I think so. Blond and gorgeous. They sound almost angelic."

"What're you trying to say?" Fred scowled.

"Nothing really. I just wondered if you ever had any arguments with the Kleins."

"No." He was certain.

"No harsh words? No petty squabbles? A little too much to drink one night? An overdue grocery bill? A joke that went sour?"

Fred's lips sliced thin for a meat-cleaver reply, but Mima gently cut him off. "It's a little hard to say, Mr. Hall. You get old and you remember what's convenient. Most everything else washes out of your system."

I turned to Fred. "One thing I'm curious about. You said the Kleins' store was successful?"

"I'll say! He had the neighborhood sewn up within a year."

"If he was doing so well, why didn't he expand into more stores?"

Fred scratched the gray thatch at the back of his head. "Damned if I know. I used to kid Al. 'Why don't you hire some more help?' I'd say. 'Advertise in the papers! Branch out!' But he would just shake his head and say, 'We're keeping it a family business.'"

"By 'family business' I assume he meant he and his wife."

"Al and Martha couldn't have children." Mima's eyes had a hollow unseeing look. "Maybe that's why we were so close. Fred and I had the same . . . problem."

The Heinleys' den seemed to tighten oppressively around me as I watched both of them.

"Martha Klein told me that her husband received strange phone calls just before they left on their trip. She also said men she didn't recognize were around the old apartment, keeping watch on him. Did you ever see anyone like that?"

He glanced at Mima, then appeared to make up his mind. "Yes, we did. For about a week before Al and Martha left, a late-model sedan parked across the street with a man in it. The car and driver changed all the time, but they were always there."

"Could you describe any of the men?"

"Too far away. And too long ago. Mima and I mentioned it to Martha. I do remember that. She seemed a little worried. The men vanished right after they left."

"Martha Klein told me their trip to Hawaii was an impulse on Al's part. Did it seem sudden to you?"

Mima wiped dust off an end table before answering. "I suppose it was. Al and Martha had a little money put back and they talked about a vacation, but they did pack up in a hurry."

"What did they do with the store?"

"Oh, Al had two or three boys helping him out," Fred said. "They could handle things for a few weeks. Mima filled in and sort of ran roughshod over the store. At least until we heard the news from Hawaii."

"This part-time help. Do any of them still live around here?"

Her head shook. "There was only one regular boy. Stanley Kallis was his name. He died at Anzio. There were a lot of others, but they came and went."

I felt my trail drying and I started making thanks-for-your-time motions. "There's one more thing you folks could tell me. Did either Al or Martha ever mention someone aboard the *Titanic* whom they knew? A passenger or even a crew member?"

"Oh, dear, I'm sure they had all sorts of friends on board. Both of them were very good with people. But I don't remember anyone in particular on the *Titanic.*"

"Wait a minute!" Fred sat up. "There was a crewman. Martha talked about him several times."

"What was his name?"

"God, let me think." He cradled his head in his hands. "It was John. John something. John MacArthur . . . no, that wasn't it. John McSomething. John . . ."

"McFarland!" Mima cried. "I remember now! It was their steward. Al used to get kind of peeved whenever Martha brought him up. John McFarland!"

7

January 17, 1962

"McFarland . . . McFarland . . ." The personnel director of Cunard Lines' New York office riffled through a husky gray file cabinet. "John McFarland. Here it is."

He opened the file on the counter and picked through the pages as if they were delicate lace panties. "Ordinarily our records are not open to public scrutiny but, seeing how Mr. Proctor called and explained . . ." His voice trailed into a reverent cough.

My fingers pattered on the counter top as his bifocals scanned through the neatly typed papers. Peter Wainwright was his name. Forty-plus and painfully sincere. Every consonant and vowel precisely pronounced through clenched teeth. A pale, pigeon-breasted type the English seem to patent.

"Yes, indeed," he was saying. "John McFarland did work for us. From twenty-three through forty-seven, actually. First on the *Mauretania* and then the *Queen Mary*." Wainwright's lips moved like a poor ventriloquist as he read further. Then his head rose from the page. "How did you know that Mr. McFarland was a Cunard employee?"

56

"Process of elimination," I said unhelpfully, "and some guesswork."

"Oh." The glasses nodded. "Yes. Yes, I see. Well, Mr. Hall, your Mr. McFarland volunteered for special service aboard the *Mary* in nineteen forty-two, when she was converted to transporting troops. After the war, he served on the *Elizabeth* until nineteen forty-seven, when he retired." Wainwright squinted at the page. "According to our records, Mr. McFarland planned to invest his small pension in an opal mining operation. He told his crew mates that he had already bought property in Coober Pedy, South Australia."

"How's that again?"

"Coober Pedy. A very small outback town."

I twisted my head to see the name. "It looks like a typo to me."

The glasses stared in icy astonishment. "I'm afraid that's just not . . . possible, sir."

Wainwright wasn't mistaken. Coober Pedy was for real.

"God, what a hellhole!" said Horace Smedly, the pilot of my chartered Cessna, as he taxied onto runway Twenty-two of Adelaide airport. "And you've picked about the worst time of the year to go there, seeing as how it's the middle of summer. One hundred twenty degrees at least."

The Cessna roared down the runway. My fingers dug into the seats in a sphincter-loosening reflex as the ground dropped beneath the plane.

Smedly aimed us north, over the eastern shore of Gulf St. Vincent. I raised my voice above the clatter of the engine.

"How about John McFarland? Have you ever met him?"

"Afraid not." He bucked an updraft as we passed over the giant stacks of Port Pirie's lead-smelting works. "Mainly I just go there to drop people and supplies. It's not a place to linger in. The folks at Coober Pedy pretty much keep to themselves."

After clearing Port Augusta, the ground beneath the Cessna quickly lost its savanna-brown richness. Within an hour we were flying over jagged foothills resembling immense bleeding gums.

The radio crackled abruptly. "This is Woomera Base. You are entering prohibited airspace. Please identify yourself."

Smedly grabbed the microphone and stuck it into his toothbrush mustache. "This is Cessna A2038 from Adelaide, heading for Coober Pedy. We've been cleared through the base."

"Roger. We have your clearance here." A pause. "We have a report from Alice Springs of a sandstorm headed south. Winds to sixty miles per hour."

"Roger. Thanks for the warning." He stashed the mike.

"What was that all about?"

"Just routine. Woomera is a weapons-testing range. Artillery and whatnot. There's also a NASA tracking station out here."

"I was referring to the sandstorm."

"Oh that! Nothing to worry about." He pointed out to the horizon. "Alice Springs is a good five, six hundred miles north. A storm could blow itself out over all that distance. Or it could switch course and veer off toward Queensland, New South Wales—any which way." He gave me a sidelong glance. "How long do you plan to stay in Coober Pedy, Mr. Hall?"

"Just overnight. We can leave tomorrow morning."

"Well, if worst comes to worst, the storm might shut the landing strip down for a day or two."

"Then let's hope the worst doesn't come."

The Cessna flew on for another hour, the sun rising higher over the bleached limestone arroyos. My eyes ached from the garish Kodachrome blue sky.

Suddenly the boulders and rolling hills vanished as we skimmed over a featureless salt pan which looked like an unimaginably huge sandbox.

"Lake Cadibarrawirracanna." He relished each syllable. "Been dry for years."

"So I gathered."

"Won't be long now." Smedly lifted the plane for a climb over the Stuart Range. I gazed down at the anonymous scrub clinging to the slopes. Then the engine dropped an octave and the Cessna drooped low over the desert, like a bloodhound on the scent.

Something sparkled in the sand. Another flash of light. And another.

"That's the place," Smedly pointed. "Those tin roofs make almost as good a beacon as any radio." He gently eased the nose down. "This Mr. McFarland of yours. How long's he been here?"

"About fifteen years, I guess."

He shivered at the thought. "Jesus. It takes all kinds. Basically, I've found two types of people in places like Coober Pedy. One is a young man with a wife and kids, full of hope, staking his claim to strike it quick in the mines and get out. Some do hit the money. The ones who miss leave anyway. Adelaide, Perth, Melbourne. Anywhere but here.

"Then there're the type who take root. It's not the promise of money. It's something about this damn desert. It'll dry you out like a smoked ham. People get out here and sit and wait for the world to leave them behind. People who desperately want to escape."

"Escape from what?"

Smedly tugged at the wheel, bringing the nose up as the dusty landing strip raced to us. Bump, bump, and we were down. He taxied to a waiting Land Rover on the edge of the strip.

"Well, see what John McFarland has to say. Maybe he'll give you the answer."

John McFarland was definitely type number two.

"Old Johnny?" The driver of the Land Rover yelled in my ear as we bounced between potholes, heading for town. "Yeah, I know him. Been out here as long as I can remember." His teeth flashed white beneath wraparound sunglasses and a khaki-covered safari hat.

"Has he had much luck in his mines?"

"Guess so. He doesn't talk much about things like that."

"What about women?" I wiped sweat off my forehead. "Has he lived alone all these years?"

"Just about. John may have done some chippy chasing in his time, but he kept it discreet like. Nothing permanent, anyway."

I kept quiet as we passed tiny stucco houses and prefab crackerboxes. The road detoured around mobile trailers and low tin-roofed shanties huddled in a clump.

"Downtown," Horace Smedly said, deadpan.

The Land Rover growled into low as we went over a rise. Then a jog to the right and we idled in front of slanting aluminum doors leading down to a burrow carved from the sandstone. It could almost pass as the entrance to a storm cellar.

"John's place," the driver said.

"Thanks." I grabbed my notebook and camera and jumped to the ground, slapping dust from my pants.

"I'll be with Jack." Smedly gestured at the driver. "They've got a couple of cots ready for us. Anyway, come on over when you're through."

"Where is it?"

"Not far. Just walk back to town and ask anyone the way."

Smedly grinned and waved, and the Land Rover was off. I squinted dubiously up at the sun. A sweat river flowed from the middle of my back down to my coccyx. While the dust still settled, John McFarland rose up through the double doors. He was a brown and weathered old redwood. Dressed only in sandals, white shorts, and a dark green baseball cap, he stepped spryly forward, one hand outstretched.

"You must be Norman Hall." His palm was dry and blistered. "A good guess."

Blue eyes crinkled. "Only an outsider or a crazy man walks around Coober Pedy in trousers and a sports coat."

"It was air-conditioned in the plane."

"Here, too." He pointed inside. "Come on down and I'll fix you a drink. Then we can talk."

I went in first, placing each foot carefully as McFarland made mind-your-head motions behind me. Five steps down and I was standing in a neat little living room filled with an old but spotless sofa and chair that would have looked comfortable in the lobby of a postwar Hilton. The ceiling barely scraped the top of my head, making me slouch. Around the corner I saw a tiny kitchen and bedroom. Every cranny gleamed with fanatic care.

McFarland latched the door behind me and climbed down the stairs. "Cozy, isn't it?"

"That I'll admit."

"It gives some people the creeps," he laughed. "Claustrophobia and all. But the underground design is pretty efficient for heating and air conditioning. Out here you can't afford to waste power." Heading for the kitchen, he glanced over his shoulder. "Something to drink? Gin? Scotch? I've got some Hennessey Four-Star that makes pretty good mouthwash."

"Sold. With ice, please, if you have it."

McFarland winced. "You Americans and your ice. How many decent bottles of whiskey have been bastardized by that dreadful combination?" As he went around the corner to rattle through his refrigerator, I took the opportunity to check out the room. No paintings or photos. An old Phillips table radio but no TV. The room mirrored the guarded facade of its owner.

John McFarland was about five-nine. Neither thin nor fat. A round face with small watchful eyes. White hair clipped short to fuzzy-dandelion length. He could pass for a young seventy. Or an old fifty-five, for that matter. His nonfeatures were already fading from my mind, like the images on an uncoated Polaroid print.

He came around the corner, ice cubes tinkling brightly from one of the two glasses. "Here we are. Take a seat." He handed me the glass, then raised his own.

"Mr. Hall, I've heard a great deal about you. All that time in the Pacific during the war. And the stories about those goddam island paradises."

"I believe you're thinking of Michener."

"Oh." He took another slug of scotch.

"I wouldn't worry, Mr. McFarland. It's you I want to talk about."

"You can call me John. Assuming I can call you Norman. Then we'll both save a great deal of tongue twisting."

"That's fine by me. What I want to know about . . ."

"I can guess, Norm." He pointed at the radio. "Once in a while I keep in touch with the outside. And now that radio keeps yammering 'Titanic, Titanic, Titanic.' As if one sinking wasn't enough. That goddam bloody Ryker is bringing it up for air."

"Well, not quite. More like a treasure hunt."

"Really?" His eyes narrowed. "What's he hope to find?"

"No one really knows."

McFarland snorted. "No one's really *saying*, you mean."

"Maybe so. But I'd like to know something about your background on the *Titanic*."

"What background? We only completed three fourths of a voyage."

"You must recall something about the ship."

"Oh, sure. After all, it's my claim to fame." He smiled ironically. "Staying afloat on the morning of April fifteenth was the most important thing I ever did in my life."

"What do you remember most?"

"She was beautiful. Elegant." He raised his hands helplessly. "Not very articulate, am I?"

I didn't answer, hoping my silence would draw out the words.

"It wasn't simply a matter of luxury," he finally said. "Both of the Queens were posh enough, much like a well-heeled men's club. But the *Titanic* served a very special clientele. English lords. Krupps and Rothschilds. Second-cousin Hapsburgs and Hohenzollerns; an incestuous pack of stuttering bleeders. American robber barons. Astors and Vanderbilts and Whitneys. The White Star Lines planned to build three sister ships to transport the rich in a style even *they* weren't accustomed to. Heavy mahogany furniture. An indoor swimming pool. Carpeting everywhere, growing thick like beige grass. An imitation Parisian cafe. The first was the *Olympic*. Then the *Titanic*. The third ship, the *Britannic*, was sunk during World War One."

"You don't sound exactly unhappy about what happened."

"Do you believe in a Divine Plan?"

"No. Not that my belief or disbelief would matter in the long run."

"Well, I do. The *Titanic* is too beautiful a symbol to be explained any way else. The ship 'God Himself couldn't sink.' Only He did. Taking all the rich and privileged down with her. A sneak preview of the future, I would say. The friends and relatives of the victims would all go down in her wake once the war broke out."

"An interesting theory, John. When you have proof let me know."

"Fortunately, such things are beyond proof," he said amiably. "What else do you want to know? My daring escape from the sinking ship? It worked, as you can see."

"Not right yet. I'm interested to know why you came here."

"No water. Dry land from horizon to horizon."

"I'd prefer something a little less facile. Like an explanation of what you did from nineteen twelve, after the sinking, to nineteen twenty-three, when you joined Cunard."

"You've been spying on me."

"Just looking at your personnel records."

"The fourteen to eighteen war, mainly. I joined the Navy and served on the *Evan-Thomas* during Jutland. Nearly got my arse torpedoed from under me more times than I can count."

"What about after the war?"

"My father died and left me some money. I took a few years to run through that."

"What did he do?"

McFarland focused on the water droplets beading his glass. "He owned a shoe store in Brighton." A shrug. "Anyway, I ran out of money in twenty-three, so I signed up with Cunard."

"What did you do immediately after the sinking? It was another two years before the war broke out."

"Oh, I don't know. Lazed about. Odd jobs and all."

"You never told me why you came here."

"I had friends aboard the *Mary* who talked nothing but Australia. The open frontier and so forth. One of them men-

tioned the fortune in opals to be made out here. Coober
Pedy and Andamooka—that's about three hundred miles to
the southeast—mine about two million pounds a year." He
laughed, slapping his stomach. "I was still strong then,
enough muscle left to handle a jackhammer, and I thought
what the hell. I bought land just north of here. And slaved
for two ball-busting years. I hit my first seam early in fifty-
one." McFarland lifted his palms. "The rest was downhill. I
hit again in fifty-seven. I've been coasting on that ever since."
He finished off his glass. "Mind if I ask you a question,
Norm?"

"Ask away."

"Why'd you come to me? Just to talk about the *Titanic*?"

"Mainly."

"There must be other old bastards left from the ship."

"Probably. But I got onto your name from Fred and Mima
Heinley, a couple who live in St. Petersburg, Florida."

"Never heard of them."

"You haven't met. But they were close friends of a young
couple who you must've served on the *Titanic*. Albert and
Martha Klein."

McFarland's eyes focused into space. "Klein. Klein." His
lips pursed. "Albert and Martha, you said?"

"That's right. They were newlyweds."

Slowly, then rapidly, he shook his head. "No, can't say that
I do."

"They were very young," I persisted. "Early twenties."

McFarland kept shaking his head. "Sorry . . ."

"Very good-looking."

"I really can't . . ." he drawled regretfully.

"Both blond."

His face was an empty smiling mold. "Wish I could help
you. But I had a lot of people on B deck portside. More than
I can remember."

"You're sure."

"Sure!" He stood and ambled for the kitchen. "You know,
Norm, I'd offer you another drink but I'm running sort of
late. I've got company for dinner. You know how it is."

Yes, I knew. With a sigh I got to my feet and headed for the door. McFarland was pouring himself a double.

"Well, John, thanks very much. If you have anything else to tell me, I'm staying at Jack Forrester's place."

"I'll surely do that!" He pumped my hand. "Let me lead the way up."

After unlatching the big double doors, he gave me a hand up the stairs.

"Glad we had our little chat, Norm." He patted my shoulder. "See you around. I might even read one of your books."

"You might try *The Death Watch Beetle*."

"I'll do that! What's it about?"

"Deceit, mostly."

"Sounds great."

"Yes, I'm sure you'll enjoy it." I wiped my brow with a forearm. "Well, take it easy."

I started off down the trail, then turned around. "You know, John, it's rather odd you don't remember the Kleins."

"Why's that, Norm?"

"Well," I said, shoulders shrugging, "they remembered you."

8

January 22, 1962

They missed me at Coober Pedy. And during the Cessna's
return trip to Adelaide. Not to mention my room at the An-
sett Hotel.

They didn't actually catch up with me until Monday morning, when I was sitting in a first-class seat of a Qantas 707
headed for American Samoa, Honolulu, and Los Angeles.

When the plane stopped in the middle of the tarmac, I
didn't pay much attention. Some traffic control problem, I
supposed. People across the aisle said an unmarked car was
pulling up to the hatch. Maybe a medical emergency. Or cus-
toms men. I resumed reading the Adelaide *Times.*

"Are you Mr. Norman Hall?"

A flashing brass badge. A stern, jowly face towering overhead.

"Yes. Yes, I am."

"Come with me, Mr. Hall." A hand on my arm. "Right this
way, please."

We marched down the aisle. Past gaping faces and turning
heads. Down the gangway and into the car. Another man
kept me company in the back seat.

"What's all this about anyway?"

66

"You'll have to speak with Detective-Inspector Vivian, Mr. Hall. He'll explain anything you need to know."

The Holden swung away from the airport and tore through graceful tree-lined boulevards.

"What about my luggage?"

"All that's been taken care of."

He hung a left on North Terrace, honking through traffic by the Parliament House and State Library. Then a sharp right down a driveway underneath a blank concrete mono- lith with little squinting windows. The Holden weaved through the parking garage labyrinth and slid into a space.

"This way, Mr. Hall."

Steel elevator doors opened. My two companions silently flanked my left and right as I watched the floor numbers light up and then die.

2 . . . 3 . . . 4

Down a neon corridor smelling of Lysol. Two doors hissed open at our approach.

"Here he is, sir."

The room was large, but I saw only the man in it.

"Mr. Hall, I'm Detective-Inspector Vivian." Neither hand rose in greeting. "I'd like you to see something."

He walked to the wall and pulled out a shining steel draw- er. I stared into one of the cautious gray eyes of John McFar- land. The remaining pieces of his face and head were wrapped in surgical catgut.

"Oh, Jesus." I felt my knees going. "Where can I sit down?"

Detective-Inspector Vivian led me to a straight-back chair in the corner of the morgue.

"Could I have some . . . water please?"

One of Vivian's men handed me a paper cup, then joined his companion by the door.

Vivian stood over me as I sipped the water. "You seem to be taking this very hard, Mr. Hall."

I crushed the cup in my hand. "How did it happen?"

"Neighbors found the body in the bathtub Sunday morn- ing. A Mauser Model 1906 fired at point blank range into the mastoid behind the left ear. We have the bullet. A 7.63 millimeter. It took a bit of digging to find."

I sighted a trash can in the corner and tossed the paper cup. It missed. "Do you have any leads?"

Vivian walked to the door where his assistants stood, moving with bearish unease. A big wrestler's body chafing within his dark flannel suit. "Would you come with me, Mr. Hall?"

He led the way, the other men staying close behind. We went up one floor in the elevator, then down a passageway filled with hustling secretaries. Unlocking a door, Vivian crooked a finger at me.

My luggage sat on a desk in the outer office. Shirts and pants lay sprawled in erotic positions on the floor. The silk lining of the two-suiter and the weekend case had been efficiently slit.

I should have played it smart but I was scared and fuming. "What the hell is this, Vivian!"

"I think you know, Mr. Hall." He prodded my clothes with one shoe. "If we had found a Mauser in your bags, it would have solved a lot of problems."

I stared open-mouthed for several seconds before I could speak.

"You know, Vivian, in my country there's a popular stereotype that all stupid cops live in the Deep South. It's reassuring to find that Australia has its share."

His jaw stubble flushed to a pink marble hue as he gave a sidelong glance to his men. "You were the last person to see John McFarland alive."

"Except for the murderer. McFarland was healthy and well on his way to getting drunk when I left him."

"Nobody remembered anyone but you visiting McFarland's house."

"Why don't you try using your head instead of cracking walnuts with your ass. The dust tracks that serve as roads in Coober Pedy wouldn't hold tread marks for five minutes. You don't have a single damn way of knowing who went to McFarland's place."

"You were the only stranger there."

"So what! Who's to say one of his fellow desert cronies

didn't blow open his skull over a crooked game of cards. Besides, the killer could've driven in from anywhere. Andamooka, Mabel Creek—any of those pestholes."

"We've considered that."

"Then what the hell am I doing here! I never met John McFarland before Saturday. Until last week, I'd never heard of him. You can talk with Proctor World Publishing if you don't believe me. Or Commissioner Bramel at Scotland Yard."

"Big-time connections aren't going to help you. You chartered a plane to Coober Pedy. You spent the afternoon with McFarland. No one else was seen with him. You shot him when he turned around, dumped the body in the bathtub, and cleaned up the blood. Then you tossed the Mauser out in the desert." Vivian restlessly shifted on his feet. "The motives are your own. But one way or another, you're the one who'll pay."

"No court this side of the Iron Curtain could work with the crap you've laid out. You admit you have no motive. No weapon's turned up. A dozen witnesses can testify about my interest in John McFarland. A fiasco like this will bust you off the force."

"I'll look after myself, if you don't mind." He looked at the officer standing behind me. "Buckley, this man's under arrest. Suspicion of murder."

I felt a prickly tremor at the back of my neck. "I assume I can make a phone call."

"Down the hall." Vivian's eyes had no more expression than two camera lenses.

It took five minutes of hassling with long distance to get my home number. One ring. Two, Four. Seven. God, I thought, what time was it in Paris . . .

"Hello." Jan had risen from the dead.

"It's Norman."

"Christ, of all the times to call . . ."

"Shut up, dear. We've got troubles. Call Frank Aylmer right away."

"In London? He won't be up."

"He will be once you call. It's time he did more important

things than divvying up divorce spoils. You should also phone Geoffrey and Tom. The American consul wouldn't hurt either."

Silence. "Norman, are we being sued again?"

"Worse."

They freed me early Tuesday morning. As I said, they had no case.

I spent the night with an amiable red-veined wino who snored and snuffled in an upper bunk. The cell smelled equally of cockroach spray, human hair, and stale sweat.

Sergeant Buckley came to get me at eight A.M. His mouth smiled anxiously as the guard jingled with the keys.

"Good morning, Mr. Hall. I hope you weren't too uncomfortable."

"I've had better nights. Have you come with the wine list for my last meal?"

"Nothing like that, sir." He held the jail door open. "Commissioner Harkless would like to see you."

The Commissioner wore a polished variant of Buckley's expression. Smile. Smile. Honed by constant practice.

"Please sit down, Mr. Hall." We shook hands and he waved at the red leather chair facing his desk. "This won't take long."

Harkless squinted at the sunlight flooding his beige office walls as he chose each careful word.

"We found an abandoned Land Rover just outside Coober Pedy. It had been stolen from Mabel Creek Saturday night. There are no tracks left unfortunately. A sandstorm from up north destroyed any traces."

"I don't suppose you found a Mauser tucked under the seat."

"Hardly, Mr. Hall. We didn't expect anything so . . . fortuitous." He peeked out warily from under his eyebrows. "Needless to say, you are no longer under suspicion."

I didn't answer. Harkless fidgeted in the silence. "I hope you weren't too upset by Detective-Inspector Vivian's rather forthright methods."

"Frankly, Commissioner, he scared the shit out of me. How many other people has he railroaded through that star-chamber court of his?"

"Vivian has been very successful for over twenty years. His success causes him to be . . . excessive at times. He's retiring soon. As a matter of fact, after this particular case, Vivian may be retiring earlier than he expected."

Harkless sat back in his chair, his have-we-made-amends face securely in place.

"You can relax, Commissioner. A false arrest suit wouldn't fit into my agenda. But you could do me a favor."

"Certainly!" He unraveled both hands, folding them serenely on the desk. "Anything within reason."

"I'd like to see any information on John McFarland."

"We don't have very much. My men tried to obtain prints from the stolen Land Rover but haven't had any luck. Our leads have reached an . . . impasse, as it were."

"I'm more interested in McFarland's early background. Such as immigration papers."

"Yes, I have those here." Harkless searched through his top drawer, then pulled out a slender file.

"Could I have a copy?"

"Of course."

I glanced through the forms, then raised my head. "It says he was born May 15, 1882 in Manchester. Is there anything here about McFarland's parents?"

Harkless craned his head across the desk, reaching out to turn a page. "There, I think."

My fingers ran across the entry. "'Parents Charles and Emily McFarland. Killed in a Manchester-Liverpool train accident, August 26, 1907.'"

"A pity." Harkless nodded staunchly. "A fellow losing his parents at such a young age."

"John McFarland told me his father owned a shoestore in Brighton and left him an inheritance shortly after the armistice."

"Well, then." His eyes were bland. "He must've lied, wouldn't you say?"

9

January 23, 1962

John McFarland, as it turned out, lied about a great many things.

He *did* serve aboard the *Evan-Thomas* during World War I. And he *was* a steward for the Cunard Lines.

Otherwise John McFarland was a cardboard man, propped up by half-truth, outright lies, and fabrication.

The meager statistics contained in Commissioner Harkless' file taunted me. Sifting through the papers as my 707 pushed across the Pacific toward Oahu, I could feel the facts slipping through my helpless fingers.

Australian Immigration had no information on McFarland's whereabouts from April 1912 through November 1914. He didn't serve on any of His Majesty's vessels during that time and he had no living relatives to support him.

Where did McFarland go from the signing of the armistice until 1932? The story of his father's inheritance was a fairy tale almost contemptuously thrown my way. Any casual checking would have exposed the lie. But McFarland hadn't seemed to care.

McFarland must have known the Kleins. The Heinleys'

72

testimony was proof of that. But perhaps he had genuinely forgotten. I had no proof, nothing to hold on to . . .

"Excuse me, sir."

I jumped, instinctively, the memory of Sergeant Buckley still unpleasantly fresh.

"Yes?"

"Your lunch, Mr. Hall." The stewardess set up the tray. Roast beef and new potatoes and melon.

I chucked the file and cleared John McFarland from all my circuit boards. Finishing my lunch, I spent the next hour watching thunderheads and turquoise atolls, content in my mild champagne buzz. I didn't sober up until I started reading the Adelaide *Times*, the same Monday issue I'd started before my arrest.

Banner headlines of a Sydney strike had crowded the story onto page three.

TITANIC FILM RECOVERED

HALIFAX (AP) A 55-year-old roll of motion picture film is the first of a remarkable series of relics obtained from the R.M.S. *Titanic* by William Ryker's salvage team.

"The 35-mm film was packed in an airtight can," announced Harold Masterson, head of the salvage operation. "It was picked up by our bathyscaph *Neptune* on the upper portside decks of the *Titanic*."

Though remarkably well preserved, Masterson stated that the celluloid film is decayed, very brittle, and will require extreme care in reproduction before a print will be released for viewing.

One rough copy has been made from the processed negative. "Another print is being flown to Geneva," Masterson said, "for Mr. Ryker to view. I'm sure he will find it extremely interesting."

Masterson added that this lost film is only the first of many discoveries to be released for public inspection as the salvage operation progresses.

I was still brooding over the article as the 707's tires yelped on the runway of Honolulu Airport.

The plane had an hour layover and I spent the time nursing a Michelob in the airport lounge. Beyond the tinted windows, the late afternoon sun cast orange-peel light across the city. I watched a formation of black clouds conduct a steamy saturation bombing over Alamoana and the Strip and my thoughts kept coming back to John McFarland.

People who say there's no such thing as coincidence are fools. About ten years ago in Las Vegas I watched a GI make twenty-eight straight passes at a Desert Inn crap table. For that matter, everytime I take the Rolls into Paris, I beat the odds by coming back alive.

McFarland's death and my visit could be mere happenstance. He could've been shot in a row over a busted flush. Maybe, years back, McFarland had sown his seed among the married women of Coober Pedy and a jealous husband commandeering a Land Rover decided to settle the score.

Maybe. I doubted it like hell. Trouble was, I liked the alternative even less. It meant someone knew I was going to see McFarland. And that somebody wanted him shut up . . .

Ah, Christ. It sounded like a bad trip through Pulpland. Faceless killers and a crooked informer and silencers going bump in the night. Starring Norman Hall as the crusading reporter, fearlessly exposing crime in time to meet the Bulldog.

Then I remembered the one unblinking eye of John McFarland. He didn't think it was quite so funny.

"Your attention, please," the Tannoy purred. "Qantas flight four twenty-eight to Los Angeles is now ready for boarding. All passengers please go to Gate eight."

I made up my mind. Spotting a vacant phone booth, I fed it a clanging meal of coins. It burped and buzzed and finally got Jan on the line.

" . . . if it's about the movie," she was saying, "I can't tell you a thing. Mike says the film will be released to the press as soon . . ."

"It's not about the film, Janice. We'll have to get into that when I get back. I called to tell you that I'm staying over in

L.A. for a day at least. I want to get more background about
Ryker. You know, under-the-fingernail stuff."

"Why L.A., Norman?

"I want to get in touch with Jerry Blaine. He'd be the man
with the dirt."

"I don't doubt it," she said stiffly. "You know, Norman, this
article is bringing you down to pigsty level. First murder and
now Jerry Blaine."

We agreed to meet at the Hotel Roosevelt's "Cinegrill." I
fumbled onto a stool, ordered a bloody mary, and waited for
my eyes to dilate.

The bartender swabbed a towel amidst the ashtrays and
pretzel bowls. The towel shambled my way. What'ya think of
the Rams game? I didn't. His eyes registered mild befuddle-
ment. He retired to his corner, drying glasses.

I finished my drink and watched the tomato juice dregs
drool down the side of the tumbler. I was about to order
another when I saw Jerry come through the door.

Jerry Blaine is tubby, sixtyish, and bald. He has a humorous potato face and canny little eyes. The past forty years of
his life have been spent searching through Hollywood's dirty
laundry and saving souvenirs.

Jerry's memory of ancient scum dates back to the Cenozoic
Era. He can tell you about Fatty Arbuckle's bizarre passions
and the strange death of Thomas Ince. Or which current
popular leading man began his screen career sword swallowing in gay loops.

In the good old days, legend has it, Cohn, Warner, and Za-
nuck all paid Jerry hush money to keep their stars out of
trouble. Now he sells tidbits to low-class fan mags and tab-
loids. The kind of stories where everyone is known as "Mr. or
Miss X" and all the people in the photos have black dominoes
across their eyes.

We shook hands, and I could see Jerry scanning his memory banks. Norman Hall: What's in my file? What past sins are
hidden from public view?

Synapses clicked in his brain. Jerry smiled comfortably.

"Norman, you old bastard!" He slapped my shoulder and popped onto the bar stool. "I never thought I'd see you back in town. How's Jan?"

"Keeping the home fires burning."

"Yeah?" He flagged the bartender. "Yeah, I guess she wouldn't want to come back here. Not after the way Mayer and Schary chewed your ass and sent you packing." He turned his head. "Hey, Jed! Jack Daniels straight!"

"Sure, Jerry." The shot glass slid down the counter. He snapped the whiskey into his throat. For a second I thought he had swallowed the glass. He made a great shuddering face, then blinked owlishly at me. "I knew you'd never make it out here as a screenwriter. You lacked the necessary well-fed eunuch look."

"Jerry, don't try to bait me with that what-price-Hollywood routine. I was at Metro exactly three months, writing the first draft for *From the Ashes.* They took the script and threw it in a pot that every hack on the lot peed in. I packed my bags and never looked back."

"So speaks His Holiness. The picture made a lot of bucks at the box office, you know."

"Yeah. Tab Hunter and Mona Freeman really pulled them in."

He laughed shortly, looking over his shoulder. "My place is down the street, just off Cahuenga. What'ya say we head down there?" He pointed at the walls. "This dump's no place to do business."

"Fine by me." I let Jerry lead the way.

Twenty years ago the architect of the Casa Alfredo tried to give the building the flavor of an old Spanish inn. Now it resembled one of Mexico's more inhospitable prisons. The stucco-adobe was peeling in big scabs and the salmon pink roof tiles were falling out like the teeth of an old woman.

A second-story tenant had a radio up full volume, blasting Jan and Dean out into the street. Surf City, Here We Come. Jerry fumbled with keys and climbed the creaking staircase, swearing in a thin stream. Those goddam kids were ruining this town. The flea-ridden little bastards should be shipped to Siberia, where they belong.

He shut and locked the door behind me, muting the blare of KFWB.

"Okay, Norm." He leaned against the door jamb. "Business talk."

I held out a fifty-dollar bill and watched it vanish. "That's for your time. There's more for any information."

"What sort?" The eyes were noncommittal.

I treaded through the heaped newspapers and magazines and settled in a musty overstuffed chair. "Do you know about my article for *World?*"

Jerry's eyelids blinked in assent. "Proctor hopes you'll help get *World* out of hot water."

"With my little story? You mean people are going to flock to the newsstands?"

"Proctor got a good deal of money from William Ryker to cover the *Titanic* story."

"Every magazine and newspaper in the U.S. would've jumped at the chance for an exclusive feature. Ryker wouldn't need to pay anyone off."

"Ordinarily not." His smile was bland. "But the money had strings attached. Ryker wanted you to write the story."

I couldn't think of anything to say and I watched him laugh at my expression.

"I've never met the man before! Exactly how much did he pay Proctor?"

"About a half million. Ryker's coffee money, you might say. Not to mention all your expenses. Proctor's sending the tab to him."

"The whole thing's crazy. Not to mention dishonest and probably illegal."

"Want to call a cop?"

"What I should do is fly to New York and wring Geoffrey Proctor's neck. Maybe, in his last dying gasp, he could supply the whys behind his little business deal."

"Can't help you there. I try to know what people are doing. Why they're doing it is their own business."

I smiled briefly. "Is that a Goldwynism?"

"Of a sort. I really don't know anything else about it, so don't corrupt me with more money. For right now, just say that with William Ryker you have one hell of a fan."

I leaned forward, hands folded. "I want to know more about him. Something besides the *Who's Who* statistics."

"Jesus!" He grimaced painfully. "Do you have any idea how many years ago all of that was? Ryker goes back to when dinosaurs roamed the earth."

"Come on, Jerry. Two months ago Ryker was just a rich old man waiting to die. But he's made the *Titanic* news. And he's brought himself into the headlines. Just tell me what you know, without the accompanying greasy con."

He chewed on a lower lip. "There's not much to tell. Not that anyone can find out. William Ryker started with a modest nest egg from a well-to-do aunt from Topeka. By age twenty-one he'd made the egg hatch into a couple of million. That became twelve by the turn of the century.

"In nineteen hundred one, Ryker married Clair Austin, daughter of a prominent but financially on-the-skids Baltimore family. Mostly it was a cool business relationship. Ryker supplied the niceties of life. In return, Clair was expected to spread her lily-white loins and moan and groan on cue."

"Quaintly put."

"Not surprisingly, this system resulted with Clair Ryker being 'with child.' Eva arrived in 1904 and seemed to shore up the marriage. For a few years, anyway. Ryker became very possessive over his wife and daughter. As a result, Clair got very indiscreet with those loins. Gardeners, dishwashers, chauffeurs—the common denominator seems to have been men who were all gonads and no brains. Word got out among polite society, and Clair Ryker found herself living a hermetically sealed life. If not for Eva, I doubt if the Rykers would've been received into any home from Manhattan to Newport.

"In the summer of nineteen eleven, Clair was vacationing on the Riviera, with Eva in tow. Endless parties, with Clair entertaining in her matchless Earth Mother fashion. Eventually she decided to go back to her husband. Guilt, maybe. Or dwindling funds. The people who would know have either one or both feet in the grave. Clair and Eva, along with her bodyguard and maid, booked passage on the *Titanic* for New York."

Jerry stood and opened the window. The neighbor's music had stopped. Distant tires hissed along Hollywood Boulevard.

"As you probably know, only Eva was picked up. Clair and her servants never surfaced."

"The maid's body was recovered," I said.

"Could be." He shrugged heavily. "You got me there. When they picked her up, Eva was a complete mess. Ryker sent her from one institution to another for nearly ten years. You know, those classy country club places with rosebushes growing up around the padded bars. Gradually she came out of it. But she swung high and low."

"Manic-depressive?"

"I guess. When she was high, Deanna Durbin charm. Then came the lows. Razor blades and piano wire and sleeping pills. In nineteen twenty-three, an Atlanta nurse struggled with Eva for a pair of scissors. Eva lost the scissors and the nurse lost an eye."

Jerry watched my face shrivel in distaste. "You wanted the facts, Norm."

"There's no law that says I have to like what you're saying."

"Anyway, the doctors in Atlanta contacted Ryker. They recommended a lobotomy to make her easier to manage.

"Ryker had other ideas. He'd been bitten by the health bug. Dandelion tea and nutmeg outlets and sitz baths. Eva went to Switzerland then stayed under lock and key at Baden-Baden for six months. They got her flying on at least a half-even keel.

"When she turned twenty-one, Eva flew Daddy's coop and took up residence in Vienna. Then Naples and Lisbon and Paris. She made the rounds through the continent, living a very fast and physical life on her old man's financial cushion. Plenty of sleek lovers. Parties and pot and the hard stuff. An abortion in Rome that went sour. She climbed out on the fifth-story ledge of Celio Hospital, clawing the police who grabbed her through an open window. The fascists permanently banished her from Italy. But Eva outlived Mussolini. She came back after the war. Italy, Portugal, Greece. Daddy's money and men kept scraping her off the pavement. But Ryker had lost heart in Eva. A bad little bitch dog he could never housebreak."

Jerry fumbled for a cigar and chomped on the stub. Puffing it to life, he spit wet tobacco leaves into a coaster perched on the sofa's arm.

"Big Daddy had his own problems. Like everyone else, he was scared shitless by the Crash. In thirty-eight, Ryker went to Switzerland to visit Eva. He never came back. An army of very expensive accountants and lawyers played musical chairs with Ryker's holdings, and when the band stopped playing, his assets were cozy and safe in numbered Swiss accounts. In no time he moved into the Château de Montreux outside Geneva. It seemed to suit him. The feudal baron and all. In June nineteen forty, he went for a morning dip in a stream running through the estate. Three days later he woke up gasping for air. Doctors in the ambulance had to cut open his throat, and even then he was nearly gone when they got to a hospital. He had the partial use of one leg and could leave his iron lung at least four to five hours a day. Many polio survivors made do with a lot less."

He blew smoke into a mushroom over his head. "Ryker went back to his château. He's never been out since."

Silence. The red cigar ash glared like a third eye. "So you're going to interview the Big Bad Ryker?"

"As soon as I can swing it."

"That could be never."

"I'd quit. Besides, Ryker must know that he has to come out of his burrow. I also want to talk to Eva. Do you have any idea where she is?"

"Spain, France, Denmark, who knows?" He threw up his hands. "The exploits of an aging fucked-out heiress aren't going to boost anyone's circulation. Even if her old man is making headlines."

Jerry grinned and licked his lips. I suddenly felt very ill.

"Thanks for the information." I handed him five hundred

dollars and made for the door. "If you find out where Eva's living, let me know."

With a shallow wheeze he heaved up from the chair and unlatched the door. "Norman, you're becoming painfully righteous in your old age. Pretty soon you'll be writing thousand-page epics about the dignity of man. Then God help us."

"Jerry, answer me one question."

"Yeah?"

"When was the last time you felt compassion for anyone?"

"Back before you were born, Norman. But I can understand your interest in Eva Ryker. After all, you do have things in common."

"What do you mean?"

"Oh, emotional problems. Traumas in the past. Things that haunt you all your life."

I stood still for a few moments, debating whether to loosen some of his teeth.

"Is this a shakedown?" I fought to keep my voice steady. "You'd be quite disappointed, Jerry. I wouldn't give you a dime."

I elbowed him out of my way. Walking down the corridor, I heard his parting words. "Give my love to Janice!"

My legs didn't break their stride. They carried me down the stairs and out into the street.

10

January 25, 1962

Jan lay waiting at Orly with more gloomy tidings. It was getting to be an unpleasant habit.

"Okay, dear, what is it?"

Keeping both eyes on the traffic, she reached behind the seat and pulled out the morning edition of *L'Express*. "It's on page three."

MASTERSON RESIGNS TITANIC POST

GENEVA (AP) Harold Masterson, the Canadian director of William Ryker's *Titanic* salvage project, announced his resignation effective today.

"The resignation of Mr. Masterson is for purely personal reasons," stated Michael Rogers, chief aide to Mr. Ryker. "All of us are very sorry to see him leave."

Masterson's dismissal comes at an unusual time, following his announcement four days ago of a lost film found aboard the *Titanic*, which was to have been released to the public.

Rogers claimed that the film, contrary to Masterson's press releases, had "deteriorated beyond any visual interpretation." He refused to say if a print would be released to the press.

In Halifax Masterson declined any comment on his resignation.

I folded the paper and glumly watched raindrops bounc-
ing off the hood like tiny Ping-Pong balls. "You know, Jan,
writing this story reminds me of knitting a sweater." My
fingers fiddled with invisible needles. "Here I am, finishing
the sleeves. Meanwhile, someone else is unraveling yarn at
the waist. I could spend the rest of my life trying to tie loose
ends."

She smiled ruefully. "What do you think of the article?"

"Isn't it obvious? You can be sure a professional man like
Masterson knew the film hadn't 'deteriorated beyond any visual interpretation.' Ryker saw something very special on
that old roll of film. Something that would make him fire a
top man and risk a stink in the papers rather than show it to
anyone else."

"So what are you going to do about it?"

"Step One will be Mike Rogers."

"The temperamental artist routine?"

"In spades. A thalamic fit that'll widen his stomach ulcer."

"I don't think Mike has one."

"Then it's time he started."

I made for the phone as soon as we got home. After running the secretary gauntlet, I got him on the line.

"Norman, am I glad to hear from you!" he said blithely.
"I've got some terrific news."

"You've got some questions to answer first."

"Just listen to me, Norman. I've just come back from Switzerland," he said breathlessly, as if he'd arrived on foot. "Mr.
Ryker wants to talk with you!" I was a good little boy being let
into the candy factory. "As soon as possible. Is tomorrow afternoon okay?"

The village of Veyrier, right on the Swiss-French frontier,
is a sleepy nursery-neat town with only one special distinc-
tion. The residents can, and do, boast that one of world's
richest men lives just outside their hamlet.

Only the twelfth richest, to be precise. But definitely not a poor relation.

The big house itself sits propped at the edge of a cliff which plummets down to the road leading between Veyrier and Annemasse. If nothing else, Ryker possesses his cherished seclusion.

Stitched on the side of the house is a low Spanish-tiled garage. Both sliding doors were left open, revealing a Mercedes pickup and a hulking Silver Phantom limousine. I felt like a minnow suckling up to a whale as I parked my rented Fiat by the Rolls.

A beauty. A '59 with a black, obsidian-shiny finish. Maybe not as much character as my Silver Wraith, but not nearly as long in the tooth. If Ryker wanted to swap, I wouldn't complain.

I looked across the courtyard at the château veiled by the thin snowfall.

Beautiful bad taste. Bell towers in Moorish baroque. Prisoner of Zenda balconies. Gothic arches over the main entrance. Big second- and third-story windows framed in shiny art deco chrome.

I rapped the knocker on the teak double doors that looked ready to withstand a Norman siege. The door was answered by a middle-aged woman with blunt features and longish brown hair tied in a bun.

"Mr. Hall?"

"Yes."

"I am Fräulein Lisl Slote, Mr. Ryker's personal nurse." A calloused handshake.

At closer inspection I saw liver spots on her hands and a faint web of wrinkles crisscrossing her face like Martian Canals. Yet her body was as taut as a trapeze artist's under the white uniform.

Her shoulders straightened under my appraisal. "How old do you think I am?"

"I hadn't really thought about it." My eyes widened innocently. "Perhaps forty . . . "

"I am sixty-five years old!" She thrust out her grapefruit breasts. "What do you think of that?"

"Remarkable," I muttered. It was her life's pride. My-name-is-Fräulein-Slote-How-Old-Do-You-Think-I-Am?

She pointed one arm at the long sweeping staircase. "Come with me, please."

Peering down vacant corridors, I glimpsed gloomy rooms trailing into infinity.

"This place seems pretty big for just you and Mr. Ryker."

"We are not alone. The château has a staff of twenty-five. Mr. Rogers also keeps him company on his visits from Paris. A most capable young man. He's also a pupil of mine."

"How's that?"

"A naturopath. Building the body nature's way. Mr. Rogers is most anxious to avoid the spreading of middle age." She looked disapprovingly at my waistline.

At the end of the stairs she turned left, marching down a passageway lined with gloomy Rembrandts and Klees. A very mixed bag. Suitable for the studied hodgepodge of the château.

I decided to play a hunch. "Fräulein Slote, did you ever work at Baden-Baden?"

Her little eyes widened. "Yes, before the war. Why do you ask?"

"Was Eva Ryker also one of your disciples?"

She stared straight ahead. "Years ago. I have not seen Eva in some time." Jabbing a hand at the door at the end of the corridor, she said, "You must be brief. Mr. Ryker should return to his iron lung within the hour. Understand?"

I nodded, stepping through and easing the latch shut behind me.

The room was bright sterile white. The sun blazed through a skylight in the roof. Huge slanting windows looked down on Veyrier, tiny in the distance. In the center of the circular room, a hospital bed sat tilted in a semireclining position. The famous iron lung lay on a gurney against the back wall. Sun lamps aimed at the bed. They made the room stiflingly hot.

Loosening my tie, I walked around the end of the bed. Naked except for sunglasses, William Ryker was a burned red lobster. Surrounded by olive green sheets, his gnarled body looked like a strip of bacon floating in a bowl of pea soup.

"Mr. Ryker?"

He stirred, reaching for his glasses. His face contained enough wrinkles to hold a three-day rain, but the eyes were pale gray and cold.

"You're Norman Hall?" A raspy voice, slow and measured.

"That's right."

One pipe stem arm rose in greeting. I gently squeezed his hand, afraid to break bones.

"I've looked forward to meeting you, young man. I said to myself after your last novel, 'That man has style.' I couldn't have been more pleased when you decided to write about the *Titanic*."

"Mr. Ryker, you paid a good deal of money to have me write this story. I'd like to know why."

"I don't quite follow, son."

"I'm referring to the half million dollars passing between you and Geoffrey Proctor."

Silence. He put the sunglasses back on. "Who told you that?"

"Does it matter?"

"Not a hell of a lot."

"In any event, I would like an answer."

"I think it's clear enough. I like your work and I wanted you on this story."

"A half million's a lot of money."

"Well, the money's relative. Hell, I had an aunt who spent ten thousand dollars putting braces on an old cat. She was a lot like me. You get to be my age and you decide to let money satisfy your whims. Once you're an old man, everyone expects you to act a little . . . peculiar." Ryker's hand patted the sheets. "One thing I should tell you right off. I'm flying out to the *Savonarola* in two weeks to inspect the salvage site."

"Is that with your doctor's blessing?"

"If I took my doctor's advice seriously, I'd need three nurses just to take a leak." Ryker coughed shortly. "Chet Kingswood—he's the new director of the project—is going to brief reporters aboard the *Savonarola* on February twelfth. You're invited."

"Thanks. I'll be there."

"Two reporters have already been picked to go down in one of the bathyscaphs to see the *Titanic*. You're one of them." A brief smile. "No claustrophobia, I hope."

"We'll find out," I said, feeling my body warm up in an adrenalin flush. "Who's the other reporter?"

"Your photographer chum, Burke Sheffield."

"How am I going to get aboard the *Savonarola*? Or does the half million include transportation to and from ship and continental breakfast?"

"Mike Rogers can iron out the details." Ryker's wrist shook feebly in dismissal.

I turned and looked out the windows. Far below, a passenger train glided on toy tracks toward Geneva.

"I'd like to know why you fired Harold Masterson."

The thin lips sourly smiled. "He drinks."

"Was this a recent vice of his?"

"I don't really know."

"You should have. Before you hired him."

The white hair fringing his bald skull rustled against the pillowcase as he spoke. "Contrary to what Mike Rogers may have told you, I'm not God. I make occasional mistakes. Masterson was one of them."

"Apparently. Did you see the film he gave you?"

"It was blank. Just random blotches. Nothing you could make out."

"Yes, that's what the newspapers said. It's odd, though. Masterson seemed to think otherwise."

"Mr. Masterson had a vivid imagination. Plus a hunger for grabbing headlines. Those two traits made a nasty combination. You might say he was riding for a fall."

Next to the iron lung sat a white straight-back chair. I dragged it next to the bed.

"Mr. Ryker, why did you start this salvage operation?"

"Scientific interest. And publicity value."

"Does Eva have anything to do with your exploration of the *Titanic*?"

"I prefer not to discuss Eva's problems. They're much too personal and they have nothing to do with your story."

"What about Mrs. Ryker? Isn't there an element of vengeance involved?"

"I don't follow you."

"Pardon my saying so, but the *Titanic* is your wife's tomb. Perhaps you have a natural grudge. The *Titanic* as an enemy. To be carved up, dissected, and conquered."

"A very colorful idea, Mr. Hall."

"Whatever your reasons, people are bound to assume that you have a morbid interest in the ship."

"People may assume what they wish." His eyes crinkled charmingly at the corners.

"Mr. Ryker, did you hear about John McFarland?"

"I sure did. That unfortunate man in Australia."

"Did you know him?"

"Who?" His brow furrowed. "McFarland? Of course not."

"He was a steward aboard the *Titanic*."

"So I've heard. But I'm sorry to disappoint you. As interested as I am in the *Titanic*, I don't keep tabs on every living survivor."

"He's not living anymore."

"Don't belabor the obvious, Mr. Hall. Are you suggesting some connection between this McFarland and myself?"

"Not suggesting. Merely curious. John McFarland's territory as a steward extended from B-eighty-four to B-seventy on the *Titanic's* portside. According to Mr. Masterson, that's where your bathyscaphs recovered the famous blank film. I interview the cagey Mr. McFarland with little success. That same day he's rather disgustingly murdered." I spread my hands. "Death is so permanent. I find it most distressing."

"You have an unfortunate taste for melodrama, Mr. Hall."

"Life *is* melodramatic. Or haven't you been reading the headlines for the past twenty years?"

Ryker lay prone on the green sheets. One finger pushed a button, lowering the bed. "You must forgive me, Mr. Hall, but I find all this conversation very tiring." His skeletal chest rose and fell. "I'm sure you understand . . . "

"Of course. But there is one more thing. Do you have any idea where your daughter is living?"

The sun lamps glinted in white-hot dots on Ryker's dark glasses. "A waste of time, Mr. Hall. Eva remembers nothing about the *Titanic*. She becomes terribly disturbed when people attempt to pry into her childhood."

"I can accept rejection. But I'd prefer it to come directly from your daughter."

Ryker tilted his head back, black lenses facing the ceiling. "I don't know where Eva is. We haven't talked in three months." He tabbed another button. "Lisl will show you the way out. Good-bye, Mr. Hall. I certainly enjoyed our little talk." His lips parted in a rictus grin. "Remember, we have a date in two weeks."

"Well," Jan asked. "What was he like?"

We were sitting at a booth at Le Béarn. I pursued an errant bite of fondue bourguignonne.

"He tried very hard to keep me from finding out. An endless variety of masks, and he shuffles through them very quickly as the occasion demands." I pushed my plate away. "Every time I think of plowing through Ryker's endless snow job, I get depressed."

We let the conversation drift to other matters until we were in the car, driving back to the Hotel Richemond. Braking at a signal, I glanced at Jan.

"Did you bring along the *Titanic*'s deck plan?"

"I think so."

"I want to take a peek at it before we turn in."

Jan searched through her suitcase while I latched the door. "Eureka," she said.

I spread the map on the bed like a third bed sheet. "Come here a minute."

"There's John McFarland's territory," I pointed. "Portside B deck, cabins eighty-four through seventy." My fingers waggled at the folder. "Do we have the passenger list somewhere in there?"

Jan fished and hauled it in. My forefinger scanned through the names. "Albert and Martha Klein were booked in B-seventy-eight. It's well within John McFarland's territory. I want to put names in these other cabins. You read them off."

Jan gave the page a blurry once-over. "Just don't rush me."

Twenty minutes later, each cabin in John McFarland's territory was attached to a name. Jan surveyed my handiwork.

"It's fascinating, I'll admit. But are any of these people connected with Ryker?"

"Not directly," I said. "Clair and Eva Ryker stayed over here." My thumb squashed the cabins. "B-fifty-three and B-fifty-five, the starboard promenade suites. Right next door is B-fifty-seven, the cabin of James Martin, Clair and Eva's bodyguard. None of them came within John McFarland's territory."

I straightened, studying the map. "No, the only connection I can see is that damn movie being found in McFarland's bailiwick."

"Exactly where was the movie discovered?"

"Masterson never mentioned the exact location to reporters. And I doubt if Ryker or Mike Rogers will enlighten us."

Her hand rested on my shoulder. "Maybe we're splitting nonexistent hairs, Norman. Ryker says the film is blank."

"Janice, you remind me of a cop directing traffic through a labyrinth." I packed up the map and put it away for the night. "If the film is really blank, then McFarland's death, Masterson's resignation, almost every aspect of this blasted story is meaningless."

The ringing phone interrupted our conversation. The hotel operator relayed a message from our Paris answering service. We had received an important long-distance call from a Mr. Jerry Blaine in Los Angeles. KL-5-7160.

"You don't seriously plan on talking to that man," Jan said.

"There's no other way of finding out what he wants."

"You can't call now, Norman. In L.A. it's about . . . " Her eyes glazed as she skipped through time zones. " . . . five in the morning."

I laughed and kept on dialing.

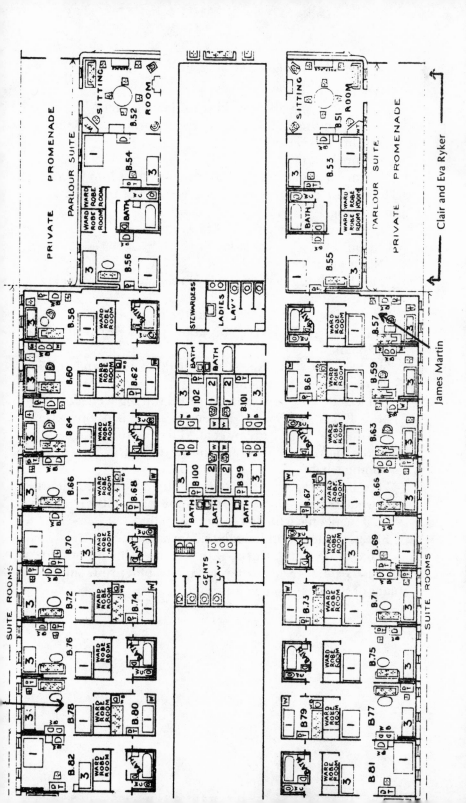

"What's so funny?"

"You. Worrying about waking up Jerry Blaine." The operator came on the line and I gave her the number. "Besides, I don't think he ever sleeps."

My hunch was right.

"Norm!" He managed to put four syllables into my name. "Thanks for calling! Say, I hope you're not sore about our last meeting."

"I've recovered nicely, thanks."

"Norm, I have a proposition."

"Name your fee, Jerry."

"Five hundred bucks for the whereabouts of Eva Ryker."

"I'm listening."

"Not so fast, Norm. What about the money?"

"Enough games, Jerry. You know very well I won't cheat you. So talk."

Silence. "All right. She's living in Madrid. Number 1402 Calle de Alcala. Apartment 510."

Jan watched me as I hung up. "And the Big News is . . . "

"Eva Ryker's in Spain." I rose from the bed, opened the closet door and hung up my coat. "I'll need to hop a plane tomorrow for Madrid. Do you mind staying here?"

"Doing what?"

"For one thing, you can start sniffing around and finding out what the people in Veyrier know about Ryker and his staff. The people who do business with him."

She gave me a lopsided salute. "It shall be done."

"One more thing. Check with the city hall here in Geneva and in Veyrier. See if they have any blueprints and floor plans of the Château de Montreux."

11

January 28, 1962

Every Sunday afternoon in Madrid twenty thousand people gather together for ritual murder.

I was a reluctant member of the herd squeezed in the stands of the Plaza del Toros. Shading my eyes from the sun, I squinted down at the ring. The bullfight was about to begin.

Behind me a chorus of bugles blew in a great groaning fanfare. Forty thousand vocal cords roared as the six matadors starring in the day's events strutted out into the ring.

One voice outshouted the rest. Or so it seemed. I focused my Nikon's 135-mm telephoto lens on the source of the noise, three rows in front of me.

The blurred image sharpened into a plump, sloppy brunette slurping beer. *"Olé!"* she yelled, suds spilling over her mouth. *"Toro! Toro!"*

With an immense gravelly laugh, she slapped the backs of her two young "gentlemen callers."

Eva Ryker had been easy to find. Unfortunately, she was equally easy to lose. I'd spent most of the afternoon following her Ferrari convertible in my anonymous rented Alfa-Romeo sedan.

My stomach began a dull ache when I saw her park near the Plaza del Toros. I hate bullfights.

But Eva was a regular aficionado. She excitedly watched the banderilleros and picadors parade into the ring. "*Ole! Bravo!*" She planted a foamy kiss on one of her companions.

Time had done a hack job on Eva Ryker. The jaw line, once ruthless and crisp, must have sagged a decade ago. Curves had turned to mounds and her long hair, wrapped up on top of her head, was dreadful in its Clairol blackness.

But the eyes, deep blue and troubled, were still good, even when glazed by too much beer. Implanted in twin craters of crow's-feet, they belonged to a girl of twenty. They would taunt her—a reminder of what she'd lost.

Leaning forward, she watched the banderilleros scamper around the bull, flinging darts into the animal's shoulders. I saw red streaks drip down the bull's black sweaty flanks and tried to ignore the bad taste in my mouth.

"*Olé!*" Eva shrieked as a dart poked a new trickling hole in the bull's back. "*Bravo! Bravo!*"

The bullring turned mellow orange as the sun eased westward. Through the Nikon's view finder I watched stale brown blood splashing on the sand. Dull and weary, the eyes of the bull stared stupidly at the advancing matador. He charged and ran, sweeping past the scarlet cape.

The matador's passes grew slower. With a jabbing flourish, he plunged the sword into black flesh. The animal lost control of its bowels in a last dying reflex as the corpse sagged into a steaming heap at the matador's feet.

Bugles screamed along with the crowd. Hats flew into the air. Crying with delight, Eva Ryker bear-hugged her boy friends.

I endured five more events. The sunlit side of the Plaza del Toros was a dull crimson when the men came into the ring to clean up the offal. I craned my head over the crowd to watch the long black hair of Eva Ryker work its way to the exit.

By the time I caught up with her, she was already getting in the Ferrari.

"Excuse me, Miss Ryker. Could I talk with you for a moment?"

Her eyes slid up to mine. "What for?"

Eva's boys puffed their pectorals. "Piss off, man." A thick Italian accent. "The lady doesn't want to be bothered."

I held out my hand to Eva. "My name's Norman Hall."

The eyes flickered with mild interest. "The Big Novelist? My, my. Don't tell me you're doing research on a new book."

"A sequel to *Blood and Sand*. You've got the Linda Darnell part."

"Shucks." Eva didn't smile. "I've always thought of myself as the Rita Hayworth type."

"Could be. But I do want to talk." I pointed in the car. "Preferably without the company of Romulus and Remus."

No one spoke. Then she shrugged. "Okay." She opened the far door. "Both of you. Out."

"But Eva . . ." they sputtered.

"Take a cab." She passed a hundred-peseta note. "Meet me at the apartment."

They looked unhappy but went. She patted the adjacent bucket seat. "Get in."

I walked around the back of the car, canting my head at the departing pair. "Nice boys. Are you buying or leasing?"

"Installment plans," Eva said blankly as I slid into the seat. "I'm disappointed, Mr. Hall."

"How's that?"

"You don't look like the coarse type."

"Implying that I am."

"I don't like leering wisecracks about my sex life."

"Sorry. But I do find my curiosity aroused by the bizarre."

Eva didn't answer. She savagely gunned out of the parking slot. My stomach slammed back in the seat as we hit the street at sixty miles an hour.

With a huge laugh she squealed a left against a honking stream of traffic.

"How did you manage to find me, Mr. Hall?"

I braced myself as we took a corner. "Don't be modest, Eva. You're a fixture of this town."

Her smile was laconic. "Then you didn't talk to Daddy?"

"I did. He said he didn't know where you were. I thought he was lying then. I'm sure of it now."

"Oh? How come?"

"We're sitting in it." I patted the dash. "New Ferraris don't grow on trees. A present from Daddy, most likely."

"So you've tracked me down." She made a face, spinning the car onto the Avenida Generalissimo. "What's the big deal?"

I had to yell above the roaring engine. "It has to do with the *Titanic!*"

"I'll tell you all about it!" she yelled back. "It sunk!"

"You were a survivor, Eva. There are things you could tell me."

The Ferrari parked at the foot of her apartment building. "Here's the place." She looked over at me. "And to answer your question—no, Mr. Hall. I was only ten at the time."

She switched off the engine. The hood popped as it cooled in the darkness.

"I gather you don't share your father's enthusiasm for the *Titanic.*"

"Daddy and I share as little as possible."

". . . 'she said frostily, lips pursed in long-accustomed tightness.'" My fingers made typing motions.

Her eyes appraised me. "Is that a taste of your style, God forbid?"

"No. Just winging it."

"How very incisive. Is that supposed to peel me down to the marrow?"

"Only if you feel like it. You were discussing your father."

"Oh, yes. Daddy." She ran her hands through her hair, peering up at the sky. "Have you ever raised pets, Mr. Hall?"

"Mostly cats," I said. "Hamsters, way back."

Eva didn't seem to have heard. "When I was a little girl we lived in a big house in Newport, and on the grounds, way in back near the boundary line, was a low swampy gully where I used to play . . ."

"Was this after the *Titanic?*"

"Of course!" Her eyebrows furrowed crossly. "Let me tell my story, will you? Anyway, in this gully in back of our house I found a baby crocodile. I don't know how it got there." She batted aside the question with her hand. "Or maybe it was an alligator. I can never tell which is which. Anyhow, I would pick up this little croc and watch it scamper through the grass. He wasn't much more than four or five inches long, and he was *so* cute! He had bright yellow eyes and a wiggly tail and sort of jaunty, grinning jaws. Of course, if you got your fingers near, he'd snap, cracking his little teeth. But he was small and harmless."

She frowned, losing herself in the ancient childhood litany. "I played with that baby crocodile all summer, pulling his tail and watching it snap at twigs. Every day his bite got a little stronger.

"One morning, I ran my hand along its back and it turned and bit me. Really hard." Eva flinched at the memory. "Later, the doctors had to take twelve stitches. I can still remember looking into the eyes of that croc as it licked my flesh out of its teeth with a pale pink tongue. The eyes weren't friendly anymore. They were wide and greedy for another bite, deciding what place to strike next. I ran screaming across the yard into the house. I suppose the servants found the crocodile or alligator or whatever it was and had it . . ."

Eva's body tensed, halting her descent over the unforeseen precipice. "Later, of course, I realized that the crocodile hadn't changed," she said with wintry composure. "Merely grown. I simply hadn't recognized him for what he was."

Her hands drooped off the wheel. "No doubt you found my father charming."

"In a heavy-handed way."

"Really?" She straightened in genuine surprise. "He used to be quite subtle. His victims were still smiling when he dragged them under the mud."

"You said 'victims,' Eva. Who were they?"

Her lips puckered defiantly. "For a start, my mother was Victim Number One."

"How so?"

"Mother was unlucky enough to be the primary object of my father's affection. He used to call her his little 'pet.'" Eva recoiled at the word. "Daddy kept her groomed and well-fed and cozy in the doghouse. He also found her useful for warming up his bed on cold nights. But Daddy grew tired of sleeping with his pet and sent it to other beds. Mostly belonging to his business partners, where she would do the most good."

"And your mother obeyed?"

"Oh yes. She was well-trained. You see, she loved Daddy helplessly, and besides, he had a nasty habit of violence when he was crossed."

"That's quite a story, Eva. How'd you come across it?"

"It wasn't just a story," she blinked defensively. "I was there and I saw it happening all around me."

"You weren't more than eight or nine at the time." I rested my arm on the back of the driver's seat. "As I remember it, at that age, I still believed babies were grown by Mr. and Mrs. Cabbage Head out in their vegetable patch."

She shied away from my arm. "I was very unsheltered."

"Downright precocious, I'd say."

Eva didn't respond. A radio played from a third-story window. *Volare . . . O-O-O-Oh.*

"Don't patronize me, Mr. Hall. In spite of what you may have heard, I'm not a child. I didn't know about my mother and father until much later," she muttered coolly. "I simply put things together I'd seen for years."

"All right, Eva. But all your woolgathering about your mother seems rather pointless. After all, she's been gone for fifty years."

"So she's gone *now!*" Eva turned on me with narrow eyes. "She was alive *then!*"

"I don't believe I'll have room in my story for the Parable of the Crocodile and Dog." I went on, sensing her stiffness. "You have much more in common with your father than you realize. Both of you like to kick those sleeping dogs just to hear them growl."

"Certain things you can't forget. But the *Titanic* isn't one of them. God knows why Daddy wants to dig around down there." She scowled in little-girl petulance. "It was the ship that killed my mother. I never want to think of it again."

"Eva, I've read all the accounts of the sinking and I've never figured out what happened to your mother. She was a first-class passenger who had first crack at the lifeboats. Why'd she stay behind?"

She fumbled for the door handle. "I'm sorry, Mr. Hall, but it's getting very late. I'm going inside. You're not invited because I have nothing more to say."

I climbed out onto the sidewalk, then leaned down into the cockpit. "Eva, too many people are interested in you. Or your past, to be precise. Three of your fellow passengers have been killed. That's a fact, not something you can wash away with cheap beer. And whoever killed them might not be as obliging about your lack of memory as I am."

Eva faced me, harshly pale under the street lights. Without another word, she jumped from her car and ran into the apartment building. She didn't look back.

I hailed a taxi to get back to my car at the bullring. Leaning back in the old mohair cushions, I watched street lights streak past the windows, remembering that last glimpse of Eva Ryker.

I'd seen something I hadn't noticed before. Eva had a faint but long scar over her right eye.

Another crocodile bite, no doubt.

12

January 29, 1962

Jan was waiting for me at Geneva Airport. On our way to the Hotel Richemond I filled her in on Eva Ryker.

"She and her daddy sound like quite a pair."

"Yes indeed." I swung the Fiat around a slowpoking Saab sedan. "A rather frightening woman. There's too much churning beneath the hood." I blinked absently. "Anything exciting happen while I was gone?"

"I take it you haven't read the papers."

I felt new knots in my stomach. "Not another bombshell. I can't take any more."

"Just a little one. Ryker released the *Titanic* film."

"The hell you say!" The Fiat swerved on the pavement.

"The film was blank. Just like Mike Rogers told the press."

"Surprise, surprise. I guess it's taken that long for Mike to find some old thirty-five millimeter film stock, expose it to light, age it convincingly, then make duplicates for release."

"That'll be hard to prove, Norman."

"I'm not about to try." I glanced away from the road. "Did you turn up anything new on Ryker?"

"You might say so." Jan had her canary-swallowing look.

"I've got a working blueprint of the Château de Montreux, for starters."

"Seriously?"

"I paid a visit to Clement and Versoix, the contractors in Geneva who helped renovate the château when Ryker moved in. One of their draftsmen, a Mr. Besançon, was very cooperative. For a few francs."

"Exactly how many?"

"Two hundred fifty thousand."

I made a rude noise. "You were had, Janice."

"So you had to dish out some money. You've still got the blueprint." She passed a large folded sheet to me. "Take a look "

"Later, dear." I handed it back. "I'd rather stay on the road. What about Ryker's staff?"

"I don't get you."

"Butlers. Maids. Bodyguards," I said impatiently, wheeling onto the rue de Granges. "They must have some time off. And they must spend some of it in Veyrier."

"I don't know. I don't think . . ." Jan snapped her fingers. "Wait a minute! Does Ryker own a black Rolls limousine?"

"A Phantom V," I nodded. "Why?"

"I saw it parked in the village. In front of a tavern. The chauffeur comes into Veyrier on errands."

"Do you remember the name of the tavern?"

"No, but I can show you where it is."

"Jan," I said, kissing her full on the mouth. "You've just answered my prayers."

Her eyes were wary. "What were you praying for?"

"A way to visit the château. Without an invitation."

"There's the place," Jan pointed later that evening.

Some fifty yards down the street yellow light spilled from a glass-paned door onto muddy snowdrifts and a line of parked cars.

A zippy accordion polka played behind the door. Swinging in the wind, the gold letters of a wood sign flashed at me in the yellow light.

"THE EICHOF," I read, pointing at the cars hugging the curb. "The place looks packed."

"Maybe there's a parking spot down the street."

We went down a half block before discovering a car taking its lion's share of room. Sandwiched between two Volkswagens, Ryker's Phantom V sat in huffy silence. Stray snowflakes perched like shy pigeons on the black sheet metal.

I braked the Fiat, listening to the exhaust echo between the buildings.

"This is where I get out. Think you'll have any problems driving?"

"No. Why should I?" Jan wouldn't meet my gaze.

I reached for the leather briefcase lying between the front seats. "Do you remember where to meet me?"

"On the road to Annemasse," she recited, "about a quarter mile past the château's entrance gate, at the soft-shoulder turnout. I'll be there at eleven-thirty and stay until two. If you're not there by then, I'll cross the border into France and call Tom Bramel as soon as I can."

"Fine." I tried to kiss her good-bye but she wasn't cooperating. "Come now, Janice, you can do better than that."

Her eyes grew grave. "I'm not sure you're worth it."

"At least wish me luck."

She squeezed my hand. "Just be sure you're there by two."

She rolled up the window. Gears ground and the Fiat moved on into the darkness, its tail lights shining through the exhaust to form a swaying red cloud that disappeared around a corner.

For the moment, at least, the street was empty. Casually, like a man who knows exactly what he is doing, I walked to the Rolls and stashed my briefcase behind the left rear tire.

People were packed into the Eichof like transistors in a Japanese radio. Dodging a snow-tanned young lady who possessed a rather improbable chest, I tried to spot Ryker's chauffeur.

My eyes scanned along the bar, then skidded to a stop. It had to be him. He was too good to be true. About thirty-five, with an Alan Shepard crew cut and a pale freckled face.

Seconds later I saw my chance. A short man next to the

chauffeur moved away, blazing an anxious trail to the men's room. I squeezed between two tables and grabbed the spot.

My man glanced incuriously at me. I smiled politely. "Hello."

"Hi." He turned his back, rapping the counter top and beckoning the bartender in very mangled French.

I noticed his chauffeur cap lying under his right elbow like a squashed animal. As he shifted his weight on the bar stool, he unwittingly moved the cap down the counter toward me.

"Excuse me." I held the cap up to him. "You don't want to lose this."

"Thanks," he nodded, smiling briefly.

I jabbed my forefinger at him. "Bet you drive that big Rolls out there!"

"Yep."

"Man, I always wanted one of those buggies."

"It gets you around."

"I'll say! Hey, you sound like a Yankee!"

His jaw stiffened. "American, yes. But not Yankee. Huntsville. The name's Jim Culhane."

"I might've known!" I pumped his hand. "Jack Warnick. From Charlotte."

"Nice place," he grunted.

"Well," I yelled above the roar of the crowd, "what brings you over here? From the States, I mean. Whoever owns that Rolls must have a lot of dough."

"It belongs to Mr. Ryker." He drained the last drop from the shot glass. "He lives up in the mountains not far from here."

"Must be a pretty easy job." My left hand eased toward his right coat pocket.

"It pays well enough," he shrugged, shifting on the stool. My hand brushed against the pocket. Empty. This wasn't going to be as easy as I thought.

"Sure," I drawled expansively. "Just look at the people in this bar." The chauffeur turned around. "Oh yeah," I grunted, my right hand delving in his left coat pocket, "the people here are prosperous enough, but they've still got to beat their brains out for everything they get." The pocket was empty.

"So you come over here and make real easy money just because you're an American. I wouldn't knock it, Jim."

He toyed with his glass. "There just isn't a hell of a lot to do."

"Can't have everything." My hand reached for the edge of his right front pocket.

"Guess so." He raised his arm, looking down the counter. "Hey, Armand! Another double!"

My fingers, probing his pocket, felt the cold brass of his key chain. The bartender came up to us with the double scotch. The shot glass slid in front of the chauffeur as his keys slid from his pocket into mine.

Culhane caught the eye of the bartender. "Let's have a beer for my friend here, too." His hand went for his right front pocket.

"No, no! Allow me!" Before he could protest, I passed a ten-franc note to Armand, who nodded and slipped unobtrusively away.

"That's mighty kind of you, Warnick." He reached for his wallet. "But maybe I should pay you . . ."

"Think nothing of it!" I beamed. I could've sworn I felt my knees knocking as his hand withdrew. ". . . it's not often that I get to talk with someone from the States . . ." My eyes suddenly went vacant and I snapped my fingers. "Christ, I just remembered. I think I left my lights on." I shoved away from the counter. "Save my place, will you? Be right back."

Shoveling like a snowplow through the crowd, I stepped out the exit. In the yellow light I sorted through Culhane's keys. Only one out of seven on the ring was of any use to me—the key with the RR crest.

I took a last look around. Not a soul in sight. In one swift motion I grabbed my case from under the rear wheels, then unlocked the trunk.

I set the case near the spare tire, then eased the trunk lid down so it wouldn't latch shut.

Culhane hadn't moved. But a new shot glass sat in front of him. I hoped drunken driving wasn't a habit of his.

"Sorry I took so long," I said, slapping his shoulder and

dropping the keys back in his pocket. "The damn lights *were* on."

"Good thing you checked."

My hand beckoned the bartender. "Another Carlsberg, please." I grinned at Culhane. "I think I deserve it."

Two hours later I knew more than I cared to about the life of Jim Culhane. Apparently Hennessey Four-Star hit him like truth serum. I eyed my watch.

"Well, Jim, I must be off." I amiably shook his hand. "Glad to have met you."

He grinned, weaving a little on his feet. "You, too, Jack. Thanks for the drinks."

"My pleasure." I stood by the door. "Good night."

I waited until the door shut behind me, then walked down to the Rolls, opened the trunk, and scrambled inside. I reached up and shut the lid.

As the trunk closed, the inside light blinked out, making it as dark as the inside of a cat. I squirmed into the fetal position and waited.

It didn't take long. Heels clicked to the rear of the car, moving around to the driver's side.

The engine whispered to life and we were off.

According to the lore of automobile enthusiasts, the noisiest part of a Rolls Royce is the clock.

Don't believe it. I can testify, from personal experience, that the loudest part of any Rolls is the trunk.

The luminous face on my watch read 12:25. Jan would be waiting on the soft shoulder not two miles away.

Minutes later the Rolls eased to a stop. Shoes scuffed dirt at the side of the car.

"Hi, Jim." The muffled voice sounded like Ryker's gatepost guard. "How're things in the village?"

"Slow," Culhane replied. "Met some gabby fellow who wanted to talk."

After a long silence the limousine accelerated. I felt myself sliding toward the rear as the Rolls twisted uphill to the château.

Tires snuffled over the courtyard cobblestones. The Rolls braked sharply, then glided for several feet and stopped.

The silence was broken by a grating roller skate noise. It stopped for a moment and footsteps faded away.

Of course! An electric garage door that Culhane shut behind him.

From what I could hear, I was alone in the garage. My palms reached up for the lid and pushed. I tottered out onto the cement floor, grabbed my case and slammed the trunk shut.

As my eyes dilated, I saw a dim rectangle of light behind the Rolls. It was a tiny window cut in the garage door. One bright spotlight shone across the courtyard from the château, casting complex patterns of light and shade across the cobblestones.

The only thing that saved me was a glimpse of the cobblestone shadows vanishing under a second source of light. I lunged away from the window, barely escaping a flashlight beam.

Two pairs of lungs panted rapidly on the other side of the door.

The guard muttered, "Nothing here, boys. Let's go." Sharp toenails scratched the cobblestones, accompanying his retreating footsteps.

Dogs. I sighed faintly, wiping my brow. Fast breathers. Dobermans, maybe?

Dobermans or not, they were an unwelcome surprise. How long between rounds? Fifteen minutes at most. Damn little time.

I took my penlight from my vest pocket and searched along the rim of the garage door for the switch. Rumbles and squeaks. Before it could make more noise, I cut it off.

There was barely a foot clearance. I got on my belly, sidled under the garage door, snatched the briefcase after me and stood erect.

Except for the single spotlight, the great gray bulk of the

château lay in darkness. I dropped to one knee and laid the briefcase on my leg. Opening the lid, I extracted a collapsible grappling hook and nylon cord. My hands worked as if detached from my body, smoothly threading four inches of the cord into the open end of the hook.

Whirling the hook above my head, I got a good idea of its weight. I backed away ten paces, gazing speculatively at the wood shingles capping the peaked roof of the garage.

Slowly, then rapidly, I spun the grappling hook over my head. Glittering in the moonlight, the hook arched over the garage roof as the cord flashed through my palm.

I tiptoed to the side of the garage and pulled the cord. It slid, then slid some more. Chagrined, I tugged harder. Now the hook caught. I gave it all my weight and it still held.

I took a deep breath, grabbed the cord with both hands and pulled myself up ten feet to the edge of the roof. Puffing like an old war horse, I yanked myself over. On my hands and knees I followed the path of the cord over the crown of the roof and down the other side.

A moving dot of light flashed in the corner of my eye. The guard patrol was back.

He passed underneath, paused, then wandered on. I waited until the last glimmer of his flashlight had gone, then sat up.

Mont Blanc and Mont Dolent glowed distantly under the moonlight. Closer at hand, chestnut and fir trees whispered and chuckled among themselves in the night wind. It was, I estimated, a good five hundred feet from the château down to the forest.

Folding the cord and the grappling hook back in my case, I gingerly crept down the far side of the garage roof. The jump down to the bedrock looked to be about fifteen feet. I hit the ground in a loose roll, landing on my butt and feeling rather foolish. I stuck close to the garage, following it around to where it met the mortar flanks of the château.

I was able to follow the slope of the mountain another twenty yards before it ended at the cliff. Perched on the edge, I watched the tips of trees beneath my feet.

Thank God the architect of Le Château de Montreux had

a flair for ornamentation! Beneath the windows was a ledge sculptured in bogus Roman scrollwork. A design horror, but very useful to me.

It was about seven inches wide—barely enough to stand on. With a mental shrug I jumped up for the ledge. I groaned and cursed under my breath, pulling myself up.

Red-faced and sweaty, I barely managed to mount the ledge. I spread my arms to keep balanced and stayed there, arms outstretched, trying to catch my breath.

The ledge seemed sturdy enough. I checked the case under my arm. No damage that I could see.

Hugging the wall in a clumsy embrace, I moved the right foot. Then the left. They both held. Right foot, left foot, right foot, left foot, I said to myself, inching along the edge of the wall.

I passed beyond the cliff face. The trees below didn't look like a very good cushion if I fell.

Don't think about falling. You're a circus performer on the high wire. You've done this for years. The crowds are cheering and the safety net is below.

The ledge came around a curve, and I knew I'd reached my destination—the windows of Ryker's sunroom. With all the lights out they were blackly opaque, like slabs of tar.

According to the blueprints of the château, Ryker hadn't bothered installing alarms on the windows facing away from the mountain. The glass cutter ground into the left edge of the window. Like a fingernail scratching a blackboard, it cut a small half circle.

I pried a thumbnail between the crack and worked the piece loose. My hand carefully reached through the razor-edged hole and pulled the latch.

The window slid aside smoothly. I grabbed the frame and stepped through. Ryker would be sleeping next door, trapped in his iron lung. And Fräulein Slote would be hovering nearby, ready for any emergency. Culhane and the domestic servants were quartered downstairs.

All in all, a good twenty-five people rattled around this mausoleum. I hoped no one sleepwalked.

The door from the solarium was locked—fortunately from the inside. It opened onto the empty corridor. The old masters on the wall slumbered in the low amber glow of bracket lamps. Ryker's office was the first door to my left.

A strip of plastic the size of a credit card is a wonderful pass key. I slipped the edge of the plastic into the door crack, found the bolt and pressed gently. The edge of the plastic caught the curve of the lock and slid it back. I stepped through and shut it behind me.

Commanding a central position in the office was a hulking walnut desk and high-backed leather chair. Two gray metal filing cabinets hugged the wall on either side of the desk.

I set up the equipment with the smoothness of an assembly-line worker. Laying the case on Ryker's uncluttered desk, I pulled out the tripod and stood it up behind the desk chair, where it tottered like a spindly giraffe.

I screwed the Beaulieu 8-mm camera into the tripod head, testing the tilt and swivel controls. It seemed steady enough.

The little lamp I removed from the case and clamped to the camera's side didn't have much punch, but it would serve at close range. I tilted the reflector to cast a white oval of light over the top of the desk. The lamp also provided enough light to see the four desk drawers, each with its own lock. Within a minute the plastic card had jimmied all four.

My first target was the long drawer directly under the blotter. Upon examination it revealed two manila folders, besides the usual quota of paper clips, rubber bands, and stubby pencils. Each folder contained about twenty typed sheets.

I rolled the chair aside and shoved the tripod in close so the camera lens pointed straight down at the desk surface. I set the zoom lens to photograph a neat rectangle encompassing the entire blotter, then kicked the aperture control off automatic and manually reset it between f-8 and f-11.

I sighed in relief after making the last setting. Now I could get on with the real job.

Placing the first manila folder beneath the lens, I fingered the twenty sheets in my left hand. As my right hand brought the camera chattering to life with the remote control, I flipped loosely through the pages, making sure each sheet was fully exposed.

The time from cover to cover was slightly less than one and a half seconds. Among the twenty-six 8-mm frames were twenty-three full-face photos of the papers. When run frame-by-frame through my movie projector, they should reveal readable copies of the original.

The amount of files and documents in the desk was staggering, but the camera made short work of them. For almost thirty minutes I settled into such a smooth pattern of piling the files on the desk, rifling through them in front of the camera, and returning them to their original location that I barely glanced at the pages flashing past me.

Done. I shut off the lamp. God, but my back was sore! I slipped the film out of the camera and arched my spine.

The doorknob rattled. Lights flashed on and Lisl Slote stood in the doorway, gun in hand.

I didn't have time to think how she'd heard me. I hit the floor, dodging the bullet yowling overhead.

Lisl, I'm glad to say, was a lousy shot. Before she could pull the trigger again, I rolled behind the desk. My hands grabbed the tripod legs and slung the camera toward the door. I heard a crackle of broken glass and bone as the Beaulieu hit Fräulein Slote's jaw. She keeled over backwards, pumping slugs into the ceiling as she went down.

I rose from behind the desk, my nose wrinkling with the gunpowder smell. Lisl lay sprawled in the corridor, tangled amid tripod legs and smashed lenses. She wasn't moving. I grabbed the grappling hook from my case and took off.

Lisl had plenty of friends. Judging from the alarms wailing outside, her pals, both human and canine, would be arriving any moment.

Everything was a blur as I ran down the hall toward the solarium. As I reached the windowsill, footsteps trod behind me. My elbow jabbed the window and it cascaded outward in a great screaming crash. Hanging the hook on the windowsill, I perched myself on the edge, grabbed the rope and swung free. My hands streamed red from broken glass, but I didn't feel a thing.

Hand over hand. Concentrate on the rope. Ignore the forest below or Ryker's guards or your aching arms.

Something dark loomed beside me. The top of a fir tree. I braved a look down. Still over a hundred feet to the ground.

I heard a voice above. "Look! Over here! This hook!"

Slowly. Don't panic. Forty feet to go.

"Get some dogs down by the road."

Thirty feet. Twenty.

The cord suddenly slack in my hands, I fell to the ground, landing flat on my back.

I lay there stupidly, blinking away stars, then moaned and groaned my way upright. Each vertebra throbbed as if beaten with a night stick.

Dogs barked in the distance. The high neurotic cries of Doberman pinschers. Their whining echoed among the encircling trees.

I tried to get my bearing. The mountain sloped to my left. Turning and running, I hit a tree trunk.

The thick blanket of chestnuts and firs cut off the moonlight. Arms outstretched before me, I ran downhill, stumbling my way between the branches.

A yellow star winked in the corner of my eye. A flashlight.

"Don't see him," a voice said hoarsely.

"He's there," a companion answered. "The dogs have the scent. He hasn't got a prayer."

I kept on running, air burning my lungs.

Leaves rustled behind me.

"Down, boy, down!"

"Ah, let him loose! He'll tear that guy to pieces."

Sweat dripped down my eyes. Not far to go.

Car headlamps lit up the snow between the trees. It was Jan in the Fiat. Maybe fifty yards away.

The barking was louder. Whipping off my jacket, I wrapped it around my right arm.

The light from the car cast shadows through the forest. From the darkness red eyes lunged.

The pinscher jumped me, attacking my arm. Long white teeth cut through my jacket into the flesh. Snarling gums. Hot panting breath.

He pushed me on my back, straddling me—shaking me like a piece of meat. My fingers grappled over the ground, squirming, grasping for a stone or stick.

My hand curled around a potato-sized rock.

Teeth slashed for my throat. The stone in my hand hit the dog behind the ear with a sharp crack.

With a shrill whimper the Doberman shuddered and died. I pushed him off me, smelling animal sweat and the last of his rotten-meat breath.

The guard's flashlight searched for me through the trees. Jumping to my feet, I threw away my tattered coat and sprinted for the car.

Two more dogs barked behind me, not far away.

Peeking down through the trees, I saw the outline of the Fiat, parked at the soft shoulder.

The dogs were closing.

I darted down the hill.

My shadow appeared in front of me, outlined in yellow.

"There he is!"

Gunshots whistled through the branches.

I broke through the last of the forest. Half running, half falling, I headed for the car. Jan leaned over, opening the door, her face terrified.

Dogs snarled behind me as I jumped in and tugged the handle. Two pinschers hit the door, their teeth scratching the glass.

"Norman . . ."

Bullets thudded into the bodywork.

"Later! Later! Get this thing going!"

Gears ground and the car lurched spastically.

"What the hell . . ."

Jan stared down at the clutch pedal. "I never could drive this damn car!"

"Get over!"

Both dogs had discovered our flimsy convertible top. Their claws made white slits in the canvas as we kicked and jabbed each other, changing seats.

"Move! Move!"

"I'm moving!"

One dog broke through, his teeth snapping at my shoulder. Jan's screaming filled my ears as I scrambled for the glove compartment. Under the impact of my pounding fists it popped open and I grabbed the flashlight.

Jan was flailing at the Doberman with her purse. I shoved her aside and smashed the flashlight against the dog's nose, then pushed broken glass into his eyes. He wrenched the flashlight from my hands, then backed out of the rip in the top and ran howling off into the darkness.

However, the other pinscher was made of sturdier stuff. As I wrestled with the balky gearshift, he bounded on the hood. The dog looked me in the eye and attacked. The windshield cracked under his impact. Glaring at me through the glass fissures, he charged again, tearing off one wiper.

The stick finally popped into first. I let in the clutch, watching the Doberman's shoulder muscles ripple in an effort to grip the hood as we got back on the road. He barked and snarled as the speedometer crept upwards.

At forty kilometers my foot hit the brakes. The pinscher flew off into space, rebounding over the radiator ornament. I caught a flashing glimpse of his wild eyes under the glare of the headlamps. Then came a sickening *bump-bump* as the car's momentum took us over the body.

Red in the afterglow of tail lights, two armed guards ran out into the road. Bullets crashed through the rear window. I pushed the gas pedal to the floor. The Fiat's little engine screamed in protest as we rounded a bend, putting the guards behind us.

The speedometer hovered at ninety kilometers. No headlights following. I eased up on the pedal as we slowed into a curve.

"We had quite a head start." I tried to swallow but couldn't. "I doubt if they can catch up."

Jan looked down at my arm. "Oh, God. You're hurt."

"No, I'm not . . ." I followed her gaze down to my bleeding hands and my arm with long teeth marks raked through the flesh. Jan wiped away some of the blood and I suddenly felt very ill.

"What happened to you?" she cried.

"I bitched it."

"You had to leave everything?"

I nodded.

She pointed at my chest. "Then what's that?"

I reached into my shirt pocket and pulled out the 8-mm magazine. Holding it in front of my eyes, I grinned raggedly, then tossed the film to Jan.

"That," I said, "is the most valuable home movie on earth."

13

February 3, 1962

First, of course, the movie had to be processed.

Jan dropped the film in a Geneva mailbox on January thirtieth to send it to Kodak's Paris lab. On February third the finished roll arrived, amid a pile of bills, at our post office box in Fourqueux.

All in all, a three-day wait. Those three days were among the most unpleasant in my life.

Two of them were spent sneaking inconspicuously out of Switzerland. Jan did most of the work, I'm afraid. I wasn't in shape to do much of anything as she drove me back to the hotel, washed my wounds, and put me to bed. While I slept, Jan paid through the nose to repair and repaint the Fiat for its innocent return to the agency. By the time I awoke, she had paid off the hotel and reserved two seats on a BOAC flight to Paris.

We took a cab straight home from Orly, locked the doors, lowered the blinds, unhooked the phone, and waited.

Nothing.

For the next two days Jan stayed glued to every TV newscast while I made cautious forays into Fourqueux to buy *L'Express* and peek at the other headlines at the newsstand.

I was beginning to think the whole misadventure was some sort of opium-dream until February 3, when the movie film arrived at our post office box.

Shoving the little yellow carton in my coat pocket, I tried to walk calmly back to the Rolls. Slowly, Norman, slowly. Let's not have an undignified scramble.

Jan met me at the door.

"It's here," I said breathlessly. "I picked it up at the post office."

"Calm down, Norman." She took my coat and put it in the closet. "You look like Moses after he saw the burning bush."

"Where's the projector?"

"In the garage. The screen's there, too." She opened the door. "If you'll stop shaking, I'll help you set it up."

Jan settled the projector on the coffee table while I rigged the screen. She flipped on the lamp and fiddled with the elevation control. The film chattered to life and she focused on the red Kodak ID letters printed on the leader.

The screen went dark. Ryker's desk flashed into life and I watched my hands reach across the blotter to turn the first stack of papers.

"Slow it down, dear."

My hand jerked across the screen at five frames per second, releasing the first page. A blur, and then it fell full-face in front of the lens.

"Freeze it right there."

Jan fine-focused. As far as I could tell, it looked like a business memo concerning Texas oil holdings.

"Okay, Jan. Go on."

For the next thirty minutes we watched the pages flicker on the screen. I chewed my lip to combat the sinking feeling of disappointment.

More pages flitted by. Stock prospectus. Dividend reports. Payrolls. Tax forms. Legal briefs. Not exactly great movie fodder.

In the middle of a huge stack of personnel records going back more than fifty years a torn, age-darkened page appeared, then vanished.

"Wait a minute, Jan. Turn back a few frames."

I rose and walked toward the screen.

QWG	RAU	WQT
PCW	BFW	IEJ
TIY	EVY	QUR
ESP	UKS	GKP
YFG	UBF	RWA
RWE	KIV	RAG
ARI	VTB	UON
OUD	IIB	WBR
TIY	PDR	ARI
QPB	WER	OBI
RGW	URP	REU
EPK	BUX	XJA
UCW	SIX	ARI
AWP	JAB	OZZ

Jan whispered. "Would I be belaboring the obvious to say that it looks like a cipher?"

"Yes. But you can say it anyhow." I bent closer to the screen. "Look how the paper's aged. And there seems to be some sort of watermark." Peering at the faint letters on the screen, I could see only the. random grain structure of the film emulsion. "If this damn thing was only sharper . . ."

"Maybe you're too close," Jan said. "Back up a bit."

I followed her advice and studied the picture as one would scrutinize a museum's Picasso. "'Marconigram,'" I finally said.

"You're sure?"

"Hardly. But look at those first letters. 'MARCO,' right?"

Jan tilted her head in appraisal. "Could be. I can't think of anything better."

I stuck my fingers into the projector's beam path, tracing the jagged edge of the paper on the screen.

"If it is a Marconigram, the departure point and destination point have been torn off." I snatched up my notebook lying on the table. "Let me copy it before the projector burns a hole in the film."

When I'd finished, Jan switched off the machine and peered over my shoulder. "Why the vertical layout, do you suppose?"

"Who knows? Maybe it's meant to be read that way."

We studied it some more in silence. She propped her chin on my elbow and muttered, "Who do we know in the cipher business?"

"No one. There's only one way we're going to crack this thing . . ."

We ended up with a slim library book called *An Invitation to Cryptograms* by Eugenia Williams.

I spent all that night and most of the following morning stumbling through the charts and diagrams. Finally, that afternoon, I placed Ryker's cipher on my desk top and decided to give the damn thing a try.

"This is our starting point." I showed Jan the chart. "It gives us a pattern of repeating letters typical with the English language."

Letter	Frequency of occurrence in 1000 words	Letter	Frequency of occurrence in 1000 words
E	591	M	114
T	473	U	111
A	368	G	90
O	360	Y	89
N	320	P	89
I	308	W	68
R	286	B	65
S	275	V	41
H	237	K	19

D	171	X	7
L	153	J	6
F	132	Q	5
C	124	Z	3

"Fine," Jan said. "But what does that prove?"

"Nothing yet. But once we know the frequency of letters in this cipher, we should be able to find some letter equivalents."

"Assuming the cipher's in English."

The corner of my mouth drooped forlornly. "Don't even think it, my dear. Just help me count the letters."

After fifteen minutes we compiled a list.

A–6	E–7	I–11	M–0	Q–4	U–10	Y–2
B–9	F–3	J–3	N–0	R–14	V–3	Z–2
C–2	G–4	K–4	O–4	S–3	W–11	
D–2	H–0	L–0	P–8	T–4	X–3	

My eyes examined the line of numbers. "The logical point to start with is the letter R, since it's the most frequent."

We substituted E for R in the cipher and continued working through the chart from that point, but, after a half hour, it became obvious that all we were creating was more alphabet soup.

I rubbed sweat off my forehead. "A dead end. R isn't our starting letter. That's for sure." I pointed at the chart. "The next most frequent letters in the cipher are I and W. Let's go with W."

Recopying the cipher, I blanked out all the letters except W, replacing it with E.

?E?	???	E??
??E	??E	???
???	???	???
???	???	???
???	???	?E?
?E?	???	???

```
???    ???    ???
???    ???    E??
???    ???    ???
???    E??    ???
??E    ???    ???
???    ???    ???
??E    ???    ???
?E?    ???    ???
```

Jan fidgeted in her chair. "Not exactly a revelation."

"Patience. We're just getting warmed up. Now let's try substituting R with T."

```
?E?    T??    E??
??E    ??E    ???
???    ???    ??T
???    ???    ???
???    ???    TE?
TE?    ???    T??
?T?    ???    ???
???    ???    E?T
???    ??T    ?T?
???    E?T    ???
T?E    ?T?    T??
???    ???    ???
??E    ???    ?T?
?E?    ???    ???
```

Her eyebrows raised. "Still a lot more question marks than letters."

"Well, let's try A for P."

```
?E?    T??    E??
A?E    ??E    ???
???    ???    ??T
??A    ???    ??A
???    ???    TE?
TE?    ???    T??
```

?T?	???	???
???	???	E?T
???	A?T	?T?
?A?	E?T	???
T?E	?TA	T??
?A?	???	???
??E	???	?T?
?EA	???	???

"We're getting somewhere," I said cautiously. "Now let's try O for I."

?E?	T??	E??
A?E	??E	O??
?O?	???	??T
??A	???	??A
???	???	TE?
TE?	?O?	T??
?TO	???	???
???	OO?	E?T
?O?	A?T	?TO
?A?	E?T	??O
T?E	?TA	T??
?A?	???	???
??E	?O?	?TO
?EA	???	???

"Now we try N for B."

?E?	T??	E??
A?E	N?E	O??
?O?	???	??T
??A	???	??A
???	?N?	TE?
TE?	?O?	T??
?TO	??N	???
???	OON	ENT
?O?	A?T	?TO

?AN	E?T	?NO
T?E	?TA	T??
?A?	N??	???
??E	?O?	?TO
?EA	??N	???

"I for U."

?E?	T?I	E??
A?E	N?E	O??
?O?	???	?IT
??A	I??	??A
???	IN?	TE?
TE?	?O?	T??
?TO	??N	I??
?I?	OON	ENT
?O?	A?T	?TO
?AN	E?T	?NO
T?E	ITA	T?I
?A?	NI?	???
I?E	?O?	?TO
?EA	??N	???

I rested my head on top of the typewriter and searched for a pattern. There was OON ENT, whatever the hell that meant. I gave up on that one and studied the vertical columns.

"Janice," I said softly. "Give me a pencil."

Snatching the paper out of the machine, I circled the letters.

?E?	T?I	E??
A?E	N?E	O??
?O?	???	?IT
??A	I??	??A
???	IN?	TE?
TE?	?O?	T??
?TO	??N	I??

?I?	OON	ENT
?O?	A?T	?TO
?AN	E̶X̶T̶	?NO
T?E	ITA	T?I
?A?	NIP	???
I?E	?O?	?TO
?EA	??N	???

"'TITA NI.' *Titantic.* It couldn't be anything else."

"Except wishful thinking." Jan scratched her head in frustration. "No, you're probably right. But I still can't read the message."

"Me neither," I confessed. "But we've almost got it licked. I'm going to type out a key and see what letters we've already found."

A B C D E F G H I J K L M N O P Q R S T U V W X Y Z

N   O   A T   I   E

We studied our six pitiful decoded letters for minutes on end. No inspirations were immediately forthcoming.

"The thing that gets me," I said, "is that there doesn't seem to be any connection between these damn letters. They're scattered all over the alphabet."

"Why don't we keep on with our substitutions, working with the frequency-of-letters chart?"

"That's fine, in theory. But look at the letter count of the cipher. There're a half dozen different letters we could choose next. We could grow old and gray chasing down dead ends."

With a sigh I began retyping the cipher, replacing E with R. Halfway down the first column I flubbed on the board with the right index finger, logjamming keys on top of the ribbon.

Jan watched sympathetically as I swore and wrangled with the eraser. "Why don't I take over?"

"Good idea," I said. We both type about the same words per minute, but she has a more graceful touch.

She reached the middle of the second column, then stopped.

"Something wrong?" I asked.

Without an answer Jan picked up the incomplete key I'd typed and held it out next to the keyboard.

"Come here and look at this," she said. I obeyed, then watched, mystified, as she tapped out every letter on the keyboard.

Q W E R T Y U I O P

A S D F G H J K L

   Z X C V B N M

Jan was beaming and exultant. I answered her smile, then shrugged my shoulders.

"So?"

Evidently I was slow on the uptake, but Jan was too happy to be annoyed. "We're looking for a connection between the letters, and it's been staring us in the face all afternoon. The letters we've already discovered are N, O, A, T, I, and E, right?"

I nodded.

"Okay. Now, where's that pencil?"

I passed it to Jan and watched her circle the letters as they were positioned on the keyboard.

Q W (E) R (T) Y U (I) (O) P

(A) S D F G H J K L

   Z X C V B (N) M

"Now look back at our key."

I looked back and forth between the key and the keyboard and it hit me. With a grin I grabbed Jan from behind, kissing her neck.

"A genius, Janice! You're a goddam genius!" I let her up, wearily shaking my head. "We make quite a team, my dear. My name and your brains."

"Come now. You would have discovered it eventually."

"Yeah. That's the operative word. 'Eventually.'"

"Well you *would*," she said staunchly. Jan grabbed the pencil and circled the key to the cipher.

She pointed at the keyboard. "All you have to do is study this and you'll see that the letters we'd already discovered are set one key to the right of the original letters in the cipher."

Jan retyped the Marconigram, her hands shifted one space to the right. Within three minutes all the question marks disappeared.

WEH	TSI	EWY
AVE	NGE	ORK
YOU	RBU	WIT
RDA	ILD	HLA
UGH	ING	TES
TER	LOB	TSH
STO	BYN	IPM
PIF	OON	ENT
YOU	AFT	STO
WAN	ERT	PNO
THE	ITA	TRI
RAL	NIC	CKS
IVE	DOC	STO
BEA	KSN	PXX

I rearranged the word groups.

WEH AVE YOU RDA UGH TER STO PIF YOU WAN THE RAL
IVE BEA TSI NGE RBU ILD ING LOB BYN OON AFT ERT
ITA NIC DOC KSN EWY ORK WIT HLA TES TSH IPM ENT
STO PNO TRI CKS STO PXX

Our momentary triumph went depressingly limp. For the first time since taking this assignment, I began to feel sorry for William Ryker.

WE HAVE YOUR DAUGHTER STOP IF YOU WANT HER ALIVE BE AT SINGER BUILDING LOBBY NOON AFTER TITANIC DOCKS NEW YORK WITH LATEST SHIPMENT STOP NO TRICKS STOP

14

February 5, 1962

Geoffrey Proctor chose a Monday to drop the other shoe.

It came in the form of a telegram delivered to our house at ten in the morning. Jan peered over my shoulder as I closed the front door on the departing delivery boy and tore open the envelope.

"From our beloved patron." I showed her the address.

"Let me see what it says."

DEAR NORMAN STOP PLEASE COME TO PROCTOR OFFICE NEW YORK IMMEDIATELY CONCERNING PROGRESS OF TITANIC STORY STOP NO APPOINTMENT NECESSARY BUT HURRY STOP LOVE TO JAN GEOFFREY STOP

"What do you think, Norman?"

"I think it's Geoffrey's equivalent of a 'Dear John' letter."

She took the telegram from my hand and read it a second time. "Notice the graceful kiss-off to me?"

"Yep. No ordinary summons, by any means." With a sigh I

dropped the wire in the trash and headed for my bedroom closet. "Maybe I should be grateful," I said, pulling out my two-suiter. "Now I don't even have to unpack."

Most visitors to Fun City return with a standard quota of horror stories. Personally, I like New York and I'm slightly in awe of people who live there. It's a testament to human adaptability. If *Homo sapiens* can live on the west side of Manhattan, he can live anywhere.

However, Geoffrey Proctor has chosen a more serene pied-à-terre. Proctor–World Publishing is housed in a seventy-five-story stainless steel crackerbox on Third Avenue that is a bad imitation of the Seagram Building.

Cooling my heels in Geoffrey's outer office, I felt like an easily digestible cog in a well-oiled machine. At my left sat Ellen Lambert, the handsome Head Secretary and ex-officio Dowager Empress of Proctor–World Publishing. Occasionally she raised her eyes from the IBM Executive and gave me a gracious Pat Nixon expression of ossified good cheer.

Much of the room was taken up by a sunken aquamarine pool, which was the home of gigantic golden *koi* that looked like mutants from a Japanese monster movie. I rose up and bent down closer, riffling the surface with my forefinger. Glaring indignantly, they swished to the opposite corner.

I heard a buzzer over my shoulder. For a moment I was afraid I'd triggered some sort of fish alarm, but it turned out to be Miss Lambert's intercom.

She tilted her incredible frosted beehive in the direction of the door. "You may go in, Mr. Hall."

Geoffrey's office is all beamed ceilings and huge slanting windows. He stood behind his chromium desk, one leg poised on the window ledge, silhouetted in front of the skyline like an Ayn Rand hero.

"Looking for me?"

"Norm! So glad you could make it!" He settled behind his desk. "Sorry to call at such short notice, but something fantastic has come up. I'd like you to start on it right away."

Geoffrey picked up an 8x10 glossy and passed it to me. It was an aerial shot of what appeared to be a big housing tract or shopping center under construction, bordered by a network of turnpikes.

"What the hell is it?"

"Flushing Meadows." He leaned forward. "Confidentially, Norman, it's the biggest story of the year. And the man I had on the assignment doesn't know a typewriter from his asshole. You've got to bail me out."

My jaw sagged, but I said nothing.

" . . . my man has most of the facts and photos," he was saying. "We just need someone to pull it all together."

I steadied myself on the arm of the chair.

"Let me get this straight. You want me to drop all the work I've done on Ryker and the *Titanic*—a story that's due in less than two months—to cook up a feature about the New York World's Fair?"

"Well, Norman, these last-minute things come up and I can certainly make it worth your while. Just name your price."

I laughed uneasily. "What is your problem, Geoffrey? Male menopause? Or simple hardening of the arteries?"

He reshuffled the papers on his desk into one neat pile. "Norman, this story is very important to me and to *World* magazine. I've tried to be generous, but I shouldn't have bothered. I should have remembered your nature."

I shook my head in wonder. "All this isn't like you. This pitiful bullshit you're holding out to me with both hands. It's clumsy, Geoffrey, and you're not a clumsy person. Nature's made you one of the Straights. The Snow Prince—chipped from ice. You should play the role."

Geoffrey slid his papers into the top desk drawer. "I see no further point in continuing this conversation."

"I'm not finished!"

"There you're mistaken," he said coolly. "In the past I've made allowances toward your temperament. But today you're being particularly tiresome. I want you off the *Titanic* story and off my payroll. Effective immediately."

"*World* has been filled with ads about the story for the past two months. So you snap your fingers and I go 'poof.' What then?"

"These things die down." Geoffrey's charming smile blossomed as easily as ever. "Don't worry, Norman. You'll be paid for the work you've done so far. In fact, I'll set it up now." He reached for the intercom.

"Don't."

His finger rose from the button. "Yes, Norman, what is it?"

"Don't force this one out in the open. You'll pray nightly for a chance to reseal it."

Geoffrey surveyed me across the expanse of desk. He picked up his Cross pen and clicked it against his teeth. "Norman, you seem to think you're immune to the real world. With a half dozen well-placed phone calls I could flush your career down the toilet."

"God, I was waiting for that one! Next comes the line about how I'll never work in this town again, right?"

"The reality may not be so humorous."

Geoffrey reached once again for the intercom. He had taken enough line. Now was time to start reeling him in.

"I know about Ryker's half million."

Every muscle froze. The eyes were round and empty.

"Jerry Blaine," I explained. "Occasionally he raises his head above the Hollywood quagmire. Whatever his personal shortcomings, he's an impeccable source."

The silver and tan face started to go limp. We glared at each other through long moments of silence. Finally, he unbent.

"Okay, Norman. It's a long story. And a complicated one."

"I'm very patient."

Reclining the chair, he stared up at a ceiling vent. "Mike Rogers first came to me at Christmastime last year. All expenses involved in reporting the salvage operation were to be paid by the Ryker Corporation. The half million was what you might call a gesture of good faith."

"I want to know exactly what strings were attached."

Geoffrey made his face look innocent. "Why, the primary condition was that you write the story."

"Yes, I know."

He smiled sourly. "You mean you've known all along?"

"Since visiting L.A. I was wondering why Ryker made the offer in the first place."

"You'd have to ask him."

"I did. He told me he was a big fan."

Geoffrey had the grace not to snicker. "For all I know, it's the truth."

"But why the big dose of payola? He was giving you a hell of a gift with the rights to in-depth coverage. Why not suggest my name as part of the package? You weren't in a position to dicker."

"The old man wanted you very badly. That's why I humored him."

"Just like you're humoring me. While you're at it, maybe you can explain why the bloom is off the rose."

"Come again?"

"You know what I mean. Ryker gave me the story and now he wants to take it away. Who did the hatchet work? Ryker himself? Or Mike Rogers?"

His lips pressed tight.

"Come now, Geoffrey. You're dying to tell me. And I'm great in the role of father-confessor. If I'm fired anyway, what difference does it make?"

"Mike didn't say," he blurted. "All he told me was that the old man wanted you out on your ass and damn fast."

"And you hastened to comply. Some *wasp*-ish Sammy Glick like Mike Rogers snaps his fingers and you have a hot flash. Such cooperation for a half million. I wasn't aware whoredom came so cheap in the businesss world!"

"I think I've heard just about enough from you."

"I can guess most of the rest. When you and Ryker closed your deal, the half million was just a chaser, designed to wash down a very large bail-out loan for Proctor–World Publishing in general and *World* in particular. Am I getting warm?"

Geoffrey sighed impatiently. "I wish you were a business-man, Norman. Perhaps you'd understand these things."

"Keep it simple, Geoffrey. You know us artists. Divine Idiots, to be handled with kid gloves."

He tried lacing his fingers together on top of the desk in an attitude of composure. "*World* is in some trouble. We need to make cutbacks, but it's damn tough to know where to cut."

I pointed over my shoulder in the direction of the outer office. "You could start by putting your *koi* on a diet."

" . . . at the same time," he was saying, "the company needs capital . . . "

"So how big a slice of the pie did Ryker get? No, never mind. I don't want to know." I glanced at my watch. "Time is getting short and I'm going to give you the bottom line. Fire me and I will take the first cab to the New York *Times* and pour out my heart in true gossip-column fashion. Since I'll be unemployed, maybe they'll even let me write the feature. All about you rolling in the sheets with a corporation which functions as a tax dodge for an American expatriate."

"You son of a bitch."

"Perhaps." I stood and grabbed my coat. "You shouldn't expect loyalty from me, Geoffrey. You've done nothing to earn it. But I shouldn't sneer at you. I'm the oldest whore on the beat. After a few years you learn to get it up and keep it there, even if a publisher gets cold feet." I slipped my coat over my shoulders. "Do you know a good place for lunch?"

He licked his lips. "There must be some way we can talk this out. Some . . . compromise."

"Why certainly. I stay on the payroll and finish the story. You publish it in April. What could be simpler?"

"I don't know, Norman. William Ryker is a very determined man."

"He is also bluffing. All you have to do is call Ryker and give him the gist of our conversation. He's a realist, mark my words." My hand hesitated on the doorknob. "By the way, how did Mike Rogers sound on the phone?"

"Damn angry. And scared."

"I don't doubt it. He must've caught it from his boss."

"One thing he never explained was why he wanted you out. I wish I could tell you."

"There's no need, Geoffrey. I know why. So does Mike. Ryker knows. And he knows that I know." I smiled, easing the door open. "In fact, the only person who *doesn't* know is you." I gently slapped his shoulder. "I think we should keep it that way."

15

February 12, 1962

My previous experience in helicopters has been limited to brief shuttles to and from airports, and I've always been able to stick my head in the sand by keeping my nose in a paper and not looking out the window.

Today, however, a newspaper couldn't serve as a security blanket. Burke Sheffield and I were five hours out of Halifax in a chartered Bell chopper, with nothing to do besides watch the sun coming up over the Atlantic breakers flitting beneath our perspex bubble at a hundred fifty miles per hour. A glorious sunrise—one to inspire a pagan worshiper to perform a virgin-sacrificing rite. I constantly reminded myself of its beauty since it kept my mind off those whirling rotor blades held in place by bolts and fasteners that wouldn't live forever and were waiting for the day when they could give up the ghost.

I also took comfort in our pilot, Ralph MacKendrick, and the confident squint lines on his fiftyish face. It pleased me to meet mellow and middle-aged helicopter pilots in the skies.

He tugged at my sleeve and pointed ahead. "There she blows."

The *Savonarola* lay less than five miles away. A very rakish lady. Ryker's Italian toy, floating amid icebergs in his big bathtub. Even seen from this distance, the flat helicopter platform dominated her stern. But no sight of the *Marianas* and *Neptune*. Presumably they were moored on the far side of the ship.

The copter lurched in the wind as I took in the scene from horizon to horizon. The ocean was pimpled with bergs, their peaks pale gold in the early morning light. Everything from Volkswagen-sized chunks to hundred-foot mountains.

The bergs were equally thick that night, at this very spot, when the *Titanic* took 1500 people to their deaths. And it was this time in the morning, almost fifty years ago, that Captain Rostron picked up the survivors aboard the *Carpathia*.

I heard a long drawn-out sigh. Burke Sheffield stared at the *Savonarola,* one eyebrow arched high.

"Just think, Norman. *Alone* on the open sea with a shipload of *sailors!*"

"No camping, Burke. Not before breakfast."

"You're right, of course." The face was weary and spent. "The last refuge of the incompetent. That reminds me. Time I got to work." Burke fired off a Gatling-volley with his Hasselblad.

Little voices buzzed in MacKendrick's headphone. He intercepted my questioning look.

"About two miles away, Mr. Hall. Be sure you're strapped down for landing."

We approached the ship from the stern and I could see a little man waving flags atop the copter pad like an auditioning cheerleader. Hopefully his hieroglyphics made sense to MacKendrick, who veered the chopper slightly to port.

I spotted the orange and white conning towers of the *Neptune* and *Marianas* suckling against the starboard side of the *Savonarola* like two remoras clinging to a shark. MacKendrick eased on the stick, the blades barking at the wind in protest.

Our target was a white painted circle on the platform. His aim was very good. Two soft bumps and we were down.

The rotors freewheeled to a stop, drooping like forlorn bunny ears. MacKendrick checked gauges and flipped switches as I tapped his shoulder.

"Remember what I said in Halifax? There's money in it for you."

"Okay, Mr. Hall. But I don't know what you're looking for."

"Neither do I. Don't try to pump anybody. Just play dumb and keep your eyes open."

He canted his head at the approaching flagman. "You two go ahead. I've got things to wind up here."

Burke and I hustled onto the deck, then hunched low beneath the rotor blades, following the flagman to a narrow flight of stairs on the edge of the helipad. The stairs led down below decks and into the blessed world of steam heat. Our anonymous flagman chose to remain unknown, but introduced us to a Commander Eric Brazier.

"Naval Liaison Officer for the salvage operation," he explained. Tight dry palm, white hair, pink healthy face. He dismissed the flagman with a snappy salute, then led us down the corridor.

"Have you gentlemen had breakfast?"

Burke shook his head. "Not before flying."

"A precautionary measure," I explained.

"Then I'll join you, if you don't mind." He pointed at another stairway. "The galley's down here."

Between forkfuls of eggs Benedict I nodded greetings and shook hands with crewmen who drifted in and out of the galley. Mostly French and Italians who manned equipment on board the *Savonarola* and the bathyscaphs.

I was pouring myself a second cup of coffee when the Commander bent low over my ear. "Here's someone you may not have met, Mr. Hall."

Facing the new arrival, I smiled softly at Brazier. "Introductions are not necessary, Commander. We're old friends."

Mike Rogers' face was an interesting study in conflicting emotions.

"You're looking good, Norm," he finally said. "The sea air seems to suit you."

"That remains to be seen." I nodded over my right shoulder. "Mike, I'd like you to meet Burke Sheffield."

They shook hands. Burke put lots of elbow grease into his grip. "Nice to meet you, fella!" he boomed in a deep butch basso profundo.

Mike aimed his grin at Commander Brazier. "Perhaps you would like to show Mr. Sheffield around the *Savonarola,* Eric."

"Certainly!" he said, picking up the cue. "Come along, Mr. Sheffield. There's a lot to see and not much time to waste."

Burke nodded and followed Commander Brazier, lenses and meters swinging from his shoulders like captured booty.

"Okay, Mike. What's up?"

"Mr. Ryker wants you to join him for breakfast."

"You should have told me earlier." I pointed at my empty plate.

"Mr. Ryker hates to eat alone. You can sit and watch him chew."

Acknowledging surrender, I held out my arm. "Lead the way."

Mike exchanged casual salutes with the crewman in the corridor as he led me past hissing steam pipes and locked cargo bays into a tiny walnut-paneled elevator.

"You mentioned breakfast. Would I happen to be the main course?"

Mike refused to be provoked. "Mr. Ryker is hardly a cannibal."

"Even beyond the three-mile limit?"

The elevator stopped. I let him lead the way down a corridor with wine-colored Wilton underfoot and unmarked mahogany doors on both sides.

Mike rapped his knuckles on a portside door.

"Please wait here." He moved on down the passageway.

I heard the door click open and turned away from the departing figure of Mike Rogers to stare into the stony black-and-blue face of Lisl Slote.

In actual fact her face was a welter of multicolored bruises and contusions. A terrific shiner just beginning to fade into the sickly saffron shade of stale rice pudding. Lots of little red scars and a line of stitches on her forehead.

Fräulein Slote was not an attractive woman, and I had done a pretty fair job of making the rest of her life even uglier. Her one good eye roved over my face, filing the image for future reference.

"Come." She beckoned with a swing of her arm.

From the far corner of the cabin, William Ryker returned my gaze—a little old mummy propped on a couch and encased in a gray, single-breasted suit.

"Don't stand there gawking!" He pushed aside his breakfast tray. "Come in and sit down!"

I obeyed but kept the Fräulein visible in the corner of my eye as she slammed the door shut.

Ryker certainly set out to sea in class. Except for the portholes, the cabin could pass for one of the more comfortable suites at the Plaza.

"Very nice," I said. "Whose cabin is this?"

"The whole ship is mine, Mr. Hall. Therefore the cabin also belongs to me."

Craning my neck, I peeked through the half-open door leading to the bedroom. Only there was no bed—just Ryker's iron lung.

"There's nothing in there to interest you," he said flatly. "You remember the old song, *Me and My Shadow?* Well, here I am and there it is."

I settled into a chair opposite the couch, mindful of the Fräulein's watchful glare.

Ryker sensed my discomfort. "My dear, Mr. Hall and I have private business to discuss. I'll call if I need you."

The door slammed shut and I listened to her footsteps clomp down the corridor into silence.

Ryker didn't speak. The pale gray eyes appraised me like a federal inspector grading a suspicious piece of beef.

"Well, Mr. Ryker, you're looking rather well."

He didn't smile. "I'm eighty-five years old and I look like hell. I will look a little worse each day until I finally die."

"I was speaking in relative terms. A change of scenery sometimes helps. Wipes away the mental barnacles."

"Perhaps. You certainly seem to be stimulated lately. Scurrying from Spain to Switzerland to New York." His fingers toyed with the weave on the armrest. "I want to know what you said to Geoffrey Proctor."

"I was very straightforward. Geoffrey can't take prolonged exposure to candor. He shrivels up. Like Judy Garland throwing water on Margaret Hamilton."

He digested my words without a change of expression. "Mr. Proctor tried to give you some sound advice. You should have taken it."

"Perhaps you'll be more persuasive."

"I hope so," he said lightly, "but to be honest, I'm not too optimistic. You see, I've run across plenty of fellows like you in my time. Young men on a Mission." His lips lingered distastefully over the word. "A Crusade to expose the Truth. All very righteous." Ryker shifted uncomfortably on the couch. "I won't try to appeal to your common sense since you haven't any. So I will make a simple statement. You will resign from this story."

". . . or else?"

"The Swiss police will be notified concerning your burglary of my house." His cheeks quivered indignantly. "Fräulein Slote got a clear view of you that night."

"Just before she fired off a shot to kill."

"You were the intruder, Mr. Hall. The Fräulein was simply safeguarding my property and welfare."

"She charged into that room with gun barrels blazing. Don't ever work late in that office without letting her know."

"I'll keep that in mind," he said dryly. "However trigger-happy the Fräulein may be, she has excellent eyesight. She'll be only too glad to sign a statement and pick you out of a lineup."

"I don't doubt it. But the whole thing is academic, isn't it?"

"What do you mean?"

"You had no intention of reporting me to the police. You still don't."

"You're a fool, son. Don't confuse me with that Ivy League twit, Geoffrey Proctor."

I didn't answer. Ryker's eyes were clear and scornful.

"Let me show you something." I dug into my coat pocket and passed a folded slip of paper to him. "Maybe this will clear the air."

WE HAVE YOUR DAUGHTER STOP IF YOU WANT HER ALIVE BE AT SINGER BUILDING LOBBY NOON AFTER TITANIC DOCKS NEW YORK WITH LATEST SHIPMENT STOP NO TRICKS STOP

Ryker read the Marconigram and his face changed. No longer merely a dried up old man, but something gaunt and haunted, like survivors of Belsen and Auschwitz. But more than that. A look of unforgiving vengeance. I began to know how Pandora felt when she first pried open the lid.

His hands twisted the paper. The words came haltingly through clenched yellow teeth.

"Mr. Hall, I won't waste time asking how you got this message. There is just one thing I want to make clear. This will never be published or made public in any way. Do you understand?"

"There are a couple of things *you* should understand as well."

"Such as?"

"Number one, the cipher you hold in your hand is a copy. One of several. The others have been slipped into sealed envelopes and sent to my attorney, Frank Aylmer, and several other lawyers connected with my business affairs. They all have instructions to send these envelopes to prominent daily newspapers, accompanied by my admittedly incomplete but highly interesting research into your past. These instructions will be put into effect upon my death, whether caused by an act of God or . . ." I shrugged lightly. "Whatever."

Staring with feigned calmness into Ryker's eyes, I could see that he had swallowed the bait. For the time being anyway. Hopefully I would have enough time once I got back to Halifax to turn an inspired line of bull into a real ace in the hole.

Ryker smiled indulgently. "If I recall, your brave words

came under the heading of 'number one.' That implies a number two to follow."

"Oh, yes. Number two is that I don't intend to publish the cipher since I don't know enough about it. Hopefully you can fill some of the gaps."

I pulled another copy of the cipher from my coat pocket and spread it flat on the coffee table between us.

WE HAVE YOUR DAUGHTER STOP IF YOU WANT HER ALIVE BE AT SINGER BUILDING LOBBY NOON AFTER TITANIC DOCKS NEW YORK WITH LATEST SHIPMENT STOP NO TRICKS STOP

"Now, as you'll see, I can piece together a very compelling story by using a little woolgathering based on the facts contained in this message."

Ryker said nothing. Rubbing my hands together, I bent over the paper.

"As you know, the destination and departure points of the Marconigram are missing, but we can assume the message was sent to you. The kidnapped daughter referred to in the message is Eva. Whoever wrote the ransom note sent it by wireless before April fourteenth, the night the ship hit the iceberg. Naturally, the kidnappers fully expected the ship to safely make its maiden crossing. They set up the ransom for the noon after the *Titanic's* docking since they were on the ship along with your daughter."

A wave smacked the porthole. Gray foam drooled down the glass.

"Eva was traveling on board ship with her mother and Georgia Ferrell, your wife's maid, as well as a bodyguard, James Martin. They all had to be eliminated before a kidnapping could take place. Which accounts for none of them being among the rescued."

I turned away from the porthole, stretching the knots out of my shoulders and back. "The Big Question is—who were the kidnappers? Total strangers? Unknown desperados? I don't think so. The kidnap note was sent to you in enci-

phered form. Of course, the message could hardly be sent by
the *Titanic*'s wireless operators any other way. But how did
the kidnappers know you'd be able to decode it?" I waved a
disparaging hand. "My wife and I puzzled it out, given
plenty of time, a little brains, and a lot of luck. But the kidnappers couldn't gamble that you would simply stumble
across the code. Logical conclusion: the cipher was something already worked out between you and the kidnappers."

Blood clotted in Ryker's face. "You filthy . . ."

"No, no! I don't mean that you were directly involved in
your daughter's abduction. But it's reasonable to assume that
you knew these kidnappers. They had used this cipher before. For what, I wonder?

"Of course, the big clue is that 'latest shipment' you were to
have brought to the Singer Building after the *Titanic*
reached New York. 'Latest shipment,'" I lingered over the
words, tasting their flavor. "A tantalizingly vague phrase.
What was the latest shipment? Bullion? Possible, but too
heavy. Narcotics, perhaps?"

Ryker's eyes were red and unseeing. He swallowed hard
but said nothing.

I smiled gently. "In a way, I suppose it's all pointless. The
kidnappers had an unlucky break, didn't they? By the time
you got the ransom note, their bodies were probably under
two miles of Atlantic . . ."

Ryker's face twisted painfully.

"Are you all right?" I asked.

"Yes, yes," he growled. "Leave me alone."

"It's very strange," I whispered, half to myself. "However
much tragedy the *Titanic* sinking brought to thousands of
people, it probably saved your daughter's life. I imagine
you've wondered why Eva was spared."

"Don't be dense, young man. Of course I have. I've had
fifty years of wondering."

"And how does she feel?"

"Eva doesn't remember." He slipped back into his iron
mask. "What little peace that child has had comes from for-
getting about the *Titanic*." The voice dropped to a reedy

moan. "And if you or any other man threaten her state of mind by repeating the contents of that cipher, I swear to God I'll kill you with my bare hands."

"I can understand your feelings, Mr. Ryker. But it was very long ago."

" 'Long ago,' you say!" Ryker struggled for breath. "It was yesterday! Do you understand? Yesterday! My daughter and I . . ." He tightened the lid on the past and looked me in the eye. "No, Mr. Hall. You have written a lot of detective fiction and you have started to believe your own books. In real life men with secrets damn well keep their mouths shut."

"Only for so long, Mr. Ryker. The tight-lipped men die, but willing listeners are always around."

"Spoken like a true phrase maker," he laughed bitterly. "You've helped me make up my mind."

"How's that?"

"I'm going down with you to see the *Titanic*."

Mike Rogers leaned against the starboard railing under the helipad, bundled in a heroic parka, tossing Fritos into the icy sea.

"Chumming for sharks?" I asked.

He spun around, then laughed self-consciously, crumpling the bag in his fist. "Sea gulls."

I craned my neck up at the swooping birds bickering among themselves. "Mike, I've got some questions."

He pitched another corn chip into the water. "I may not be able to answer."

"The subject is noncontroversial. Right up your alley. Your boss' crazy submarine jaunt."

"Oh. That. I never pry into Mr. Ryker's personal affairs."

"Very noble. But what do his doctors say?"

"They did a lot of yelling, naturally. But, when you get to be that age, what *will* the doctors let you do?"

"It's still a bad decision on his part."

"That may be. But I can't see that it's any of your business."

"Quite true, Mike. However, the field of journalism is built upon the divine right to be meddlesome. Readers tend to yawn at unerring good taste."

The gulls brayed impatiently. Mike flung the Frito bag overboard. "Suppose I told you to shove your readers' questions up your ass."

"I would be mildly offended. And slightly awestruck. A very indiscreet choice of words for someone with PR ambitions. Be sure and check with your boss before putting me on the Shit List."

His face whitened. "What are you . . ."

"Ryker and I have reached a mutual understanding. Or armed truce. You might be wise to follow suit."

"I didn't . . ."

". . . know. Of course not. But I'm more worried about Ryker's health than your occasional lapses of tact."

"It's his life to risk, Norm."

"Suppose he has a seizure down there? Even if it was minor, he could be very dead by the time we'd make it back to the surface."

"I've discussed the risks with Mr. Ryker. But he won't back down. If something happens, you'll just have to wing it."

"Inspirational, Mike. Much thanks."

Just past noon I settled down to a corner table in the galley by a fastidious gentleman named Alvin Spears. He wasn't exactly eager to talk about his work, but finally confided that he was an engineering consultant for the remote manipulative tools used by the bathyscaphs.

"Tell me," I asked, "are there any special problems using waldos under such extreme pressure?"

Spears blinked dully at me. "I'm afraid I don't understand."

I spent the next five minutes explaining how remote-control tools got their nickname. But he had never heard of the term before, which, to put it mildly, seemed very odd.

Before I could pursue the matter any further, Burke

joined me at the table, watching me down the last of my salmon.

I folded my napkin on the table. "Want to go for a walk?"

"Sounds fine." He jumped up to lead the way.

Alvin Spears nodded to acknowledge my words of farewell and kept on chewing.

Turning my collar against the wind, I let Burke lead me by the elbow as we walked along the deck.

"Norman," he whispered in my ear. "I know you think I'm totally paranoid, but we're being watched. I mean one particular man. My personal shadow."

"Maybe he's a . . . friend. Perhaps your reputation precedes you."

Burke's eyes narrowed. "Very shabby, Norman. Actually, he's not my type. Very ethnic, warty and swarthy, with matching five o'clock shadow. He's been milling about in the corner of my eye for the last two hours."

I glanced along the deck. "Well? Where's he now?"

Burke patted the guardrail. "Just stay put. He'll show up."

I'm glad I didn't bet. I would have lost. He appeared within five minutes. Nodding brusquely, he swept past us, stopping to pick up an empty cigarette carton left on deck.

"Any comments, Norman?"

"Only the obvious ones. That he's keeping tabs on you. Me too, most likely. Probably one of Ryker's men. But you never know. The Navy can be so damn touchy on a project like this. He could be working for Brazier."

Burke laughed mirthlessly. "I've thought of all that. I was hoping you'd have some bright ideas."

"Shoot him." I pointed at his camera . "When we get back to Halifax, we'll have a crack at tracing him down. Provided you're still interested, of course."

At one P.M, I met Burke Sheffield and William Ryker on the starboard deck of the *Savonarola*.

The principal characters milled together like theatergoers at intermission. Lisl Slote steadied her boss' wheelchair and wrapped blankets around his thin shoulders. From what I saw of Ryker's face, he could use the extra warmth.

Commander Brazier fussed over the crew securing the rope ladders attached to the conning towers of the *Marianas* and *Neptune,* bobbling above the gray-blue swells.

One of Brazier's starched-white ensigns compressed all of Burke's camera gear down to one bundle, fitted it into a nylon sling, then lowered it down to a crewman braced atop the *Neptune's* conning tower.

He straightened, looking Burke in the eye. "You're next."

He made a show of independence, but welcomed a steadying arm as he inched down the long swinging ladder. The man atop the *Neptune* grabbed Burke's leg and guided him down the steel rungs, disappearing into the innards of the bathyscaph.

Seeing Burke was safe, Commander Brazier crooked an arm at Mike, who bent anxiously down to his boss.

"You're sure you're feeling all right, sir?"

Ryker's voice was deadly chill. "Rogers, you're not my mother, wife, or lover. Mind your own damn business."

I tried to help Mike with the wheelchair but Ryker shooed me away. His wrinkled, shrunken neck corded with strain as he rose like a miracle man in a Katherine Kuhlman revival meeting. The pipe cleaner legs trembled like tuning forks and Mike and I lunged for his arms. But Ryker stayed erect, taking one step and then another.

A special winch was rigged above the rope ladder, complete with a harness usually used for air-sea rescue. Commander Brazier and Fräulein Slote buckled the harness across his shoulders and under his arms. Ryker grinned triumphantly at me. An old banty rooster with a few tricks still in him. I found myself returning his grin.

"All right, Mr. Hall," said Brazier. "You go on ahead."

The conning tower of the *Marianas* seemed a very long way down once I swung one leg over the edge of the ship. I took one rung at a time and tried not to think about falling.

An electric motor whined above me. Looking up, I watched Ryker swing out over the sea.

"Grab the ladder!" I yelled. And he did so in his feeble fashion.

I lowered my foot to the next rung but felt nothing. The deck of the *Marianas* rose and fell beneath my feet as the crewman reached for my legs. I waited until a swell rolled the conning tower to me, then jumped, grabbing hold of the crewman's arm. I clambered down the access tube to the observation sphere under the main tanks.

A broad-shouldered man, hunched over a blinking instrument panel, looked up quizzically through the opening.

"Welcome aboard, Mr. Hall." A Boston accent. "Come join the party."

Captain Phillip Toffler was red-haired and freckled, with a ginger mustache that went well with Navy tans. He watched my eyes rove within the little sphere. "Homey, wouldn't you say?"

"Very." Two little circles of cool light caught my attention. I bent forward and bumped my nose against the glass.

Dark and threatening, the hull of the *Savonarola* faded into the mist. The surface sizzled like quicksilver butter frying in a pan.

"How thick is this glass?"

"About a foot. Very safe."

Ryker arrived at the hatch with a wheezing clatter. We guided him into one of the two chairs.

The old man seemed shaken by his descent but was too stubborn to admit it.

"Well, Captain?" he rasped. "Are we going to get this thing underway or not?"

"Soon, Mr. Ryker." He bent down to examine the seal of the hatch, then slammed it shut. It must have weighed the good side of three hundred pounds. Now I knew how it felt to be trapped in a bank vault.

The captain checked the instruments. "We're just now opening the flood valves. That fills the access tube with seawater. Then Mr. Noiret, who helped you two aboard, opens the valves of the water ballast tanks just before he jumps back onto the *Savonarola*."

We sat still for a moment. The small rocking motion that I had taken for granted stopped.

Toffler checked the depth gauge. "We're off."

There was no feeling of movement. Ryker and I stared through the viewing ports. Slowly the hull of the *Savonarola* seemed to rise up and out of sight. The surface faded away until I could see only a pale blue light. I figured the *Neptune* must be very close, but it was out of our line of sight.

A large swordfish swept in front of me, and I heard a strange hollow gurgling in the cabin.

"Hydrophones on the hull," Toffler explained.

A vast school of flounders floated by. Then nothing.

"Have you had much experience with deep-sea salvaging?"

Ryker kept his eyes to the port. "Captain Toffler has a ship to run, Mr. Hall. I think we should let him do it in peace."

Toffler looked at me, then at Ryker. He shrugged and returned to his instruments.

"*Neptune* calling *Marianas*." A voice rattled from a hidden loudspeaker. "Passing one-hundred-fifty-foot depth."

The captain grabbed the microphone. "*Marianas* calling *Neptune*. Ship at, mark, one hundred seventy-four feet. Out."

I still couldn't see the *Neptune*. Sitting back, I watched the light slowly fade beyond the port.

Two hundred feet. Two hundred twenty-five feet. Three hundred feet.

All trace of sunlight vanished. Toffler switched on the external spotlights.

Five hundred feet. Twelve hundred feet. Eighteen hundred feet.

Tiny white flakes flashed up past the port, resembling a snow flurry in reverse.

"Plankton." Toffler answered my unasked question. "It appears to be moving up as we descend through it." He eyed the depth gauge. "In fact, we're descending a little *too* fast."

He released ballast and a volley of steel pellets bubbled up by the port. The *Marianas* was falling faster than the weights Toffler had released. He increased the ballast until the pellets fell steadily away and vanished into the darkness below.

Twenty-one hundred feet. Twenty-five. Thirty-five. Forty. Fifty-five. Over a mile down. Six thousand feet.

"The halfway point."

A long red snipe eel writhed under the lights and was gone.

Seven thousand. Seventy-six hundred. Eighty-two hundred. Nine thousand.

I flinched instinctively as a huge fish with long fangs and an immense bloated stomach chased by.

Ten thousand. I glanced at my watch. About an hour since our descent began.

"*Neptune* calling *Marianas*. Eleven thousand feet."

"*Marianas* calling *Neptune*. Mark, ten thousand, three twenty-five feet."

Eleven thousand. Far below I spotted a glow worm of light.

"The *Neptune*," Toffler staunchly replied when I pointed it out to him. He gestured at the echo sounder graph, which showed a few dark streaks. "There's the bottom."

Still over a thousand feet to go. Eleven thousand. Eleven five.

The floodlights seemed to brighten.

"We're reflecting off the sand and silt."

Toffler released more ballast, lowering the bathyscaph to the bottom with almost erotic care.

"Well, we have arrived. A little off the mark. The *Titanic*'s about a mile away, if I reckon correctly."

The bottom of the observation sphere hovered about three feet from the sand. I watched a hatchet fish scamper away from the light.

"Peaceful, isn't it?" Toffler said softly. "It's hard to realize that an unprotected man out there would be pulped so quickly he'd never feel a thing."

The hydrophones picked up the propeller's whir as Toffler inched the *Marianas* forward, raising her slightly at the same time until we rested about a hundred feet from the ocean floor.

The seabed was no longer smooth. Huge boulders glided

beneath us. Once again I spotted the yellow light of the *Neptune*.

It was then that the misty silt below cleared and the *Titanic* congealed out of the haze.

The ship lay on its starboard side, on an eighty-degree angle. Although rusted to a brown-orange and encrusted with sea animals and ancient slime, the *Titanic* was still intact.

No one spoke. There didn't seem to be adequate words. The bow of the ship crept past thirty feet below the port. A tangle of twisted steel from the crow's nest had smashed into the bridge, where Captain Smith had stood fifty years ago, watching his ship founder.

A teacup drifted by, stirred by our passing. Our floodlights poured down on the Boat Deck, revealing the lifeboat rigs. The four funnels had been torn away, but I saw two of them on the rocks, attached to their supporting cables.

Lovers once walked the surface of the Boat Deck—now all I saw were two lobsterlike prawns lazily skimming about, searching for prey.

The light in the distance grew stronger. The *Neptune* was cruising over the *Titanic*'s stern. I could imagine Burke frantically running through his bulk film magazine.

The *Marianas* moved over the exposed portside flanks of the ship. Porthole after porthole. A few with glass still in them. I remembered that the iceberg struck the ship on the starboard side; thus the three-hundred-foot gash in the hull remained hidden by the sand and rocks.

We inched our way over the Promenade Deck. I noticed the first evidence of Ryker's salvage operation. Long acetylene torch scars had cut into B Deck, burning away sea life and rust to expose bright shiny metal.

"Isn't this where you found the blank movie film?"

"That's right," Toffler volunteered.

Moving toward the forepeak of the ship, I saw further torch marks around the bow, where freight had been stored.

"You're interested in the cargo hold, I suppose."

Ryker didn't look away. "Many priceless items were lost aboard the *Titanic*. The passengers carted some very expensive trinkets. Many have decomposed by now. But other things remain for the taking. Automobiles lying down there in the hold, for example." His canny eyes wrinkled around the edges. "How much would you pay for a restored Silver Ghost rescued from the *Titanic* after fifty years?"

"It sounds a little ghoulish to me."

"Fortunately, others will not agree. I know human nature."

The *Neptune* passed our starboard side. We skirted around her, resting over the *Titanic*'s poop deck and elegant stern. A length of chain waved languidly in our wake.

For the first time in my life I suddenly knew why primitive people established taboo grounds. The *Titanic* smelled of death. I'd seen dozens of people killed before my eyes in the war, but I'd never felt such remorse as I did staring at this broken metal dinosaur lying gutted on the ocean bottom.

Ryker stared out the port with wide unblinking eyes. Ever since our meeting I felt that he was a possessed man—now I knew the cause. The dead ship provided a dreadful, obsessive image, and I could almost see it enter through his eyes to fester in his brain, stirring old memories and filling his waking and sleeping hours.

We swept past the *Titanic*'s huge triple propellers, then turned to begin another pass of the ship. And another. And another.

Toffler finally brought the *Marianas* to a halt. "Our batteries are running low. I'm going to head for the surface."

He adjusted the ballast controls and the *Titanic* slowly faded away in the darkness.

"Soon," Toffler said, "we'll begin a thorough interior exploration of the ship. Sometimes I think of the keepsakes and mementos lying in the darkness all these years. Mail openers and loose change. The pillboxes of the old woman and the doll of the young girl. Things that meant so much and now mean nothing."

I smiled at Toffler's unexpected poetic urge, but Ryker paid no mind.

"There's something else down in that ship." He kept staring down even as the *Titanic* vanished. "My wife."

* * *

I leaned comfortably back in the rear seat of the Bell chopper and watched the *Savonarola* dwindle beneath me.

"Mr. MacKendrick," I asked, "did you have any trouble refueling?"

"Not at all. A very cooperative crew."

"Anything unusual to report?"

"Not really." He absently ran his fingers through his hair. "I hate to disappoint you, Mr. Hall, but the whole operation looked aboveboard to me."

"What do you think?" I asked Burke.

"About the *Savonarola?*" He shrugged. "Except for our tail on board ship, I didn't see anything suspicious. But what can I say? If Ryker had something to hide, he'd be damn sure you wouldn't stumble across it."

"Not intentionally, anyway." I rubbed my chin, realizing I needed a shave. "But one thing Ryker couldn't cover up. That ship on the ocean floor. The *Marianas* and *Neptune* have been tearing the *Titanic* apart and they're going about it in a very strange manner. No one has ever given a plausible reason why they started exploration on B Deck portside."

"Isn't that where the roll of film was recovered?" Burke asked.

"That's right." I gazed out the window for a last glimpse of the *Titanic's* burial ground. "And it's also where Albert and Martha Klein spent their honeymoon."

Five hours later the helicopter passed over the outskirts of Dartmouth.

"Almost home, gentlemen," MacKendrick grinned. "And don't think it hasn't been a pleasure."

He swung the copter in a wide arc across Halifax harbor, taking us over the path of the departing RCMP ship *Alberta*. The captain hooted three times in greeting.

"Everyone get his gear together. We'll be landing in a couple of minutes."

I peered over MacKendrick's shoulder, trying to spot the

helipad amid the jumble of waterfront buildings, but was distracted as he tapped the tachometer in irritation.

"Hell of a time for the thing to go haywire."

My nose stung with an acrid odor.

Burke smelled it, too. "What in God's name . . ."

Smoke drifted from under the instrument panel. MacKendrick swore, tugging at his seat belt.

"Quick!" He pointed at the fire extinguisher. "Over here!"

Gripping the extinguisher in both hands, I passed it to MacKendrick. The image of my fingers clamped around the metal cannister was stamped on my retina as blue sparks strobe-flashed from the instruments.

The roar of a million igniting gas burners. Black clouds filled the cockpit.

Hands and arms scrambling around me. High screams through smoke.

Blistering faces. Flaming hair. A stench of burned plastic and roast meat.

Thrashing rotor blades. Hitting the roof, the floor, the roof. Fire licking my face.

A life preserver in my hands. A door handle burning my palm. Falling—metal hunks following me. A rush of blue. Freezing water down my lungs.

Then nothing. Nothing at all.

16

February 22, 1962

White. My eyes opened upon an infinite expanse of white.

Oh, God. I'm blind. My gaze moved down.

Still more white—the white of a sheet-covered bundle. My body stretched out before me on a bed.

Thick bandages covered both arms. Under the bedsheet my legs had a curiously bulky look, as if in a cast. I tried wiggling my toes but the sheet draping my feet didn't move.

"Nurse!" I heard myself shouting. "Nurse!"

A startled female face appeared at the white-painted door, vanished, then reappeared a few moments later with a man in tow.

"Mr. Hall, I'm Dr. Malle. I'm very glad to see you've regained consciousness. At least your vocal cords sound healthy."

The doctor watched my eyes rove dazedly around the room. "I imagine you're curious to know where you are. This is the Burn Unit of Victoria General Hospital in Halifax." He walked to the window. "You've been here nine days."

I blinked densely at him.

"You're very lucky to be alive." Dr. Malle ran his fingertips over the windowsill. "In fact, some of my colleagues are still

154

debating the fact. By their reckoning, you shouldn't be. Second-degree burns on your legs, arms, shoulders, and chest. Half-drowned and exposed to near-freezing seawater. If it wasn't for a very competent medic aboard the Mountie ship that picked you up, you would be the concern of the mortuary down the street, not me."

"My wife," I asked quietly. "You've notified her?"

"She's waiting outside," said the nurse.

Malle and the nurse checked the catheter bag by my bed and spirited away. Low voices muttered on the other side of the door, which then swung open as Jan entered the room.

Her hands were strangling the straps of her handbag and her eyes and nose were red. She looked wonderful.

"How do you feel?"

"Numb. How about yourself?"

She smiled feebly, dabbing at her eyes with a knotted handkerchief. "Damn it, I promised myself not to cry."

Canting my head toward the end table, i said, "There's some Kleenex. Blow your nose."

Jan grabbed a handful of tissues from the dispenser. "You must think I'm a silly ass. I've been very square-chinned until now."

"I'll tell you what I think of you when I'm able to feel it."

She dropped the tissues in the wastebasket and kissed me on the cheek. "You always were a horny bastard."

I scowled at the heaped bouquets in the corner. "Who sent all these damn flowers?"

"Oh, you'd be surprised. Your folks. Your son. Your ex."

Nodding dully, I pointed at a huge bunch of lilies planted in a silver tankard. "Not from you, I hope."

"No. I know you can't stand them." She read the accompanying card.

"Well?"

"'Best wishes for your speedy recovery,'" she said softly. "It's from Ryker."

My answering laugh was brittle. It brought back an unpleasant subject to mind.

"Jan, what happened to MacKendrick and Burke?"

She sat on the bed. "MacKendrick is dead, Norman."

I swallowed hard. "And Burke?"

"He's in Intensive Care. Burke's been burned very badly." She fumbled for the words. "They've had to . . . cut . . . I mean both his legs are gone. And his right arm."

Her teeth chattered in a strange little titter. "Doctors can do wonders these days. Burke can be fed through tubes, with the latest machines to suck the waste away. Why, he could live for years."

Slowly I let air hiss through my teeth. "I want to see him."

"Later, Norman. When you're stronger."

I painfully pulled the sheet snug under my chin. "Did the police recover any remains of the copter?"

"That's what I understand. A Captain Lincoln cornered me here this morning. He wants you to appear at the inquest on the crash as soon as possible."

Police inquest. I felt a tightening in my throat. Of course, I wouldn't be on trial this time, not in any sense, but the very words hit me like an ancient curse.

Jan read my mind. "Captain Lincoln promised me everything would be kept low-key."

"A pious hope, my dear. Unfortunately, the whole story has the making of a press circus."

Silence. Her hand kept stroking my hair.

"Something's on your mind, Janice. Are you going to come out with it, or do I have to play guessing games?"

"Oh, Norman, don't . . . "

"Right now you're planning strategy once I leave this place. If you had your druthers, I would hand my resignation to Geoffrey and retire to a cottage by the seashore, writing Harlequin Romances until age ninety-five."

Jan laughed grudgingly. "You're making the last part up. Romance was never your strong suit."

"We'd collaborate."

"No, Norman." She patted my shoulder. "We'll have to thrash this out, but not here and not now. At the proper time and place I'm prepared to pull my hair, scream, and throw dishes. You will set your jaw and gird your loins and nothing will change." A lingering kiss before she stood. "In the meantime, get some sleep."

* * *

OTTAWA (UPI) After an exhaustive investigation spanning two weeks, the inquiry into the loss of the Halifax Air Charter Company's Bell helicopter, which killed one man and injured two, adjourned today, no closer to a verdict than when the inquest began.

"We were faced with conflicting evidence," explained Chief Investigation Officer Glenn Lincoln, "which seemed, and still seems, very inconclusive. The Board of Inquiry simply didn't have enough material on which to base a satisfactory verdict."

The helicopter was returning to Halifax after visiting William Ryker's research ship, Savonarola, on what was described as a "journalistic mission" by Geoffrey Proctor, Chairman of the Board of Proctor–World Publishing. Mr. Proctor was the employer of both Norman Hall and Burke Sheffield, who were injured in the crash.

The board heard today from Hall, who related how a fire broke out on board the copter, engulfing the cockpit in seconds.

"The details are all very jumbled," he stated, "but the fire was definitely sudden, almost explosive."

Hall went on to testify that the position of pilot Ralph MacKendrick may have cost him his life.

"Both MacKendrick and Mr. Sheffield were sitting in the front seats, directly behind the controls. Since the fire seems to have started under the instruments, they had very little time to escape."

Only scattered pieces of the helicopter have been found by recovery teams. No evidence was found as to the cause of the explosion.

Simon Harriman, representative of the Bell Corporation, testified before the board that no design fault in the copter could conceivably cause an explosion such as Hall described.

"Things such as fuel lines and electrical circuits are protected by insulators. I don't see any way for this particular explosion to be considered an accident."

However, police investigation can find no direct indication of sabotage.

"Lack of facts puts the whole inquest at an impasse," said Chief Investigator Lincoln.

Ralph MacKendrick is survived by his wife and son. Burke Sheffield is under continual intensive care at Victoria General Hospital.

I spent the next two months in Halifax, stitching together the scattered pieces of my life.

With Dr. Malle's encouragement I was able to sit up in bed by early March. Another two weeks of sitz baths, bouts in an oxygen tent, and lube jobs with tannic jelly passed before the bandages came off for good.

All the doctors and nurses kept telling me how fortunate I was not to have facial burns. Much of my body hair had been scorched away and the freshly-healed skin resembled a shiny sugar-coated glaze. I tried flexing my biceps. It was like bending a sausage.

Weeks passed before I could walk normally. But I couldn't just sit and vegetate. Time was running out on the *Titanic* story.

On March 10, I swallowed my pride and called Geoffrey. In the end we compromised. I gave and he took. I coughed up the article by the end of the week. Fast and breezy and a piece of shit. In return, he agreed to announce that it was only the first part of a forthcoming serial to conclude in *World* by Christmas.

Jan jet-shuttled between Paris and the hospital, bringing our background notes. With papers stacked high on all sides of the bed, I sat my portable on my lap and typed for two days straight. A rehashed sinking, culled from other books. An emasculated account of my meeting with Eva and her daddy. Although haunted by half facts and half hunches, I wrote nothing about the Kleins. The *Marianas* trip served as capper, with a P.S. plugging the next promised installment. You—the reader—ain't heard nothin' yet!

I chucked the pages into an envelope, licked the flap shut, and passed it to the night-duty nurse to mail. Sagging back against my pillow, I turned off the table lamp and watched snowflakes bounce off the window, lit by the blue glow of the night-light.

I had a sudden desire to get roaring drunk. Anything to blunt this fall into my personal black pit.

I spent the night thinking of that story on its airmail way to Geoffrey's desk. A god-awful work compared with what it could have been. But what could I have done? Wrapped and mummified in the hospital, I'd been helpless. An act of God . . .

I remembered Ryker's words aboard the *Savonarola*, thought about the sabotage rumors, and felt sick with apprehension.

By sunrise I'd worked out a tentative battle plan for my followup article. Check out the identity of the man tailing Burke on the *Savonarola*. Talk again with Eva. Badger the Australian police about new leads on the McFarland murder. Interview other *Titanic* survivors who stayed in cabins close to the Rykers or Kleins.

It was a formidable checklist. Once escaping from this damn place, I would once again be an all-around nuisance to a great many people. That thought cheered me considerably.

Those last weeks at Victoria General became a teeth-gritting prison stretch. Malle and his crew filled my morning hours with treadmills, barbells, endless Jacuzzis, and pummeling masseurs.

In the afternoon came visitors. Most were pleasant, some tiresome, and a few very painful. Geoffrey arrived with bundles of advance *World* copies bearing my bastardized story. A masterpiece, he said. The editorial board couldn't wait for Part Two. Keep up the good work.

My parents flew in from Honolulu, followed shortly thereafter by Ron, away from USC for Easter. And, most astonishingly, my ex-wife. She wept demurely, squeezed my hand, told me to take care, and ran from the room. To my surprise, I found myself oddly moved.

I saved the worst for last. The night before my release I limped up to Intensive Care to see Burke. He had asked for me. The whole experience was something I'd rather not discuss.

Finally, on April 24, I held Jan's hand in my left and a walking stick in my right as Nurse Rhoades wheeled me down the front steps of the hospital to our waiting car. Pure foolishness, of course, since I could walk fine. Steadily if not gracefully. But regulations were sacrosanct, and outgoing patients must never leave under their own power.

Jan's rented '62 Impala waited curbside at the bottom of the steps. She got the door as the nurse locked the chair's wheels and eased me upright.

"Any problems, Mr. Hall? Just let me know."

I promised, while she and Jan exchanged brave parting words. Then we were off.

Jan fiddled with knobs and got the heater roaring. "Well, how does the outside look?"

I peered through wiper streaks at the slush and traffic. "A godsend. I feel freshly hatched and ready to tackle the world."

"A terrifying image, Norman." She turned right onto Connaught Avenue.

"Where in the world are you taking me?"

"Something I ran across a few days ago."

She wouldn't elaborate as we made a left onto Chishom Avenue, skirting the edges of what at first seemed to be a handsome city park. The Chevy swerved and braked in front of a brick signpost. I rubbed frost off the window with my coat sleeve and appraised a blue-tarnished plaque.

City of Halifax
FAIRVIEW
Lawn
CEMETERY
1893

"I find this in poor taste, Janice."

"Please don't be angry." She eased the car forward onto the snow-slippery driveway. "Just sit tight."

The road cut straight between columns of shivering elms. Beyond the trees, tombstones jutted out of the snow like petrified toadstools.

A white paint-chipped sign hugged the right side of the road. I squinted at the black letters as we pulled over and stopped.

TITANIC

"My God, Jan, what have you got us into?"

"Bear with me, Norman." She coached me from the car and led the way toward the deserted graveyard.

Most of the markers curved up the gentle slope in unassuming rows resembling immense granite dentures. A mere handful of marble stones stood above the crowd. Jan brushed ice off the chistled words of one monolith.

> IN LOVING MEMORY OF WILLIAM HENRY HARRISON
> BELOVED HUSBAND OF ANN ELIZABETH HARRISON
> WHO LOST HIS LIFE IN THE TITANIC DISASTER
> APRIL 15, 1912
> 'IN THE MIDST OF LIFE WE ARE IN DEATH'

I huddled within my coat to fend off the chills. I smelled the old dreaded scent. I'd come across it on the ocean floor. And in the closet at the Moana Hotel. After twenty years, I still couldn't wash it away.

"Nearly two hundred of them," Jan explained. "Picked up two weeks after the sinking by a Halifax cable ship, the *Mackay-Bennett*. Some, like this man, were identified. Others not." She turned over her shoulder and watched a lonely tanker chugging out of Halifax harbor. "Quite a spot, isn't it?"

We walked past row after row of faceless headstones. LOST ON THE R.M.S. TITANIC APRIL 15, 1912. R.I.P. I had an uneasy vision of buried corpses wakened by our footsteps, whispering among themselves. Complete nonsense, of course, but even so . . .

A Plymouth sedan nosed in back of our parked car. The woman driver locked it up and moseyed our way. She kept her distance, inspecting the gravestones.

Minutes passed and we wove between rows like shoppers in a Christmas tree lot, drawing steadily closer to the woman.

She still hadn't acknowledged our presence. A pause at each stone and then she moved on. Jan and I found ourselves imitating her pattern. I began to feel like a pawn in some elaborate board game.

An approaching freight train howled on the other side of the fence. The woman paid it no mind. The next row would take her by us.

Warning bells rang at the Chishom Avenue intersection as the freight roared by, shaking the cemetery fence. The ground under my feet trembled as the wheels rolled over gaps in the rails. Under the cover of the noise I examined the woman more closely. Horsey and fiftyish, with a doughy face marked by years of good living. The type who would accompany her husband on hunting trips, bagging two ducks to his one.

The freight hooted mournfully to silence. She was coming our way.

"Hello," I said.

"Morning." She didn't look up. "You folks come here often?"

"No." Jan held onto my arm. "We're from out of town."

"You're lucky. It not being crowded, I mean. This poor place has been a tourist trap ever since the *Titanic* business cropped up. Nothing but that old fool Ryker on the news. It's no wonder the locals shudder at the thought of a *Titanic* graveyard right in the heart of town."

I tapped the headstone with my shoe. "The residents don't look capable of much mischief."

"Not quite true." She crooked a finger. "Come with me."

We followed her to a plot tucked in a far corner, where the fence ran along Windsor Street. The headstone had a tiny brass plate on its base. The woman pulled a handkerchief from her purse and wiped off some of the tarnish. We bent closer.

GEORGIA BETH FERRELL
1880-1912

IN APPRECIATION FOR SERVICE BEYOND THE CALL OF DUTY

ABOARD THE R.M.S. TITANIC APRIL 14, 1912

R.I.P.

W.A.R.

"Notice the date." She underlined it with a forefinger. "One day earlier than all the others. The ship sank early in the morning of the fifteenth. I sometimes wonder what she did on the fourteenth to rate such approval."

I stood erect. "Who are you?"

"My name's Ruth Masterson." She shook my hand. Her eyes were canny and alert like a wise old eagle. "I've been following since you left the hospital."

"I'm afraid . . . "

"No, we never met. But you know my husband, by reputation at least." She led Jan and me by the arm. "I can explain better in the car. Harold is very anxious to talk to you. But we thought it safer if I was the one who picked you up."

"Harold . . . ?"

"That's right. He's got an old movie at home. And you're invited to a private screening."

17

April 24, 1962

We agreed to follow Ruth Masterson's Plymouth to the apartment, where her husband waited. The path took us downtown, across the Angus MacDonald Bridge into Dartmouth, and finally to a low stucco triplex near Little Albro Lake.

She waited out front while we parked on the street, then led the way to the back apartment. A record player blasted behind the closed curtains of the front unit. Vaughn Meader's uncanny impersonation of JFK, followed by shrill canned laughter.

"College kids," Mrs. Masterson explained. "They raise quite a racket, but you learn to live with it."

The back unit had a closed and abandoned look, but it came to life when she tapped the front door.

"Who is it?" asked a muffled voice from within.

"It's me, Halley."

Chains rattled and the door opened into stuffy darkness. Mrs. Masterson made introductions and I peered through the gloom to see the man shaking my hand.

Harold Masterson had shrunk since his appearance on television, when he was pink and flushed by success. The

164

chubby face had turned pale gray and his eyes were wide and dazed, like a near-sighted man who has lost his glasses.

"I'm so pleased to meet you. Both of you." He finally released his grip and pointed to the couch. "Please sit down."

Sunlight seeping through the dark green drapes filled the living room with an aquarium glow. Masterson stood over us, rubbing his palms together.

"Now! Just make yourself at home. Would you like something to drink?"

"No, thanks."

He settled into a lumpy chair, then smiled uncomfortably. "I'm sorry, but I'm rather anxious about this whole thing. Once you see that film, my head is on a chopping block. I want your word that you'll wait at least five days before making the contents public."

"That seems fair."

"Good, good." Masterson exhaled deeply. "You see, I need time to get out of the country."

"I don't understand."

"It's Ryker. The man's ruthless. He'll . . . " Masterson blotted his forehead with a shirt sleeve. "Maybe I should start from scratch." He coiled both hands together. "Last year I was working at the New York office of Brubaker, Hutchison and Adler. One of the top execs in charge of the Savannah-Co account. As it turns out, William Ryker dabbles in oil. He's a major stockholder. He drafted me last November to work on the salvage project. The job's title was 'Executive Director,' but Mike Rogers and the technical boys did most of the directing. I was hired as a high-powered PR man. Not ego-building, perhaps, but most lucrative.

"We kept the lid on all the news until the *Marianas* and *Neptune* located the *Titanic* and began retrieving relics. Then a controlled trickle to the networks and wire services. Absolutely routine. I never heard a ripple from Ryker in Veyrier.

"The *Neptune* discovered the film on January twenty-first. Everyone on my staff knew it was a terrific find. I personally took a plane to New York to deliver it to the DeLuxe labs. Their technicians took fantastic care of the original neg when they made the dupes."

"Wait a minute," I interrupted. "How many people saw the movie?"

"At the lab? Three that I know of. Security was pretty tight. My orders." He laughed grimly. "And, as it turned out, my undoing. Fewer men for Ryker to smother under all his money."

"Bribes, I suppose."

"And threats. An iron-fisted sugar daddy. Ryker's found the combination most effective." Harold crossed his legs and fidgeted into a new position. "In any case, after viewing the film, I held a press conference explaining the movie and promising release prints within two days. We flew a copy to Ryker that night."

Masterson swallowed bitterly. "Twenty-four hours later I got a long-distance call from Veyrier. Ryker had seen the film as well as my press conference."

He laughed, staring at the smudged ceiling. "I can still hear his voice. 'You're through, Masterson. Your pay'll be sent through the mail. Get out of my life. And if you say one word about this,' he said, 'I'll kill you.'"

Jan said, "Maybe he was just blowing off steam."

I nodded. "Murder threats seem to be Ryker's standard expression of disaffection."

Masterson studied his folded hands. "After that call, I cleared the hell out, but quick! I knew I'd jumped into the frying pan. The first thing I did was mail my copy of the film to a post office box in New York. It was my high card in this mess."

"How many copies exist?"

"Three that I know of. One to Ryker. And two for me. All sixteen millimeter reduction prints."

"What happened to the original neg?"

"Gone." He shrugged helplessly. "DeLuxe did their best, but the celluloid was fifty years old, after all. It jammed in the printer and crumbled into a million banjo picks."

He stooped under the coffee table and pulled out a film can from the bottom magazine rack. "There it is. One of three prints in the world. Assuming Ryker kept his."

"I'm sure of it. He never throws anything away."

Masterson held the can up to me. "I want you to have it. As insurance." He beckoned us with a finger. "The projector's set up in the bedroom."

Even at high noon the room brooded under clotted ivy vines snaking across the windows. Ruth drew the drapes and subdued the sunlight to a thin gray rumor. She and Jan settled on the king-sized bed facing the home movie screen while Harold fiddled with an old Bell & Howell.

I craned over his shoulder. "Anything I can do?"

"Nope." Film chattered through the gate. "We're rolling."

Masterson clicked on the lamp and a blurry number 9 flickered past, followed by a sharper 8 and 7 as he focused the image.

6

5

4

3

2

1

A blotchy black and white image appeared of the English countryside seen from a moving vehicle. A wood windowsill wobbled in and out of the picture. A flashing railroad crossing sign.

"The boat train," Harold said, leaning toward the screen. "It left London for Southampton dock on April 10, 1912. Astor, Guggenheim; all the cream of the *Titanic*'s passenger list were on board. Whoever our cameraman was, he had money."

The movie cut to a cat's cradle of train tracks writhing outside the window.

"Terminus Station. Southampton."

A complex of sheds, gantries, quays, cranes, and warehouses glided past. The train eased to a stop and the camera trained on three plumes of smoke puffing from tall funnels jutting up from behind the dock.

A cut to rough wood planking. A pan up a wall of black metal to the bow of the ship, proudly inscribed TITANIC.

The rattling projector made the only sound in the bedroom.

The camera panned to the right, revealing the entire looming length of the ship, finally stopping at the gang-planks.

A tall brunette in her mid-thirties, with amused, provoca-tive features, held the hand of a little girl as they walked to-ward the gangplank. The lady wore an elegant hat and long dress of another time. Turning to the camera, the girl laughed and waved.

The scene switched to the Boat Deck aboard the *Titanic*. Rigging ran from the four towering funnels down to the white lifeboats. The camera made a restless sweep of the rail-ing.

A shot down to the dock far below. Men and women jubi-lantly waved caps and scarves. The little figures began slowly shifting within the frame.

"They're off."

The film, momentarily absorbed with Southampton's pass-ing scenery, cut back to the Boat Deck.

Long funnel shadows slanted across the lifeboats. A rather pert girl in her late teens or early twenties leaned against the railing and watched the teetering horizon. She wore a cap and a heavy coat.

Cut to the little girl standing nearby, wrapped up for cold gusty weather. The same child we'd seen before.

The attractive woman reappeared from the side of the frame as she bent down to turn up the collar of the little girl's coat. She then glanced up and gave the photographer an odd and secret smile. Standing, she led the little girl by the hand to pose beside the teenager. All three grinned and waved awkwardly.

The hand-held camera unsteadily followed the teenage girl as she walked in front of the other two, tapping the shoulder of a passerby. She pointed at the camera, and I gathered she wanted the man to hold it so the photographer could get in the picture.

Cut to four people standing by the railing.

On the left, the thirtyish brunette. Next to her, the cute teenager, who pulled off her cap, shaking long blond hair. To her right, the little girl, now being held piggyback on the shoulders of a new face—a straight-spined young beefcake in his mid twenties. Scrubbed, square-jawed, and white of teeth. Hair either dark blond or red. Pure, humorous eyes. Caressing the knees of the girl straddling his shoulders, he mouthed unheard instructions into the lens and out from the screen to us.

The foursome frayed into a scratchy mess, then vanished like an uncertain vision. Trailing leader clicked through the projector.

"That's it," Masterson said.

"Like hell it is!" I lunged around him and reversed the machine. The final scene reappeared, then froze as I turned the switch to 'single frame.'

"Well, Jan?" I felt a rising bristle of excitement. "What do you make of it?"

She looked uncertain. "It's your show, Norman."

"Okay." I walked in front of the screen. The four faces swam over my forehead as I shaded my eyes against the beam. "Can you crank it up, Harold? That's fine." I pointed over my shoulder. "Now, let's start with the older woman on the left. Harold, I'm afraid you've skimped on your homework. That's Clair, Ryker's wife. And that little girl is Eva." I pointed at the grainy little face. "No scar above the right eye, but it's her, all right."

I turned to Jan. "Now, the other two. A worthy challenge. Any ideas?"

"Is this Twenty Questions, Norman?"

"I'll give you a hint. Think they'd look good atop a wedding cake?"

Insight flashed into her eyes. "Mima Heinley!"

"Right." I stared at the two faces fifty years in the past. "Their neighbors didn't exaggerate. Albert and Martha were a beautiful couple."

18

April 30, 1962

"How can you be so sure?" asked Tom Bramel.

I switched off the movie projector and the image of the Rykers and Kleins faded from the wall of his Scotland Yard office. "They match Mima Heinley's description. According to Masterson, the film was discovered on B Deck in the area of their cabin. And although I can't prove it, I'm sure both William and Eva Ryker could verify their identities. If you believe Masterson—and I do—Ryker is prepared to commit murder rather than let anyone see that film."

"You're swinging pretty wild, Norman."

"I haven't mentioned the most important thing. I'll testify, under oath if need be, that the young girl in that movie is the same Martha Klein I met in Honolulu."

". . . twenty years ago." Tom pressed his hands together, peering through the finger-steeple, then put both palms face-down on the desk. "I don't doubt your sincerity, Norman, but we'd be relying entirely on your memory."

"Goddamit, Tom! That's unfair and you know it."

"Sorry, Norman. I'm trying to grab on to facts, and there are damn few of them."

"The Kleins had to have passports to board the *Titanic*. That would give us the pictures we need."

"Which probably went down along with the ship."

"But wouldn't the State Department have some sort of record?" I asked.

Tom tugged thoughtfully at his chin. "Could be. I don't know if they keep photo files that far back, but it's worth a try." He scribbled on his memo pad. "While we're at it, we'll check any files from the British Inquiry of the sinking, as well as records from the Board of Trade. Between all of them, something will turn up."

A thought then occurred to me. "Tom, we've neglected the most obvious answer. Mima Heinley. I can have blow-up stills made from the movie. She and her husband are the only two people alive who are willing and able to identify the Kleins."

"It may not be that simple, Norman. The film's pretty grainy. And it'll look worse, not better, as a print." Finding an errant match stick, he scuffed it to life on his shoe and puffed at the pipe. "By the way, what's the second favor?"

"Need there be one?"

"You have an unsated look, Norman."

"All right, Tom. It's really quite simple."

"Aren't they all?"

"No, no," I said. "The mouth's too wide. Smaller. And turned down at the corners."

"More like this?" Sergeant Rand, the operator of the Identikit machine, peered at me through the darkness of the little room just down from Tom Bramel's office.

Up on the wall screen the mouth disappeared and the Identikit projected a new one below the eyes and nose.

"That's better. But the hair's too curly. Wavy, not kinky. Parted well up on the left side of the head. And longish sideburns."

As Sergeant Rand pushed the necessary buttons, Tom leaned across the battered table. "Anything else, Norman?"

I studied the face on the wall. A little sketchy, but the best I

could muster from the images in my head. A passable facsimile of Burke's tail, the crewman with the smooth white
hands that hadn't seen a day's hard work.

"No," I said, "that's about all I can add."

With one sweeping stroke Sergeant Rand pulled the Polaroid tab from the Identikit machine, counted off sixty seconds on his watch, peeled the finished print from the back
door, and passed it to Bramel.

"Fine. Get that on the drum and off to Paris, will you
please?"

Tom sighed mildly once Rand left the room. "Well, we
shall see. Interpol may be feeling diligent today." He stood.
"Meanwhile, lunch calls."

We spent the best part of two hours at a groaning buffet at
Mirabelle's. Loosening my belt, I watched Tom polish his
plate and began to wonder if I was feeding a tapeworm.

Tom checked back with the Yard while I paid the bill and
dispensed tribute to all outstretched palms. But he said nothing to me until we returned to his car.

"Paris came through with your picture, Norman."

I held onto the seat as we roared past the Hilton and
wheeled around Hyde Park Corner. "Already? I hardly expected . . ."

". . . yes, I know." Tom kept both eyes on the road. "This
one was easy."

He passed me the top page of the report when we returned to the office. "That your man?"

It certainly was. In both full and profile positions shot by
the Rome police.

"Alfredo Petacchi." Tom read aloud from the dossier, a
forefinger underlining vital statistics. "Born June 18, 1915,
in Palermo. Married to Maria Scalisi, daughter of Carlo Scalisi, April 24, 1935." He scratched the back of his head. "Curiouser and Curiouser. Have you heard of the Scalisi family,
Norman?"

"Not just 'a family,' I gather. The Family?"

"Precisely."

Alfredo Petacchi glared at us from the surface of the photo as we peered into the details of his life. Arrested for armed

assault in Corleone, 1947. Dismissed for lack of evidence. Held on suspicion of homicide in Milan, 1952. Acquitted. Suspected in Trieste gang slaying, 1957. Never indicted. Believed to be an enforcer and important lieutenant for the Scalisi family and its interests in both Sicily and New York state. Investigated by the Kefauver Commission, but no definite evidence on which to base prosecution.

Tom released the folder and wiped his fingers on the blotter. "Like I said, this one was easy." He studied the photo once again. "And you say this man was crewing aboard the *Savonarola*?"

"Ostensibly."

His head shook. "Ryker runs a tight ship, doesn't he?"

The ringing phone cut in on our thoughts. A long-distance Paris call from Jan.

"Jerry Blaine called this morning," she explained. "I still can't believe it, but I agreed to wire him money."

"Now what?"

"Eva Ryker slit her wrists last night. The doctors in Madrid don't think she'll make it."

19

May 1, 1962

Madrid's Hospital de Clinicas sits quietly on the Paseo de las Delicias. From any window facing northeast, patients have a pleasing view of the Botanical Gardens, the zoo, and the Buen Retiro Park.

I turned away from a fourth-story window and looked down at Eva Ryker. Except for the slight up-and-down sighing of the sheets covering her, she could have been dead. The white bandages taped around her wrists closely matched the color of her skin.

Eva's eyes opened without any demure fluttering and began their survey of the room. The dilated pupils swiveled my way.

"What the . . ." A broken smile. "It's you."

"How do you feel?"

Eva blinked dully at the bed. "God. How did I get here?"

I took one wrist and held it up for her to see. She crouched down in the covers at the sight of the bandages.

"What the hell are you doing here?"

"I heard you were in trouble."

"From who? Daddy?"

My head shook.

174

"Mike Rogers, then?" She laughed feebly. "Mr. Clean's been around, you know. Tidying up. He came last night to pay his respects. Kicked him the hell out. And you're about to get the same boot." She fumbled for the room buzzer.

"Don't, Eva." I took it from her hands. "I want to talk."

"What about?" she sneered. "My precarious teetering between life and death?"

"And your strange brand of good fortune. Your landlord found you in time, lying on the bathroom floor. And you've got nice run-of-the-mill O-type blood, which the hospital has sitting around in gallon jugs. That's why you're here with catheters up your twat, swapping *bon mots* with me."

"Jesus, Hall." Her lids blinked desperately in an effort to blot the seeping moisture. "You really are a son of a bitch."

"Possibly." I handed her a Kleenex. "But I may also be the only friend you've got. Not that Daddy and Company aren't useful. Your hospital bills are paid off. Mike also stuffed green down the throats of your greasy young studs and other survivors of your recent bash. But even Daddy's money couldn't buy off the landlord. You've been tossed out." I spread my hands. "La Dolce Vita is all gone."

Eva's lips pressed tight. "Get fucked, Hall."

"Act your age. What are you going to do when you get out? Sure, the Ferrari's gassed up and Mike left some cash, but what then?"

"Just what are you proposing?"

"Something more than what you've got."

"How very righteous! And you've cast yourself in the role of Holy Father!"

"By necessity, Eva. I'm not letting you out of my sight." I reached out a finger and gently touched her forehead. "You see, locked up in your skull is a memory. Fifty years ago you threw away the key."

"Shut up!"

I grabbed her arms and shook them before her eyes. "That's the reason for this! And it's why you've tried to turn your entire life into a pile of shit!"

She turned from my grasp and clamped both hands over her ears. "Leave me alone! God damn . . ."

"I can help . . ."

"No!" she screamed hysterically. "Just get out! Get the hell out of my life!"

She bent double as the dam broke. I found myself sitting on the bed, stroking her hair. Murmuring guilty words of comfort. Wiping the eyes of a face stretched like pulled taffy under the weight of tears. Let it all out, Eva. It's all for the best. Catharsis, courtesy of Norman the Good.

I held her hand in mine and tried to ignore any lingering taint of treachery.

Five days later I watched Eva Ryker walk toward her Ferrari parked in the hospital lot. She already had the key in hand before jumping in. The engine turned over. And over and over and over.

I knocked on the door and held up the distributor cap for her to see. "This joins us at the hip."

Leaning against the car, I waited for her string of swearing to end. "Are you through?"

". . . you miserable bastard. I'm . . ."

"That's enough, Eva. You're going to at least pretend to be a civilized human being, or you're not going anywhere."

She slow-boiled in a dormant state. "Just what do you have in mind?"

I bent inside the car and snatched the keys from the ignition. "Move over."

Walking to the front of the Ferrari, I installed the cap. A quick slam of the hood and I slipped in the driver's seat. The engine caught with typical Italian shrieking and propelled us out of the parking lot onto the Paseo de las Delicias.

Eva slumped down in the bucket seat. "Okay, Hall. I consider myself kidnapped. What next?"

"Oh, don't fret, Eva. Just a little spin down to Balerma. I've rented a beach house there."

Her eyes widened. "That's over three hundred miles away!"

"Quite right." I smiled, dodging a produce truck as we

crossed the bridge over the Manzanares River. "Nothing so therapeutic as a change of scenery."

"Oh really?" She folded her arms tight across her chest. "And what if I decide not to play along with this farce?"

"I don't think you'd leave your car." My thumb pointed backward. "And all your clothes are in the trunk. Not many alternatives, I should think."

Her frown cracked a little. "Don't expect me to sleep with you."

I accelerated around a Fiat sedan, then throttled down to cruising speed. "Believe me, my dear, I have no designs on your virginal white flesh."

Eva cinched her seat belt tight as the Ferrari sped south, away from Madrid.

Spain was up to technicolor-travelogue standards during the long drive south to the Mediterranean. The shadow of the Ferrari grew longer and longer on the road as I pushed at a steady hundred twenty kilos through Getafe and Pinto and Aranjuez and Ocana and Madridejos and Puerto Lapiz.

Headlights flashed on as the orange glow faded in the west and the big Italian engine boomed out the stretch through Manzanares and Valdepeñas and La Carolina.

We stopped for the night at Bailen, registering at La Plaza de la Naranja, just off the main road. Eva stormed unceremoniously to her room, but did agree to eat dinner with me, a minor improvement in our cold war.

At the risk of seeming provincial, I've never approved of Spanish dining etiquette. A late supper *cum* midnight snack doesn't agree with my digestive tract. Eva and I squinted at the menus in the semidarkness and finally managed to order Cochinillo asado, Pollo al Barco, and sangria by a quarter to eleven.

I glanced at a neighboring table. "The food looks edible, anyway."

"Are you speaking as a gourmet?"

"Not really. But my wife's cooking does spoil me."

"Oh, yes. Janet, isn't it?"

"Janice."

She turned her head to study me. "For some reason, I can't see you married. You have the look of a rumpled, unpressed bachelor."

I smiled as the sangria arrived. "Sorry to break your heart." I passed her a glass. "Fifteen years of matrimony. Sixteen in September."

Eva took a healthy gulp. "A whirlwind courtship, I suppose."

"Naturally. She was too good an agent to lose."

"Such an unbridled romantic." Another sip. "Kids?"

"None with Jan. A son by my first marriage."

Her eyebrows arched in surprise. "You? Twice-bitten?"

"Sad but true."

"The girl back home, right?"

"In Honolulu."

Eva's glass made a wide swing toward her mouth. "Are you sure you're from Hawaii? Shouldn't you be . . . blond and sun-kissed?"

"Not necessarily. Among rich haoles, you do well to be nondescript and unethnic. Eastern Seaboard Wasp, with a mere hint of a tan, is considered very proper."

Eva grinned. "Did you qualify?"

"We both did. Louise and I." I toyed with my fork. "But . . . things happen. We separated before I went into the Army. After the war, I didn't come back. We still see each other every year or so, when I visit Ron." I shrugged. "Christmas and birthday cards and all that. My son doesn't understand, I'm afraid." I laughed tightly. "Unlike Louise, who understands *everything*. Or so she tells me when we meet. All knowing and forgiving." My hand dropped the fork. "Somehow, though, I get the feeling she wouldn't care too much if I dropped dead."

Eva sighed and settled back in her chair. I felt very comfortable in the room-within-a-room we were building out of sangria and small talk.

"Tell me something, Hall."

"Hm?"

"Do you find me attractive?"

"Women! This afternoon you sweated over your fate worse than death, and now you want me to meter your sex appeal?"

Eva flushed pale pink. "Well?"

Candlelight cast a kind glow on her face and bare shoulders, framed by a simple black dress.

"The answer's yes. You're very lovely."

Her lips curled in Gioconda irony. "How earnest, Hall."

"I'm sorry," I said gently. "But I don't feel safe letting it warm up."

"That's very pure. And quite unworldly."

"Maybe."

"Then why the unbreakable vows with Wifey?"

I raised both hands. "We're hot for each other."

"I can imagine! A regular duel of the titans."

"Cut it out, Eva. You don't have to play slut queen for my benefit. You don't love me. I'm not even sure you like me. So it's all moot sparring."

"You know," she drawled, "I'm not sure you're entirely normal."

"Such veiled barbs. You're a master, Eva."

The wine glass circled in for a landing. "Once I read someone—a literary critic, I think—who said that American novelists form a long daisy chain of failed queers."

"Then I must be the missing link."

Wine sputtered across the table. I jumped up and pounded her on the back as clattering dinnerware died and people stopped, food in hand, to stare at us.

Eva finally regained her breath. There wasn't a sound in the dining room. Every eye trained on us.

We glanced at each other across the table and broke up.

"Good God, Hall, how much did we drink last night?"

The car's exhaust boomed along with my head as I maneuvered out on the road leaving Bailen. "I lost count after the third pitcher."

Eva gingerly cradled her skull. "And you were supposed to reform me."

After a stop for coffee we felt slightly more human.

"Well, I told you my life story last night." I glanced at Eva as we slowed while passing through Padul. "How about reciprocating?"

Her eyes lost their focus as she gazed out the window. "Where do I begin? There's so much to tell! I was born of poor and humble parents . . ."

"Spare me your wit. Before lunch, at any rate." I braked the Ferrari as we entered Durcal. "Did you have many friends as a kid?"

"Friends? Sure, plenty. Mostly rich snots, though. One time . . ."

She chattered for the next two hours as we flew down the empty road to Motril and cruised along the Mediterranean toward Balerma. All about her girlfriends who ripped up her paper dolls and her airedale, Skipper, who died of kidney stones and her first date and college and her moving to Switzerland and her sex life and her money and how her father was driving her to ruin.

But never in all the welter of half truths did she mention a thing about the *Titanic*.

It was late afternoon when we arrived at the little beach house just past the outskirts of Balerma near the Punta del Moro.

Eva walked through the living room to the big glass doors sliding onto the balcony facing the sea. I sat the luggage on the floor and stood behind her.

"Quite a scene," I said.

She silently studied the orange cliffs loping down to the huge crescent beach curving around us. An urgent wind blew off the sea and the breaking waves were some of the largest I'd ever seen on the Mediterranean. There wasn't another human in sight.

"It's beautiful," she whispered, before her voice resumed

its hearty badgering mold. "So this is your torture chamber. Very plush."

"I'm glad you approve." I tugged the suitcases toward the bedrooms. "No talkathons tonight, Eva. Ferrari lag. We'll get a fresh start in the morning. There's something I want to show you tomorrow. You'll need your energy."

Eva's first surprise came at seven A.M., when I showed her the carport at the side of the cottage.

"A jeep?" She blinked incredulously as I climbed behind the wheel. "Where in hell are you taking me?"

"Where finicky Italian sports cars fear to tread." I held out my hand. "All aboard."

We cruised along a paved highway to Almeria, then over unmarked dirt tracks into the desert roads of boulders and sand and wishful thinking. Fortunately, I'm blessed with a boy scout's canny sense of direction.

"Hall, have you lost your mind?"

"Patience, Eva." I kicked into four-wheel drive, skidded us atop a sand dune, and cut the motor. "Come with me."

I carried a picnic basket and helped Eva through the blasted Martian landscape, trying to ignore the painful chafing of clothes against scar tissue as we rose over the last knoll. Then I pointed. "Curious, no?"

She gaped at a scene of war and devastation. The snaky skeleton of railroad tracks, blackened by dynamite scars, lay twisted like coat hangers. An old steam locomotive sprawled on its back, with upturned steel wheels sparkling in the sun. A drunken conga line of splintered passenger coaches trailed behind the engine at crazy angles. Two crows circled warily above, but we were the only people in sight.

"What in God's name happened?"

I steadied her as we plunged through the sand toward the train. "It's a movie, Eva. They shot here last summer. 'Lawrence of Arabia,' it's called. Due for release this Christmas." I threw out my arms at the wide open spaces. "Tourists haven't got wind of it yet. But it'll be picked clean before too long. I thought you'd like to see it. Illusions like this don't last forever."

We spent the next couple of hours poking through the rubble. She climbed atop the roof of one of the coaches and forced me to follow. The perfect picnic spot, she said.

Eva was not a shy eater. I spent most of my time passing her hard-boiled eggs, pepper, and celery stalks.

"Hall," she mumbled around a mouthful of roast beef, "how could you give all of this up?"

" 'This?' "

"The movie business, I mean. You were in it, weren't you?"

"In my flaming youth."

"Didn't you like it?"

"Most of the time I spent under house arrest at the writers' block at Metro. I saw myself as a latter-day Algonquin wit fighting the corrupt temple of Mammon. But it didn't play; so I got out."

"Ever regret it?"

"Hell, no!" I slapped my thigh in mock gaiety. "Look at all the swell folks I've met. You, for one. And your father, not to mention the interesting company he keeps."

She frowned gravely. "What do you mean?"

"In the last few months I've learned some marvelous things about William Ryker. Get too close and you end up singed. Scarred for life."

"I could have told you that," she chortled.   .

"But I meant it literally."

I unbuttoned my shirt to the waist. Eva turned my way and flinched.

"Jesus Christ," she whispered. "How did it happen?"

"You could call it a boating mishap, I guess." I filled her in on the details.

Eva bleakly examined the distant sand dunes. "And you think my father deliberately arranged it?"

"I don't know. Maybe it's better for my peace of mind that I don't."

She seemed lost in thought as we packed up and headed back for the jeep. We didn't exchange ten words on the return drive to Balerma.

The sun floated on the western edge of the Mediterranean as we headed down the last stretch to the beach house.

I pulled off onto the soft shoulder and put the stick in neutral. "Look at that."

Eva's eyes followed my outstretched arm. About seven miles out an ocean liner furrowed through the choppy water, its superstructure orange against the slanting sunrays, heading for Gibraltar and the distant Atlantic.

"Beautiful, isn't it?"

She didn't answer.

I peered out to sea. "Italian registry, I think. Maybe the *Cristoforo Colombo,* the sister ship of the *Andrea Doria.*"

"The one that sank." Her voice was hollow. "People are such fools."

"How's that?"

Eva's eyes clouded. "Like on board that ship. Wrapped up in their little worlds. And all the captain has to do is make the wrong slip, and those fine civilized folks would turn into rats before your eyes. Tearing at your face, gnawing at . . ."

Eva hunched low in the seat and trained both eyes on the tired red sun. "I'm cold. Let's head back. Please."

She had nothing to add during our drive home.

The wind kept blowing off the sea even after a half moon rose from behind the cliffs.

Eva came in from the porch and watched me put away dinner dishes in the kitchen. "So you can cook, too. My, Mr. Hall, you are a man of surprises."

"An old Army talent." Drying my hands, I followed her into the living room.

"Well," she said, "what now? We've ruled out sex. No TV. No records. What do you suggest—Parcheesi?"

I settled on the couch. "Want to talk?"

"Not really."

"Okay." Standing, I headed for the closet. "Then you can watch my old movies." I pulled out a 16-mm projector I'd rented in Madrid. "Absolutely fascinating."

"Good God, Hall!" She sank to the floor. "You've got to be

kidding! Let me guess. The kiddies on the front lawn? Your honeymoon at Niagara Falls? Aunt Sadie at Mount Rushmore?"

"Not quite." I set the projector on the coffee table. "They're someone else's; not mine."

Adjusting the elevation control, I plugged in the machine, then walked back to the closet, grabbed the film, and spooled it on the projector.

"What's it about?" Eva leaned forward in her chair.

"You'll see."

I threaded the film onto the take-up reel, then got the lights. The projector flashed a solid white beam onto the cream-colored wall.

Leader clicked through the projector and the first scene flashed to life.

"God, Hall! How old is this film?"

"Over fifty years."

"I believe it! Where were these train pictures taken, anyway?"

"England."

The scene shifted.

"That looks like a dock. Some big ships there."

The scene cut to the dock, panning up to the black bow of the ship.

"Titanic." Eva's voice was low and threatening. *"Titanic!* Hall, if this is your idea of a joke . . ."

I didn't answer. The camera trained on the thirtyish brunette and the young girl.

I froze on the scene. "Do you recognize anyone in this picture?"

"No." Her lips trembled. "No!"

"That's you, Eva." I pointed. "And that's your mother."

"You're lying! You're just trying to trick me!"

"No, Eva." I flipped the projector forward.

In the shadowy light of the projector lamp I watched Eva's fingernails dig into the fabric of her chair.

Cut to the young blonde girl in her twenties out on deck. Eva's eyes blinked furiously as she stared at the image, as if forcing herself not to see.

Cut to Eva and her mother.

"It's a fake!" Tears rolled down her cheeks. Her voice was curiously whiny, like a child's.

"No."

"Yes it is! It is! It is! You're lying!"

The film showed Eva and Clair with the young girl.

"It's a fake! A fake!"

The final scene flickered on the wall. All four people. Eva and Clair Ryker with Albert and Martha Klein.

Eva stood, staring at herself perched on the shoulders of the handsome young man.

"No!" The scream was a little girl's—a scream of mindless maniacal terror.

Eva ran through the open door and into the darkness.

The film was flopping in the take-up reel as I ran after her. Standing on the balcony, I searched the moonlit beach.

A figure fleeing across the sand. Heading for the breakers.

I kicked off my shoes and tore after her. The wind blew sand into my eyes, blinding me, but I kept on running.

Left? Right? Straight ahead? Which way? I blinked at the obscuring grit.

A splash of white as a body plunged into the surf.

My legs waded through the sand-quagmire. Blood pounded through my temples.

A face broke surface, then went under.

I hit the water without breaking stride. A wave crashed over me. I tumbled to the bottom, scraping my arms and knees.

My face broke surface, choking in air. Eva was just ahead, thrashing to get away from me.

Diving under, I grabbed her legs. She hit me in the side of the head. My skull rang as I grabbed her by the shoulders. She fought me with a tiger's strength. I felt myself losing my grip on her, but clamped my arms around her waist. Her elbow smashed into my mouth, loosening teeth. Going under, I clenched my jaw against the salt water burning down my throat.

I backstroked and held onto her like a sack of gold. Rough

pebbles suddenly brushed beneath my toes and I stood, hauling Eva up on the sand.

My chest heaving, I sank to my knees beside her.

Wherever she was, she wasn't here with me.

The eyes trembled blindly back and forth. Her tongue hung loose in her mouth.

"No, no!" she cried in a high childlike voice. "Don't hurt me! I don't know! I don't know anything!"

"Eva!" I shook her shoulders. "You're all right! You're safe with me!"

"No!" She screamed at terrible visions up in the night sky. "Leave me alone! I don't know anything! Mommy! Mommy! Please! Take me away!"

I slapped her across the face. "Eva!"

"Mommy!"

I hit her again.

"Take me away!"

And again.

"Leave me alone!"

And again.

Along silence. She watched me as if she'd never seen me before.

"Come on, Eva," I whispered. "I'll take you back to the house."

Without a word she crumpled into my arms.

20

May 7, 1962

Dr. Margaret Sanford's Tokyo office is on Nakasando Avenue, not far from the Koishkawa Botanical Gardens. Her chauffeur wheeled Eva and me into an underground garage, then up an elevator, and down a lush carpeted corridor to the third door on the right.

Implanted behind a desk stacked with disheveled files and reports, Margaret glanced up over the top of her reading glasses and rose to greet us.

"Norman!" She pecked me somewhere behind the left ear. "How are you?"

"Coping."

"And Janice?"

"Fine. She indulges me shamelessly."

"Everyone does, my dear." She patted my hand, turning her attention to Eva.

I made introductions and tried to interpret Eva's reaction to Dr. Sanford. Most people initially see her in a well-meaning, befuddled light. Good-hearted but not terribly bright. But it didn't take long to taste gristle beneath the Eleanor Roosevelt mush.

She shuffled behind the desk and shut drapes across the

floor-to-ceiling windows overlooking the city, then picked forlornly at the clutter on the desk top. "You must forgive all this," she muttered. "People ask me for a psychological definition of *Homo sapiens,* and I sometimes think 'a paper-wasting animal' would be as good as any." She settled into the chair and folded both hands in front of her. "Now, Eva, what has Norman said about me? Or perhaps, knowing his talent for gossip, I should ask what he left *out?*"

"Well . . ."

". . . Freudian Wonder Woman, adept at untying all the knots that bind, etc., etc . . . ?"

Eva blushed, smiling wanly. "Something like that."

"Yes, Norman was always full of testimonials." She leaned back with a deep sigh. "But I may be a little rusty for this sort of thing. One of the hazards of specialization is that it constipates you when something new turns up. I've spent nearly ten years in Japan, up to here in the problems of these people. First the Etas, and later studying the impulses behind their dreadful suicide mystique." She gestured at the files and shook her head. "Page after page of learned conclusions backed up by years of meticulous research. And I sometimes still have the feeling I'm talking through my hat."

"What are you trying to say?" Eva asked.

"I think Margaret is trying to scale herself down from Olympian heights."

"Nicely, if sarcastically put, Norman." She removed the glasses and rubbed her eyes. "I myself prefer the allusion of cards on the table." She polished the lenses with a stray Kleenex. "Now, Norman explained your background in some detail, including the events in Spain. I'm afraid his . . . stratagem of showing you that old film was unorthodox, brutal, perhaps, but it certainly jarred the mental defenses you've set up against your experiences aboard the *Titanic.*" Margaret resettled the glasses on her nose. "Do you remember anything about the ship?"

Eva shook her head.

"You recall the film, don't you?"

She squirmed in the chair. "I remember watching it. Then

I blanked out, I guess. Next thing I knew, Norman was slapping me."

Margaret made a face as she stood and paced slowly behind the desk. "I understand that you want to undergo hypnosis. To try and recover your memories?"

Conscious of our appraisal, Eva's head lifted firmly. "That's right."

Margaret switched on a desk lamp that filled the room with a low amber glow. "Well, there's a number of approaches we can use. Scopolamine, Pentothal, straight hypnosis, hallucinogens. But whether it's advisable or beneficial to you is another question. Forcing your brain to explore a past experience it's tried to obliterate for fifty years. I've seen people who've placed themselves at the disposal of . . . incompetents. Some are mumbling vegetables in hospital wards."

I watched her resolve begin to wilt.

"Eva," I said, "don't do this as some sort of obligation to me. You're the only person you've got to please."

She smiled thanks and tightened the grip on my hand.

Eight o'clock the following morning I walked with Eva into Margaret's inner office.

It was a small, square windowless room. A low modern lamp hung above a long leather couch, an expensive Sony tape recorder on a rolling stand, and two chairs.

I sat in an unobtrusive corner while Margaret took charge.

"Now, Eva, the first thing I want to do this morning is called a suggestibility test. It'll give us some idea how receptive you are to a light trance state and a simple capacity to relax. Would you come over here please?"

Dumbfounded, Eva obeyed.

"Fine. Now, dear, just stand facing this wall. That's perfect. Now, look straight up at the little black circle painted on the ceiling. Right over your head. Okay, Eva, please stand straight, with your feet together and your arms at your sides. Don't take your eyes off the circle. You're doing fine, dear."

Margaret quietly moved behind her. "All right, Eva. Now I

want you to keep very still, and don't move. The only thing I want you to do is close your eyes. Keep your head facing toward the ceiling, but close your eyes. That's wonderful. Don't be tense, dear. Try to relax. I am now going to place both my hands on your shoulder blades. Gently, very gently. You will feel a force pulling you back toward me. Don't worry and don't resist. We'll catch you when you fall. You are falling, falling, falling. Drawing back . . ."

Eva began swaying like a skyscraper near collapse.

"You are falling back," Margaret said, "back, back, all the way. We'll catch you, dear; falling back . . . back . . ."

Feather-light, she began to topple. I bolted upright to help Margaret cushion her fall.

"Wow." Eva grinned sheepishly and shook herself upright. "Are my heels round enough?"

"That's putting it mildly, my dear. I think we'll make good progress."

Late that afternoon I joined Margaret in her outer office. We had gone through three reels of tape. Eva lay asleep in the other room.

Margaret opened the drapes behind her desk. Tokyo was turning into a neon firecracker in the fading light. Winking Kanji and Hirigana signs blinked their unfathomable sales pitches our way.

She lit a cigarette, then waved the pack. "Smoke?"

"No thanks. You got me to quit, remember?"

"Oh, yes. Sorry. I wasn't enticing you."

"Sometimes I resent it. The tobacco cure, I mean. There are times when it gives you . . . something to hold on to."

"I thought you were beyond crutches, Norman."

"Not yet. Probably never."

We watched a high silver plane searching through the smog for Haneda Airport.

"You'll get duplicates of the tapes," Margaret said. "I want you to understand I would never allow such a thing if Eva hadn't requested it. I'd like her to stay with me for a while. A couple of weeks at least. Together we can talk this thing out. Put it together a piece at a time." She smiled, patting my shoulder. "It's called Crawling before Running."

"Of course." I watched her drag deep from the cigarette. "Margaret, you better be sure what you're doing, every step of the way. If she breaks down over this . . ."

"Don't underestimate Eva. A very resilient lady. She'll survive."

I took refuge in the glorious view and tried to ignore my misgivings.

Two days later the last of the seven hours of tape flipped onto the take-up reel of the recorder in my den.

Jan struggled up from the leather chair by my desk and turned it off.

I didn't say anything. She nervously fiddled with my letter opener while trying to collect her wits.

"My God, Norman. How could you stand it?"

"I couldn't. But I did." I reached for the flask in the bottom drawer. "Join me?"

Jan grabbed our empty coffee mugs. "A double."

I poured two fingers of Jack Daniels into her cup and three for myself. "Well? What do you think?"

She touched bottom with one giant swig, then came up for air. "I wish I knew. The tape raises two questions for every answer."

The phone rang. I tried to shake off my mental storm clouds as I picked up the receiver.

"Tom Bramel, Norman. Good news! We scrounged up a picture of Albert and Martha Klein!"

"You're kidding! Where?"

"Well, the FBI and State Department were dry wells. But the Cunard Line came through, if you can believe it. Their London office has some of the old White Star Line's records in storage. They came across a company duplicate of the Kleins' original passport!"

"Have you seen it yet?"

"It's on its way over. I'll mail you a copy."

"Jesus, Tom, I can't wait that long! Can't you speed it up somehow?

"Well . . ." The receiver crackled thoughtfully. "Do you know how to get to the Sûreté Nationale's headquarters in Paris?"

"At the Ministry of Interior? Sure."

"All right. Be there as soon as you can. Within the hour if possible. Ask for Chief Inspector René Bresson. I'll phone ahead. The Sûreté can pick up the picture by facsimile and give it to you."

"Thanks very much. You're a lifesaver."

" . . . again. Yes, I know. After a while I lose count. 'Bye."

I hung up and intercepted Jan's question. "Not now. I'll explain in the car."

We were courting disaster with the traffic cops by the time we got to the Ministry on the rue des Saussaies.

If Chief Inspector Bresson noticed that both Jan and I were out of breath, he gave no sign. After polite formal introductions, he led us up an elevator and down a corridor to a telex room filled by two teletypes, a phone connected directly with Interpol's radio station, and a Phillips facsimile printer. The phone, I noticed, was off the hook.

Attaching the receiver into the printer's cradle, the operator waited a moment, then pushed a button. A paper cylinder about the size of a piano roll started spinning beneath the glass cover of the machine. The scanning head started at the left side of the roll and moved slowly along the length of paper, receiving signals from the identical machine transmitting across the English Channel.

Complete transmission took two minutes. Its task completed, the machine sighed gently to a stop.

The operator passed the picture to Inspector Bresson, who gave it to me. I took one glance, blinked, then looked again. My stomach had a curious sinking feeling.

"Norman? What's the matter?"

I numbly passed the photo to her.

"It can't be!"

"I quite agree. Now, if we rip this up, we can pretend it never happened."

The left side of the photocopy was marked "Albert Cassius Klein," the right "Martha Vanella Klein."

Albert Klein was a handsome fellow with thin, narrow cheekbones.

His wife was a pert, cute girl with a short nose and a full face.

Mr. and Mrs. Klein were black.

21

May 9, 1962

"Norman, you aren't going to solve anything by crying into your popcorn."

Jan's words and the accompanying "shushes" from surrounding theatergoers did little to break my shell shock. She had suggested staying in Paris and going to see *West Side Story* in an effort to cheer me up, but so far the doomed Super Panavision romance of Maria and Tony wasn't doing the trick.

At intermission we loitered outside the main entrance of the Gaumont Palace to avoid the hubbub and cigarette smoke. On the Champs-Elysées Citroëns and Peugeots zipped insanely through the chrome-plated night.

"Janice," I finally said, "I don't understand any of it. Why would Martha Klein lie to me about she and her husband being aboard the *Titanic*?"

"What makes you think she did? We saw both of them in the Masterson film."

"What we saw was a good-looking blond couple who matched the description Mrs. Heinley gave me. 'Handsome as two figures on a wedding cake!'" I laughed grimly. "Hardly a definitive portrait."

194

Blinking lobby lights beckoned us back to the further adventures of the Jets and Sharks. Through the rest of the film thoughts of Rykers and Kleins circled through a muddled holding pattern in my head. Driving home, I grew obsessed with a mental image of a great gray snake twisted into a loop and biting its own tail, swallowing its way to self-extinction.

I had just veered the Rolls off the Autoroute onto D-98 when the Gestalt hit me.

"Norman? Norman!"

With a start, I steered us out of the soft shoulder.

"If you don't mind, I'd like to stay alive! Are you all right?"

"Janice," I said slowly, "when we get home, I want to go over the HPD files."

Jan made coffee while I pawed through the rubble in my desk drawer. It took only a moment to locate the photocopied passports of Albert and Martha Klein picked up by the HPD in 1941. By the time she entered with the cups and cream pitcher, I already had long distance on the line.

"Who are you calling this time of night?"

I didn't answer. The phone was ringing on the other end.

"H'lo?"

"It's Norman, Tom. Were you asleep?"

"Until you called. I think your initial charm is beginning to wane."

"I apologize. I really do. But something big has come up."

"You mean the Kleins in blackface? I've already had my belly laugh for the day."

"Not that, exactly. But it got me thinking." I flipped through the HPD file on my desk. "When you get to work in the morning, look through the original Honolulu report on the Klein murders. You should see a passenger list of Pan American Clipper Flight 208 from Los Angeles to Honolulu on November 24, 1941."

"That's the flight the Kleins took, isn't it?"

"Right. I've got my copy in front of me now." I read down the column of nineteen names, hoping for a clue, but none was forthcoming. "It's a tall order, I know, but I need an FBI check of everyone on that list."

"Norman . . ."

" . . . it's crucial. Trust my hunch."

A tired sigh. "What is the FBI looking for?"

"A missing person. Someone who flew to Hawaii and never came back."

"I'm not sure I understand."

"Neither do I, really." I rubbed my eyes. "But I need the information yesterday. To simplify things, start with the men's names first."

"All right, Norman. I'll be getting back to you."

"Jan can take a message if you call in the next week. I won't be here."

"Where are you off to now?"

"Honolulu."

"To do what?"

I plugged my ear against Jan's sputtering protests. "Something I should have done months ago."

I rose to my feet when Claudine Jarmon entered M's Smoke House to keep our luncheon date. The reaction was more than mere chivalry. Mrs. Jarmon, *née* Claudine Maurois, was one of the most self-possessed, formidable young women I'd ever seen. Clad in a beige suit cut in unrelenting good taste, she walked with the assurance of a lady who expects the cosmos to part in twain at her approach.

"Mr. Hall." A cool, white-gloved handshake and a cultured smile which accented her Eurasian eyes. "I'm so pleased to meet you. Have you been waiting long?"

"Not at all." I let the host lead us to our table on the mezzanine. Drinks arrived and I watched Mrs. Jarmon lunge for the martini as if it was heavenly manna.

"Christ, that's good." She sighed in demure heartiness. "Ever spend the morning with ten Eastern Star biddies?"

"Not that I recall."

"Oh, I'm sorry." She squeezed my palm. "You didn't fly nine thousand miles to talk about me." She blinked oddly. "Or did you?"

"Not exactly. I . . . ."

"If I had to guess, I'd say you want to talk about my mother. Am I getting warm?"

"Amazingly so."

She swirled the ice in her glass. "I can't claim any ESP powers, Mr. Hall. Just ordinary common sense. And a pretty fair memory. You see, when I was a young girl, I distinctly remember reading about a certain HPD patrolman who resigned under a very dark cloud just about the time my mother flew the coop." Mrs. Jarmon held the martini aloft. "Ready for a refill?"

"An excellent idea," I said unsteadily.

When the second round arrived, she smiled and patted her lips. "Enough cat and mouse, don't you think? What do you want to know?"

"Where is your mother, Mrs. Jarmon?"

An impatient frown. "She was declared legally dead in 1948. No one's arisen to dispute it."

"I'm not prepared to debate the point. But your mother vanished into limbo. What did the police do to find her?"

The waiter arrived with two salads. I sensed her body coiling tight as she spread the napkin on her lap.

"Mr. Hall, I will synopsize my mother's life as concisely as possible. You will not interrupt and we will get this unsavory business out of the way. Agreed?"

"I'm listening."

"Very well. My mother, Catherine Maurois, was a very drab lady to possess so aristocratic a name. Not, as you might imagine, a descendant of some French plantation baron but a laundress from Montreal. She moved here in 1922 to improve her fortune, without much success. After a series of odd jobs, she hired on as a maid at the Moana Hotel in 1924.

"Mother lived just off Hotel Street, and it was a rowdy place even then. Soon she found herself supplementing her income by entertaining men. Not exactly a prostitute but a very talented amateur." Her lips drooped mordantly. "You see, I grew up with an astonishing variety of 'uncles' in the family tree. I don't know which one was my father." The almond eyes glinted. "Although I can make some pretty shrewd guesses."

"I'm sorry."

"Of course. Mother was always pretty careful at work, but she wasn't above calling in sick if she could get away with it. And on that November afternoon she told the boss, Mr. Pendergast, that she *had* to go home. Menstrual cramps was the standard excuse." Her eyes crinkled with mischief. "Men are so terrified of women's trouble. He always let her go, like she was carrying the plague." Mrs. Jarmon sprinkled pepper on her salad. "So she left work and I never saw her again."

"But you must've worried. You reported her missing to the police."

"She never turned up. HPD had no leads. And once December seventh rolled around, they had other things on their minds. After Pearl Harbor, I resigned myself to the fact that she was dead."

"I don't understand."

"One of my mother's friends lived on McCully Street. 'Uncle Tashima.' She spent a good deal of time there. And on that December morning an antiaircraft shell from the *Nevada* missed its intended target and landed on that McCully Street apartment. Uncle Tashima's room was ground zero."

"But no bodies were ever recovered."

"No. But perhaps you can see why I never pursued the matter." She beamed at our approaching steaks. "Ah, ambrosia! Now maybe we can change to a different topic of conversation?"

"If you wish." I cut into an improbably tender porterhouse.

"How about the upward climb from poor little poor girl to my present happy state?"

I trimmed away some fat. "To be honest, my interest is marginal."

"I can sum it up in two words." She chewed thoughtfully. " 'Marry rich.' "

"I'll keep that in mind. Also, I have a favor to ask."

"Yes?"

"Do you have any keepsakes of your mother's? Things that you packed away soon after her disappearance. Glasses. Silverware. Jewelry. Items few other people would've handled."

"You have an unexpected morbid streak, Mr. Hall."

"I can see how it might seem that way. But please indulge me this once. It could be very important."

The eyes studied me for traces of deceit.

"My husband won't be home until six," she finally said. "I have Mother's things in the garage."

Claudine wafted me in her pink Coupe de Ville to Waimanalo Bay, where the Henry Jarmon residence sat like a steel and glass jukebox washed ashore. I reluctantly turned my attention from the impossible blue sky and matching ocean as she slapped the remote control on the Caddie's dash and berthed us in the four-car garage.

She climbed out of the car. "If I recall, the box is over here." Her fingertips pointed up at a cabinet high above a gleaming walnut workbench festooned with shiny Black and Decker tools. "You'll need a ladder."

She held the aluminum legs and made meaningless coaching noises as I grappled with an old pineapple crate filled with dusty relics of her humble past.

I settled the crate on the cement floor and carefully picked through the clutter. Clothes and shoes wouldn't do. Nor did dishes and silverware look promising. I finally picked a bud vase of smooth green glass. Wrapping a handkerchief around the stem, I held it up to the light.

"Was that your mother's?"

She smiled wistfully. "We bought it on a trip to Maui in 1937."

"Did you use it after the war?"

"Once I found myself alone, I tried to use as few of Mother's things as possible."

"I'd like to borrow this vase, if I may."

"What in the world for?"

"I can't tell you that right now. Please trust me. I'll ship it back to you undamaged within two weeks."

Claudine examined my face for any clues. What she saw apparently satisfied her.

"All right, Mr. Hall. Take it with my compliments. Someday, I hope, you will tell me what the hell this is all about?"

I gently folded the vase in the handkerchief and slipped it in my coat pocket. "You'll be among the first to know."

Rain without end was turning St. Petersburg into a swamp with delusions of grandeur as I plodded through sandy mud toward the Bahia-Belle Cabanas and pounded on Fred and Mima Heinley's front door.

They still kept the thermostat at barbecue level, but today I welcomed the warmth. Fred pumped my hand as I found myself shaking like a sodden spaniel.

"I tell you," he beamed, "you could have knocked Mima and me over with a feather when we got your call. You sure picked a hell of a day to come." Fred pointed at the storm doors nailed over the windows. "This is about as bad as you can get without being caught smack dab in a hurricane. You'll be lucky to catch a plane home."

Mima rushed in from the kitchen to rescue me with a cup of hot chocolate. "Here, drink this. It'll take out the chill."

"Thanks, but I won't keep you two long . . ."

"Nonsense!" she said. "You're staying for dinner."

"Well, I appreciate it, but right now I have a couple of things I want to get out of the way." I stood on tiptoe and rapped my knuckles on their attic door. "If you've got your ladder and flashlight, I need to get up here again."

Fred and Mima braced the frame as I did a repeat performance of my act three days earlier in Claudine Jarmon's garage. Spreading the spoons and books and shoe trees and ashtrays on an open newspaper, I was struck with the similarity of this junk with the dusty flotsam of Catherine Maurois. Not that it could be anything but coincidence.

"There's a favor I need to ask you both. May I take this crate home with me? I promise I'll return it in a few weeks."

"Of course," Mima said, "but what is this all about, Mr. Hall?"

I felt I owed them some sort of explanation. "It may help me find who killed Albert and Martha."

They couldn't think of adequate words as I folded the top of the cardboard box and stood, slapping my hands.

"Now, I have something to show you." I pulled out a slightly damp manila envelope from the coat's inner pocket. "First of all, I'd like you both to look at this." I passed them an unlabeled photo of Albert and Martha Klein, the Negro couple who boarded the *Titanic* at Southampton. "Have you ever seen these people before?"

Mima and Fred handed the picture back and forth between them. "Never." Her face wrinkled in puzzlement. "Who are they?"

"I wish I knew." My fingers slipped the second photo out of the envelope. "How about this one, Mima?"

She squinted hesitantly, holding the 5 x 7 in both hands. Then her eyes filled with tears.

"Where did you get this, Mr. Hall?"

"I'm sorry, Mima, I can't tell you. I'd be breaking a promise."

She wasn't overly concerned with the origins of the picture. "Honey, look at this. It's Al and Martha."

Fred gently took it from her hands, holding it by the edges. "It's wonderful." He swallowed. "It's just like I remember them."

"It's not too sharp, I'm afraid." The custom lab in Paris had been lucky to get a halfway decent print from Masterson's 16-mm movie. "You can have it if you like."

She picked up the photo and rested it in both of her hands like an infant child. "You have no idea how we appreciate this. It's the only picture of Al and Martha we've ever had." Mima chuckled, wiping her eyes. She looked again at the photo, and I watched the question form on her lips.

"By the way, who are these other people?" Her finger pointed them out. "The woman and the little girl."

"I think they were friends of theirs. Aboard the *Titanic*."

"Friends." She took obscure pleasure in my words. "Yes, Al and Martha made friends wherever they went." Still smiling, she rose from the sofa and laid the picture flat against the wall behind Fred's chair, amid the grim Puritan faces of relatives gone by. "What do you think, honey? We'll get a silver frame and put it right here."

The picture seemed to bring a little joy into both their lives and I was grateful for that. But I also owed Fred and Mima a great deal. They had provided the first proof positive identification of the young couple accompanying Eva and Clair in the Masterson film.

I made one last pit stop in London before jetting home. Two errands weighed heavily on my mind. One was a visit to Frank Aylmer, my attorney. I gave him a hulking sealed envelope containing photocopies of every document I possessed dealing with the Rykers and Kleins, with instructions that it be opened upon my death.

That afternoon I dropped by to see Tom at the Yard. He zeroed in on my wavelength as we shook hands.

"Yes, Norman, I know. You're chomping at the bit over that Pan Am list. I haven't heard anything from the FBI. Legwork like that can't be rushed."

"I'm sure you're doing all you can, Tom. That wasn't my immediate concern."

He sagged into his chair. "Lord, what now?"

"I don't like to impose, but this one favor could make or break my whole career. Yours, too, for that matter."

"Have mercy, Norman. Out with it."

I breathed deep and took the plunge. "How do we go about having Albert Klein exhumed?"

Four months later, on September 12, 1962, I mailed the following letter:

Mr. Norman Hall
Post Office Box 2344
Fourqueux, France

Mr. William Alfred Ryker
Le Château de Montreux
c/o Post Office Box 1865
Veyrier, Switzerland

Dear Mr. Ryker:

You are invited to my home at 11 A.M. on September 20, 1962, for the purpose of discussing the contents of an upcoming article written by Janice Steiner and myself which will appear in the Christmas issue of *World* magazine. Geoffrey Proctor will be present, as will your daughter. Our topic of conversation will include your salvaging operation of the R.M.S. *Titanic* and the murders of Albert Klein, Martha Klein, and John MacFarland.

If, for reasons of ill health, you are unable to attend, I will gladly make new arrangements. However, if your absence is due to nonmedical reasons, I must inform you that Assistant Commissioner Thomas Bramel of New Scotland Yard will also be present. At this time he plans to be at my house out of personal curiosity. But, if you choose not to meet with me, you may become a prime object of Commissioner Bramel's official scrutiny.

I also wish to remind you that any of the information to be confidentially discussed can just as easily be released en masse to the press.

Since I relish neither of these drastic possibilities, and I'm sure we're as one in agreement on this issue, I shall look forward to seeing you on September 20.

Sincerely,

Norman Hall

Norman Hall

P.S. Bring a lawyer

PART II

The Puzzle

22

September 20, 1962

"He's coming."

I joined Eva Ryker at my living room window. Far down the road a Rolls Royce radiator glinted imperiously in the morning sunlight.

"Eleven o'clock." I glanced at my watch. "Right on time."

"I haven't seen him in three years," Eva said as we watched the limousine's approach. "It won't be easy, will it?"

"I don't know."

"Don't worry, Norman." Her smile was laced with sadness. "You don't have to play nanny."

The big black Rolls Royce swung into my driveway, gravel popping under the weight of its tires. Ryker's wrinkled face peered suspiciously through the tinted glass.

Jan came in from the den. "Should Tom and Geoffrey come out?"

"No." I made for the door. "You'll do fine."

My wife and Fräulein Slote had worked out the logistics of Ryker's visit. In an emergency his medical supplies and iron lung lay waiting at a clinic in Fourqueux, not five minutes away.

Jan and I moved furniture to clear a path into my den as

Mike Rogers, Fräulein Slote, and Jim Culhane wrangled the Old Man into his wheelchair. Ryker paid no mind to Tom or Geoffrey as we wheeled him to the other side of my desk. He was preoccupied with the sight of his daughter.

"Hello, Eva." The voice was light and cracked.

"Father." Her fingers twisted tightly together. "You're looking . . . tired."

"I hope you aren't taking Mr. Hall's charades too seriously."

"I'm keeping an open mind."

Mike diplomatically sat between them. Ryker glared at the two tape recorders, the big Mercator world map pinned against the west wall, and, most of all, the four-foot model of the *Titanic* in the center of the room.

"What is this?" he growled. "A goddam floor show?"

I perched on the edge of the desk as Jan shut the door. Each of the six watchful faces waited to hear what Norman hath wrought.

My thumb punched on one of the recorders. "Merely for the record, Mike."

I thoughtfully stood over the *Titanic* model. "Well," I said slowly. "Where to start? It's a long story. And it's taken a long time to track down. Over nine months. Even now I can only guess at some of the fine print. But, in many ways, all the puzzle pieces fit around this man."

Picking up an Identikit sketch from my desk, I showed it to Ryker. "Do you know him?"

He was defenseless with momentary surprise. "I'm not sure."

"Yes, you are. I ate lunch with him aboard the *Savonarola*. He introduced himself as Alvin Spears and claimed to be an expert in remote manipulative hardware. But when I asked him about 'Waldos,' he didn't know what the hell I was talking about." I passed the picture to Tom. "Even in my ignorance I've read enough science fiction to know 'Waldos' are named after devices described in an old story by Robert Heinlein. There and then I made a vow to check up on this man so blissfully ignorant of his stock in trade."

Tom Bramel cleared his throat and held up the sketch.

"We ran this through Interpol and came up with a positive make. 'Alvin Spears' is actually George Van Treese, a highly reputable appraiser and cutter of diamonds. Although clean himself, Mr. Van Treese has occasionally placed his services at the disposal of some very questionable clients."

"Which brings us to a fascinating question," I said. "What is a diamond expert doing on board the *Savonarola?*"

Ryker's mouth opened, then smiled. "No comment."

"Well, in the absence of any contradicting statement, I can only assume the obvious. Mr. Van Treese was hired in the anticipation that diamonds would be recovered from the *Titanic.*"

He showed his Great Stone Face. "Assume anything you want."

Mike flared impatiently. "Stop baiting my client, Norman."

"Let me finish. Then we'll see who's baiting whom."

I walked toward the map. "Where did the diamonds come from? Fortunately, the De Beers Central Selling Organization, which markets about eighty percent of the world's diamond production, had some very useful information on both present and past smuggling syndicates. One particularly interesting operation ran from 1905 until 1912. After the pipeline collapsed, De Beers security was able to trace its roots."

My index finger pointed at South Africa. "It began here. The Premier diamond mine, newly opened in 1903. Leaving by ship at Capetown, the smuggled stones proceeded to Dar es Salaam." I pointed at the East African coast. "A transfer to Mogadiscio. Then through the Red Sea to Cairo. A short trip to Beirut. Then to Istanbul. On the Orient Express through Sofia, Belgrade, and Venice. Through Switzerland and on to Paris. Calais and across the channel to London. Put on a ship at Southampton, the diamonds reached the end of the pipeline in New York, where they mixed and became undistinguishable from the legitimate market.

"The De Beers Organization had no idea who ran the operation. So Jan and I did some checking. From Capetown to London the only ships transporting the stones were ratty little tramps belonging to the Quelimane Shipping Company, which was owned entirely by a front company called the

Southwest Africa Corporation. Every share of Southwest Africa stock was owned by you, Mr. Ryker."

Not a muscle moved in the old man's face.

"The diamond operation was a highly profitable sideline to your 'conventional' business interests. For a few years, at any rate. But trouble was brewing that would bring about the collapse of the pipeline and your personal fall from grace." I circled the British Isles on the map. "Right here. London, and your two contacts who transported smuggled stones from the Dover-Calais ferry."

With a sigh I settled back on the corner of my desk. "Who were they? Well, you hired them in New York City in June 1909 under the names Steven and Julie Herrick. One of their many aliases. A young couple of unknown origins struggling on the West Side. In bad times Julie played a hooker to keep them both eating. Later, her husband became a leader in a minor-league protection racket specializing in small store owners near the Bowery. Two tough fish rapidly outgrowing their little pond. But all that changed when they met one of your trusted employees. A Mr. Martin Brockway."

"That's a lie!"

Mike drawled scornfully, "I resent you trying to implicate . . . "

"Your boss *is* involved, right up to his scrawny little neck. Martin Brockway was a predecessor of yours, Mike. One of an illustrious line of brownnosers stretching back to the turn of the century."

Ryker hunched low in his wheelchair. "All right. Brockway did work for me. I fired him because he was incompetent."

"No doubt. His biggest mistake was recruiting Steven and Julie Herrick. In later years, as Brockway became trapped in . . . uncomfortable events, he found himself pensioned off and relegated to nonperson status. And so he Told All to his wife. Sarah Brockway is still alive, as I'm sure you know. Retired in Flagstaff, Arizona. Jan and I went to see her this past July. She's exhaustively well-informed about the whole affair."

I stood and paced in front of Ryker. "Steven and Julie Herrick happily settled into their assignment in London. Once a month they shepherded a packet of smuggled stones from the ferry to another unknown contact at the Southampton docks. The pipeline flowed smoothly for nearly two years. It took that long before the Herricks decided to nibble off some of the cheese for themselves.

"Who made the first move?" I chuckled sadly. "Knowing a little about them, I'd say it was the girl. As you know, Mr. Ryker, there was a great deal more to Steven and Julie Herrick than met the eye. More than the cunning resourcefulness you and Brockway sensed. A terrifying moral blankness. I have no real idea what caused it. One can bandy about words like 'psychopath' without doing them justice. I can't dispute their intellect. They were smart enough to know they couldn't simply snatch a shipment and run." I raised an eyebrow at Ryker. "I doubt if they would've lived long enough to spend their loot. No, their plan was a good deal more labyrinthine than that. And it all revolved around the fact that your wife and daughter were about to leave England on the biggest ship in the world."

I tossed a paper to Mike. "That's the tentative passenger list of the R.M.S. *Titanic*, the same list reprinted in the London *Times* on April eighth. And here is the final roster, compiled after the *Titanic*'s departure at Queenstown."

I pointed out the circled names on both lists. "You can see that a Mr. and Mrs. Ralph Carmichael canceled at the last moment—to be replaced by a Mr. and Mrs. Jason Eddington."

I hefted a bulky dust-encrusted book up off the blotter. "You might be curious as to the identity of these two couples. The Carmichaels were easy. They're listed right here," I said, opening the book to where a marker lay and passing the volume to him, "in the *Who Was Who: 1898-1915*."

Mike read the entry:

CARMICHAEL, Ralph Eubank. b. June 17, 1875. d. May 14, 1942. Board member of Monsanto and Union Carbide

1926-1941. Married Esther Townsend July 12, 1892. Son
Phillip born June 23, 1893. Phillip Carmichael graduated
Munich University with honors on June 19, 1912.

I smiled at Jan. "My wife called Mrs. Carmichael, who's
now living in Philadelphia, to find out why she canceled their
booking. According to her, she and her husband were staying at the Dorchester in London when they received a telegram on April 9, 1912, from the Munich police. Phillip, their
son, had been killed in an automobile accident. Would they
please come to make the necessary arrangements?

"They dropped everything and rushed to Munich. The
police, naturally, had never heard of Phillip Carmichael. No
one had sent the telegram. The Telefunken wireless office
was checked; no such message left Munich. The telegram,
everyone concluded, must have been a forgery. Phillip was
located on the Munich campus, in perfect health and thor-
oughly baffled."

I frowned sternly. "No harm done, of course, except for
the near-breakdown it caused Mrs. Carmichael. The origina-
tor of the prank, if you'd like to call it that, was never found.
But the net result was that the Carmichaels lost their booking
on the *Titanic*, which was quickly taken by Jason and Lisa Eddington."

I handed a facsimile sheet to Mike. "These are duplicate
passport photos of the Eddingtons; American passports—
allegedly, anyway—which were photographed for the files of
the British Foreign Office."

Mike carefully examined the pictures, then gave them to
Ryker.

Wrinkles around the old man's mouth deepened as he
stared at the handsome blond couple, losing himself in the
faded black and white images.

"Let me see, Father."

"No!" He snatched them away.

"I'm all grown up. You don't have to shelter me."

Ryker bent forward and thrust the pictures into my hands.
"Some things you never outgrow."

Passing the pictures to Tom Bramel, I said, "Mr. Ryker, I understand your instincts. But Eva's right. It's unnecessary."

"That's for me to judge!"

I let the issue pass, not wanting to provoke him so early in the day. "Well, it's not hard to imagine how the Herricks . . . " I smiled apologetically, taking the photos from Geoffrey, "pardon me, 'the Eddingtons,' sent the phony telegram to the Carmichaels. The passport copies you saw were forgeries. If they had contacts who could fix that for them, then the forgery of a simple telegram was no problem. And the Carmichaels, being socially prominent, were sadly vulnerable."

Taking off my coat and rolling up my shirt sleeves, I faced the model of the *Titanic*. My hands grasped the bow and stern, pulling off the A Deck, Promenade, and Boat Decks. The bridge, the four smokestacks, and the entire superstructure came with them. I put the model section of the floor behind Tom Bramel's chair. B Deck was exposed like the guts of a great dissected fish.

"Now," I huffed, standing up, "there's B-76, the Eddingtons' cabin. On portside, as you can see, Mr. Ryker. Across on the starboard side is cabin B-57, belonging to James Martin, the bodyguard of your wife and daughter. And right next door are cabins B-53 and B-55, forming the starboard promenade suite." I glanced up at Eva. "That's where you and your mother stayed."

Her feet stirred uneasily, as if poised for flight.

"So, ladies and gentlemen, there you have it. Our stage is set." Bending down by her chair, I held Eva's hand. "I think it's time to hear your tape."

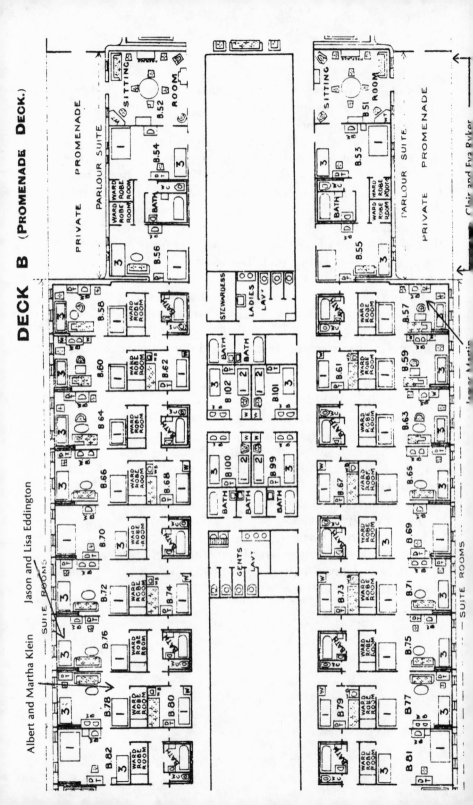

DECK B (PROMENADE DECK.)

Albert and Martha Klein   Jason and Lisa Eddington

Clair and Eva Ryker

SUITE ROOMS

PRIVATE PROMENADE

PARLOUR SUITE

SITTING ROOM

B.52

B.54

B.56

B.58

B.60

B.62

B.64

B.66

B.68

B.70

B.72

B.74

B.76

B.78

B.80

B.82

STEWARDESS

LADIES LAV.

BATH

BATH

B102

B101

B100

B.99

BATH

BATH

GENTS LAV.

SITTING ROOM

B.51

B.53

B.55

B.57

B.59

B.61

B.63

B.65

B.67

B.69

B.71

B.73

B.75

B.77

B.79

B.81

PRIVATE PROMENADE

PARLOUR SUITE

SUITE ROOMS

Isaac Martin

23

She walked to the window and watched the salvia and lobelia shivering in our front flower boxes.

"It'll be the first time, you know, without Dr. Sanford's help." She smiled feebly. "A triple somersault, with no safety net."

"Eva," I said, "if you're not ready . . . "

Her head shook. "No, Norman. Don't be 'kind.' I've had fifty years of understanding. What I need is a firm push."

Ryker snapped at me. "Perhaps you'd like to explain what the hell you're talking about?"

I stood by the second recorder and recounted our visit to Japan.

"God damn you! You had no right without my permission!"

"Your daughter's not an infant. She asked for help and I took her to the person I thought would do the most good. The tape you're about to hear was recorded during a session with Eva under deep hypnosis. You'll hear both Dr. Sanford and myself on the recording. I should also mention that it was edited from seven hours down to one to cut out the chaff."

Silence as the leader hissed through the tape heads. Then a low undertone of three people breathing in a small room.

"All right, Eva," Margaret said. "Just relax on the couch and keep your eyes closed. I'm going to ask some questions. How old are you?"

"Sixty-one."

"Have you ever been married?"

"For two days. I don't want to talk about it."

"Both Norman and I are here. You don't have to worry. I want you to go back. Think back to the past. It's your fortieth birthday. What do you see?"

"It was the first anniversary of my annulment. A year of total freedom!"

"What are you doing, Eva?"

"Drinking!" She giggled shrilly. "Drinking and drinking and drinking. A Gay Annulmentee. I ran off with a gardener. Daddy was *very* angry!"

I watched Eva as the recorder spun between us. Her face was ancient and unreachable.

Dr. Sanford broke in. "We're going back a long way now. But don't be afraid. I'll be with you. You're floating in a black void. No light. No sound. Nothing. Your body feels like gossamer. It's dissolving, vanishing like dew on the morning grass. Floating, spinning. You're ageless. A hundred. Five. Both and neither. You can rove back in time like skimming through back pages in a book. Do you understand?"

Soft and languid, the reply came. "Yes."

"You're flipping through those pages, Eva. A page at a time. You're fifty-nine. Now fifty-eight. Fifty-seven. Let's flip the pages faster, Eva. Fifty. Forty-two. Thirty-nine. Twenty-seven. Twenty-one . . . "

Whimpers of protest.

"What's wrong, Eva?"

"Don't hurt me!" It was a young woman's cry. "Tell them to go away! I want out of here! Talk to my father; he'll get me out of this place! Tell the doctor! I tell you, I cut her by accident! She shouldn't have scared me that way! Talk to my Daddy!"

The look Ryker gave me was as dark and brooding as a black abscess.

"Eva," Margaret said, "no one's going to hurt you. Forget about the hospital. We're going back some more. Seventeen. Fifteen."

"No." The voice was hesitant at first, then firm. "NO!"

"Don't be afraid," I blurted out. "I'm with you."

Hysterical sobbing. "Leave me alone! Leave me alone! I want my Mommy!"

"Your mother's with you," she said, gentle, yet insistent. "She's standing next to you."

"No!"

"Yes, Eva," she whispered. "She's standing next to you, holding your hand. You're ten years old. It's early in the morning and you and your mother are on a long platform. A railroad platform. You're at a train station in London. You're boarding the train. The boat train. People are all around you. Big locomotives are puffing. You're holding very tight to your mother's hand."

The little-girl voice was peevish. "Where're we going, Mommy? I'm tired of waiting! Why can't we go on the train? You promised we could see the train! You promised! You promised! You promised! You . . . "

Clair Ryker sighed, leading her ten-year-old daughter by the hand. "I know I promised, dear."

Eva gazed curiously around London's Waterloo Station, watching the train screeching to a stop on Platform eleven. Her nose wrinkled at the oil-coal-sour milk-horse chip smell of the place. All these stations looked alike, she thought glumly. She hadn't really seen one new thing this spring.

But, for the first time this year, she'd found some excitement in traveling. Curiosity, anyway. Not everyone got to sail on the first voyage of the biggest ship in the world!

Eva peered down the platform. Porters wheeled trolleys past the elegantly attired crowd loitering by the train. She turned up to her mother.

"Where's Georgia and J.H.?"

Clair frowned wearily. "I don't want to tell you again, Eva. Our maid's name is Miss Ferrell. And it's 'Mr. Martin,' not 'J.H.?'"

"That's what you call him!"

"True enough. But a ten-year-old girl doesn't call a forty-year-old man 'J.H.' Mr. Martin went ahead to the ship. Daddy had some business for him. Miss Ferrell went along to make sure our cabin is ready for . . . "

Eva wasn't listening. Walking behind a young man handling a Pathé movie camera, she watched him crank and pan across the expanse of the station.

"Hey, mister!" She pulled his coattails. "You wanna take our picture?"

"Eva!" Clair snapped. "Stop it, that's . . . "

"Oh, that's all right." The man bent down and flashed a toothy smile. "What's your name, honey?"

Eva raised her eyebrows and lowered her lids, imitating her mother's expression at formal gatherings. "Miss Eva Clifton Ryker."

He solemnly offered his hand. "Mr. Jason Eddington. Pleased to meet you."

"You must excuse her," Clair moaned ruefully. "My daughter has all the makings of a perfect snob."

"That's quite all right," he laughed, running a hand through his straw-colored hair. "Maybe that's what the world needs; a little class."

Eva frowned, watching Eddington give her mother that strange look. So many men looked at her that way. And, for the briefest second, she saw her mother return the glance. Eva's grip on her mother's hand tightened.

"Jason! There you are!" Down the platform, a pretty young blonde rushed up to Eddington. Huge fawn eyes blinked curiously at Eva and Clair.

"Mrs. Ryker," said Jason, taking the girl by the arm, "may I present Lisa, my wife."

Introductions and explanations were duly exchanged. Jason and Lisa, it turned out, were taking the boat train to Southampton for a honeymoon journey on the *Titanic*. Un-

der Eva's prodding, they were persuaded to share the Rykers' private pullman compartment.

The minute hand of Waterloo Station's big clock reached
the hour mark and the guard waved his green flag. With a
shrill whistle the locomotive hauled the White Star boat train
away from Platform twelve.

By eleven o'clock the train began its gradual downgrade
from Basingstoke's Plateau toward the coast of Eastleigh.
Sticking her head out the window, Eva watched smoke from
the locomotive settle in a black shroud over beeches and elms
flitting past the train like shadowy figures painted on a rotat-
ing drum.

"Eva! Get back inside."

She frowned and turned back to the window. Somehow
she felt funny when Jason and her mother were together.
She wasn't sure why, but . . .

Eva forgot the nagging feeling as she pointed at the sign
marked TERMINUS STATION. "We're there!"

Jason's camera exposed footage as the train glided over
Canute Road and through the ugly tangle of telephone
poles, cranes, rail tracks, boxcars, and low sheds fringing the
Southampton dock.

The boat train puffed to a final stop by a platform built
alongside the quay. Eva ogled the four yellow and black smokestacks jutting head and shoulders above the clutter of the
port.

"That's it! There's the *Titanic!*" She bolted for the door,
dashing from the train toward the dock.

Suddenly Eva stopped, her head craned back. Her long
black hair whipped in the cold wind as her mouth sagged
open.

A black, rivet-studded steel cliff rose seventy-five feet up to
the bow, on which gold letters spelled TITANIC. High above,
the Stars and Stripes fluttered on the foremast.

She only half felt Jason's hand on her shoulder. "Quite a
sight," he said quietly.

Eva impatiently posed with her mother for Jason's camera,
then broke away. Running inside the White Star shed, she
darted up a flight of steps, dodging startled couples on the

first-class gangway, then dashed into the ship, past the purser's office.

She roved through the endless decks of the ship, marching down the grand staircase and snooping along the labyrinthine corridors surrounding the first-class staterooms.

The random prowling eventually brought her up to the Boat Deck. She peeked under the railing, watching men load crates and trunks from the dock up to the forecastle hold by means of electric cranes.

A burly man in an expensive Simpson Crawford suit shook his fists theatrically as a crate tottered on a crane high above his head.

Jabbing a thumb and forefinger in her mouth, she emitted a window-shattering whistle. "Hey! J.H.!"

He reconnoitered over his shoulder and caught sight of her waving hands. With an impatient wave at the rattling cranes he clambered up a ladder to join her.

"Howdy, Eva! Does your mother know where you are?"

She shrugged, her eyes lowered.

"I thought so." He took her hand, marching along the deck. "We'd better find her before she tans your ass. Not to mention mine."

Eva grinned at Martin's language. "What's in the box, J.H.?"

"Huh?" He barely swallowed his surprise.

"Back there on the dock."

"Oh, you mean the crate!" He pressed a finger to his lips in the gesture of a conspirator. "Hush, hush. Some things your father wants delivered to New York." Martin sighed in mock weariness. "Your daddy's a cruel taskmaster, Eva."

After considerable trial and error they reached their destination. Eva warmed up her innocent and woebegone expression as she spotted her mother standing by the purser's door.

"There you are! What have you to say for yourself?"

"Sorry." Eva strived for the proper combination. Contrite, yet winsome.

Clair stepped into the purser's office, thanking Hugh McElroy and Martin, then led Eva to the elevator.

"Where're Jason and Lisa?" Eva asked, pushing the call button.

She held her daughter's hand as they stepped aboard. "We're meeting them now."

Five minutes short of noon the deep, gut-shaking horn of the *Titanic* boomed through the corridors of the liner, echoed into the bright April air, and finally bounced into silence between the sheds of Southampton dock.

Lifting her eyes from the Boat Deck up to the four thrusting smokestacks, Eva felt a tense flutter in her stomach.

Crowds lined the port railing, blocking her view. She tugged Jason Eddington's trouser leg.

"Can't see?" He smiled, bending down. "Hop on."

Sitting atop his shoulders, Eva was hoisted high above the crowd. She clung to his collar as he handled the Pathé.

Suddenly a pack of men—crew members, to judge from their clothes and tattered baggage slung over their shoulders—ran along the quay, waving and yelling desperately as the last gangway was being lowered.

Jason pointed them out to Eva, Clair, and his wife. "Poor devils! Look, the officer on shore's not letting them on! Serves them right for being late." He laughed grimly. "I wouldn't like to be in their shoes."

As the last gangway was hauled ashore, Eva felt a tremor run up from the decks as the *Titanic*'s great engines turned over. Cheering floated up from the dock; a cheer returned by those on board.

Inch by inch the chasm between the ship and the quay widened as tugs heaved at the hull.

Two gigantic screws, with a combined weight of seventy-six tons, churned the water behind the *Titanic* into a swirling indigo whirlpool.

The giant liner crept away with agonizing slowness, under the anxious attendance of the tugs, and crawled toward the entrance of the dock.

The maiden voyage had begun.

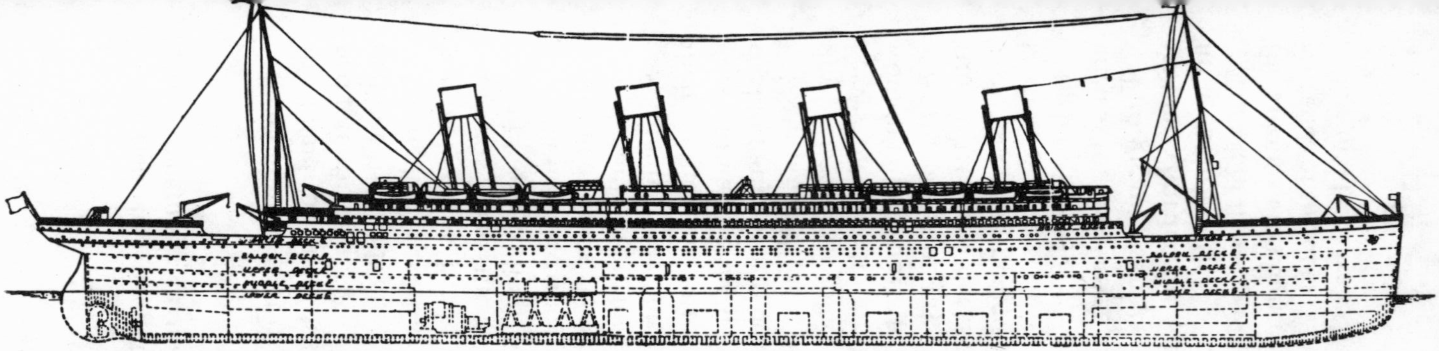

FIG. 1. LONGITUDINAL SECTION

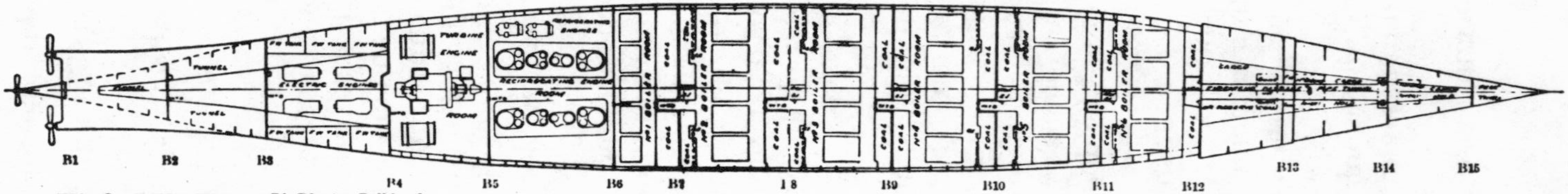

FIG. 2. TANK TOP   B1, B2, etc., Bulkheads

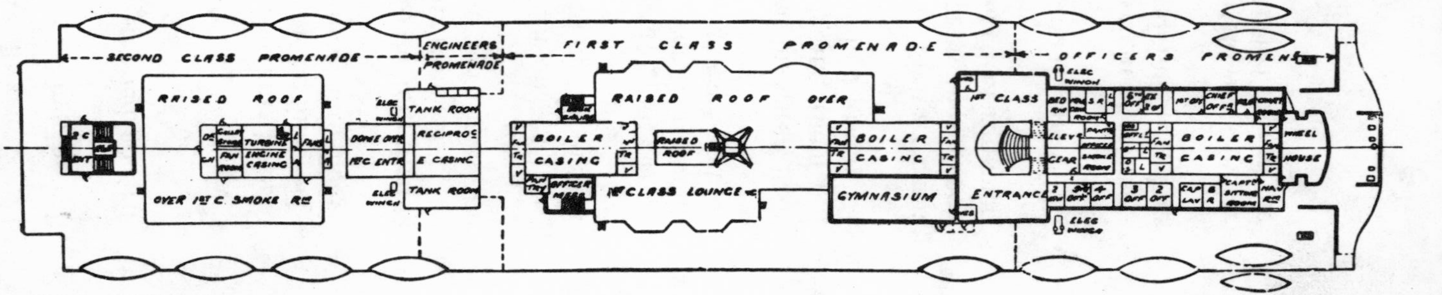

B1   B2   B3   F4   H5   H6   H7   I8   H9   H10   H11   H12   H13   H14   H15

No. 1 BOILER ROOM
No. 2 BOILER ROOM
No. 3 BOILER ROOM
No. 4 BOILER ROOM
No. 5 BOILER ROOM
No. 6 BOILER ROOM

COAL

FIG. 3. BOAT DECK

SECOND CLASS PROMENADE

RAISED ROOF

OVER 1ST C. SMOKE RM.

ENGINEERS PROMENADE

TANK ROOM

FIRST CLASS PROMENADE

RAISED ROOF OVER

1ST CLASS LOUNGE

BOILER CASING

GYMNASIUM

1ST CLASS ENTRANCE

OFFICERS PROMENADE

BOILER CASING

24

As the *Titanic* swept across the Channel toward Cherbourg, Eva peeked through the windows of the Promenade Deck, watching St. Catherine's Head sink behind the stern like a fallen soufflé.

The long afternoon was whittled away playing shuffleboard with Jason and Lisa, followed by a visit with her mother to Maud Slocombe's Turkish bath down on G Deck. As the orange sun lowered itself into the sea, Eva curled up in a wicker chair on the Ryker suite's private promenade and studied the whitecaps floating lazily by.

She thought of the Eddingtons and small lines of concern deepened in her brow. A memory darted through her mind, a vision from early in the day, when Martin was introduced to Jason and Lisa in the Cafe Parisien. J.H.'s smile was cordial as he shook Jason's hand, but, for a fraction of a second, his face had gone slack and his eyes filmed over in an inward-looking glaze. The moment was gone in an instant, then everyone settled back to polite parlor chatter. But Eva still noticed a slight tightening around Martin's eyes that wouldn't go away.

*   *   *

On Thursday afternoon, April eleventh, the *Titanic* anchored at Queenstown Harbor, two miles off the Irish coast.

Along with the two tenders, *Ireland* and *America*, a fleet of bumboats nestled up against the liner's hull, their owners propping up a jury-rigged market on the Promenade Decks, selling Irish linen and lace.

Eva peered down at the steerage passengers coming into the ship from one of the tenders. Girls in rough dresses and young men in soiled shirts and heavy shoes gaped up at the liner. Some cast lingering glances back at the shore. They looked sad, she thought. And a little scared.

She raised her head to watch sea gulls swoop over the stern. Galley scraps spit out of the ship's waste pipes and the birds raucously squabbled among themselves over the floating potato peelings and wilted lettuce.

Roaring over the water, the *Titanic's* horn shooed away the tenders and bumboats. Propellers thrashing a white trail, she arched a graceful quarter circle, then steamed westward.

The great liner proudly cruised between four to five miles off the coast of Ireland. Skirting the Sovereign Islets, laden with herons and terns. Passing the jagged cliffs of Courtmacsherry Bay, the Stags, Toe Head and Kedge Island.

Hunched in a deckchair on the Promenade Deck, Eva saw two familiar figures sit together about five chairs away. She was about to wave, but instead pulled her coat high over her face. Eva felt very smug in her role of eavesdropper. Jason and her mother would never spot her!

"Beautiful, isn't it?" Clair Ryker calmly watched the distant gray cliffs. "A pity Lisa couldn't come."

"She's very sensitive to cold," Jason said stiffly. "Probably better off in the library."

Eva peeked over the edge of her collar. Her mother still had her eyes trained on the sea.

"I'm sorry not to invite you to our suite, but our maid is a frightful gossip and so are the stewards. You understand?"

Silence. Jason shifted toward Clair but didn't meet her

eyes. "I wouldn't want to cause you any trouble, Mrs. Ryker. I never had anything like that in mind."

Clair's laugh was short and amused. "Oh, my dear Jason, you're a prize; you really are! At the train station, when you found out who I was, I saw the way you looked at me."

An awkward pause. A puzzled frown slowly replaced Eva's smile.

"You're the wife of a famous man, Mrs. Ryker. Naturally I was surprised."

"Don't be tiresome, my dear. I'll tell you what you thought. 'Clair Ryker?' Why I can hear the penny papers whispering this very minute! Of course, Willie has paid millions wallpapering over my indiscretions, but still everyone seems to know the same tired stories. There's Clair Ryker, child-stealer. Apparently my preference for the continent is depriving Eva of her American birthright. A 'loose environment,' it's called. As opposed to a tight one.

"Then we have Clair Ryker, nymphomaniac. The carnal chaser for my husband's business deals." Smiling, she raised an eyebrow. "You've heard that one, no doubt."

Sweat beaded on Jason Eddington's forehead as he inspected the horizon. Far in the distance sat a crumbly signal tower planted on a headland, a remnant of the Napoleonic Wars. "I suppose so."

Clair put her hand on his. "Jason, I want you to look at me. Do I look like that sort of woman?"

Eva watched his face over her mother's shoulder. At first he blushed, then his lips flattened. "You sure as hell do, Mrs. Ryker."

For a second Eva thought her mother was going to hit him. Then she laughed, loudly and vulgarly. "Jason, you're an honest man! There're damn few of them left!" Her laughter died as quickly as it began. "I just wonder if you're honest enough."

"I don't understand."

Clair's eyelids eased shut. "You see, I'm right. A long row to hoe, Jason."

Her fingers ran gently down his arm as she stood. "Give my regards to Lisa."

"Hey!" he called, but she didn't look back. Fists jammed in his pants pockets, he brushed, unseeing, past Eva.

Amber sunlight splashed across the Rykers' private promenade, slanting long railing shadows across the deck.

Eva stared out at the ocean, eyes blinking at the sun. The Fastnet Tower stuck up feebly, dwarfed by the distance. Cape Clear Island jutted up to the north, a green quilt of tidy farm plots. She glimpsed the silhouette of Mizen Head and Dursey Island, and—so far away she thought she was imagining it—a phantom vision of the Skellig Peaks and the Kerry Mountains.

John McFarland, the steward for the Eddingtons, had pointed out the landmarks as the last sight of shore until the *Titanic* reached the coast of Nova Scotia. Eva felt a sorrow she couldn't explain as she watched the hazy green mountains slip from her grasp.

A knock on the parlor door distracted her thoughts. "Who's there, Georgia?" she called over her shoulder.

"Just J.H."

Eva hurried into the sitting room at the sound of his voice. Dressed for dinner, he squatted down and pecked her cheek. "Hey, kid. Get ready. We're keeping the chef waiting."

As Eva ran to her room, she heard Martin chatting with Georgia Ferrell. "Where's Clair?"

"Oh, off somewhere." Her voice was elaborately casual. "She said she'd meet you and Eva in the dining room."

Eva buttoned her pink dress and listened with one ear.

"Do you know what I spotted on B Deck?" J.H. was sour with disgust. "The cabin right next to the Eddingtons? Niggers! In first class. A couple of coons! Named Klein, if you can believe it."

On Friday the twelfth the *Titanic* skimmed like a flat rock on a mill pond, cutting through the placid Atlantic at twenty-one knots. The ship's passage through fresh morning swells stirred Eva awake.

Slowly rising to her knees, she blinked sleepily at the gunmetal sea, then padded out on deck and looked down sixty feet to the racing, foaming waterline. The railing beneath her hand trembled as the engines drove the *Titanic* faster than ever before. She grinned and darted back for her clothes. It looked like a beautiful day.

The sea breeze blowing through the corridors swept away early morning drowsiness as Eva ran up the grand staircase to the Boat Deck's gymnasium. Children were usually allowed only from one until three, but Eva, seeing the gym was vacant, aimed her mournful eyes at instructor T. W. McCawley, who finally gave in. She rode the electric horse and camel, paddled an exerciser cycle, and rowed stationary oars until blood pounded in her head.

Barely halting to catch her breath, she ran below decks, stopping at the sight of Lisa Eddington in the tailor's shop. Curiosity drew her inside.

"Hi, Eva." Lisa paid off the clerk and took a small gift-wrapped box. "You're up early."

Eva pointed at the package as they headed for the door. "What's that?"

"A gift."

"For whom?"

Her lips puckered in a look of censure. "It's for Mr. Martin, Eva."

"But what is it?"

Lisa glanced at the clerk behind the counter. "It's a knife. A pocket knife."

Her nose wrinkled. "What's he need a knife for?"

"You never know when it might come in handy." Lisa took her by the hand. "Come on. We'll be late for breakfast."

Seventeen feet wide and thirty-three feet long, the swimming bath was burrowed down on G Deck, aft of the racket court. It was a tremendous coup for the White Star Line; besides the *Titanic*, only her sister ship, the *Olympic*, had such a facility.

Clair Ryker, dressed in a long frilly pink bathing suit that made her look like someone about to be shot out of a cannon,

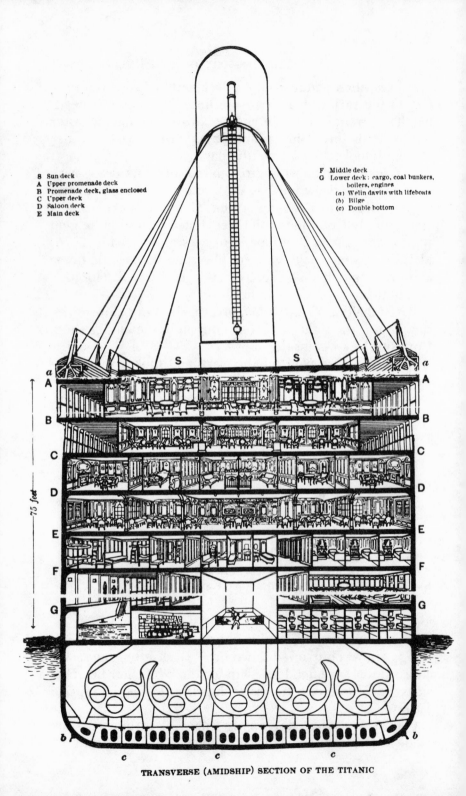

8 Sun deck
A Upper promenade deck
B Promenade deck, glass enclosed
C Upper deck
D Saloon deck
E Main deck

F Middle deck
G Lower deck: cargo, coal bunkers,
        boilers, engines
   (a) Welin davits with lifeboats
   (b) Bilge
   (c) Double bottom

TRANSVERSE (AMIDSHIP) SECTION OF THE TITANIC

stood at pool's edge and raised her voice at the swimming attendant. "What do you mean, no men allowed?"

The young girl's mouth drooped in disapproval. "Mixed
swimming is against company policy. Men's hours are from
two to six, women's from ten to one."

Clair smiled painfully and pointed at the Eddingtons.
"This girl is a dear friend of mine, and this is her husband.
Surely you don't expect to separate a married couple, do
you?"

Lisa spoke up. "Clair, maybe we should . . ."

"Nonsense," she said severely to the attendant. "Now, my
dear, you can see there's no one else in that pool. No one is
going to know we're here. If you simply cooperate with me,
your services will be appropriately rewarded. Do you understand?"

The girl's determination crumbled. "All right. But only for
a half hour!"

With a shrill whoop Eva broke away from her mother's
side, held her nose, and plummeted into the pool. She shivered at first contact, then paddled around, becoming accustomed to the water.

Ignoring the watchful eyes of the attendant, who stood at
the far end of the room, Clair gingerly eased down the step
ladder. She waded at the edge and caressed her sides. "I
thought this thing was heated!"

The Eddingtons dove in gracefully. He surfaced, shaking
drops from his hair. Shoulders rippled in casual power as he
swam to Clair.

"You know how to swim, don't you?"

Eva dog-paddled next to them, laughing. "Are you kidding? You should see her. She sinks like a rock!"

"No, she won't. There's no big trick to swimming." He
gently took her arm. "Come on, I'll show you." He blushed.
"Free of charge." Jason turned to his wife. "We'll be glad to
help; won't we, honey?"

"Sure, Mrs. Ryker." Lisa's eyes glinted. "Jason's a great
Good Samaritan."

"Okay, then." His hand lifted her off the tiled edge. "Put
your arms around my neck. That's fine. Now hang on."

Deciding to watch, Eva sat up on the railing surrounding the pool.

"Now don't worry. Fear of water's perfectly needless if you know what you're doing." He held her at arm's length. "Lay on your back."

Lisa joined Eva at the railing. Her facial muscles trembled with the weight of her smile.

"That's it," Jason muttered lowly. "My arms are right below you. Relax. Arch your spine. Chest up. Breasts high." His ears burned. "You're doing fine."

His fingertips glided along the small of her back. "Let your arms float alongside. Keep your chest up. Chest up! That's fine. Now relax. Relax . . ."

Slowly his arms moved away from her. Clair floated for a minute, then panicked. She went under. Jason dived for her. Moments later they broke the surface. Shaking, she wrapped her arms around his shoulders, her face pressed against his chest.

Smiling gaily, her incisors showing, Lisa stood at the pool's edge. "You know, your daughter's right, Clair. You do sink like a rock."

She spun on her heel and stalked for the dressing room.

Eva Ryker stood on the Boat Deck, hands jammed in her coat pockets against the southwest wind. From horizon to horizon the Atlantic sparkled placidly in the afternoon sun.

An elderly man passed Clair and Eva, tipping his cap. "Afternoon, ma'am."

"Afternoon," Clair muttered, her attention directed some fifty feet along the deck, where Jason Eddington was filming footage of his wife.

"I heard some talk from my steward," the man said. "Ships to the west, he says, wired reports of ice."

Eva glanced up. "Really?"

He smiled, the orange sunlight cutting shadowy creases in his cheeks. "Nothin' to worry about, miss. Routine this time of year."

With a polite bow the man walked on, stopping some thirty

feet away. He leaned at the railing and stolidly watched the sea.

Eva perked up at Jason's approach. He patted the movie camera in his hands. "Some good scenes. Almost out of film. Hey!" he beamed. "How about a group shot? Just to finish up the roll."

Clair nodded, holding Eva to her. "Both of us?"

"Sure. Bend down by her." Cradling the Pathé on his shoulder, he focused, then turned the crank. "Okay, just act natural."

Eva stuck her tongue out at the camera. Clair smacked her on the shoulder, then nestled Eva's collar closer to her ears.

"Fine. Now get up and walk toward Lisa."

The three stood together.

"Okay, ladies! Everyone smile and wave!"

They grimaced, flapping their hands.

"Jason, you should be in this!" Lisa ran along the deck and tapped the shoulder of the man at the railing. Eva couldn't catch her words, what with the wind roaring in her ears.

He trotted back with her and gingerly took the camera from Jason's hands. "Nothing to it," he said, showing the man the controls. "Everything's set. Just crank. There's a built-in governor, so it doesn't matter how fast you go. Okay?"

The man nodded. Jason jogged over and joined the group.

"Ready?"

"I can't get you all in the picture!"

Jason hoisted Eva on his shoulders. "How's that?"

"Fine." The man turned the crank, exposing everyone's smile and wave just before the roll ended.

Thanking him, Jason took the camera and led the way back to B Deck. Eva hung back, watching the sun easing toward the horizon.

"Eva," Clair called, "come on! Time to get dressed for dinner!"

"Oh, all right," she moped, walking away from the last glimpse of sunlight the *Titanic* would ever see.

* * *

After dinner the Rykers, the Eddingtons, and Martin rode the elevator up to A Deck to catch the evening concert in the Louis XVI lounge. The adults sipped coffee from thimble-sized cups as the orchestra offered a medley from *The Merry Widow.*

Eva yawned and slouched in her chair. Her mother and Lisa sat stiffly at opposite ends of the little wrought-iron table. Jason watched one woman, then the other, as if appraising the combustibility of two volatile chemicals. Martin studied Jason's straying eyes and smiled his sympathy at Lisa.

The orchestra stopped amid polite applause. With a tap of his baton Wallace Hartley led his little group through Offenbach's *The Tales of Hoffman.*

Eyelids drooping, Eva's head rocked back and forth with the music until it reached a climax. The conductor bowed to loud clapping. The crowd frayed around the edges as families made their way to their cabins.

Clair sipped the last of her coffee and surveyed the elegant lounge with an air of proprietorship. "It's beautiful. It really is. You know, Martin, we must do all our future crossings on this ship."

"I know how you feel, Mrs. Ryker." Lisa smiled. "It's certainly been lucky for you."

She glanced over her cup. "What do you mean, dear?"

"Well, being all alone on this big ship." She pointed across the table. "I don't mean you, James, or you, Eva. But I figure it must get very lonely traveling without your husband and all."

Clair's expression didn't change. "We're going home now."

"And I'm sure your husband misses you very much!" Lisa grinned at Eva. "Don't you want to see your daddy again?"

She didn't answer. Something in Lisa's voice discouraged her.

"Anyway, I'm sure this trip's been a godsend for you." Lisa patted Clair's hand. "What better place to circulate?"

"How's that?"

"You know. We're like goldfish swimming in a bowl. Swishing our tails and giving each other the eye. Unfortunately, if you don't want to join the fun, there's no place to hide."

"You're being slightly cryptic tonight." Clair blinked at Martin. "Shall we go?"

As she reached for her purse on the table, Lisa grabbed her hand. "Don't, Clair! The party's just starting. Isn't that right, darling?"

Jason's eyes fixed on the bottom of his teacup. "Every person in this room must be watching you, Lisa."

She ignored him, aiming her smile at Clair. "Tell me, do you find my husband attractive?"

"That's hardly for me to say."

"Of course it is! I just asked you."

Getting no response, she turned to Eva. "*You* tell me! Isn't Jason Eddington the most handsome man you've ever seen?"

He didn't move a muscle. "Shut up, Lisa."

Eva seriously regarded Jason. Her smile was shy.

"You see! A charmer of both young and old."

Clair put Eva's coat around her shoulders. "Take her to her cabin," she told Martin.

"Oh no!" Lisa placed a restraining hand on his arm. "It's early yet. And Eva's getting to be a very adult young lady. She can stay and watch the grown-ups play."

Her eyes trained on Clair. "But we were talking about you. You and my darling. Do you know how I roped this prize bull?"

"I'm not really interested."

A high laugh. "Oh, Clair! Consider your reputation for candor and . . . stamina. You've a legend to live up to."

Tendons stiffened in Clair's neck. "My dear, absolutely nothing has happened between Jason and me."

He grabbed Lisa by the upper arm. "Don't make a complete fool . . ."

"That's what you want, isn't it?" She shook him off. "A docile cow who turns a blind eye while you're out spawning with this million-dollar slut!"

Round as saucers, Eva's eyes darted uncomprehendingly from face to face.

Clair rose to her feet. "Martin, take Eva down below *now*."

Spirited toward the door, Eva still heard the mad bad talk behind her back.

"Very touching, Lisa." Jason's voice rose. "This plucky snit of jealousy. About as touching as the nautch dance you've been performing for Martin!"

J.H. stopped in his tracks, letting go of Eva's hand. "Now see here, Jason . . ."

Lisa's slap cracked across her husband's cheek. "You know, Clair, I think you were telling me the truth! Otherwise you would know . . ."

Eva stood shivering as Martin went back to join the fray. Huge towering men—stewards and stern mustachioed patriarchs—rose to restore order.

The voice cried high and shrill over the surrounding wall of bodies. " . . . otherwise you would know that this great blond god is all advertising and no product!"

Eva trembled at the meaty sound of a fist striking flesh. Teacups and silver spoons flew, crashing to the floor. A wild, incomprehensible scuffle of bodies. Arms reaching to raise Lisa from the table. White linen smeared red. Hands scrambling at Jason, who shook them off and stumbled away, with Clair in pursuit.

Between the encircling men she glimpsed Lisa's head tottering upright. Slowly, her hand blotting blood from her mouth, she staggered from the lounge with Martin's help.

A hot trickle of tears streamed down Eva's face as she sprinted away in blind flight.

25

The tape reels turned with calm clockwork certainty, unraveling the panting torrent of words. " . . . Georgia, it was awful . . . I ran and ran . . . they were yelling . . . screaming . . ."

My hand punched the recorder's stop button. No one in the office made a sound as I walked to the window. Ryker's limousine shimmered chilly under the noonday sun.

Eva's voice was almost timid as she broke the silence. "It's . . . hard to describe. Like little jigsaw pieces worn away by time that don't quite mesh. Snatches of it are clear, yet so far away. As if I'm looking through the wrong end of a telescope. And yet other things . . . I can practically reach out and touch." She rubbed her arms. "Like that awful fight . . ."

I nodded. "A particularly awful fight because it was prearranged. The final act of a well-choreographed routine worked out by Jason and Lisa."

With a sigh I sat on the edge of my desk. "In many ways it's the oldest game in the book—Double-barrels of Sex and Jealousy. Aimed at an unattached wife and her tough but oddly vulnerable bodyguard. An explosive brew, especially since it was common knowledge that Clair Ryker and James Martin were having an off-and-on affair over the years."

Ryker sat hunched over in his chair, weighed down and shrunken. His mouth opened but no words of denial emerged.

"With a combination like that," I said, "the Eddingtons didn't even have to breathe hard. Even as a little girl, as we heard, you sensed the moth-and-flame gambit between Jason and your mother. Although you weren't privy to them, we can assume similar maneuvers between Lisa and Martin. Unfortunately, both Clair and J.H. seemed to imagine themselves as the flames in this unwholesome ménage. As we'll find out later, they were sadly mistaken. Along with Georgia Ferrell, they were hardly more than pawns to be swept off the board. The object of capture was you, Eva."

She sat very still. "Go on, Norman."

"At this point," I gently explained, "your tape fails to tell us what happened that night. Georgia Ferrell put you to bed and you slept through the next hour and a half. And yet that time, from nine-thirty to eleven, may have been the most important ninety minutes in your life.

"So, how to find out what happened? One segment of the tape which we'll hear later provides part of the answer. As for the rest, I can only do some woolgathering based on the available facts. We know from you that Jason left the lounge with your mother not far behind. You saw him heading for the stairs which led to the Boat Deck. . . ."

Moonless, the sky formed a black tent over the Atlantic, the stars sparkling pinpoint holes in the fabric. Black upon black, oily smoke poured from the black and yellow funnels.

Jason Eddington clamped his teeth as he shuffled along the Boat Deck. Tiny ice shavings glinted around the deck lights. The crew had a name for them, he remembered absently. "Whiskers 'round the lights." It meant ice was near.

He rested one hand on the white tarpaulin of Lifeboat thirteen and gazed toward the stern of the *Titanic*. White and faintly phosphorescent, her wake trailed off into the darkness.

Footsteps tapped behind his back. He ignored them. Clouding in the cold, Clair Ryker's breath blew over his shoulder.

"So much for the blood feast, Jason."

His head turned a fraction, eyeing her mordant frown. "How's that?"

"I thought you might need company after the unleashing of the demons." A sad smile. "Walpurgis Night isn't supposed to be until the end of the month."

"I guess we just couldn't wait." His hand wearily kneaded the back of his neck.

Clair shoved both hands in her coat pockets, looking down at his feet. "Jason, I'd like to say it was all my fault, but it wouldn't be true. The two of you together are a very sick pair."

Air hissed through Jason's teeth as he faced her. "Just what do you want from me? You heard Lisa's little speech. Plenty of other men will be only too happy to give you what you need."

Clair leaned on the railing. "People say things when they're angry. I don't place much stock in them." She looked up at him. "It isn't true, is it?"

Jason's face was haggard. "God, no."

Clair watched the ocean, her hands close to his on the railing. Then she shivered and shied away. "You're not going to prove anything by freezing out here. I've got some champagne in my suite. It'll soon go flat." She looked over her shoulder. "It'd be a shame to waste it."

"I thought you were worried about gossiping stewards."

"After this fight, I don't think any of us have a reputation left to protect."

"Lisa won't be with me tonight. Why don't you stop by?"

She nodded. "Give me a call."

Jason waited until she was out of sight, then moved across the ship to the starboard deck. He skulked in the shadows and peered down the long railings. His lips tightened as he saw them; two figures silhouetted against the night sky. Jason recognized the voices of Martin and Lisa. A few more words were lost in the distance. Then Martin kissed her and left.

Lisa stood alone at the railing. Her eyes, dark and empty, regarded Jason as he approached.

"I'm sorry," he said, "I didn't mean to hurt you."

She didn't react to his apology. "Is everything set?"

"Yes. I'll call her in about fifteen minutes."

Without another word, they fell into step together, heading below decks.

Clair Ryker caressed a magnum of Tattinger '05 and tapped her knuckles on cabin door B-76.

Jason's eye ogled her through the open crack in the door. She smiled and held up the bottle.

"Room service!"

His grin was forced. "Come in."

Brushing past him, she idly gazed around the cabin, then walked to the porthole, peering out into the darkness.

"Look at the sea," she whispered slowly. "I've never seen it so smooth. Have you, Jason?"

"No . . . no, I never have." His hands shook slightly as he popped the bottle and filled two champagne glasses on the end table next to the bed.

Clair saw his face and was amused. "My, my, Jason. Stage fright?"

He grinned in spite of himself. "Opening night jitters."

Slowly Clair moved to the door, turned the latch, and dropped the key in the cleavage of her gown. "You see," she said, spreading her hands, "I've taken the initiative. You're my prisoner."

Her low laugh stopped as she spotted a Victrola sitting on its stand opposite the beds. She curiously thumbed through the records. "Jason, you didn't tell me you had one of these things."

His words were brittle. "It's my wife's."

"Sorry I asked." She scooped a record out of the pile.

Putting the disc on the turntable, Clair fiddled with the

crank, then threw her hands in the air. "I give up. How do you work this thing?"

"It's a special model," Jason answered, fumbling with the Victrola, "mounted on gimbals so it'll work aboard ship. You have to release the turntable like so . . . then turn the crank."

He wound the spring, adjusted the horn, and set the tone arm onto the disc. Harsh and brassy, the band rasped out of the Victrola's horn.

Clair snapped her fingers to the music and leaned against Jason, a glint of alcohol in her eyes.

"You're still my prisoner, you know."

He held up his wrists. "Want to handcuff me?"

"Oh, I don't think so," she murmured, feeling his hands stroking her hair. "You look safe enough to me."

Their lips met. Softly. Barely a touch.

"Is that a compliment?" His hand skimmed along the curve of her back.

"Jason," she whispered, her lips wet along the lobe of his ear. "Shut up."

His tongue slid over her teeth, gliding along the silky inside of her mouth.

The Victrola bellowed gaily. *"Casey would waltz with a strawberry blonde . . . "*

Rough, tanned fingertips grappled with dress lacings.

" . . . and the Band played on . . ."

Untying the strings. Rustling brocade petticoats.

" . . . He'd glide cross the floor with the girl he a-dor'd . . ."

Metal corset snaps. Petticoats swishing over the carpets. Gown sagging, slipping. On the carpet in a heap.

Saxophones blew gaily.

Kneading hands on wool jacket. One sleeve. Two. Flung on bed. Celluloid collar snapped. Top button. Second, third, fourth. White shirt, dark under armpits, hung on bedpost.

A trumpet rattled the horn.

White bra straps against white skin. Long brown hair spilling over shoulders. Left. Right. Snap at the back.

Moist nipples against brown chest. Soft. Red, slushed. Stiffening.

Plunk-plunk-plunk of bass.

Last clothes on floor. Trousers on chair back next to bed. Red tongue along blond chin stubble. Bare toes clutched white against blue carpet.

" . . . *But his brain was so loaded it nearly exploded . . .* "

Blunt fingers piercing black thicket. Low groan in her throat.

" . . . *The poor girl would shake with alarm . . .*"

Sinking. Silently, in two. Tiny squeaks of mattress springs.

" . . . *He'd ne'er leave the girl with the strawberry curls . . .*"

Nails probing blond pubic hair. Curling gently.

Leg muscles clenched hard against soft thigh. Brown palms along white flanks, drawing shiny sweat line glinting in faint yellow light.

" . . . *and the Band played on.*"

Kneecap pushing inside of leg. Slender fingers at groin, stroking, guiding.

The tone arm reached the end of the record and moved toward the hub. *Sigh-pop-hiss* from the Victrola's horn. The big needle bounced heavily in the groove.

Thrust. Slow and measured. Fingernails clutching, furrowing rippling back. White scar lines, welling pink, then dusty salmon.

Red lips drawn away from white teeth and pink glistening gums.

Clenched buttocks thrusting, driving. Blond and black curls mixing, gnarling wetly. Blue and brown eyes meeting; vacant, vast, and piercing.

Sigh-pop-hiss. Trapped in a circle. *Sigh-pop-hiss.*

Tangled pale and tanned legs in rhythm on white silk sheets. Sea pounding. Sighs deep in throat like shore-breaking waves.

Tongue curling slowly, lingering around nipple. Pink and shining.

Light and dark flesh riding the wave. Through crests and troughs. Crests and troughs. Crests and troughs.

Rictus grin, teeth sinking gently into brown corded shoulder muscle. Sweat darkening blond hair, down forehead and cheeks, collecting in amber stubble.

Sigh-pop-hiss. Sigh-pop-hiss.

Brown palm cupped hard on breast. Rising and falling. Crest, trough.

Hand off breast, roaming along mattress to the nearby chair.

Drive deep and silky. Brown hand delving in back pocket of pants on chair.

Crests and troughs. Plum-taut glans advancing, retreating.

Hand taking bottle from pocket, flipping cap with a thumbnail. Little white pellet jostling into palm.

Painted toenail gliding along brown sole. Crests and troughs.

Pill dropping into champagne. New bubbles rising, frothing. Thin film around glass, then nothing.

Legs intertwined, pushing through mattress. Rising, falling. Red lipstick smudge on brown earlobe. Crest and trough. Long thrust.

Sigh-pop-hiss.

Rising, falling. Rising, falling. Crest, trough. Rising, rising. Crest, cresting. Wave breaking, writhing, curling, frothy white foam. White against open dark triangle, across tan belly.

Wave crashing on shore, foam slowing on sand; thin, tired, and flaccid. Hard muscles softening wearily against flushed skin. Moist air pumping through lungs.

Hiss of bodies against silk, turning on sides. Head sagging, leaning gently against breast.

"You know what, my darling Jason?" Laugh lines fanned out from the corner of her eyes. "Lisa's even dumber than I thought."

He chuckled, low and sleepy. They lay together for a moment, listening to the expiring noise from the phonograph. Finally Jason propped himself up, reaching between her shoulders and the bedboard for the champagne glasses. He gave one to Clair and took the other.

She smiled smugly, her eyes distorted through the champagne as she held it up to the light. "What shall we drink to?"

Jason stared at the ceiling, then grinned, pointing to the Victrola.

Clair giggled, leaning against his chest.

Jason smiled, his eyes watchful. Her throat rippled down the wine.

He slipped out of bed and padded to the bathroom. Clair lay propped against a pillow, listening to the stream of water from the washbasin.

"Where might Lisa be?"

He walked back to the bedroom and stood impassively before her. His eyes regarded her for a moment, then turned dully away. "You don't have to worry about her, Clair." His voice was calm as he bent down and put on his underwear.

"You know, for a doting husband, you're very casual about all this."

Sitting on the edge of the bed, he grappled with his socks. "I can hardly be concerned over something that doesn't present a problem."

"That's a fine . . ."

Suddenly she doubled over in bed, her face pale. Face muscles grimaced as she straightened.

"God, I feel sick. It must've been something I ate."

"Or drank." Jason snatched his pants off the chair back.

Clair bent over again, a thin scream hissing from her throat. "Get my dress! I've got to see Dr. O'Loughlin!"

Jason's face was impassive as he buttoned his fly. "You're a big girl. Do it yourself."

"You stupid bastard!" She fell off the mattress and knelt, naked and shaking. "I'm sick and . . ."

Convulsions began and Clair writhed on the carpet. Jason bent down, felt the bodice of her dress for the cabin key, and pocketed it.

Arms and legs thrashing, she retched over and over, saliva wet and glistening on the carpet as she staggered for the door.

Clair fell to her knees and fought with the knob. Another spasm hit and she shivered on the deck, bile bubbling green and ugly over her lips.

Jason's fingers fastidiously buttoned his shirt.

Her face turned a motley purple.

He looped his tie into the tight Windsor knot.

Eyes bulging almost out of their sockets, her lungs strained for air.

Jason spotted his gold clasp on the dresser. He stepped over Clair, snatching it up to align it on his tie.

A deep gurgle in her throat and Clair Ryker was gone.

He took a mirror from her purse and thrust it under her nose. No vapor. Tanned fingers gently felt the neck. No pulse.

Jason was satisfied. He grabbed both arms and dragged the body across the cabin. The bare feet traced scuff marks on the carpet. Kneeling, he shoved it under the bed. The fabric fringing the box springs hid it from sight.

He rose and gathered up Clair Ryker's clothes. Jason chucked the Madame Lucille evening gown under the bed with the body, followed by the shoes, coat, lingerie, and the heavy laced corset.

Carefully, Jason inspected the cabin, kicking an errant foot back under the bed. The Victrola was winding down. *Sigh-pop-hiss. Sigh—pop—hiss. Sigh . . . pop . . . hiss.*

Lashing out, he ripped the arm off the record. The big needle etched a screaming gash through the grooves.

Except for the low rumble of the *Titanic*'s engines, all was quiet. Jason poured himself more champagne from the Tattinger bottle, then went to the telephone on the end table and lifted the receiver.

"The library, please." His enunciation was slow and deliberate. "Yes, I know it's late."

A click and a pause. "Library. May I help you?"

"Is Lisa Eddington there?"

"One moment please."

Jason waited, the yellow bulb of the bed lamp reflected in each eye.

Another click in the receiver. Lisa's voice was low. "Yes?"

His mouth moved slowly. "The bitch is no longer with us."

"Fine. Yes, I'll see you soon, darling."

Bidding the librarian a brief good night, Lisa walked down the grand staircase to B Deck, donning long white evening gloves. A glance down the starboard corridor revealed only locked doors receding into the distance. She made sure no one could see her before she knocked on cabin door B-57.

It opened quickly. Martin hustled her inside. They stood in darkness relieved only by a table lamp in the living room. She clung to him with one arm, the other clutching her purse.

His lips nestled tenderly by her ear. "Did you have any trouble with Jason?"

Light from the lamp cast long shadows across Lisa's face, hiding her eyes. "I haven't seen him since . . . since . . ."

Tears crept down her cheeks as she lay her head on his chest, the drops streaking on the silk lapels of his evening jacket.

"Ssh. Ssh," he whispered, stroking her long blond hair. "Come on. What you need is a drink."

Martin led her into the bedroom. He quickly grabbed a decanter of scotch and poured her two fingers' worth.

Pale blue eyes stared doubtfully at the amber liquid.

"Go on. Drink it. It won't kill you."

She smiled away her tears and swirled the scotch down. "I'm . . . I'm sorry I acted so silly."

He laughed indulgently, turning around and throwing his jacket on one of the beds. As he began unknotting his tie, Lisa opened her purse. Her hand reached for the lamp switch. A click and all was black, except for the stars twinkling through the porthole.

Martin frowned in puzzlement, then grinned, tossed his tie on the bed and turned to her. "Lisa, darling . . ."

A surprised little sigh bubbled over his lips as a knife stabbed him between navel and groin. Lisa thrust until the blade scraped against his spine.

He had no time for pain. A femoral artery ruptured, rushing red over her white gloves. He sagged like a puppet with cut strings.

Lisa released the knife still in his stomach and stood, wrinkling her nose in disgust as she peeled off the gloves. Red and white, they flashed out of the porthole.

She swung the glass shut, then went to the bed and plucked a monogrammed handkerchief from Martin's coat, dabbing away leftover tears on her cheeks. She walked to the door and listened for any sound. Nothing. She pocketed the handkerchief and walked out of cabin B-57.

Next door were cabins B-55, 53, and 51, which formed the Rykers' suite. Lisa loitered in the corridor until a steward passed by, pushing a dinner tray toward the kitchen, then knocked on the door of B-51.

A curt and sleepy Georgia Ferrell answered.

"What do you want, Mrs. Eddington?"

"Is Clair here?" Lisa slurred nastily. From the corner of her eye she could see the steward fiddling with the tray, working busily at not listening.

"No." She started to close the door. "It's late. Please go . . ."

"That whore and my husband are in there! Let me in!" She struggled past Georgia and slammed the door behind her. "Where are they!" she yelled, searching frantically around the dark and vacant parlor.

" . . . Mrs. Eddington . . ."

" . . . don't lie to me! They're here! Tell . . ."

" . . . Eva is next door. You'll wake her . . ."

" . . . tell me, goddam you!" Lisa shook her by the shoulders, then stopped, spotting the private promenade. "They're out here! Hiding!"

Georgia followed her outside, hands fluttering. They stood at the railing, framed by the stars.

"You've hidden them! You've taken them away!" Her hair blew beserk in the wind.

"You're upset, Mrs. Eddington. Go back to your cabin and get some sleep. Please."

The madness slowly left her eyes. Chin trembling, she managed to smile and kiss Georgia on the cheek. "You're right. I'm so sorry. You must think me a terrible fool."

She smiled in understanding, turning to look out at the Atlantic. "No need to explain . . ."

Lisa slashed both her hands across Georgia's neck, toppling her over the railing. The robe and pajamas flashed down into the night. A single splash seventy feet below was immediately lost in the *Titanic's* churning wake.

Lisa turned her attention to the rattan furniture on the promenade. She tipped one chair on its side. Her hand shut the glass door as she stepped back into the parlor. A settee toppled. A table jostled. A vase crushed on the carpet; white porcelain and red roses ground under her heel. But quietly! Not to disturb Eva.

She surveyed her work. Satisfied, she took Martin's monogrammed handkerchief, dropped it near the door leading to the promenade, and left the cabin. The steward was still shuffling dishes in the corridor. Lisa turned back to the black interior of the suite.

"Thank you so much, Miss Ferrell," she said warmly, wiping her tears. "You must forgive me. I'm . . . I'm very, very sorry. Good night."

Lisa closed the door behind her and headed down the corridor—a woman with a destination—giving the steward a haven't-you-got-something-better-to-do look. He vanished guiltily into the kitchen.

As he disappeared, Lisa walked down the hallway to the elevators and rode down to the purser's office on C Deck.

"Excuse me," she said to the assistant on duty, "I'm retiring for the night. Would you please send this up to the wireless office?" She passed him a half sheet of onionskin paper.

"Yes, of course." The assistant nodded graciously.

"Thank you. Good night."

Her message snuffled up the pneumatic tube from the purser's office and clinked into the "Incoming" basket in the wireless room as she returned to the starboard corridor of B Deck. A glance both left and right. Totally vacant.

Smiling, she reopened the door of B-51, and eased herself back into the parlor. Lisa didn't make a sound as she tiptoed through the interconnecting cabins to B-55, where Eva Ryker slept.

26

" . . . of course, we have no way of knowing the exact strategy Jason Eddington used to maneuver Clair Ryker into his cabin." I sighed, wiping my face with a handkerchief. "From what we know of their relationship, she didn't need much persuasion. And, of all the things that may have happened in B-seventy-six, all we can say for certain is that Clair came to a very bad end. As we'll hear, the tape testifies to that.

"The fate of James Martin and Georgia Ferrell is even more mysterious. J.H. simply vanishes from the scene. None of the survivors remember seeing him when the passengers were mustered to the lifeboats early on the morning of April fifteenth. But the almost offhand comments Jason and Lisa later made to Eva very strongly suggest that he joined Clair in the rubbish heap. More waste material in the Eddingtons' Grand Plan."

Scowling, I tugged at my chin. "I suppose Lisa did the actual work. Her very public purchase of a knife as a gift to Martin was more than mere coincidence. And, from studying a timetable of those last few hours before the *Titanic* struck the iceberg, I think we can safely assume that she also handled the murder of Georgia Ferrell.

"Our evidence is a little more concrete in the case of the Ryker maid. Several weeks after the sinking, the *MacKay-Bennett,* a cable-laying ship out of Halifax, picked up about two hundred bodies. She was among them." I stared at Ryker. "It must have taken a very discriminating eye to pick her out of the anonymous pile."

He folded and refolded his hands in a gesture of helpless and ancient grief. They were pitifully white, with gnarled blue veins snaking between the liver spots.

"Have you ever been to Halifax, Mr. Hall, to see their graves?"

"Last April," I replied.

"I used to take the train up every month. Row upon row. At one time I thought she was there. Hiding. Clair hid from me frequently, you know. After a while I gave up the search and never went back."

Ryker's lips creased tight like an old wound. "To answer your question, Mr. Hall, yes, I did meet the *MacKay-Bennett* when it returned to Halifax. No Clair, of course; but there was Georgia Ferrell. I made the necessary arrangements at Fairview Cemetery. The headstone and all. And before the burial I had a pathologist look at the remains. She was definitely killed by a sharp blow that snapped her neck." One hand flapped impatiently. "The old fool didn't want to commit himself, but both he and I knew it was no accident."

I settled behind my desk. "Even with the scattered facts we have, I think they can be welded with some strong hunches to reconstruct the Eddingtons' plan. To do that, of course, you first have to imagine what would have happened had the *Titanic* never met with an iceberg on its maiden voyage."

Leaning back in my chair, I scratched my head. "It doesn't take any deductive feat to know that Jason Eddington had to get rid of Clair Ryker's body. Yet we know that he hid it under the bed, thanks to Eva's discovery a few hours later."

She impassively absorbed my words, her face as blank as an Easter Island statue.

"In my opinion, the bed was a temporary hiding place," I continued. "It was no simple matter to shove a carcass out the porthole. Though it was terribly cold that night, passengers were still up and around. Jason and Lisa would have to wait until the early hours of the morning before dumping Clair. In the meantime, the body had to stay out of sight. Under the bed was as good a place as any.

"On April fifteenth, the morning after the murders, a steward would have discovered Martin's body in his cabin. The calls would immediately go out to Captain Smith, Dr. O'Loughlin; the whole ship in an uproar.

"The same steward would run next door to the Ryker suite with the news and discover that Clair and Eva, along with their maid, are missing. There are obvious signs of a struggle. Perhaps, as an added refinement, the steward or one of the investigating officers would discover an object—a tie clasp or cigarette lighter—establishing Martin's presence in the room.

"At this point Jason and Lisa come on the scene, Eva with them. They tell Purser McElroy that she banged on their door late last night, in shock and screaming something about J.H. and her mother having a fight.

"The captain questions Eva—uselessly. She would appear to be in shock, partly in bafflement and partly because Jason and Lisa would've kept her doped up. With Eva unable to tell the truth, the officers aboard the *Titanic* would have little choice but to buy the Eddingtons' story. I can hear Captain Smith talking to both of them.

"'I understand you had a very serious fight with Clair Ryker last night.'

"'That's right,' Lisa would say, 'but I went to her cabin later to apologize. I acted like such a fool!'

"The captain would check with the Rykers' steward, who'd corroborate her statement. Captain Smith then would show Lisa the murder weapon. Let's assume for the moment it was a knife.

"'Of course, I recognize it,' she'd reluctantly answer. 'I bought it for Mr. Martin as a present from the gift shop here on board ship.'

"Captain Smith would check with the clerk at the gift shop, who'd agree with Lisa. Eva herself saw Lisa buy the knife, but she would be in no position to testify. With such limited information Captain Smith would reach the pat, but inevitable, conclusion.

"Someone, probably Purser McElroy, who kept his nose to the deck, would whisper old rumors. All about James Martin being one of Clair Ryker's ex-lovers. The fight with the Eddingtons would have brought things to a head. Late that night, they would speculate, Martin went next door to talk with Clair. They fought. First words, then fists. Eva overheard and ran to the Eddingtons' cabin. Martin went berserk and killed Clair. In panic, he murdered Georgia Ferrell as a witness and tossed both their bodies overboard.

"Back in his cabin, Martin realized what he'd done. He took the easy way out; or the hard way, depending how you look at it; disemboweling himself with the knife Lisa had given him."

I shrugged. "It would have suited Captain Smith, at least for the time being. Being a stickler for discretion, he'd keep the press out of the affair. The only people he'd notify would be the widowed Mr. Ryker and the police in New York, who'd meet the *Titanic* at docking.

"Somewhere along the line Jason would offer to take care of Eva and make sure she'd get to her father safely. As Jason might've said, she really had no one to turn to.

"And so the *Titanic* would wire the sad news to you, Mr. Ryker. But what the officers on board wouldn't know was that you were already informed."

QWG	RAU	WQT
PCW	BFW	IEJ
TIY	EVY	QUR
ESP	UKS	GKP
YFG	UBF	RWA
RWE	KIV	RAG
ARI	VTB	UON
OUD	IIB	WBR
TIY	PDR	ARI

QPD	WER	OBI
RGW	URP	REU
EPK	BUX	XJA
UCW	SIX	ARI
AWP	JAB	OZZ

I held the cipher up for the Old Man to see. "You know the key, I believe. Like to translate?"

"Son, you can go to hell."

I passed the deciphered message to him. Pale eyes blinked over the lines.

WE HAVE YOUR DAUGHTER STOP IF YOU WANT HER ALIVE BE AT SINGER BUILDING LOBBY NOON AFTER TITANIC DOCKS NEW YORK WITH LATEST SHIPMENT STOP NO TRICKS STOP

Ryker read the message as if contemplating an old enemy.

My voice was soft. "The 'latest shipment' refers to the diamonds, of course."

Oblivious to Mike's warning grimace, his lips slowly moved. "Yes."

I put the paper on my blotter. "The Cape Race Wireless Station has a record of the message, since they saved their logs for the Senate inquest of the sinking. It was transmitted from the *Titanic* five minutes before she struck ice. The destination was Pittsburgh, where, to gather from newspaper accounts, you were staying to wrap up a purchase of new coal holdings. The Eddingtons kept pretty close tabs on you. Closer than the tabs you had on them."

The Old Man's eyes grew red and misty. I tried to remember how I'd felt an hour earlier, before he arrived. The avenging angel armed with Truth. And already I felt tarnished. I had the Norman Touch; the opposite of King Midas' talent. The gold was turning into shit even as I watched.

"In any event," I said lowly, "all my second-guessing is academic. The Eddingtons' scheme went wildly astray. By the time their cipher reached you in Pittsburgh, the *Titanic* had already carried fifteen hundred people to their deaths."

I kept my eyes on Eva as I rose and returned to the tape recorder. "Are you sure you want to hear the rest?"

"No, I'm not entirely sure at all." She nervously brushed the hair back off her face. "Even with Dr. Sanford's help, it's not easy. For years I've been fleeing the bogeyman in the dark. One step ahead of its snapping at my heels. Now you want me to stop in my tracks, turn around, and ask 'who's there?'" Eva turned up to me. "Would you have that kind of courage?"

"I don't know."

"Noncommittal candor. A Norman Hall trademark." Eva's lips hinted at a smile. "Go ahead."

"I don't want to play it straight through. As you know, the session with Dr. Sanford became increasingly . . . disjointed. And it's restrictive in viewpoint, if we're to get some idea what happened on the *Titanic* early that morning of April fifteenth." I tapped the recorder. "That's why I'll stray away from this if it becomes too fragmented or too . . . painful.

"Eva, you were a sound sleeper that night. Totally oblivious even to the murder of Georgia Ferrell. A slight crack of an opening door was the only thing that disturbed you . . ."

Snug under the covers, Eva Ryker opened her eyes. There was nothing but the blackness of her bedroom and the low rumble of the *Titanic*'s engines.

Reassured, she buried her head in the pillow.

Eva heard a small hiss from the corner of the cabin. She peeked over the covers.

Another tiny hiss. And another. And another. It was breathing. Inhale, pause. Exhale. Inhale-pause-exhale. Inhale-exhale. Inhale-exhale. Damp and hot, by her ear.

She sat up, crying, "Georgia! Georgia, is that you?"

A hand grabbed her throat, fingers digging for the carotid artery as it forced her face into the pillow.

"No, no!" Eva screamed, thrashing out of bed. As she jumped off the mattress another hand, unseen in the darkness, clutched at her. The corner of the end table hit her above the right brow, but Eva felt nothing. Blood trickled from the cut into her eye, pooling in the socket as the pillow pushed over her face. She struggled uselessly. Eva tried to fight, to run, to stop her descent into the swirling maelstrom, sucking her down through the frothing water, turning to black.

Eva fell through the abyss and was gone.

27

The light hurt her eyes. Eva raised a hand to shield them. A star burst of yellow light focused into a lamp on an end table. The open orifice of a Victrola's horn yawned from one corner. Two shadowy giants loomed overhead.

Eva's fingers dug into the bedsheets beneath her as a woman's hand reached out to examine the cut above her eye.

The shadow giants turned slightly and light fell across their faces.

"Oh Lisa, Lisa! I had an awful nightmare . . ."

"It's all right, darling." Lisa cradled her head by her breasts and stroked her hair. "Ssssh . . . ssh. Don't cry. Everything's all right."

Her sniffling slowed, then stopped. Jason sat on the bed next to her.

"Hey, Eva," he smiled gruffly, tweaking her under the chin. "Big girls don't cry, do they now?"

"Nope." She wiped her eyes with the sleeve of her nightdress, not noticing the bloodstain. She glanced around at her surroundings and frowned. "What am I doing here?"

Jason looked serious. "We hoped you could tell us. You

came pounding on the door, screaming something about Mr. Martin and a fight. You passed out for a few minutes. We were about ready to call a doctor. That's a nasty cut on your eye."

Eva grimaced and held her hand over the scar. "I can't remember. I thought I was asleep. Someone was . . ." Breath quickening, she stared around her. "Where's my mother? And Georgia?"

"I don't know Eva." He rose and went to the door. "But I'm going to find out."

Jason looked at his pocket watch.

Eleven-forty.

In the *Titanic*'s crow's nest Lookout Frederick Fleet glanced away from his watch. Only twenty minutes left in his shift. His eyes strained out beyond the ship's bow. But there was nothing except the stars and the black becalmed sea.

Mist clouded out of his cheeks. He turned to Reginald Lee, partner on his watch, who grinned and shivered in sympathy. Neither man noticed the faint black-on-black patch in the ship's path.

He returned to examining the horizon, slowly scanning left to right. His eyebrows raised at the dull gray vision straight ahead. Must be seeing things, he thought. No . . . he wasn't. It was small, just a chunk. No . . . no, by God, Christ, it was a monster!

Fleet spun and rang the crow's nest bell three times, then lunged for the bridge telephone. The patch grew even as he grappled with the receiver.

"What did you see?"

"Iceberg right ahead."

"Thank you."

On the bridge First Officer Murdoch heard the news. Fast, fast, a voice yelled in the back of his skull as he yanked the brass telegraph handle to "Full Speed Astern."

"Mr. Hitchens!" he yelled. "Hard-a-starboard!"

"Aye, aye, sir!" The Quartermaster's hands flew at the wheel.

A quick hard jab at the button brought down the watertight doors.

Alarms rang down in the bowels of the ship. Stokers glanced up, startled.

Fleet put down the phone, stood by Lee, and waited.

It was closing . . . closing . . . by God, we'll never make it . . . the engines are throbbing, spinning . . . it's not so big really, maybe we'll mow it under . . . this ship's strong, unsinkable . . . Sweet Jesus, how big is that thing . . . fifty . . . no seventy . . . almost a hundred feet out of the water . . . white and craggy like giant salt crystals . . . closer . . . we're still not turning . . . Goddamit, how slow can a ship be . . . closer . . . high and threatening above the forecastle . . . turn . . . turn . . . my God . . . TURN!

Shearing through the water at over twenty knots, the *Titanic's* bow began to come around. Slowly, agonizingly. Swinging to port.

Underwater, white knuckles of ice swept past the *Titanic's* hull. Gliding, scraping, ripping. Steel buckled, crumpling like foil.

Engineer and fireman jumped up at the sound of alarm bells ringing throughout Boiler Room Number Six. The side of the ship peeled open with a groan of tortured steel. Encroaching water churned among the gauges and fittings. The sea at waist level, both men cleared the watertight doors before they ground shut.

Like a thousand trash cans rolling down stairs, the noise rang through the steerage quarters, toppling screaming women out of their bunks.

Jason braced his feet on the carpet and listened to the long ripping noise. Lisa watched the shivering chandelier overhead, mouth agape. Eva felt the bed quivering beneath her but was strangely unafraid. She threw open the porthole and stuck her head out into the darkness.

The iceberg reared above the *Titanic's* stern, silhouetted by the stars. It vanished in the night even as she watched.

"Eva, close that!" Lisa slammed the glass and settled her on the bed.

Jason said, "I'm going to find out what's going on. You two stay here."

He shut the door behind him. Lisa bent down by Eva and smiled weakly. They both examined the cabin, as if plumbing it for safety.

In the smoking room, men filtered back to their highballs and bridge, reassured that the ship seemed as safe as ever.

In the galley Chief Night Baker Walter Belford swore feebly and picked up Parkerhouse rolls littered across the deck.

Marching down the B Deck corridor, Jason approached the steward on duty. "Say, what was that noise all about?"

John McFarland smiled in reassurance. "I've heard talk about an iceberg, sir, but I'm sure it's nothing serious."

Jason's eyes hooded over, his voice hollow. "Yes, you're probably quite right. Good night."

"Good night, sir." With a nod and a smile McFarland continued on his way. Jason watched the steward go, his face tight and unconvinced.

The *Titanic,* ablaze with lights, still raced through the water as Captain Smith ran from his cabin near the wheelhouse to the bridge.

"Mr. Murdoch, what was that?"

His face was slightly shaken. "An iceberg, sir. I hard-a-starboarded and reversed the engines and I was going to hard-a-port around it, but she was too close. I couldn't do any more."

"Close the emergency doors."

"The doors are already closed."

Captain Smith stepped closer to the light, worry lurking in the corner of his eyes. "Stop all engines, Mr. Murdoch."

The first officer nodded. "Stopping all engines." His hand wrenched the telegraph.

The ship's three props, ninety-eight tons of steel churning the sea white in their wake, glided to a halt.

The wind ceased its whistle through the wireless antenna stretching far above the smokestacks.

Walnut and teak paneling in first-class cabins stopped the telltale squeaking that had lulled passengers to sleep since the ship left Southampton.

The glass dome covering the A Deck foyer no longer clattered within its frame.

Eva Ryker felt the gut-deep purr of the ship slow, then die.

"We're stopping." She sat up and peered out at the blackness beyond the porthole. "Lisa, why are we stopping?"

Lisa took her by the hand. "Lie down, dear. I'm sure it's nothing."

Laying in bed, Eva solemnly regarded her. "Where's my mother? I want my mother!"

"Yes, I know, dear." Lisa patted her forehead gently. "I know."

With a thundering hiss that cut through the freezing night air, three of the four funnels shot steam from the boilers into the blackness as the *Titanic* stood still amid the millpond calmness of the ocean.

Jason Eddington stood on the Boat Deck and studied the funnels and the starlit sky. He was one of the handful of people wandering about. Jason looked over the railing, down the rows of lighted portholes, to the water far below.

"Well, Mr. Eddington, what do you think?"

He glanced over his shoulder to see fellow passenger Jack Thayer, dressed only in an overcoat and pajamas. His adolescent face looked tremendously excited.

"Oh, hello, Jack." He gestured casually at the ship around him. "I don't know what's going on. Everything looks all right." He buttoned up his coat, mist clouding by his lips. "I've heard some chatter about an iceberg, but . . ."

"It's more than chatter! Haven't you seen the ice?"

Jason scowled, shaking his head.

"Come on!" Thayer led him all the way forward on A Deck, where they looked down on the starboard well deck near the foremast. Steerage passengers tumbled laughing among tons of crushed ice on deck, like characters in a Currier and Ives engraving.

"You see?" Thayer laughed. "It's a major tourist attraction. Christmas in April!" His laughter died when he saw Jason's frown.

Captain Smith wasn't smiling either. From the bridge he watched the playful passengers, then turned away and looked evenly at Fourth Officer Boxhall. "Go down and find the carpenter and get him to sound the ship."

Boxhall was saved the trouble. Carpenter Hutchison brushed past him on the bridge ladder. He panted as he stood in front of the captain. "She's making water fast!"

Captain Smith said to Boxhall: "Get me Mr. Andrews."

Thomas Andrews, Managing Director of Harland and Wolff, the builders of the *Titanic,* sat in cabin A-36, surrounded by a pile of papers and blueprints of the ship. The phone rang. Andrews glanced up from a floor plan of the first-class writing room, then turned back to his work. It rang again. And again.

"I hear you, I hear you," Andrews muttered, grabbing the receiver. "Hello?"

"Mr. Andrews, the captain wants you." Boxhall's voice was crisp. "Quickly please."

Jason Eddington smiled patiently at Jack Thayer as they stood gazing down at the *Titanic*'s bow.

"No, I don't feel like souvenir hunting, Jack. You go on."

"Okay, Mr. Eddington!" Thayer ran for the stairs leading below decks. "I'll save you a piece!"

"You do that," Jason murmured absently. Standing alone, he took one more look around him. There was nothing more to do out here. Maybe he could corral one of the officers and learn something.

Turning his collar up around his ears, Jason wandered back toward the stairs.

In an effort to avoid curious passengers, Captain Smith and Thomas Andrews clambered down the crew's stairway leading to the innards of the ship.

They inspected the flooded mailroom on F Deck, then moved down to G Deck and stood in the spectator's gallery of the squash court. Seawater sloshed over the floor of the court like a big shallow bathtub.

"Eleven fifty-five." Andrews checked his watch. "A little over ten minutes after the collision." His voice was dry; he studied the water, then swallowed, and met Smith's eyes. "Let's see how the boiler rooms are doing."

Coming down the grand staircase in the A Deck foyer, Jason glimpsed the huge clock, flanked by bronze nymphs symbolizing Honor and Glory. Nearly midnight.

His eyebrows raised in surprise as he saw the crowd, clad in everything from Gimbels long johns to ermine stoles, standing around waiting for some word. No one seemed troubled, he thought. Just curious. Probably being silly, getting worried . . .

His thoughts were interrupted by the passage of Captain Smith and Thomas Andrews through the foyer. No one asked any questions. Something about the two men's faces told them not to. People simply stood and sniffed the air for any omens. As the men left, on their way to the bridge, the crowd chattered softly in bright, hearty speculation.

In the chart room near the bridge, Andrews pulled out a longitudinal section blueprint of the ship and spread it flat on the table, grabbing a pencil from his vest pocket.

"All right, Captain, let's see what we've got." He began marking the chart. "Water is in the forepeak, the first two holds, the mail room and the fifth and sixth boiler room. And by the time we got below decks, the sea was already well above keel level." Andrews' eyes held no emotion as he drew a line from the forepeak back on the starboard side. "That means the berg sliced about three hundred feet from there to there, doing in the first five watertight compartments."

Smith studied the chart silently. Then he looked up at Andrews. "Where do we stand?"

He pursed his lips, then threw the pencil on top of the chart. "We don't."

"Goddamit it, man! Are you trying to tell me . . ."

"Captain, the simple fact is that the *Titanic* cannot float with five compartments open to the sea. Take a look at this." He pointed with the pencil. "Here you see the bulkhead separating Compartment Six and Compartment Five. It's only built as far up as E Deck. These five compartments will settle so water will naturally spill over the top of the bulkhead into Compartment Six. Then Compartment Seven, Eight, Nine . . ." Straightening upright, he shook his head. "It's as inevitable as the next sunrise, Captain."

Smith bent over the chart, examining every detail. Finally he drew back.

"How long do we have?"

Andrews' voice was hollow. "An hour and a half to two hours. At most."

Neither man spoke. Captain Smith walked out of the chart room onto the bridge and gazed at the ship's commutator. It showed the bow seven degrees down at the head. Even as he watched, the figure changed to eight degrees.

"Mr. Wilde," he said to the Chief Officer, "uncover the boats."

When Thomas Andrews went to his cabin to get his lifeboat, a young man waited in front of the door. He looked familiar . . . ah yes, it was Clair Ryker's latest young buck.

"Good evening, Mr. Eddington. Can I help you with something?"

"I want to know what's wrong."

Andrews put a fatherly hand on his shoulder. "Now, I'm sure . . ."

"The truth, Mr. Andrews."

"Well, I would get my life belts and report on deck. Not that I . . ."

" . . . is it serious . . ."

"I'm sure panic isn't . . ."

" . . . are we . . ."

" . . . I wouldn't . . ."

" . . . is this ship sinking?"

Andrews' smile flattened. "Get your wife up on deck. Get any valuables, too. We don't have more than a couple of hours."

Pushing past, he went inside and slammed the door behind him.

The news spread quietly. From First Officer Murdoch to Purser McElroy to the stewards, on duty and off. Down through first class, second class, and steerage.

John McFarland got the news from the chief steward during a coffee break. The two men sat alone in the steward's quarters on the port side. He didn't speak until the chief rose to leave.

"Uh, sir?"

"Yes, Mr. McFarland?"

"How serious is all this?"

The chief made a face. "Oh, I don't know. Probably just a precaution. By the way, one more thing. Don't spread any gossip among the passengers if you can help it."

McFarland nodded, eyes glazed, as the chief left to brief the starboard crew.

Well, he thought, there's no use wasting time. Walking to the faucet, he plucked a glass off the rack, filling it halfway. He gulped the water, then looked down at the glass shaking in his hand. Why, he was being an ass! A grown man quaking like some bloody schoolgirl!

His fingers fumbled and the glass fell on its side, water drooling across the surface. He swore a little under his breath and grabbed a rag. The pool was only half blotted when he stopped and studied the glass. At first he wasn't sure why. Then it came to him. The overturned glass was rolling to the end of the counter.

McFarland snatched up the glass and returned it to the rack. Why would a glass be rolling toward the bow like . . .

Rolling toward the bow.

McFarland stood still for a moment, his face expressionless. Then he turned and walked, briskly, to warn his passengers.

Stepping into the corridor, he saw a familiar figure. "Mr. Eddington!" he called as Jason brunted past. "I say, Mr. Eddington . . ."

McFarland's voice died as Jason rushed into his cabin and the door crashed behind him.

Ah well, he thought. He had other passengers to muster awake. The Eddingtons could wait a bit.

The table lamp threw Jason's torso shadow over the bed as he drew close to Eva. His skin looked gaunt and membrane-tight, like drying leather stretched over bones.

"Come here," he said to Lisa in a raspy whisper. "I want to talk. Alone."

Eva clung to her hand. "Don't leave me, Lisa! Please don't!"

She shook away. "Don't be silly. Nobody's leaving you!"

Lisa joined her husband in the semidarkness of the bathroom.

He licked sweat off his lip. "We're going to sink."

"What do you mean . . ."

" . . . I talked with Thomas Andrews . . ."

"But we can't be! We just . . ."

"He was telling the truth . . ."

"But sinking . . ."

"God damn you!" He shook her. "Don't you understand? We don't have more than a couple of hours!"

Lisa stared at him, her face sagging like a wax mannequin in a hothouse.

Eva Ryker sat up in bed and watched them tower over her. She frowned. She wasn't sure why. Then she could see it in their faces. The lips. Around the eyes. They were strangers.

Jason and Lisa both reached for their life belts stashed under the bed.

Eva looked alarmed. "What're you doing?"

Jason grappled with the belt and glanced at her in irritation. "Everyone has to get to the lifeboats."

"But why?"

He stood above her, arms akimbo. "Why in the hell do you think?"

Scared by the tone of his voice, she began to sniffle. "I . . . I want my mommy!"

"For Christ's sake, Eva," he mumbled, fiddling with the life belt strap, "will you please shut up?"

"I want my mommy! Let me go!" Tears brimmed over her eyes. "I want my mommy!"

Lisa looked dully at her as she put on her jacket. "You can't see her."

"I want her! I want to see her now!"

Jason tapped one of the bedposts with his foot and broke into a smile of a sort that Eva had never seen. "You want to see her?" Walking to the door, he unlocked the latch. "You go out and find her."

Eva gaped uncomprehendingly.

"You little bitch! Get out of here! We don't need you anymore. Just get out!"

"I thought you were my friend."

He snorted in disinterest.

"You just wait!" she yelled, her face red. "Wait until I see J.H.! He'll beat you up real good!"

He grinned at Lisa. "I'll bet."

"You'll see!" Eva bounded for the door. "One word from J.H. and my father'll get you!"

Jason helped his wife with her life belt. "Sure, kid."

"He'll tell my father all about you!" Eva's fingers curled around the doorknob. "He'll see him right away! As soon as we dock! He's got a package he's giving him right from the ship!"

Smiles vanished on the Eddingtons' faces. Leaping across the cabin, Jason dragged Eva, kicking and screaming, away from the door and locked it behind him. He threw her on the bed and Lisa held her down.

"A package?" Teeth flashed in Jason's face. "What sort of package?"

She said nothing.

His fingers lightly massaged her throat.

"You're going to tell me, Eva. And you're going to tell me now."

Surrounded by the calm sea, the *Titanic* sat motionless in the water. Seen from the distance with its lights ablaze, the ship resembled an improbable stage prop pasted on a starry backdrop. Even up close it seemed sublimely confident. But the lowest portholes were no longer parallel with the waterline. They slanted toward the bow. With painful slowness the forward porthole sank underwater.

Deep within the flooded forecastle hold water seeped into the crate marked "Ryker Industries."

The passengers gathered out on the Boat Deck; first class in the middle of the ship, second class to the rear, and steerage at the stern and bow; covering their ears against the noise of the steam hissing from the funnels.

Under Officer Wilde's direction crewmen started uncovering the boats. There were four near the bridge, both port and starboard. The same number toward the stern. Completely full, they could accommodate 1,178 people

The *Titanic* carried 2,207 on this maiden voyage.

Passengers watched the crewmen bustling around the boats, unsnarling lines, stashing lanterns, and pulling off tarpaulins.

New arrivals up on deck stood by the railing and watched the boats begin to totter away from the ship's side. Roused from their cabins by the stewards, some scrambled into their clothes while others dawdled.

The couple in B-78 were going to be dawdlers. John McFarland could sense it as he knocked softly on their door. Mr. Klein peeked through the crack.

"What is it?"

McFarland patiently explained.

Considering his words for a moment, Klein eased open the crack. Through it McFarland could see Martha Klein sitting up in bed. Albert Klein bent down and whispered the news to her. In her nightgown she rose and gathered her best dress from the closet as her husband returned to the door.

"It'll be a few minutes."

"Please don't take too long," McFarland called, but the door had already shut.

In B-76 Eva Ryker struggled uselessly against Lisa's arm as Jason's blue eyes examined her coolly. His lips smiled in reflex action.

"The package, Eva. You know something. Tell me."

"No!"

"Don't be clever, Eva. We don't have the time. You said J.H. had a package. I want to know where it is!"

"No! Leave me alone . . ."

Eva's words ended in a scream as his hand crashed across her face. Lisa's hand clenched over her mouth.

"You stupid twat! Do you think this is some sort of game?"

Two eyes stared, terrified and unbelieving, over Lisa's palm.

In B-78 Albert Klein tied his shoes, then grabbed his suspenders, while his wife tugged at her corset strings. Out in the corridor John McFarland stood waiting, one foot tapping impatiently. He heard the low voice of Jason Eddington in B-76, but paid it no mind.

"Now, I'm going to ask you once more," Jason whispered. "Tell me where the package is."

Lisa eased the grip over her mouth. Jason turned one ear toward her.

"Well?"

Eva said nothing.

His face grew red and clotted. "Come on, Eva!"

No answer.

"I'm warning you!"

She bit down hard against any escaping words.

Jason's chest rose and fell. He smiled slightly, lips trembling around the gums. "All right, Eva. Have it your way."

Full force, he hit her in the mouth. Across the face. Again and again. The cut opened, blood dripping down her eye. Again and again. Forming screams were stopped by the next blow. Again and again.

Out in the corridor McFarland ignored the faint noises coming from B-76. Albert and Martha Klein were finally emerging from their cabin.

"Fine, fine," he nodded, examining the life belts tied around them. A strap needed a tug here, a pull there.

Eva blinked the blood away from her eyelids. Tears running down her cheeks shone in the lamplight. Her lips were slack and bleeding.

"Up front," she groaned like a Victrola near death. "In the front."

Jason's face thrust up next to her mouth. "Tell me again, Eva. We can't hear you."

"Up front. A big crate. He was lowering a big crate."

"Up front? You mean the bow?"

"Up front." Eva shut her eyes against the pain. "Where . . . where the crates are."

Jason and Lisa glared at each other in the common knowledge that they were too late.

Up on the bridge the commutator clicked off sixteen degrees. A baby grouper, sucked through the gaping gash in the *Titanic*'s hull, swam curiously among the cargo in the forecastle hold, his tail brushing by the crate labeled "Ryker Industries."

Jason stood erect, his eyes averted from Eva. "Come on. Let's get out of here."

Lisa nodded, went to the closet, and rummaged through suitcases for their ready cash.

Eva lay motionless and blankly watched them bustle around the cabin. She tried to move. An arm. A leg. Nothing happened.

"So long, Eva." Jason bent down close and wiped the hair matted with brown blood on her forehead.

She snapped at his hand and sliced down to the bone, tearing away meat by his thumb.

His lips snarled slowly; a low feral growl. Bloodstained fingers grappled his trouser buttons.

"Jason!" Lisa ran to him. "What in God's name . . ."

Eva's scream tore through the cabin walls, stopping John McFarland in his stride. Spinning away from the Kleins heading upstairs, he ran to the door.

"Open up! What's going on? Open up!"

No answer.

McFarland kicked through and rushed in. Light from the corridor cut through the cabin.

The figures within strobe-flashed onto his retina, pinned down and frozen under the light.

Slumped against one wall, Lisa Eddington stared at the bed.

Eva Ryker lay on the mattress, blood dripping down the side of her face, down scratches on her arms, down in a thin stream from between her legs. The face was shrunken and dark.

The door slammed behind him, cutting off the horror images. McFarland had time to see a shadow behind him before a fist hit the base of his skull. Without a sound he crumpled at the foot of the bed.

The Eddingtons stood together, ignoring Eva's soft whimpering.

"Is he dead?"

Jason bent down and felt his pulse. "No."

"Leave him. Leave both of them."

He rifled through McFarland's pockets and took his pass keys. Eva cradled her stomach, crying, but they didn't turn around.

"Are we ready?"

"I think so." They surveyed the room.

"Okay, let's go," he said briskly.

"Don't forget to lock the door behind you."

Eva watched them pass through the door, silhouetted by the corridor light. A last glimpse of Jason's back and he was gone. The door shut. A key rattled in the lock. Footsteps faded down the hall.

Eva Ryker's eyes were wide with inexplicable dirty terror. Her breathing was the only sound in the cabin. Inhale. Exhale. Inhale. Exhale. Inhale-exhale. Inhale-exhale. Faster and faster.

A low wail rose in her throat, rising up and up as she curled into a tight shrieking ball.

28

I ran to stop the recorder as Eva's brave armor began to crumble. No words; just a cry like a trapped animal as she tried to shrivel into herself.

"Eva, stop it!" I knelt by her. "You're all right!"

The little-girl eyes were filled with unspeakable nightmare memories. I held her face up to mine, shaking her, making her see me.

Mike and Geoffrey had that wishing-they-were-elsewhere look, like dinner guests who stumble into the midst of a deadly family quarrel. Tom blinked and wiped his eyes. Ryker hid his face behind his hands.

My wife dug into the desk drawer for our decanter of Jack Daniels and handed me two glasses. I held one up to Eva.

"Drink. Emergency plasma."

She reached for the glass with both hands and took a tentative sip. She coughed, then tried some more.

"Are you okay?"

Eva wiped away the last of the tears, throwing hair back off her face. "Sure. A very gutsy broad."

"Do you want to talk about it?"

She considered the question for a long moment. "It's been

a one-woman hell for so long. Then Dr. Sanford pried her foot in the door. And now you." Her head shook as she pointed at the tape. "I don't want that part of my life to go on display."

"Eva, I think you know that was never my plan. We don't need to play the tape any further. Fair enough?"

She smiled her relief.

"Your recollections," I continued, "combined with the firm historical facts, enable us to state with a good deal of certainty what happened early that morning of April fifteenth. After the Eddingtons locked you and John McFarland in the cabin, they joined the crowd up on the Boat Deck . . ."

The roar of the steam from the funnels stopped as suddenly as it began, echoing across the water into silence.

Babbling chatter arose from the first-class passengers on the Boat Deck. Jason and Lisa, emerging from the grand staircase entrance, brushed through the crowds, catching odd phrases.

". . . this is perfectly ridiculous . . ."

". . . a precaution surely . . ."

". . . this wasn't my idea to take this trip, Harold . . ."

". . . did you see the ice near the bow . . ."

". . . really? Say! Meet you tomorrow morning for a snowball fight! Loser pays for the dinner . . ."

Jason prodded his wife's arm, eyes on the string of lifeboats being readied by the crew. "Excuse me, pardon me," he kept saying, but people were slow to move.

Davits moaned as Boat Six swung free from the ship and eased down until the lip of the boat was level with the Boat Deck.

Second Officer Lightoller rested one foot on the boat, turned, and surveyed the passengers. "All right! Women and children first! Step lively, please!"

Women shook heads at each other.

". . . out in that little boat . . ."

". . . on a night like this . . ."

"I'm no fool! You're not getting me out there!"

". . . we're safer here than out in that little thing . . ."

The Eddingtons pressed between two elderly couples, nearing the boat.

Women, some with children, gingerly stepped aboard.

"Excuse me," Jason said, "let us through, please."

Lightoller looked around and saw no more volunteers. "All right, lower away."

The crew bent over the cranks.

Jason and Lisa ran up to the railing, out of breath, to see Number Six already descending past the Promenade Deck.

Chest heaving, he faced Lightoller. "You've got to get us on board!"

The second officer scowled at Jason. "It's women and children first, sir. Your wife'll have to go alone. But there's plenty of time. No need to panic."

As he turned away, Jason heard a crash of music over his shoulder. The orchestra had assembled, only half the members in their uniforms, their torsos made huge and puffy by life jackets. They stood near the grand staircase entrance, scraping through "Alexander's Ragtime Band."

Eva Ryker lay on the bed in B-76, taut and brittle like a drawn bowstring. Her wide eyes took in everything and nothing. She clutched herself, ignoring John McFarland, sprawled at the foot of the bed, and she watched the crystal chandelier hanging at an odd angle.

A golden trail of light hissed up from the bridge's starboard side at twelve forty-five A.M. Conversation on the Boat Deck died as heads averted to watch.

Past the superstructure it flew. Over the black and yellow funnels, the masts, and the gossamer-thin wireless antenna. A crackle and it blossomed into a blue-white nova, its light shimmering on the water.

"Rockets." A low sigh escaped from Lisa's lips, as if in worship.

The white star slowly fell and shadows of rigging and cables shifted across the Eddingtons' faces as they watched.

A little boy oohed somewhere in the crowd. "Fireworks!"

"All right!" Officer Lightoller faced the crowd as he stood by Boat Number Eight. "Women and children first!"

Women gave husbands a quick kiss, a few words, then left. Wives without husbands. Children without parents. Quickly the boats filled.

Jason Eddington nudged Lisa as they peered over the heads of the crowd clustered in front of Boat Number Eight.

"Come on, let's try the starboard side."

Eva Ryker's crying gradually ceased. She spread her arms wide across the mattress. It was tilting.

Moments later, Eva was at the door, pulling at the locked doorknob. It wouldn't budge. She twisted. She banged. She kicked the door with her bare feet. Nothing.

Jason and Lisa passed Albert and Martha Klein, sitting placidly together in deck chairs.

"Good evening, Mr. Eddington," Albert Klein nodded politely. "Or perhaps I should say good morning."

Jason gave him a preoccupied frown. "Uh . . . hello, Mr. Klein. Aren't you two going to try for the boats?"

They looked at each other and smiled. "Oh, there's plenty of time yet."

"Besides," Martha Klein said, "I'm not leaving without my husband."

Second Officer Lightoller watched the loading smoothly progressing in Boat Ten, near the stern. Taking a momentary break, he wandered to the top of the emergency stairway leading down to E Deck. Green water was rising step by step, covering lights that kept burning below the surface of the sea.

On the starboard side, a woman tottered on deck and plunged over the Titanic's railing, vanishing in the darkness.

Women screamed and leaned over the side, but a hand grabbed her. She hung there like a slaughtered chicken being carted to market. Men finally gathered on the Promenade Deck and dragged her aboard.

On the second attempt, she stepped into the lifeboat without so much as a bumped shin.

"Can anyone hear me? Help! Help me!"

The voice echoed down the empty slanting corridors of B Deck.

Bruised hands drummed on the door. Still pounding, Eva Ryker sank to her knees.

Another rocket sputtered high above the *Titanic* as Jason and Lisa made their way to the starboard side of the ship.

Far below several lifeboats hugged the hull, slowly disappearing into the darkness.

Jason pulled at his wife's arm. "Come on! This way!"

First Officer Murdoch strode quickly by and leaned over the railing, addressing the crew below on the Promenade Deck.

"Lower away, then row back to the gangway and wait for orders."

"Aye, aye, sir."

Murdoch swept past, nodding absently to the Eddingtons. They gazed bleakly over the railing and heard a voice below yelling "Any ladies?"

The voice came from Boat Number Thirteen, hanging level with the upper Promenade Deck. Lisa squinted at the boat. There were some crew and a few men, but mostly women. Almost full, she noticed.

Lisa shook away from Jason, vaulted over the railing, and tumbled into the boat.

"Goddam you! Wait for me!"

Even as he swung himself on the railing, three more women, a man, and a baby reached the boat from the deck below. It lowered away, the ropes creaking.

Jason felt a hand on his shoulder, pulling him back. He struggled but was dragged off the railing.

A burly crewman shoved him across the deck. "You crazy fool! Jump when the boat's lowering and you'll swamp all of them!"

Jason dodged the man and ran back to the railing, but it was too late. Boat Thirteen was already thirty feet below him.

He glared at his wife in impotent fury as she sank from sight.

Eva heard a low groan as she huddled by the door of B-76. She turned and saw McFarland. His arms moved a fraction, then stopped.

She went to him on hands and knees and shook his shoulders. "Mr. McFarland?"

He didn't move. A prod in the back.

"Mr. McFarland!"

No response.

Foot by foot, Boat Thirteen eased down the side of the black hull. Lisa listened to the ropes yelping through the pulley blocks. A porthole passed by, a brightly lit suite beckoning beyond the glass. Then it vanished over her head.

The crewman at the tiller spoke up. "We'll be coming down to the water by the condenser exhaust. We don't want to stay in that long or we'll be swamped. Down on the floor there's a pin which frees the ropes. Pull it as soon as we're afloat!"

"What pin? Where?" Everyone searched fruitlessly.

Lisa looked down over the side at the water gushing from the condenser.

Settling in the swirling water, the boat became mired in the whirlpool.

"I don't see any pin!" a passenger bawled. "You find it!"

Lisa heard ropes squeaking above her. Boat Number Fifteen was coming down directly overhead.

"Stop! Stop Number Fifteen!"

Seventy-five feet above, the crew still spun the davit cranks.

Passengers in Number Fifteen, seeing the other boat below, yelled up at the crew.

The words were lost. The crew kept on cranking.

The two boats were less than twenty-five feet apart.

"Stop that bloody cranking!"

Twenty feet.

"Goddam it, can't you hear up there?"

Fifteen.

Ten.

A second-class passenger and a stoker jumped up as the keel of Number Fifteen brushed their heads, trying to push it away. It was no use.

Another stoker leaped to his feet, a glinting knife slicing the rope. "One!" he yelled, scrambling to the stern.

The keel of Boat Fifteen grazed Lisa's hair.

"Two!"

The rope snapped.

The wash from the condenser tossed Boat Thirteen like a matchbook in a gutter, thrusting it away from the ship. As Lisa regained her balance, she saw Boat Fifteen settle into the same exact spot on the surface.

Jason watched the scene from above, his face gray. A rocket hissed and crackled over his shoulder.

He turned in frustration and watched the crowd at Boat Number Nine. First Officer Murdoch's policy was to let men through, but only if there was extra room. Women and children filled the boat in seconds.

Two hundred yards out on the Atlantic, Lisa Eddington watched the *Titanic,* its lights still bright. Brassy strains of "Oh, You Beautiful Doll" floated away from the ship. On the bow the gold letters spelling TITANIC vanished underwater.

An ashtray on the end table of B-76 slid to the deck and crashed into pieces. As Eva jolted and spun around, the fragments slid into a corner of the cabin.

"Mr. McFarland!" She shook his head. "Mr. . . . ."

The words faded in her throat as she stared across the cabin. Something under the bed caught her eye.

Long strands of black hair trailed from under the mattress fringe.

Eva's eyes narrowed in puzzlement as she crawled over the slanting deck. She bent down closer.

Eva Ryker raised the fringe and looked into the unwavering eyes of her mother.

Another rocket fired above the ship, flashing to its death.

Down in Boiler Room Number Four a trimmer worked frantically to avoid a boiler explosion. Drawing the fires, he felt a clammy chill through his socks. He glanced down at the water oozing up through the steel floorplates.

The last rocket arched over the *Titanic.* When the final sparks died, Lisa turned in frustration to the sight of red and green lights low on the distant horizon.

". . . it's a ship, all right," she heard a crewman mutter in the dark. "About ten miles out, I'd guess."

"Why doesn't it come?" A woman cried. "Why can't it see?"

No one could say.

The scream that tore through B-76 reverberated against the cabin walls and into the eardrums of John McFarland.

His eyes jumped open like a frightened animal's. With a low groan he sat up.

Eva squatted on the floor in front of the bed, with her back to him.

John McFarland's face darkened in concern as he stumbled toward her. "Eva, what in God's name . . ."

The words stopped when he drew near enough to see over her shoulder. On her lap rested the head of Clair Ryker.

Slowly Eva's gaze rose from her lap. "Where's my mommy, Mr. McFarland? Can you help me find her?"

He watched for long moments, probing for answers beneath the waxen mask of her face. Then he noticed the cuts covering her mouth and the bruises over her body.

"What did he do to you, Eva?"

She couldn't answer.

"I'm going for help." He rose to his feet, grimacing as he felt the lump at the back of his head. "Stay here."

McFarland strode across the cabin and reached for the door. The knob rattled but would not turn.

With a grunt of exasperation he reached for his coat pocket. His face grew pale as he searched for the key that wasn't there. Not until he finished the search did he notice the water seeping beneath the door.

Lisa Eddington's eyes were blank as she watched the sea wash over the *Titanic's* bow. Tiny waves shimmered around the cranes and the base of the mast.

In addition to sixteen regular lifeboats, the *Titanic* carried four collapsible boats. One of these, Collapsible Boat C, was being attached to the davits used by Boat Number One, and attracted a huge mob. Jason Eddington stood amid the crowd. The talk was ugly.

". . . we'll stay here and die . . ."

". . . I've got a wife in the boats . . ."

". . . if they had enough room . . ."

". . . we can't take this . . ."

The men roared forward like a lemming invasion. Jason slugged First Officer Murdoch in the kidneys and dropped into the boat.

Purser McElroy punched an attacker in the face, firing two pistol shots over his head.

"Get out of this!" Murdoch yelled, as the mob drew back from the boat. "Keep out of this!"

Two first-class passengers, Bjornstrom Steffanson and Hugh Woolner, shoveled through the men.

"We saw the flashes . . ."

". . . what in hell's going on . . ."

". . . those bastards in the boat . . ."

Jason lashed out at them, his fist thudding in Woolner's stomach. He grunted but kept on coming. With Steffanson, he grabbed Jason by an arm and leg and tossed him and another man out of the boat.

Rising to his feet and wiping blood off his mouth, Jason heared the distant blaring of the band.

"Won't you come home, Bill Bailey? . . . won't you come home? . . . She moans the whole night long"

The sea surged around the bed Eva stood on, splashing at the legs of the Victrola and the end table. Amazingly the table lamp still burned brightly.

"All right, Eva. Get out of the way." McFarland waded to the far end of the cabin, bracing himself on the bulkheads. He poised for action.

McFarland's shoulders hit the door with a faint thunk of wood. It refused to budge.

". . . *Remember that rainy evening, I threw you out . . .*" Band leader Wallace Hartley tapped his foot to the beat. ". . . *With nothing but a fine-toothed comb?*"

Jason Eddington stared over the port railing at Boat Number Four, level with the upper promenade. A man stacked deck chairs across the gap.

John Jacob Astor loaded his wife aboard, then faced Second Officer Lightoller. "Can I please join her? My wife's in delicate condition."

"No, sir. No men are allowed in these boats until the women are loaded first."

Jason mulled over the words as Astor walked away. He fretfully chewed on a thumbnail. Boat Number Four and Collapsible Boat D were the last two boats left.

Low red light suffused B-76 as power drained from the table lamp. The sea rose past Eva's waist as she stood on the bed. She gave no sign of noticing Clair Ryker's face and the graceful underwater motion of her black hair.

"Eva!" McFarland spit water by his chin. "Can you swim?"

"Yes . . . yes!"

"Come over here!"

In a frantic dog paddle she flapped across the cabin.

"Good! Good! Come on!"

The light flashed out with an evil-smelling hiss and Eva's scream filled the darkness.

"Stop it! You're all right! Over here!"

"I can't find you!"

"There! Take my hand! Now hang onto my shoulders!"

Guided by the faint strip of light shining underwater from the bottom of the door, McFarland tugged at the knob. It was coming! It was coming! He could feel it!

The doorknob came off in his hands.

Boat Number Four eased down into the ocean. The ship was so far gone that the lifeboat had a mere fifteen-foot drop to reach the water. The sea gushed through C Deck and into the first-class staterooms, swirling around the Chippendale chairs and swamping walnut and brass beds.

Jason watched from above and made up his mind.

"Hey!" A voice yelled behind him. "You can't do that!"

He ignored the shout and the footsteps pounding his way. Jason jumped over the railing, dropped twenty-five feet into the water by Boat Number Four, grabbed the edge, and pulled aboard.

Women meekly made room; they were past caring. At the bow a trimmer glared contemptuously, then bent over his oars.

"Everybody row! We've got to get away or the ship's suction will take us down!"

John McFarland shook his head, fighting the water rising

past his collarbone. His fingers fumbled at the exposed lock mechanism.

Eva started to slip off his shoulders.

"Come on! Hold tight!"

Her hands flexed around his neck as the door gave a faint crack. Arms straining, he tugged hard. Nothing.

Muscles rippling under the strain of the oars, Jason watched the huge dripping propellers at the stern slowly creep from the water.

"I can't make it!"

"You can Eva! Just hang on!"

McFarland's hands were bloody from jabbing at the door lock. In the blackness he searched his mind for the layout of the cabin.

"Now keep calm, Eva. And hang on."

He pushed away from the door and treaded water to the end table. His hands reached down and touched the milk glass rim of the table lamp. Breathing raggedly in the stuffy air trapped at the ceiling, he felt the heavy weight of the lamp's brass base.

McFarland paddled back to the door and rammed the base against the lock. The cabin seemed to flinch at the noise. Again. And again. The door cracked slightly.

Hand grasping hand, crewmen joined arms to form a circle around Collapsible Boat D. The last boat. Forty-seven seats. Sixteen hundred people. Second Officer Lightoller wasn't about to risk an ugly scene.

Women and children seeped through the barrier. Two babies were passed to safety by their father.

Deck lights began to cast a reddish glow, reflecting bright orange on the brass trumpets and trombones. The band followed Wallace Hartley's lead and broke into "Alexander's Ragtime Band."

Like surf breaking on shore, tiny waves washed up the slanting corridor of B Deck, foaming pink against the red carpeting. Glasses crashed in the distance.

"Help me! Mommy! Mommy! Help me!"

Eva choked on the water at her lips.

McFarland gritted his teeth and kept hammering the door. Wood splintered against his hand.

Crowds aft watched the little boat disappear in the night. They huddled inboard, away from the railing. Men struggled with Collapsibles A and B on the roof of the officers' quarters as water rushed toward them.

Lisa turned from her oar and watched the mob cluster toward the poop deck; scrambling army ants in the distance.

Albert and Martha Klein sat quietly on a bench near the aft funnel.

John McFarland had to breathe through his nose. "Sit on my shoulders!" he managed to sputter. "Breathe deep, Eva! In and out! That's the way!"

A huge jagged crack cut through the door.

"Need a light?"

The match flame flared yellow in the face of Bellboy Jock Croyn. His friend nodded, puffing on his cigarette. They grinned at each other. For the first time on the voyage no one bawled them out for smoking.

Blood slammed through McFarland's temples as he fought with the door.

Water must be to the ceiling, he thought. Hang on. Don't breathe. Don't no matter how much you want to. Just hope to God Eva can hold on . . .

The door gave way with a crackle, chunks floating past his face.

Faster! Faster! Ignore the purple spots before your eyes. That's right! Throw the lock out! Quick! Now push!

He grabbed Eva and swam through. The sea stung his eyes as he peered up at the reddish lights above the surface.

Kick! Drag Eva after you!

The quicksilver surface beckoned; then he broke through. McFarland's fingernails dug into the red carpet as he dragged himself from the water.

Eva lay still next to him. He bent over her. Christ, she was gone! No . . . she coughed, shaking her head. Slowly her eyes opened.

"Come on, Eva!" He slung her over his shoulder.

The sea tugged at his feet as McFarland struggled up the debris-strewn corridor. His shoes lost traction. He sank to his knees but managed to grab onto the doorknob of B-78. Knuckles popped as he dragged himself away from the water.

Spreading his legs, he clung onto a door frame. Then a wall lamp. Another doorknob.

A pullman case tumbled down the hall toward him. Hanging with both hands to the knob, he side-stepped the case as it plunged by, splashing into the rising sea.

On the Boat Deck Wallace Hartley rapped his violin. The band was silent for a moment, then softly began playing the Episcopal hymn "Autumn."

The sea surged over the bridge, washing away Officer Lightoller and a dozen others struggling to free Collapsibles A and B. The boats tumbled into the water along with the men.

Waves rushed up the Boat Deck as the bow gained momentum in its downward plunge. A woman kept ahead of the water until flying deck chairs toppled her overboard.

* * *

Hands grasping the bannister, McFarland tripped and stumbled up the staircase to A Deck. The sea boiled and foamed at his heels.

Sweaty palms slipped from the railing. Eva fell off his shoulders, screaming. She landed on her back and started rolling down the stairs.

"No, Eva! Grab the railing!"

Her hands lashed tight around the wood. Water cascaded at her feet as she stood and struggled. Together they made the first flight.

Chef John Collins braced his legs in an effort to keep footing on the wildly slanting Boat Deck. He scowled at the baby in his arms. His damn luck! Where was that woman from steerage?

The wave began its advance up the deck. Spinning to run, he slipped. Icy water surged over his head. Crying rose, then died as the baby was tossed out of his arms. A quick flash of a pink blanket in the white foam and it was gone.

McFarland and Eva thrashed up the last flight of the grand staircase and reached the Boat Deck. The Honor and Glory Clock in the A Deck foyer spilled and crashed behind them, the bronze nymphs smashing into great yellow chunks.

Eva ran around the still-playing orchestra and searched the deck. "We must find Mother. She'll know what to do."

"No!" McFarland snatched her off the deck. "I've got to get you to . . ."

His voice died as he saw the empty davits, those forward already sinking under the sea. He put Eva down, but she still struggled in his arms.

"Stop it!" Holding one wrist, he shrugged out of his life jacket. "Here, put this on! I'm a better swimmer than you."

Eva spotted the wave rising behind McFarland as he tightened the lacings. She tore away from his grasp.

He yelled after Eva, but she couldn't hear. Dodging the careening deck chairs, she searched the swirling faces around her. "Mommy! Mommy!"

Shrieking, shadowy figures roared around her as she ran astern toward the poop deck. Rosary beads glittered in the red light.

". . . Hail Mary, full of grace, the Lord is with thee . . ."

". . . Our Father, who art in heaven . . ."

Voices cried above the crash of breaking glass.

"God help me! God help me! I can't swim!"

"Get out of my way . . ."

". . . Ave Maria . . ."

". . . jump! Jump!"

Eva crawled between the crush of helpless bodies. Her fingers curled around a cable supporting the aftermast. Next to her an old man trembled on his knees, clutching a gold St. Christopher.

Jason sat and watched from Boat Number Four as the *Titanic* swung on its center of gravity for the final dive into the sea.

Eva clung to the cable, losing her footing. A little boy slid down the deck. People grabbed onto ventilators, cranes, railings—anything in the rusty glow of the lights.

"Autumn" halted amid a clattering heap of brass and woodwinds.

In Boat 13, Lisa saw the ship's lights blink off and on, as if tolling the end of an intermission, before vanishing for the last time. All was black aboard the *Titanic,* except for the last kerosene lamp burning on the aftermast.

Twenty-nine boilers moaned and twisted free from their moorings, crashing through the bulkheads. Everything within the ship somersaulted toward the bow, the noise rumbling in Eva's ears.

The cable cut into Eva's fingers as the deck slipped out from under her.

Swimmers already thrashing in the water groaned as the forward funnel snapped its cables and collapsed into the sea, sparks spraying over the deck. It hit the surface with an immense splash. Albert and Martha Klein each raised up an arm in reflex as they swam, before being pulped under tons of steel.

The *Titanic*'s triple screws gleamed under the stars as she stood totally erect with the water rising between her funnels.

Eva stared, mouth slack, at the frothing water four hundred feet below her dangling legs.

The old man with the St. Christopher lost his grip and tumbled past Eva. A flash of his screaming face; then he dwindled; a tiny speck hitting the water below.

"Let me go! Get away! There's only enough room . . ."

A war veteran fell, his hooked arm flailing through the air and catching on the steel superstructure arching sparks as he vanished in the sea.

Twenty feet below Eva an old woman swung from a ventilator port, tongue lolling blue from her mouth, strangled on her diamond necklace.

Hundreds of people writhed around the aftermast, those slipping off plummeting to the water.

The sea embraced them all. Up over the third funnel. Then the fourth.

Blood drooled down from Eva's wrists.

Over the davits. Spouting through the portholes.

A hundred feet below. Eighty feet. Seventy-five.

Past the fourth funnel. Seventy feet.

Eva's fingers slackened on the cable.

Men and women plunged, struggling into the wake.

Sixty. Fifty-five. Surging around the aftermast.

Eva's fingers slipped. Shouts spiraled around her as she tumbled over and over in a tight ball.

The sea hit, driving through her body like a million needles. Breaking surface, she snarled with the cold.

The *Titanic* dove past her, the poop deck railing gliding before her eyes. By instinct she grabbed it and felt herself being dragged below, following the ship.

No! No! A voice in her skull yelled. Let go! Let go! Her hands were free but still she was dragged down. Life belt straps were snagged around the railing.

Eva struggled, air bubbling from her mouth. Sinking in

the cold. Her hands grasped the belts, throwing off the jacket.

She kicked to the surface. Huge pieces of cork mat and deck chairs floated in the way. An unseen arm hit her face. Her teeth clenched tight. Lungs aching, dying. Water seeped into her mouth.

Eva broke the surface with fifteen hundred men, women, and children crying in agony under a gray shroud of fog. The noise roared across the water.

"Save one life! Save one life!"

"Help me! Somebody help me!"

Eva flapped past a baby floating face down.

A Japanese man swept past, tied at the waist to a door.

Hands grappled around her, a voice panting in her ear. She glimpsed panic-bulging eyes as she kicked him away.

A low black shape loomed ahead, shadowy figures scuffling on top. Eva's hand reached out and grasped the edge of the overturned Collapsible B. Men crouched in an effort to balance the hull.

"Help me!" she cried. "Help me!"

No one heard her amid the clamor of voices. The boat sunk lower in the water with each new arrival.

"Lean to port; we're losing balance!"

Eva knew the voice. "Mr. McFarland! Mr. McFarland!"

No one answered. The boat floated away in the night.

Eva half-swam, half-drifted, unaware she was even moving. Cries faded away and bodies littered the sea. The white jacket of a steward. A young French girl from steerage. An old man in a tuxedo. The war veteran, his hooked arm spread across the water.

Still she swam, arms moving by rote, no longer under the control of their owner.

Her hand hit wood planking with a hollow knock. Eva turned dazedly, aware of something blocking her path, but too far gone to respond. Her arms battered feebly at the side of the boat.

"Over here!" a man yelled, as footsteps pounded to her. Hands grabbed her arms and dragged her aboard Number Four.

"Who is it?"

"A little girl. Half dead. Anyone got a blanket?"

Eva felt cloth wrapping around her. Lamp trimmer Samuel Hemming called out to the stern.

"Is there some room back there? The girl's got to lie down."

Women chattered and dresses rustled. "It's all right. We've made some room."

Eva vaguely felt herself being passed from Hemming to another man.

"Put her over there. By the women."

Looking up, she saw the man's head silhouetted by the stars.

"She looks pretty bad," Jason Eddington said. "I don't think she's going to make it."

Eva screamed and screamed as the stars whirled around her, flinging away like water drops from a spinning wheel as she fell through a blackness that had no end.

29

The eighteen lifeboats drifted across a five-mile area of the black sea. Most were alone, wandering aimlessly, their grief-stricken passengers listening to the dying cries of hundreds of swimmers freezing to death in the dark. Very few boats went back to pick up the helpless. Many erroneously feared a suction in the *Titanic's* wake, which would drag them under if they returned to the scene. Others, more rightly, had visions of being swamped by panicky swimmers fighting to get aboard. So they sat and listened and wrestled unsuccessfully with their consciences.

There were some exceptions. Boat Number Four was moored with Ten, Twelve, Fourteen, and Collapsible D in a rescue attempt under the leadership of Fifth Officer Lowe.

"Consider yourself under my command!" he barked, standing at the bow of Boat Number Fourteen. "We're going to go back and pick up any survivors we can find. I'll need some men to volunteer."

Scattered figures rose from the boats.

The fifty-five passengers in Number Fourteen stood uneasily, tottering and jumping one at a time to the other boats.

Mumbled words and the low clunking of oars drifted into the ears of Eva Ryker as Boat Fourteen cast off on its errand of mercy. Sitting in the lap of a woman, unseen in the darkness, she didn't move. Her face was upturned to the bright dispassionate stars overhead.

The boats floated on through the night as the passengers scanned the horizon.

"Be on watch for two lights," said Trimmer Hemmings in Boat Number Four, "one just below the other. That'll be the mast lights of a ship."

Everyone intently watched the sharp line between sea and sky.

"Over there!" Jason Eddington pointed southeast.

Hemmings turned and examined the sparkling light. It slowly drew above the water, but no second light appeared beneath.

"A star," he said dully.

Through the still air the cold bit into Eva's marrow. She clutched the blanket and bit the corner to keep her teeth from chattering. Her hair crackled with every move, the strands frozen stiff.

"Keep a lookout for icebergs," Quartermaster Perkis was saying.

Icebergs . . . icebergs . . . icebergs . . . icebergs . . .

His voice waned into blackness as Eva slumped against the woman's breasts.

She awoke with a jolt. Breathing heavily, Eva stared at the gray-black shadows surrounding her.

"Ssh . . . ssh," the woman whispered, tightening her embrace. "Be still. It's all right."

A fuzzy patch of light glowed on the horizon. Mrs. Astor pointed. "The sunrise. It's morning."

The light grew, then faded, only to flare again.

"No." Hemming's voice was cold. "It's the Northern Lights."

Eva watched the glow fan across the northern sky, faint streamers stretching toward the Pole Star.

The night wore on as the passengers huddled together to escape the cold. Far in the distance Fourth Officer Boxhall fired flares. Green sparks reflected in long streaks across the water.

Ghostly white shapes of other boats materialized, only to be lost again. Boats Four, Ten, Twelve, and "D" were still strung together like trinkets on a bracelet. The last wild cries in the night faded like the buzz of a dying fly. Officer Lowe and Boat Number Fourteen had been swallowed in the darkness.

A crewman lay in the bottom of Boat Four, looking up pleadingly at Mrs. John Thayer, the woman holding Eva. "One of you ladies wouldn't happen to have a little drink handy, would you?"

No one replied. Eva smelled a strong brandy breath.

The air grew colder and everyone on board hugged themselves against a rising breeze. Timbers creaked as they wobbled on a newly choppy sea.

A light flashed in the southeast, followed by a distant explosion. Eva shuddered and clung to Mrs. Thayer.

A pinpoint peeked over the rim of the water. Then one below it. Jason snapped to attention, eyes trained on the distance.

Lights rose row upon row over the edge of the world. Firing rockets, the big steamer throbbed toward the boats. Cheers and cries of relief echoed among the boats as the ship hove to, three miles away, revealing deck after deck of lighted portholes.

A band of gunmetal gray shimmered to the east and a soft golden glow spread in all directions. Thin clouds stretched along the horizon, growing pink as Eva watched them.

The stars faded as if their power supply was failing, leaving Venus gleaming low near a pallid new moon.

Gold and pink rays shone across the bright blue sea and revealed an incredible scene. Throughout the night the survivors imagined themselves floating in limbo. But the lights now sparkled off a vast field of surrounding icebergs ranging from icy handfuls to two hundred-foot mountains looming over the boats.

Five miles away solid field ice stretched to the north and west horizons. The ice gleamed in the sunlight—white and pink where the beams caught an outcropping; purple and blue in the shadows.

The *Titanic's* eighteen lifeboats were little dwarfed specks among the bergs as they rowed toward the steamer. Lisa Eddington watched the rescuing ship come into view as Boat Thirteen steered around an icy mountain.

A crewman pointed at the bands on the ship's single funnel. "It's a Cunarder."

Lisa could already see other boats reaching the liner's gangway.

Four miles away men balanced precariously atop Collapsible B, rolling in the roughening surf. It sank lower with every wave.

"Ship ahoy! Ship ahoy!" the men on the overturned collapsible yelled, but no one responded.

Feet spread catlike on top of the hull, Second Officer Lightoller dragged his whistle from his pocket. The sharp piping blew across the water, turning the heads of crewmen in Boats Four and Twelve.

Trimmer Hemming wheeled around at the noise, then jabbed the shoulder of the Quartermaster, who jumped to the bow and pulled off the mooring ropes.

The two boats drifted from the others, oars splashing in the water. His back bent from rowing, Jason Eddington squinted at the twenty little figures standing in the middle of the sea.

They were on a cake of ice . . . no, it was some sort of wreckage, a lifeboat. Didn't look like they were doing too well . . .

As the boat closed the distance he could make out faces. Lightoller was easy to spot . . . Jack Thayer . . .

His face tightened as he saw John McFarland near the stern of Collapsible B. Jason watched him shivering in the cold as the boats drew close, nearly tossing the men overboard in their wake.

The collapsible wallowed as each man flopped into one of the rescuing boats. Jason stared down at the floorboards, hoping to look inconspicuous. Eva watched the men scramble next to her, shadowy figures flashing before her eyes.

Jack Thayer fell into Boat Twelve, not noticing his mother eight feet away in Number Four, as McFarland jumped and landed next to him.

Lightoller was the final man off the collapsible, dragging a corpse with him onto Boat Twelve. He grabbed the tiller as the boat drew away, rowing toward the still distant ship.

As Boats Four and Twelve parted, McFarland spotted a familiar face.

"Eva!" he yelled across the water.

She didn't answer. She merely shook in Mrs. Thayer's arms.

Scanning the passengers in Boat Four, McFarland's face went slack.

"Eddington! Eddington, you bastard!"

Jason met his eyes, the distance growing between them.

"Grab that man!" McFarland pointed. "He's . . ."

"Sit down!" Lightoller yelled, pulling him off his feet.

"You don't understand. That man . . ."

"McFarland, any quarrel you have can wait."

No further words were spoken as the white boats drew apart.

At about eight-fifteen A.M. Boat Number Four nestled alongside the gangway of the Cunard liner. Jason looked up the side of the ship at the letters on her bow: CARPATHIA.

A long line of people leaned over the Boat Deck railing. He spotted Lisa in the crowd. They didn't smile. Or wave. They warily appraised each other as the *Carpathia's* crewmen lowered a rope ladder.

Hands reached out to Eva from the descending ropes. Voices swirled around her.

"Grab her there . . . careful . . ."

" . . . she looks dead to me . . ."

" . . . almost . . . get her to the doctor . . . here, get her arm . . . that's it . . . "

The sky and ship flipped end over end.

"Watch it! Don't let her fall . . . "

" . . . I'm trying . . . "

A strong hand grabbed her waist. A rough wool shirt bristled her face. Puffing lungs mixed with the tang of sweat. Feet clomped the deck.

"Here. Get her to Dr. McGhee. Quick."

Passed from hand to hand. Sky, rigging, and faces reeled about her; then wood, electric lamps, stewards, and cool hands.

"Easy. Keep her head up."

Smooth white table linen brushed Eva's cheek. A walnut-creased face peered from above, lifting her eyebrow.

"Get her clothes off and into something dry. And get some bandages."

The *Carpathia* turned and steamed a snaky course between the bergs, smoke from its funnel trailing a black strand across the sky.

Churning away, its wake fanned over the sea. Aqua bubbles and pale gold foam bubbled under the rising sun. In orderly waves the wake spread, splashing feebly among the ice, jostling the chair cushions, the abandoned lifeboats, and the hundreds of corpses. The famous and unknown drifted together, buoyed by life jackets.

Two weeks later the *MacKay-Bennett* would come from Halifax and recover some two hundred of the bodies. Those left behind scattered over the Atlantic in the next weeks and months.

Flesh rotted under the sun and the skeletons still floated until their water-logged, sun-bleached life jackets at last gave way and the bones plummeted miles to the ocean floor.

In the decades to follow, ships' captains would still avoid the region as a place of half-seen ghosts and uneasy folklore.

It would be another fifty years before men sought out the *Ti-tanic*'s grave.

The news traveled fast. The ether crackled between the Atlantic ships—*Frankford, Olympic, Mt. Temple, Virginian, Burma*—relaying the impossible news toward the shore.

Telegraphs and phone lines buzzed across the country, and the news was forged into hot lead for the presses.

Clamoring headlines hit the stands. New York *Times*. Chicago *Tribune*. Los Angeles *Times*. Pittsburgh *Post-Gazette*.

William Alfred Ryker sat behind the desk in his Pittsburgh hotel suite, staring out the window at the smoke smudging the city skyline.

A yellow Marconigram lay under his outstretched hands on the desk top. Next to it was a lockable volume, much like a diary, opened to a page which contained a cipher key. The key rendered sense from the jumbled letters on the Marconigram.

WE HAVE YOUR DAUGHTER STOP IF YOU WANT HER ALIVE BE AT SINGER BUILDING LOBBY NOON AFTER TITANIC DOCKS NEW YORK WITH LATEST SHIPMENT STOP NO TRICKS STOP

Ryker didn't speak. Or move.

The doors flung open and Richards, his manservant, bolted into the room, fighting for any remnants of aplomb.

"I . . . I'm very sorry, sir. I had to see you . . . I mean to tell you . . . "

He held out a copy of the Pittsburgh paper.

Ryker frowned at the shadow cast over the enciphered message on his desk. Looking up, he saw the front page in Richards' outstretched hands. Ryker took it and studied the headlines.

Neither man said a word. Ryker let the paper fall on his desk. He looked up at the butler.

Ryker giggled. Helplessly. Peeling laughter over and over

as he slumped on the desk, oblivious to Richards' astonishment.

"Are you all right, sir?"

Guffaws shook him as if stricken. Rolling on the floor, he held his sides.

"May I please be excused, sir?" His face grew red around the collar.

Whooping laughter ran on and on as if Ryker was gagging. He waved a hand in dismissal.

Richards turned on his heel, took his coat from the closet, went down the hall, rang for the elevator, rode down to the lobby, and left the hotel, searching for the nearest bar.

Jason Eddington leaned against a davit strut and watched the field ice gliding past, a mere two hundred yards away as the *Carpathia* steamed southwest for New York. His lips were pressed tight to keep his teeth from chattering as the wind blew his hair. He was alone. No one else would brave the cold without a reason.

But Jason had a reason. The deck on which he stood led to the wheelhouse and the captain's quarters.

A tiny figure appeared at the opposite end of the deck, marching toward him. It grew in the corner of Jason's eye. Turning, he stood in the figure's path.

The man halted at the sight of Jason, then pushed on. As he drew near, John McFarland's face was murderous. And a little frightened.

"Get out of my way, Eddington!"

He smiled lazily. "Where're you going, John?"

The steward didn't answer. He brunted past.

Whiplike, Jason grabbed his arms and pinned them both behind his back, forcing McFarland hard up against the rail.

"You don't have to tell me," he whispered in his ear. "I already know. You're going to tell the captain all about me." He pulled harder on the arms and McFarland's joints creaked.

The steward gritted his teeth but said nothing.

"I wouldn't try it, John." Jason's grin flashed white. "A push over the railing. That's all it'd take."

"You can't do a damn thing to me," McFarland spat. "The last thing you can afford is another murder on your hands."

"Very clever, John. You're a regular detective."

"Then let me go."

"Oh, I can't do that. Not until you listen to me. You're not going to tell anyone what you saw on the *Titanic*." His grip tightened. "Because it's your word against Lisa's and mine. And both my wife and I lie beautifully. You'll have no back-up witnesses. No evidence. Least of all Eva. I talked with Dr. McGhee. The kid can't even speak. All you'll have is your word and a police investigation that'll end in a smear on your work record for slandering a passenger."

The courage drained from McFarland's face.

Jason released him, smiling as McFarland straightened his clothes. "I'm glad you have some common sense. It's such a rare commodity these days. Now get the hell out of my sight."

"How did it go?"

Standing on the poop deck with his wife, Jason glanced away from the *Carpathia's* wake, dribbling along the edge of the ice that stretched whitely to the horizon.

"McFarland shut up quickly enough," he said. "He won't be making any more trouble."

Lisa Eddington turned her collar up against the wind. "That's the least of our worries right now."

"I know."

"Ryker will have men waiting at the dock in New York."

Jason eyed the *Carpathia's* superstructure. "Maybe not."

"What do you mean?"

He tapped her shoulder and pointed. Lisa followed his finger up two decks, where Second Officer Bisset was leaning over two women in shawls, a clipboard cradled in his arm.

"So?"

"He's compiling the survivors list. They'll wire it to New York."

Lisa still looked baffled.

"Ryker will only be after us if he thinks we're alive."

Second Officer Bisset swore under his breath as he fought with the clipboard sheets whipping in the wind. Thank God this was almost over!

Bisset leaned over the railing. There was a couple on the poop. God knows what they were doing out in this cold. Impossible to see who they were. Ah well, he'd better check it out!

The couple smiled at his approach.

"Sorry to intrude," Bisset said, "but I'm compiling the survivors list. You are from the *Titanic*, aren't you?"

Lisa nodded happily, both arms around her husband's waist. "Boats Four and Thirteen."

Bisset warmed to her infectious smile. "You're very lucky. I've talked with a lot of widows this morning."

"We're just thankful to be alive," Jason said.

The second officer held his clipboard, pen point poised over paper. "Your names, sir?"

Jason tightened the embrace on his wife. "Mr. and Mrs. Albert and Martha Klein."

Sobbing women and frenzied men thronged the front of the White Star Line's New York office on Broadway, ringed by a human chain of police reserves, blocking the path of William Ryker's black Packard limousine.

Not waiting for the car to stop, Ryker jumped from the back, running past newsboys hawking the April sixteenth paper. Their cries reaffirmed the huge black headlines.

He had no luck shoveling past the mob until someone recognized him.

"It's Ryker." The words whispered from lip to lip. "Ryker . . . Ryker . . . Ryker . . . "

The crowd slightly parted, making a path to the front door.

About to pass through, he was pushed aside by a school of

reporters, all trailing long pieces of paper as they scattered in all directions.

The White Star Vice-President, Phillip Franklin, still stood in the foyer. The door to his office stood open to reveal total chaos. Telephones yammered throughout the building.

"Mr. . . . Mr. . . . Ryker." Franklin looked near collapse from exhaustion. "I had no idea . . . "

"What were those men carrying?"

Franklin dazedly brushed hair from his eyes. "It just came in. Relayed from the *Olympic*." He picked up a page from the reception desk. "It's the survivors . . . "

Ryker tore it from his hands. All he saw were the names, in neat rows:

Rheims
Robert
Rolmane
Rosenbaum
Rothes
Rothschild
Ryerson
Ryerson
Ryerson
Ryerson

The entry leaped at him. "Ryker, Eva (child)."

Even as he spotted the name, Ryker noticed an absence. No Mrs. William A. Ryker. She wasn't there. Swallowing hard, his eyes flashed up the list. Hawksford . . . Hays . . . No Herrick.

He smiled savagely. "The bastards are dead."

"I beg your pardon, sir?"

Ryker paid no attention as he spun and slammed the door behind him.

On Thursday night, April eighteenth, Albert and Martha Klein braved the night air of the *Carpathia*'s deck, watching the Statue of Liberty's torch cut through the night.

Ten thousand people watched the ship's approach from the Battery. Tugboats surrounded her, each weighed down with reporters yelling questions at Captain Rostron and the crew through megaphones.

The ship remained silent to the reporters as it turned up the North River to Cunard Pier 54, where thirty thousand milled under umbrellas in the pouring rain. Police cordons struggled with the mob. Hoofs clomped on rain-slicked cobblestones as mounted policemen rode down scattered men and women scrambling to get closer to the pier.

Outlined against a red sign flashing on the Jersey shore, the *Carpathia* crept to the dock. The umbrellas jiggled in excitement at her approach.

Finally visible under the spotlights, the ship bumped against the pier and every photographer triggered his flashlamp. The gangways were eased across under the magnesium glare.

One by one the survivors filed off the ship. Seventy widows. Henry Sleeper Harper and his dog, Sun Yatsen. Irish farmers and Turkish peasants.

William Ryker watched each face as he stood at the foot of the gangway with his personal physician.

He then spotted his daughter on top of the ramp. Carried by Dr. McGhee, Eva blinked fearfully at the magnesium flares and the searchlights and the roaring voices around her.

McGhee gave her to Ryker. His tears and kisses were ignored. Eva's face remained blank.

"I've got to get her out of this rain!"

"Go on!" McGhee nodded, yelling above the crowd. "I want to have a word with your doctor."

With Eva in his arms, Ryker ran back to the Packard.

McGhee unfurled his umbrella, then held out his hand. "Pleased to meet you, Doctor . . . "

" . . . Stevens."

" . . . I need to give you some facts about your patient."

"Yes?"

"From what I can determine, Eva's not physically ill. Run down from exposure, of course. And she has some nasty abrasions and contusions which I've tried to deal with. But it's her state of mind I'm worried about."

Dr. Stevens nodded. "She looks very frightened."

"Frightened! During the past four days she hasn't said a word! Not one word. I don't understand it." McGhee glumly rubbed his five-o'clock shadow. "Or maybe I do and don't want to."

Under his dripping umbrella, Stevens scowled. "What do you mean?"

"I've given Eva a rather thorough examination. She's no longer . . . intact."

"I . . . I don't follow."

"Goddamit, man," McGhee snapped. "Don't give me that! Of course you 'follow'!"

"Such an occurence isn't unusual, considering the strenuous experience . . . "

"Trust me to know some simple anatomy, Dr. Stevens." His voice lowered to an indignant whisper. "I'm familiar with the clinical details of . . . cases like this. What I *don't* know is the emotional stability of her father. You'll have to decide when—and if—he should be told."

Dr. Stevens looked uneasily over his shoulder. Ryker stood one leg on the Packard's running board. The car's exhaust smoked impatiently.

He listened for a long moment to the rain drumming over his head, then turned back to McGhee.

"Thank you for your advice, Doctor." Stevens formally pumped his hand. "I'll have to think it over."

With a final parting nod, he headed back to Ryker's car.

Albert and Martha Klein stood at the head of the *Carpathia*'s gangway and watched the red tail lights of the Packard vanish in the rain. Walking arm in arm, they sidled through the crowd.

Up on the Boat Deck John McFarland studied them until the blond heads were lost in the field of shiny black umbrellas.

Ten days later, in St. Petersburg, Florida, Mima Heinley

eased open the screen door of her apartment off Central Avenue. "Yes? Could I help you?"

The Kleins stood together and smiled diffidently. Albert spoke up. "The apartment next door's for rent, I hear. Folks downstairs said you have a key."

"Sure do! Be right with you." Mima scurried into the bathroom and fished the key from Fred's pants.

"What now?" He grunted from the tub.

"A young couple to see the apartment."

Fred splashed soap off his handsome black mustache. "More trash, I suppose."

"Oh, hush up!" She playfully slapped his muscular shoulders. "Fact is, they look real nice. The clean bright type this neighborhood needs."

As Fred dried himself and yanked on his pants, he heard Mima's high, thrilled voice in the living room. "Oh, I just know you're going to settle right in and make yourselves a fine home!"

30

". . . unfortunately, the exact method of escape off the *Ti-tanic* used by Jason and Lisa is lost in the past."

I walked across the den and opened the window, breathing the cool afternoon air. Lurking mental cobwebs blew away.

"We know from Eva's tape that Jason Eddington wound up in Boat Number Four, one of the last to leave the ship. Lisa made her exit earlier in the evening, although it's impossible to pinpoint the exact boat. Both of them were very good at covering their tracks."

Sitting behind my desk, I drained the last of my whiskey glass. I held it up to the window light. Water beads dripped coolly between my fingers.

"So, after the rescue by the *Carpathia,* we had another metamorphosis. From Steven and Julie Herrick to Jason and Lisa Eddington to Albert and Martha Klein. One can't help being struck by their audacity." I cocked an eyebrow at Ryker. "They knew their only chance of escaping your vengeance was to lose themselves among the anonymous ranks of the seven hundred five *Titanic* survivors. Of course, from the beginning, their identities as the newlywed Eddingtons had been a cooked-up façade to serve their purposes aboard ship. But it took a very peculiar sense of irony to adopt the names of Albert and Martha Klein.

"I suppose the ruse had its own crazy logic. The Kleins were certainly easily verifiable as not being among the rescued aboard the *Carpathia*. All Jason and Lisa had to do was give the new names to Second Officer Bisset, who was compiling the survivors list. I imagine they took the elementary precaution of telling Bisset their new names out of earshot of any fellow passengers from the *Titanic*. Paper work and passports were a total mess after the disaster, of course." I shrugged. "All in all, Jason and Lisa—or should I call them 'Albert' and 'Martha'?—must have found it very easy to shuck off their previous guises.

"One thing puzzles me," I said to the Old Man. "You knew something about their past. Why were you so ready to accept their deaths? Simply because the names 'Steven and Julie Herrick' weren't on the survivors list?"

He massaged the swollen knuckles on one hand. "You're so frightfully sure of yourself, Mr. Hall. At the time . . . no one was thinking very clearly during those dreadful days."

"I can understand that. But there's another mystery surrounding Al and Martha's escape. What became of John McFarland after his brave confrontation with Jason out in mid-Atlantic?

"It's fair to state, I think, that McFarland lost his courage. Probably not through threats of physical violence. He was working closely with the crew aboard the *Carpathia* and would be quickly missed if he fell victim to Albert and Martha. But I'm sure they quickly told him the score. Their word against his and all. McFarland struck me as a man who'd bow a little too quickly to the inevitable.

"In any event, Albert and Martha Klein nimbly dodged all obstacles and vanished once again when the *Carpathia* reached New York. Ten days later they quietly surfaced in St. Petersburg, Florida, as the new neighbors of Fred and Mima Heinley. They remained good neighbors for the next twenty-nine years.

"The records I've found on the Kleins over that period are rather sketchy. They applied for a business license to open a produce store on May 9, 1912. The new Albert and Martha certainly weren't strapped for cash. When they left London on the *Titanic,* they must've brought along quite a nest egg.

"But the Kleins resisted all pressures to expand their little business. Fred Heinley told me of Albert's determination to keep it 'in the family.' By running a nice clean business and refusing to grow, they kept a very low profile."

Mike Rogers leaned forward. "What exactly are you driving at?"

"Come now." I impatiently stood, then leaned on the edge of the desk. "Use your head. Better yet, ask your client."

Mike turned in appeal to Ryker. The Old Man at first didn't seem to hear. His eyes were mannequin-blank. But the lips slowly moved.

"In those first days after Eva came back to me, I wasn't thinking too clearly. She was home and their names didn't appear on any survivors list. That was enough. But then Stevens told me what they'd done to my daughter, and I prayed they'd be alive." He painfully swallowed. "Every night I got down on my knees and pleaded to God to make them be alive, so I could personally find them and tear out their living guts . . ."

"Mr. Ryker!" Mike warned. "For Christ's sake . . ."

"That very week I was rewarded." He cocked a brow my way. "It's damn odd, Hall. I've never had another prayer answered before or since."

"Things even out in the end. You answered John McFarland's prayers by making him a rather wealthy man."

Ryker showed no surprise at my good guess. "Son, the money was nothing compared with the news McFarland brought me."

"Your generosity enabled him to take rather large chunks of retirement in between both world wars."

"McFarland wasn't a greedy man." Ryker's eyes were trained elsewhere and elsewhen. "He came to my house in Newport. Important information, he insisted, which he had to tell me personally . . ."

* * *

John McFarland and William Ryker sat sipping Irish coffee at a white-painted wrought iron table on the sun terrace of the white rococo Ryker summer cottage. They looked upon bright clipped grass sloping down toward Narragansett Bay. Out on the lawn a black housemaid guided Eva on a spring stroll.

Ryker kept both flint-eyes on his daughter as McFarland talked and talked, spinning his horror tale. Eva clung tight to the maid's hand. Her back was turned and each foot plodded mechanically in turn. Left, right, left.

Ryker closed his eyes, then realized McFarland had stopped. "And you saw both of them leave the *Carpathia*?"

"Yes, sir."

"Any idea which way they went?"

"No. There were thousands of people, you remember. And the rain . . ."

". . . yes, I know." Ryker watched the front yard for a long moment, then bolted upright. "Carrie! That's quite enough for today. You can take her in."

McFarland smiled awkwardly as Ryker settled back down. "How is Eva doing, sir?"

"She's . . . on the mend." He followed Eva's halting progress inside and out of sight. "Well, Mr. McFarland, you're a brave and resourceful man."

"Mainly I was scared, Mr. Ryker. Sometimes sheer fright can keep you going."

"I was speaking in a larger sense." He fingered the china cup on the glass tabletop. "It's most fortunate that Dr. Stevens already told me of Eva's condition. I've had several days to absorb the shock, as it were. If you had come and told your story cold . . ." Ryker raised his eyes. "Did you know in ancient times, if a king received disastrous news, he would order the messenger of evil tidings beheaded?"

McFarland smiled uncomfortably. Really?"

"Oh yes. Mercifully we live in a civilized world. I'm deeply grateful that you confided in me." He pulled his checkbook from an inner coat pocket. "If not for you, Eva wouldn't be alive today."

McFarland watched Ryker's scribbling pen, then blinked at the check for ten thousand dollars.

"Really, Mr. Ryker, I had . . ."

". . . of course not. But I feel obliged to offer it. And I'd be honored if you'd accept."

The steward stammered his thanks, folding the check in his wallet. Ryker stood and shook his hand.

"If there's ever anything else, you let me know."

". . . and he did." The Old Man chortled. "In 1920, '26, '35, and '49. Hell, the money didn't matter. Didn't add up more than fifty, seventy-five thousand over the years. It was the dues I paid to have my daughter alive, pure and simple."

"Yes, I know. The complicated part was figuring how you made use of McFarland's knowledge that Albert and Martha Klein were alive." I picked up a second Identikit sketch and showed it to Ryker. "How about this man? Do you recognize him?"

"Yes, I think so," he drawled carefully. "A crewman aboard the *Savonarola,* isn't he?"

"That and much more." I passed the drawing to Tom. "As Inspector Bramel can tell you, his name is Alfredo Petacchi and he's a suspected enforcer who's been seen with organized crime figures on both sides of the Atlantic during the past twenty-five years."

"Norman," Mike blustered, "I'm sure my client . . ."

"It's late in the day," I said to Ryker. "Can't we cut through the crap?"

The weathered hands wearily gripped the bars of his wheelchair. "He wasn't aboard the *Savonarola* by my choice," he finally said. "Petacchi serves as a representative of . . . interested investors."

"The Scalisi Family?"

He nodded.

"Among others, I suppose."

"I never asked." A hint of a smile. "You learn not to after a while."

"And I suppose you closed your eyes when Petacchi decided to sabotage our helicopter."

"No!" His forehead clotted red. "I know nothing about that! For all you or anyone knows, it could've been a dreadful accident."

"One man knows," Tom snapped. "Is Petacchi still aboard your ship?"

"I couldn't say for sure. He comes and goes." Ryker turned to Mike. "Rogers, have you checked?"

"Not lately." He examined an imaginary grease spot on his tie. "There are a lot of people on the *Savonarola*."

"And the facts just slip through your mind like a sieve. Right, counselor?" More scribbling on Tom's note pad. "We'll send out a bulletin, Norman. See if we can turn him up."

Eva leaned forward and placed a hand on Ryker's arm. "Father, how could you get involved with a man like that?"

He wiped his eyes. "I did it for you, darling."

"I don't understand."

"When McFarland told me both of them were still alive, I hired the best detectives in the country. Name your price, I said, but find them."

He laughed bitterly. "But for once, my money didn't help. A year went by. Two. Five. Nothing." His fists tightened. "You have no idea how . . . impotent I felt. The bastards bled me white with nothing in return.

"But the search made a big splash. In 1933 a representative from the Scalisi Family came to see me. I never learned his name. The family had heard of my problem. They had 'contacts' not open to me which might prove helpful." He snorted at the memory. "Those were the little man's exact words. 'Contacts.' An open invitation to join the sewer rats of this world. I said, 'How much?'

"A fateful question as it turned out. I paid dearly, but more empty years passed. You went to Switzerland, Eva, for treatments with Fräulein Slote and I followed you abroad in '38. I turned my back on the whole stinking country." He braced both skinny arms on the wheelchair. "And then this."

He looked up at me. "You're right, Hall, about things evening out in the end. Six months later, as I lay in that iron lung, I got a call. A young punk named Alfredo Petacchi—cheap strong-arm stuff working the rackets for the Scalisi Family in Miami and St. Pete—had found them in their produce store. Prosperous little shopkeeping bastards. Petacchi and his friends were keeping a close eye on them."

"At least *that* much of Martha Klein's story was true," I said.

"The voice on the phone asked me what I wanted next. If I liked, a 'final deal' could be arranged immediately."

"Father, no." Her head shook. "Please, no."

"Mr. Ryker, as your attorney . . ."

"Shut up, Rogers." The afternoon sun lit up the crevices in his face. "I'm an old man. My doctor tells me I'll be dead in a year. Why should I care who knows? What are you going to do? Throw me in jail? Unplug my iron lung? I paid Petacchi's price. He was most anxious to please me and his family bosses. Unfortunately, he was sloppy. The Kleins got wind and took off. But he followed them to Hawaii. They were fat and careless with middle age. He got the man first. Then the woman. And it was finished."

Ryker's chin rested on his chest. No one spoke. I looked down at my hands and watched them tremble.

"You old bastard." I grabbed his arm, forcing him to look at me. "You've always known, haven't you? That I found both of them."

The gray eyes were unwavering. "Son, you're a bit slow on the uptake. Of course I knew. Why do you think I had Geoffrey Proctor hire you?"

Jan must have seen something very ugly in my face for she stood and drew us apart.

Proctor spoke up. "Norman, I want you to know . . ."

"Later, Geoffrey. Much later." My voice wavered as I perched on the edge of the desk. "This whole damn story has been some sort of joke to you, hasn't it? See Norman Run! Like a squirrel on his treadmill, going nowhere fast."

Ryker pursed his lips. "Maybe in the beginning. I've been following your career for a long time, son. Not many people could emerge from disgrace and pick up the pieces like you did after the war." His head drooped at a melancholy angle. "And, I must confess, I've always felt some sense of responsibility for your unpleasant experience in Honolulu."

"My God! Was all this supposed to be my *reward*?"

"No! Oh, no, no," he yammered. "You don't understand! It was never supposed to happen this way. You were to write about the *Titanic*, nothing else. That and the salvage project. The story was going to be the perfect publicity for the diamonds, when they were discovered." Greed slow-boiled to the surface. "Five million dollars on the market; that's what they were worth even in 1912. And now? How much would people pay to own jewels snatched from the depths of the *Titanic*? That's all it was—a simple business venture. How'd I know you'd go charging off in all directions, tracking down the Kleins? You weren't even supposed to know they'd ever been on the *Titanic*!"

I felt the pulse pounding through my throat, but I tried to keep calm. "Ryker, you were a little too subtle for your own good. She told me, you see. Martha Klein told me in Honolulu. Why, I'm not sure. But I've always known."

Ryker seemed to shrivel within his skin. I'd seen that look before; in fact, I'd shared it myself. When the best laid plans go very wrong very fast.

"Have you found the diamonds?" I asked.

His head shook. "Originally, they were shipped as patent medicine pills. They're still down there. Waiting with unlimited patience. Unfortunately, time is taking the ball away from all of us. Especially me."

"Father," Eva said, "how long have you known?"

"A couple of months. It's a relief, really. An end to all the playacting." He met my eyes. "You may not believe it, Hall, but I don't enjoy hatchet work."

"Such as Harold Masterson?"

"Among others."

"I understand your concern. If the film had been released to the press, the shiny faces of Albert and Martha Klein would've appeared on every TV screen in the Western world, along with Eva and Clair."

"How in the hell do you know about that?"

"Masterson gave me a copy. Your daughter's seen it, too."
I pointed at my filing cabinet. "I can run it if you like."

"God, no." He coughed. "Do you think it matters now? I've
spent fifty years trying to squash the memory of those two.
That's why I never begrudged Petacchi, even though he was
a millstone around my neck. I've always appreciated services
efficiently rendered." He snorted in contempt at Tom. "So
now you can pick him up and be a big hero. Not that I give a
damn."

Eva examined her father's face. "Is revenge all you ever
lived for?"

"You of all people ask me that?"

"Am I supposed to be grateful? 'My Father the Murderer!'"

"What did you expect me to do? Do you have any idea how
you looked when I brought you from the *Carpathia*? I can
still remember Dr. Stevens—oh, how circumspect he was—
breaking it gently. But how delicately can you phrase the
news that your ten-year-old daughter's been in a gang shag-
ging?"

His shouts tore at the room. "Do you know how I felt for
fifty years? Taking you to endless specialists. You didn't say
one word for two years. Two years, Eva! Paying off quacks
who advised me to drop you in some snake pit. Hearing you
scream in the night. The suicide attempts. The look of ungodly terror in your eyes when I, or anyone, tried to show a
little affection. And you're asking me to feel guilty?"

"You're the one who hired them!" Eva cried.

"You're a child in these matters . . ."

"Bullshit!" She flung an arm my way. "After all he's said today, you have the goddam nerve to preach to me? Without
your help the Kleins would probably have ended up in a padded cell, where they belonged. So you put them on your payroll and got burned. You lost your wife. You received your
daughter as damaged goods. But you still had one more
game to play!"

I rose from my desk. "Eva, cut it out!"

She ignored me, pacing before her father. Her shadow swung back and forth across the skeletal face.

"You could play gangster! All in the name of sweet vengeance. How delightful to be a righteous killer. Was it a thrill? Did it give you a kick, Father?"

"Are you telling me you don't feel anything? After what they did?"

Eva stood still, gulping in air. "It's a little late, isn't it? I'm not sorry they're dead, except when I think how they died. But I can't nuture hate for the rest of my life. I'll leave that to you."

Ryker said nothing. Air rasped through his windpipes. His eyes were oddly triumphant, trapped in a dying body.

"Whatever anyone says, they're gone. They paid very painfully."

My wife glared at me. She was angry—really angry—like I hadn't seen her in years. And I knew why. Disgust over this day of thrust-and-parry.

Well, she was right. I felt a little disgusted myself. I said to Ryker: "There's one thing you've forgotten."

"What?"

"Who killed John McFarland?"

"McFarland! I had nothing to do with it. He saved Eva's life!"

"That's right. You don't have a motive. So the question remains. Who killed him?"

"Son, what are you saying?"

I regarded him mildly. "I haven't said anything, have I? I can't state for sure who killed McFarland; not anything I could prove in court. But the prime suspect is Albert Klein."

Mike Rogers snapped to attention. "What!"

"Or Martha Klein." My shoulders shrugged. "Either or both. I don't know."

"Goddamit!" Ryker spat. "What do you mean?"

His voice still rang in my ears as I sighed. "Albert and Martha Klein aren't dead."

31

A low growl bubbled from the depths of his chest. "What are you trying to pull, Hall?"

"Nothing. I merely stated a fact."

"'Fact' shit! The fact is that Petacchi killed both of them!"

"No, Mr. Ryker. Alfredo Petacchi took credit for two murders in Honolulu because the victims were identified as Albert and Martha Klein."

"Christ, what are you talking . . ."

"Tom," I said, "will you please explain?"

He unclipped a Thermofax copy from his notebook and showed it to Ryker. "This is an FBI missing persons report dated January 25, 1942, made by a Margaret C. Kerans of Glendale, California. Her father, Mr. Brian G. Winter, age fifty-two, left Los Angeles that previous November twenty-fourth on Pan American Clipper Flight 208, headed for Honolulu as the first step in a long overdue vacation. The plane arrived safely in Hawaii, but neither she nor anyone else has seen Brian Winter since . . ."

Turning away from the great bloated clouds racing past the sunlit window, Brian Winter reclined his chair, held both hands over his eyes, and listened to his thoughts.

Forget her. You're on a holiday. That trip to the islands you always promised the kids you'd take. Forget the mastectomies and the X-rays and the doctors with their hearty, taxidermic smiles. Forget the radium treatments and the morphine and her gray dry skin and the look in her eyes the last time you saw her.

Forget the funeral, with the black Cadillac limousines and the lilies and the damp words of pity and the fifty-dollar-a-minute pieties and her thin body, the raven-black wig against the purple satin, wrapped in a Nieman-Marcus suit, the face smeared with rouge, pink and waxy, like a freak out of the circus . . .

Winter bolted from his seat and unsteadily wobbled toward the first-class lounge. A blue-uniformed stewardess smiled in casual concern, then let him pass. Patting his forehead with a silk handkerchief, he settled on a couch.

"Anything I can get you, sir?" Another stewardess bent down to him.

"A . . . a Beefeater's and tonic, please."

As she hustled away, he leaned back, breathing slower and taking vague comfort at the spinning props and roaring engines beyond the window.

Winter looked up at the middle-aged couple playing euchre across the aisle.

"Your drink, sir."

"Oh! Thanks."

Holding the glass in one hand, Winter listened to the tinkling ice cubes and watched the couple. She grinned wickedly as her husband failed to make his third trick.

"Ha! Two points for me. You oughta go back to playing Fish!"

"I'd be even better off if you stopped cheating."

"Sour grapes! Nothing but *kvetching*."

Winter smiled as the man redealt each of them five cards. Midwesterners, he thought. Airborne toward that time-of-your-life vacation. No, maybe East Coast. New York? Jersey?

"Excuse me."

Winter blinked away his daze. "Yes?"

"I'm sorry," the woman beamed, "but you look so lonely sitting there I couldn't help but noticing. Would you like to join us?"

"Well, I . . ."

"Oh, I'm sorry!" She flushed. "I'm Martha Klein and this is my husband, Albert."

"How 'do."

"Uh, hello." Winter shook Klein's bearish hand. "I . . . I wouldn't want to impose . . ."

"Oh, come on!" he boomed. "You do know how to play, don't you?"

"Yes." Winter scooted into a chair facing the table between the Kleins.

"You know Railroad?"

He scratched the back of his head. "I'm a little rusty . . ."

"Cutthroat, then! You know that?"

Winter nodded.

"Fine!" Albert slapped him on the back. "Cutthroat it is!"

Three hours passed and the doodling on the score pad reached toward the bottom of the page.

Martha Klein looked up from her cards. "Well, so you're a widower, you poor man." She clucked her tongue at Albert. "Lately it seems like so many men are losing their wives."

Winter took no pleasure in picking up the trick. "One of the hazards of getting old."

"I'm afraid so. That's why Al and I decided to take this trip."

Albert grunted. "Are you going to play, or have you turned into a pillar of salt?"

"Oh, hush up!" She turned back to Winter. "We scrimped and saved for the kids year after year. Finally we decided it was our turn, before it was too late."

"You're very wise." Winter focused unseeingly at his cards. "I waited just one year too long."

"Yep." Albert made the fifth trick, then entered his three

points for the march. "Time steals up on you. After Martha and me got rescued from the *Titantic,* we never took so much as the next sunrise for granted."

"Really?" Winter glanced up in interest as he passed the turn-up for trump.

"Really. And here we are, nearly thirty years later, playing euchre at ten thousand feet." He chuckled. "Life's funny sometimes."

Winter straightened in his chair. "Are you kidding about being on the *Titanic?*"

"What? Hell, no!" Albert scowled as his wife made the trick. "God's Truth!"

Four hours later the Clipper landed at Honolulu Airport and the Kleins had become "Al" and "Martha" to Brian Winter. He grabbed his two-suiter from the terminal's baggage claim and looked rather forlornly out upon the stormy night on the other side of the windows.

Martha Klein's face was sympathetic. "Where will you be staying, Mr. Winter?"

"The Royal Hawaiian."

"Oh! We're booked at the Moana. Practically neighbors! Would you like to have dinner with us tonight?"

About to beg off, Winter took another look at the desolate terminal.

"Why yes, Martha. I'd love it."

Brian Winter was drunk. Roaringly. Rum and vodka and pineapple juice poured from the Trader Vic's bar in an unceasing flow of deadly "tropical coolers" which resembled a Carmen Miranda headdress. Canny bastards, these Hawaiians!

He giggled while red blowfish lamps and rattan walls wheeled around him. The Kleins swam up from the bottom of a wine-dark pool.

". . . one last drink!" Al was saying. "We've still got some champagne left."

"Champagne?" Winter held his head. "On top of all this booze? My God, Al . . ."

The Tattinger '32 frothed pinkly in each of the upheld glasses.

"A toast!" Albert Klein laughed.

Martha sidled closer to Winter. "What to?"

"To us. True-blue, but fading fast!"

Foam trickled down his throat as Brian Winter laughed and laughed, unaware of Martha Klein's fingers snatching the passport from his jacket.

Brian Winter told the Kleins the bad news when they met for breakfast at the Royal Hawaiian.

Al frowned in sympathy. "When did you notice it missing?"

"This morning. I hung up my jacket and went through the pockets, but no passport. I searched everywhere; the poor maid turned the room upside down." He swirled cream into his coffee. "I simply don't understand why anyone would steal something like that."

"Maybe you just misplaced it," Martha eagerly offered.

"'Misplaced it' and then some. I'm going to go to the State Department and file a report . . ." His voice trailed off into concern. "Al, what's the matter? You don't look so good."

"I said the same thing myself." Martha worriedly felt her husband's forehead. "Maybe we should see the doctor here . . ."

He pushed her away. "Pipe down, woman! Jesus, you'll have the hearse coming any minute!" Sighing, he nursed his coffee. "It's called a hangover, my dear."

As the waiter approached with orange juice, Al pointed a finger at Winter. "Don't let me throw a wet blanket over your vacation. Martha wanted to go see the Pali this morning. You two can run along and let me die in peace."

"I shouldn't leave you alone," she said.

"Bull." He chucked the keys of their rented car across the table. "Brian, take the Ford and have a good time. You can even check out the State Department on the way home."

The waiter passed juice glasses to the Kleins and started to walk toward Winter.

"Allow me," Albert said, taking the glass off the tray. A tiny white pellet hidden between his index and middle finger dropped into the juice as he passed it to Winter's hand.

"Well, if you're sure you want to stay . . ."

"I'll cope, with a little luck." He rubbed his temples and watched Winter down the juice. "Just take the concerned Mrs. Klein away. As the Eskimos say, she's all yours."

Hedges of syringa lined the soft shoulders of the Pali Highway as the Ford chugged up the Nuuanu Valley.

"Beautiful, isn't it?"

Martha Klein nodded. "If I could only grow them like that back in St. Petersburg."

Winter glanced away from the wheel. "Homesick?"

"Oh, gracious no!" She sighed. "I can't wait to see the Pali. From all the pictures I've seen, it must be breathtaking."

"Breathtaking and full of bloody history," he snorted. "Like most landmarks."

"I don't like to think about things like that," Martha said in gentle disapproval.

The car rounded a slow curve. As Winter turned into the straightway he suddenly winced.

"Maybe I shouldn't have eaten breakfast. Seems to be kicking back on me."

"Is that a fact?"

Trembling, his lips parted. "I don't feel so good . . ."

From that moment Winter was unable to talk. Sinking on the seat, he wretched over and over, hands sliding off the wheel.

The car steamrollered down the road as Martha Klein grabbed the wheel. She kicked his writhing feet from the pedals. A low blubbering sound drooled out of his mouth, then faded when she brought the car under control.

She glanced both ways. The Ford had the highway to itself. Quickly she drove into the roadside ditch, switched off the engine, then turned the key back to the ignition position.

Brian Winter lay facedown. She straightened him up, pulled the doctored passport from her purse and slipped it into his breast pocket. In one swift moment he had become the late Albert Klein.

She gently felt for the pulse in his throat. The eyes had no more expression than two pieces of carved soap.

Satisfied, Martha Klein grabbed Winter by the lapels and flung his head against the windshield.

Glass flew—delicate snowflake patterns crackling through the pane. The fissures radiated back to a red dripping center.

She dropped the body and picked up a glass sliver. Carefully inspecting herself in the mirror, she gave her face and arms a few strategically placed cuts.

Martha let the sliver tinkle to the floor. Except for the metallic pinging of heat dissipating under the hood, there was silence.

She left the car and started walking down the highway toward Honolulu. Martha cast a wary eye on the big gray clouds boiling over the mountain crests, but she plodded confidently onward. Rain or no rain, a car was going to show. She had her story all prepared. It was only a matter of time.

32

". . . as usual, Albert and Martha chose their victim with exquisite care," I said. "Brian Winter was recently widowed, unattached, and unknown in Hawaii. Of course, he also bore a rough physical resemblance to Albert Klein.

"No doubt, he found them charming. As you know, Eva, they could turn good cheer on and off at will. It was child's play to sweep Winter into a fast vacation friendship. And, in a carefree moment, very simple to snatch up his passport. The Kleins always had a talent for forgeries. In the privacy of their hotel room they merely airbrushed out the signature and pertinent information on Brian Winter and substituted Albert Klein's. Soon after, they slipped something into Winter's food or drink before he took a nice Sunday drive with Martha.

"The bitch." I smiled bitterly. "That bitch with the trickling tears and the voice crackling with shell-shocked grief. I can still hear her. 'My husband did not have a heart attack. He was murdered; poisoned. You've got to find them, officer. You've got to find whoever did it.'

"So the ambulance came and took the body away and, lo

and behold, the doctors diagnosed nicotine sulfate poisoning."

I stared up at the ceiling, then sighed and rubbed my eyes. "And I bought it. At least the part that mattered. I was twenty years old and *so* damned worldly. Martha Klein was filed under 'Distraught but Harmless.' I still believed it when I went to pick her up at the Moana Hotel, where she and Albert had finished disposing of yet another newly acquired friend."

Reaching into my desk drawer, I pulled out a green glass bud vase wrapped in a clear plastic bag. "This belonged to a maid at the Moana Hotel named Catherine Maurois, who was HPD's prime suspect in the murder of Martha Klein. She called in sick to her manager and went home early in the afternoon of November thirtieth, a few hours before I discovered the . . . corpse in Room 307." My finger shook as I set the vase on the blotter. "No one ever saw her again. She followed Brian Winter into limbo. But I was lucky enough to get this vase from her daughter. Tom and his people at the Yard were able to lift some good latent prints."

Tom cleared his throat. "There are prints belonging to a half dozen different people on that vase. But at least two—a right thumb and little finger—match those in the HPD and FBI file. The Late Great Martha Klein, needless to say."

William Ryker looked very ill.

My words came slowly. "It's not hard to imagine how Martha Klein drew Catherine Maurois into her confidence. Some kind words, along with a big tip.

"'Oh, my dear, it's so refreshing to receive real service these days! You've been simply priceless. What is your manager's name? I'll certainly pass a good word on to him!'

"Once Catherine Maurois gave Martha that information, her remaining time on this earth could be measured in minutes. All she had to do was turn her back on the bereaved widow. Just long enough for Martha to blow her spine into little pieces with a silenced .twenty-five.

"Then a call down to the manager, Mr. Pendergast, with a voice disguised through a handkerchief. Followed by a second call to her beloved Albert, wherever he was hiding at the time. Would he please come and help 'tidy up'? "

I struggled to speak, ignoring the foul taste in my mouth. "The police had to be able to identify the body solely on the basis of fingerprints. Of course, Catherine Maurois' prints were all over Room 307, since she tended it day in and day out. That simplified the task. All they had to do was wipe Martha Klein's passport clean, then press it into the hands of the dead woman. Maybe some extra items for good measure—luggage handles, cosmetics, watchbands. Also, they had to remember to scrub clean the belongings of Albert Klein. The police might never check them against the prints of Brian Winter, but the Kleins hadn't lived so long by taking chances.

"So. One more thing to do before slipping out through the side entrance of the Moana Hotel. One of them peeled off a rubber sheet on the mattress, while the other took their dress carrier from the closet. Then they rolled Catherine Maurois onto the sheet." I heard my voice going thin and reedy. "Grabbing the sharp knives . . . maybe the same ones that sliced artichokes and salami in their St. Petersburg store . . . Albert was always strong, but we shouldn't forget Martha's resourcefulness . . ."

". . . Norman," said Eva, "this isn't necessary . . ."

". . . they worked swiftly but carefully, almost like surgeons. Nothing could splash beyond the sheet, you see. Swing and chop and dice until Catherine Maurois was a jigsaw puzzle no one could ever put together . . ."

"Stop it," my wife pleaded quietly.

". . . then roll the sheet over the remains, like folding a tortilla . . ." I chuckled wildly. "Finally, one at each end, they eased the mess they made into the dress carrier and hung it in the closet. Such a surprise for the person who finds it! What juicy headlines!"

Something in my face must have told everyone in the den not to offer lame words of understanding. I poured myself another whiskey, took a generous slug, then sat and waited until I could continue.

Tom's voice blessedly filled the void. "This July Norman and I were granted an exhumation order on the Honolulu grave of 'Albert Klein' . . ."

". . . Martha really planned ahead," I explained dully. "She had all the arrangements laid out with a local undertaker. That body had to be planted in the ground before the wrong people, such as Fred and Mima Heinley, could come pay their respects."

"Naturally," Tom said, "we couldn't get any fingerprints from a twenty-year-old corpse. But, by a stroke of luck, Margaret Kerans is still alive. At the time, she was still keeping vigil for her father. Mrs. Kerans helped us in every way she could, even though she must've known where our investigation would lead. Through her, we obtained the medical records of her father at the Physicians and Surgeons Hospital in Glendale. Brian Winter had a left clavicle broken in two places during the Battle of the Somme. Those hairline cracks still show on the skeleton of 'Albert Klein.'"

He stopped, waiting for me to pick up the trail of the story.

"I didn't enjoy severing those last threads of hope, any more than I liked telling Catherine Maurois' daughter the facts she knew but never wanted to hear. But it was especially hard for Mrs. Kerans. You see, she had been clinging to a single mystifying lead. The FBI head discovered that Brian Winter had boarded Pan Am Clipper Flight 702, leaving Honolulu on the evening of December 6, 1941, for Los Angeles. Strangely, he was now in the company of a Mrs. Edith Winter.

"Mrs. Kerans was distraught. The poor girl actually thought her father had met and married a woman in a whirl-wind Hawaiian courtship. But Mr. and Mrs. Winter stepped off that plane in L.A. and simply evaporated. Neither the FBI nor private detectives ever picked up the scent."

Against my will I found myself smiling. "You know, Albert and Martha—I refuse to call them 'Brian and Edith'—had one of the narrowest getaways on record. History was always snipping at their heels. First the *Titanic,* then Pearl Harbor. The Pan Am Clipper that lifted off the Honolulu runway on Saturday night passed within spitting distance of Admiral

Nagumo's fleet, cruising off Oahu. Ten hours later they would've been sealed tight on the island. I doubt very much if they could've pulled off their shell game with corpses under the military curfew.

"But Alfredo Petacchi *was* left behind, just as I was, to sift through the rubble of red tape and 'official inquiries.' Of course, he and his men were completely baffled. He had followed the Kleins to Hawaii for one reason, and now someone had seemingly beaten him to the punch. He was, I'm sure, suspicious as hell, but the HPD *did* make what seemed like a definite ID of the bodies. So Petacchi accepted the kindness of fate with good grace. Naturally he embroidered on the truth when he reported back to you, Mr. Ryker. I'm sure it must have been an unusual experience for him—boasting of two murders he never committed."

Ryker wouldn't reply, but his body tightened like a coiled watch spring.

"So Petacchi got his reward," I sighed, "which effectively sealed the lid on the whole affair for another twenty years. Albert and Martha bubbled up into polite society on the mainland with new names and backgrounds. To this day I still don't know where they went and who they became. I don't suppose it's terribly important. They didn't emerge into the foreground until this January, when the *Marianas* and *Neptune* discovered the *Titanic* and the Ryker name was plastered once again on the front pages. I'd give a good deal to have seen their faces when they learned about the project and that I was going to write the background story. Old Home Week, you might say."

Pacing in front of the desk, I said, "Al and Martha certainly didn't waste any time. That same day the story broke, I was deluged by reporters over the phone, only some of whom I personally know. I was able to give most of them the cheerful brush-off, but one man—ostensibly from AP—wouldn't drop it, so I offhandedly told him I was going to St. Petersburg for an interview.

"The wrong reply to the wrong person at the wrong time. I can't prove it, but I'm sure that Albert Klein was on the other end of the line. No other explanation makes sense. He was the only person to know that my flying to St. Pete meant a meeting with the Heinleys. That in itself might not seem threatening to Al and Martha, but I certainly bore watching."

I held up three papers to Ryker. "These are passenger lists of three flights I took in January. Delta from Idlewild to St. Petersburg, National from St. Pete back to New York, and a Pan Am from New York to Adelaide, Australia, via Honolulu. Looking down all these lists, we come across a name in common. Besides mine, that is. 'Mr. Walter Shirer.' I could dismiss the coincidence on two flights, but not three.

"Albert Klein didn't have to worry about being recognized, since I've never met the man. Theoretically, I suppose I might've spotted the same elderly gentleman on all three trips, but I have no memory for faces of fellow travelers unless someone is sitting in the next seat. Sometimes not even then.

"'Walter Shirer' must've checked with the charter company in Adelaide to know I was scheduled to fly to Coober Pedy. Albert has always been enterprising. He took a plane to Mabel Creek, then hired a Land Rover to pay John McFarland a visit. I suppose he imagined himself having settled a grudge with McFarland by blowing his skull off. It's hard to anticipate a mind like that. He must've worried about what McFarland might tell me. Perhaps he was even a little frightened."

I turned to Ryker. "That's the last known whereabouts of Albert Klein. Tom and I have beaten the bush, but they're keeping well hidden. Waiting for another crack at those diamonds. Just like you, Mr. Ryker. Persisting in the old shopworn follies right to the end."

His lips drew back. "You miserable bastard. Do you have the slightest idea what you've done?"

"To you? Yes, I think so."

"I had them. They were mine." A faint tremor shook his face. "Every night I prayed. Until the early hours of the morning. 'Give them to me,' I asked. What was the sin? Wasn't I justified?

"Then He answered my prayers. After more than twenty

years. It was worth it. All the hell. They were going to pay.
And I could die a happy man . . ."

His voice faded as he sat staring at his memories. The poor
maligned father. The gods had frowned upon him.

I stood and watched the spinning tape reels, wondering if
I would ever have the stomach to play the recording again.

"You know, Mr. Ryker, there's a way to get them back."

September 25, 1962

HALIFAX (AP) Over $5 million worth of uncut diamonds
were recovered today from the R.M.S. *Titanic* by the bathyscaph *Marianas* in what may be the most important salvage find in recorded history.

Debeers' Diamond Experts in London, when informed
of the discovery, hesitated to make any appraisal without
seeing the stones, but estimate that the gems' background
alone will raise the price five to ten times over their original
value.

According to the captain of the *Marianas*, Phillip Toffler,
the bathyscaph found the diamonds in a glass apothecary
jar deep within the remnants of the *Titanic*'s B Deck
cabins.

After the stones were returned to the research ship *Savonarola*, the news was relayed to industrialist-in-exile William A. Ryker, backer of the project, who expressed surprise and delight at the discovery.

"Of course, we had no idea such a thing was aboard the
Titanic," Ryker said. "There's no written record of these
diamonds by any of the authorities on the sinking. We may
have uncovered a rich historical vein, as well as a financial
one."

The diamonds are being flown by helicopter to Halifax,
where they will be transferred for shipment to London.
Once there, experts from Boucheron will appraise the
stones, cut them, and eventually arrange for their auction.

According to a Boucheron spokesman, the diamonds will
be on public display for the next two weeks in their London
headquarters.

The diamond find of the century sat surrounded by purple velvet and glass. It was a star attraction, beyond any
doubt, but a star attraction in a refined and very British
mode.

No sticky-fingered kids pressed noses against the glass. No
tourists snapped flash pictures. The red ropes around the
display and the impassive, hulking security guard discouraged such vulgar rubbernecking. But the elegant crowd
circulating through Boucheron was definitely curious.

After a quick perusal of the routine merchandise—
Fabergé eggs and emerald necklaces—the gentlemen and ladies stationed themselves in front of the case. Gazing at the
rather ugly uncut stones beneath the glass, they would read
the accompanying plaque:

> These diamonds, of unknown origin, were recovered
> from the R.M.S. *Titanic* on September 25, 1962, by the
> bathyscaph *Marianas,* belonging to the Ryker International
> Corporation.
>
> Owned by William A. Ryker, the diamonds are believed
> to originate from South Africa. Estimates on their uncut
> value begin at 2 million pounds. Considering their histori-
> cal value, the diamonds are currently appraised at any-
> where from 20 to 30 million pounds.
>
> Boucheron wishes to express thanks to William A. Ryker
> for allowing the public display of the collection while they
> are here for cutting, a final appraisal, and auction.

Finished with the reading, the public would eye the diamonds with cool hunger, then meander out the door.

I watched this ritual from a television monitor in the security office. Four days of eyestrain was all I had to show for
standing guard at this damn tube.

I was still feeling sorry for myself when I glanced at the
screen and saw that my waiting was over.

An obliging gentleman-customer held the door for her.
Martha used a cane and hobbled painfully.

My fingers jabbed the videotape machine's "Record" button as I leaned forward. The camera, hidden high in the corner, followed her wandering around the display. I zoomed in on her face.

There she was, sweet and grandmotherly. I found myself grinning. She was too good to be true.

Martha moseyed around Boucheron, giving her just-passing-through smile to the clerks. I squinted at the picture tube as she discreetly appraised the case and the guard. In a few casual glances she fixed the location of all exits in her mind. Martha Klein blinked thoughtfully at the photo cells rimming the diamonds. She even stared into my eyes, searching for hidden cameras. I felt nape hairs bristling on my neck.

Her face registered polite awe at the sight of the diamonds. Long moments passed. She seemed to be satisfied, and turned to go.

I grabbed the microphone of the transceiver at my side. "This is Norman. She's here. She's leaving just now."

My words were beamed to the unmarked patrol car parked across from Boucheron's front entrance.

"Relax, Norman," said Tom. "We see her. A woman in a beige suit, walking with a cane."

"That's right."

"We're on her." Sergeant Rand's voice briskly rattled the speaker. "Just stay there. We'll keep in touch."

"Yeah. Do that."

They both laughed, cutting me off.

I must have converted five pounds of fat to sweat before they called back.

"Yes, this is Hall. Go ahead."

Tom's voice was tense. "We've found both of them, Norman—702, London Arms Apartments."

33

Prowling through Soho at one in the morning, when the fog's as thick as boiled Kleenex, does wonders for the nervous system.

Fidgeting in the front seat of an ancient Daimler patrol car, I watched the hood plow into walls of eiderdown and prayed this night errand wouldn't blow up in our faces.

The orange parking lights, oversized and blazing as in all European cars, picked out macabre images which scuttled into the shadows like hermit crabs. Gothic iron fences with arrowhead crowns crept by our flanks. A sycamore, pitifully naked except for a coat of smog. Cobblestone gutters and cigarette butts. Three Teddies woven out of gray blankness who closed ranks and insolently watched our passing.

The car swept past Old Compton Street, pushing deeper into Soho. Tom, Rand, and Sergeant Morley, our driver, all had that same look I'd seen on veteran GI's at Messina and Anzio—a sweaty-palmed expectancy.

"I must be certifiable," Tom moaned lowly, "being sweet-talked into this lunacy."

"You'll get ulcers yet," I chided. "Didn't I promise to stay out of everyone's way?"

"Norman, you're a professional meddler. Don't try looking guileless and obliging; it's too late in the game."

"Sir?" Morley broke into the conversation. "Is this our turn ahead?"

Tom squinted through the windshield. "No, the next one down. Left turn. The apartment's on the right."

The Daimler slithered around the corner and sighed past fire hydrants and the spattering of lighted windows which formed a crazy-quilt pattern in the fog.

Tom pointed across the street. "Here's the place."

We rocked gently to a stop.

He leaned forward, murmuring gravely into my left ear. "If I ordered you to wait here with Morley, would you stay put?"

"I hope the question's hypothetical. You know very well what this means to me."

"That's not what I asked, Norman."

"Then I can only shrug and make no promises. You wouldn't want me roaming around alone. The streets aren't safe at this hour."

Tom uttered a weary monosyllable. "'Dogged' is the word that describes you, Norman. And 'relentless.' Like tidal erosion and the coming of the next ice age." Easing open the door, his lips bent in a frigid smile. "Come along, my friend. Just be damn sure you stay behind both Sergeant Rand and myself. 'Bringing up the rear,' it's called."

"An honored position, Tom. You won't even know I'm there."

"That's my fervent wish," he muttered as we got out of the car.

The Daimler's doors shut with a muted thump. A freighter despondently lowed from the Thames. Piccadilly Square distantly grumbled, even at this hour, with omnibuses and taxis. A cricket preened its legs, then shut up. No eyes peered from lighted windows. None that could be seen, anyway.

Across dank cobblestones we approached the apartment building. Room 702 on the seventh floor. No lights.

A pale yellow glow filtered sickly through frosted panes unimaginatively etched LONDON ARMS APTS. Empty milk bottles sprawled on seven grimy steps leading from the sidewalk.

I shut the front door behind me. Wood steps painted a cheap light green curved up and out of sight. An elevator also yawned open. The apartment smelled of human hair and boiled cabbage.

Sergeant Rand seemed oblivious to the squalor, his face flushed with the sweet smell of pursuit. "Do we take the lift?"

Tom nodded. He punched the button as I slipped through the doors.

Two . . . three . . . four . . . five . . . six . . . seven.

The doors clattered open like old boiler plates, revealing a gray corridor, finger-smudged and muggy with gas heat.

Numbers ran to the right. 706 . . . 704 . . . 702. A corner apartment.

Tom's knuckles rapped the door. "Police. Open up, please."

Silence. He knocked again.

"Open up, Klein."

No answer.

Sergeant Rand and Tom backed up two paces, then hit the door with one blow.

The architect of the London Arms must have been in cahoots with the local gentry. The door was the only sound part of the building.

"Once more!" he bellowed. "Give us a hand, Norman."

The chain latch flew across the grimy flat as we burst through amid splintering wood. My eyes searched out details in the gloom.

An empty rumpled bed. Wind stirring curtains through an open window. Martha Klein's cane propped against the coffee table.

I stood stark still and heard footsteps clanging up the fire escape.

Either I set the land speed record or my companions tripped. I found myself charging up the stairs that faded into the fog.

Suddenly I seemed to soar above above the fog like a jetliner over a cloud bank as I reached the roof of the building.

A bumper crop of TV antennas sprouted in the moonlight. The Kleins crouched on the other side of the metallic jungle. They sprang like two cornered badgers and sprinted for the edge of the rooftop.

I immediately grasped their plan. London Arms Apartments did not stand alone but were flanked by twin sisters, each separated by a ten-foot gap. Between the apartments was a makeshift oak beam that served as an emergency walkway across the roofs.

Martha scampered across to the neighboring roof, then Albert followed. As I jumped on the ledge, he kicked the beam into the fog-cushioned chasm between the apartments.

Tom and Rand puffed and wheezed next to me. "What the hell happened?"

I didn't answer. I was halfway down the fire escape before I heard them following.

The fog crept over my head as I stumbled down the stairs. Flat iron bars forming the fire landing loomed beneath my feet. My eyes blinked blearily in the fog as I fumbled through the windowsill.

I took one look and fought the temptation to go back the way I came.

Have you ever been in the middle of a drunken, carousing party? A real orgy which ends in at least three divorces? The swirling bodies in the apartment were bawling and screaming like the return of Bacchanalia.

Gray matter clicked and I realized they were yelling at me. Prune-faced cronies. One old man with incredible John L. Lewis eyebrows. Pitiful children scampering around with runny noses.

The oldest and ugliest whore in the world breathed beer in my face. "What the 'ell is all this? Can't the decent folk get some sleep around here!"

Decent folk. Ah yes—the Kleins' neighbors. Everyone and his aunt must have come to see the show.

The iron steps clanging behind me wiped away momentary blankness. I dodged around the old woman with the beer breath and tore down the hall.

Bodies cringed out of my way like cows brunted from the

path of a train. I gave a longing glance at the elevator. No time. As I headed for the stairs, a little kid in matted clothes grabbed my trouser leg and hung tight. Swearing feebly, I pried him off, tossed him at his mother and careened down the steps.

Tom's ragged breathing was behind me.

"How many exits does the building next door have?" I panted.

"It's just like this one. Fire escapes on every side."

Then they could get away by four exits. Plus the front door.

Steps advanced and receded beneath my feet—three at a time. Fifth floor. Heads peeked out of doors as we twisted down the next flight.

There were no bystanders on the lower floors, not that I much cared. Hollow wood steps, clomping like horse hoofs, formed a dull mallet jarring my skull.

A dusty letter racing by said "Fourth." Then it was "Third," "Second," and "Lobby." Back where we started and nothing to show for it except fallen arches.

Tom slid open the lobby door. "I don't see anyone."

What did you expect, I thought bitterly, as the full hopelessness of the situation hit me. "You can't see beyond your nose."

The fog had lifted very slightly, but there was no more visibility than the Black Hole of Calcutta.

Tom and Sergeant Rand dove into the darkness. I hesitated a moment, hearing their feet cracking twigs on the sidewalk, before scrambling in pursuit.

I caught up with Sergeant Rand, standing alone.

"Where's Tom?"

"Checking back with Sergeant Morley."

Two hot orange eyes bore down upon us. Shielding my brow against the glare, I saw the chromium grimace of the Daimler grill. Tom materialized by the side of the patrol car, wielding a flashlight resembling a blunderbuss. He took careful aim.

Pearly light splashed into the cul-de-sac between the apartments. Shadows of the fire escape crisscrossed across the alley like prison bars as two amorous cats caterwauled over garbage cans and a dirty picket fence.

"Nothing here," Tom said unnecessarily. "Let's go."

The approaching apartment building was a black monolith against a field of charcoal gray. Window boxes, their contents folded up for the night, neatly faced the street. One corner of sandstone was immortalized by an engraved heart proclaiming, "Barney Williams Loves Wilma Rutlage." I was feverishly wondering about Barney and Wilma's ancient passions when I noticed that the 'G' of the glass doorway spelling out BRIGHTON GARDENS was blotted by a man's silhouette.

My hand grasped Tom's shoulder as I pointed. He moved to comply, but it was much too late.

The Kleins shot through the door, eyes glittering. Wheeling about, Albert spotted us, grabbed his wife's arm, and bounded to the pavement. Tom darted after them as Martha lost her footing, but they straightened up and plunged into invisibility.

"Listen to me," he yelled, "both of you! We've blocked the streets. No one's going anywhere!"

Tom's empty words echoed among the encircling buildings.

"You'll never make it, Martha!" I cried desperately. "Tell Al to give up!"

We stood still, listening for any reply.

The answering shot tore through the air like a rusty scythe. Hitting the cobblestone pavement, I heard an angry yowling ricochet that splintered concrete by my ear. As the sound ebbed to silence, the fog mooched back in place, smothering all traces of violence.

Even as I jumped to my feet, bedroom windows glowed with curiosity. All we need, I thought savagely, are spectators.

The fog blanket was fraying at the edges, twisting into ground level thunderheads one moment and thin gauze the next. It was a fog that distorted sound badly.

Breathing through my open mouth to avoid telltale wheezing, I concentrated upon the unearthly quiet. Nothing. Then the faint mewing of a baby, cut short with harsh words and a slamming door. A tepid trickle of water gurgling down a gutter. And something else. Sharp rustling. Then silence numbing my brain. Another rustle. Then another. I couldn't resist a grim smile at the sound of heels clicking on the leaf-strewn sidewalk.

Tom appeared from the orange gloom of the squad car. "I guess we lost them."

"Shut up," I said. "They're at the end of the intersection on the right side."

"How . . ." he began, then thought better of it, turning to Rand. "Sergeant, get back to the car and radio backup units in Piccadilly. We're going to have to track them on foot. Get Morley to follow us."

Fog rushed to fill the hole where Rand had been.

"Norman," he whispered, "stay on the right side of the street, parallel with me."

Running into the misty shroud, Tom, Rand, and Morley faded in my mind. There was just me and the Kleins in the dark. I could hear their footsteps, which had abandoned all pretense; thrashing and stumbling down the pavement. I couldn't tell how much of a head start they had, and I began yearning for Sergeant Rand's youth; at least the physical advantages.

I also started wishing for some firepower to match the Kleins. Not for myself; I haven't pulled a trigger since the war. The experience was like a purgative; a necessary but deplorable evil to be repeated only in the direst of emergencies. But as for Tom and Rand . . .

All those TV documentaries flashed through my head. See the genteel, unarmed bobbies. Guarding the bastions of Pax Britannia with a mere nightstick. How jolly civilized!

But, here and now, I had misgivings. Big ones. In the Old West they called guns "equalizers." More than ever I appreciated the nickname, with all its dreadful implications.

The fog had turned spotty and halfhearted as I paused for breath at a stop sign at the end of Archer Street. Mercury vapor lamps strung out toward Shaftesburg Avenue filled the blackness with brackish pools of light. Two figures under one of the lamps cast long shadows toward me.

Tom jogged across the intersection to the left side of the street. Jesus, I thought, he made a tempting target. Moments later my misgivings came to pass.

A pale yellow flower of light flashed his way. The bullet and its noise blasted Tom off his feet. For one hideous instant arms and legs flailed the air like those strobe photos of race horses with all four hoofs off the ground. Then he crumpled. A wad of old clothes tossed down a laundry chute.

I rushed to him. A red-black blotch fluttered across his left side. My fingers felt his throat. Thub. And again. Once more.

"God," I said painfully. "Just stay still." The orange fog lights swerved our way. "The car's coming. You'll be all right."

Tom groaned wonderingly. Deep neural shock. He didn't realize his arm was a boneless mass.

The car screeched up as I slung him in the back seat and jumped in front. Sergeant Rand looked thunderstruck.

"What the hell happened?"

I didn't bother to answer the obvious. Morley scrambled for the first aid kit. As Rand pulled off Tom's jacket and shirt, I leaned over the seat with a wood stake and bandage and began twisting the tourniquet around his left arm. Mercifully, he was out cold.

Rand blinked in wary approval. "You're pretty handy with that."

I grunted, turning the stake vise-tight.

"Which way were they heading?"

"Down Shaftesburg toward Piccadilly."

He impatiently slapped Morley's shoulder as the driver let out the clutch and growled into first.

My eyes raised. "Aren't we taking him to a hospital?"

Rand chewed on his lower lip. "The bleeding's stopped. Nothing anyone can do for a while. Do you want those two running loose?"

"Fortunately, Sergeant, the decision's not mine to make."

Gears grumbled as we ate up the pavement. The fog was losing ground.

"They'll try to lose themselves in a crowd," he said, leaning anxiously forward, "so the car's useless. The Circus will still have its share of people." His head shook. "God knows how they keep going."

The Daimler squealed on to the avenue. Bawdy signs beckoned patrons to strip shows, folk singers, and jazz sessions. London was no longer a ghost town and everyone on the street was a potential victim. Dark crannies between buildings offered no assistance. How to spot anyone in the crowd? Look for the black suit? A light gray dress? All cats are gray in the dark.

But not gray enough. Cruising slowly past the corner of Shaftesburg and Great Windmill Street, I spotted a familiar head of white hair. "She's over there!"

"This is the police!" grated the megaphone on the car's roof.

They didn't need to be told. I got a glimpse of Albert's snarling face before a gun barrel snapped at the Daimler.

The noise of champagne glasses tossed into a million fireplaces. The windshield collapsed in razor-sharp sheets. Rand I were out of the car and on the sidewalk as Morley pushed the glass off his face and wheeled in closer to the tangle of traffic.

People were everywhere, funneling into Piccadilly, screaming and scattering in terror.

There they were, a few yards ahead, shoveling through the crowd. I flung people aside left and right, cursing and swearing.

Suddenly the Kleins and I burst into the Circus. My mind received disjointed, garbled images of vast walls of light. A giant pendulum carved out a neon path. Grant's Scotch. Gordon's gin. Garish yellow letters of the London Pavillion. Max Factor. Persona Blades. Wrigley's Spearmint Gum; Healthful, Delicious, Satisfying. Young people gathered with nocturnal pigeons around the blackly gleaming Eros Fountain.

The Kleins began a heedless dash through the encircling moat of traffic. Scream of brakes and horns mixed maddeningly with the yelling bystanders. They were trapped in the center of the stream of cars as I bounded into the street.

Angry bawling of English motorists hit my ears as a lane of cheese-box cars jerked sullenly to a stop. A whirlpool of Cortinas, Fords, and Austin-Healys swarmed before me. Albert Klein was just a hood's width away.

I flagged the cars to stop, with negligible results. Furiously jumping on the bumper of an Austin Cooper, I slid over the hood and grabbed his sleeve.

There was a break in the traffic as he smashed the back of his fist into my face and leaped for the curb with Martha. Stumbling off the hood and onto my feet, I couldn't have been more than five yards behind. I remember a vague collage of gaping, incredulous faces.

Jesus, how did they keep the pace! But then, I wasn't the one being hunted.

The Kleins approached a tube entrance as Martha aimed a fearful glance over her shoulder. I grimaced as they charged down the steps. The subway was a rat's warren of endless hidey-holes.

The stairs leading to the Underground belched with Piccadilly fun-seekers. I plowed into their midst. In the background Rand distantly cried, "Police! Move aside!"

They moved, all right. In every way imaginable. There was no time for courtesy. I mowed people down like bowling pins. Where the hell were they? Ten yards down the ramp I got a glimpse of her dress.

Martha's face still held untapped reserves of cunning. She grabbed her husband's arm and rode through the jostling crowd like an icebreaker, disappearing down the second flight of stairs.

I kept pushing through the mob like a salmon swimming upstream and gradually rounded the corner. Blessedly, the flow of people stopped. I struggled the rest of the way on my fading rubber legs as they pushed into the porcelain-tiled catacomb.

"Police! Grab that man!"

His eyes bulged whitely like those of a terrified horse as he broke away from his wife and jumped over the guardrail onto the tracks.

Red-faced and sobbing, Martha Klein collapsed to her knees.

"No, Al! My God, don't leave me alone!"

I had no time for her. Vaulting over the railing, I ran to the crowd leaning over the platform like a chorus line above an orchestra pit.

Albert Klein sprinted down the tunnel. He had barely gone five steps when his left leg caved in under him, his face smashing on the steel rail. Exhausted and dazed, he still managed to look back at his left foot caught on a rail tie. He wrenched desperately at the ankle, lips gnarling in pain, but he was doing nothing but tearing ligaments.

Strange and devious is the human mind. Push-button morality gets people in the damnedest fixes. One moment I watched him flutter like an impaled butterfly, and the next instant I jumped over the railing, tugging at his leg.

Far down the tunnel the northbound train greedily winked at us.

Al thrashed at me, avoiding my grasp.

"Keep still, goddamit! Don't you know the far rail's electrified?"

He stiffened into virtual rigor mortis.

Loosen the shoe. I grappled with the laces. If only those idiots would shut up! What were they worried about? And why was that woman screaming? Couldn't they leave a man in peace?

Red blotches of fatigue clouded my vision and I shook them away. My palm pushed the back of the shoe down over his Achilles' tendon. I ignored his painful grunt. It was coming!

My whole universe was the shoe, the greasy rail tie, and, overwhelming me, the glare and lurching rattle of the train with its twin Cheshire cat eyes.

Less than ten feet away. A burning image of two headlamps, the conductor's horrified face, yanking at the air brakes, and screeching, sparking wheels.

Steam from the air brakes tugged at my trouser cuffs as I jumped and landed on the platform. Either the train or an air pocket buffeted me. A scream from hell tore through my head as red and blue lights flashed and all went black.

As the crowd clustered overhead, my eyes blinked open. Ceiling lamps hung down in greeting and a dark figure loomed in the foreground.

". . . you all right?" Sergeant Rand was asking.

I sat up dazedly. "Is he . . ."

His head shook. "You tried, Mr. Hall. There just wasn't any time."

No time . . . no time . . . no time . . .

His words echoed as I wobbled to my feet. The train was stalled, its scattered occupants craning their heads out the windows. I pushed through the chattering throng on the platform. The conductor and station manager stood at the front of the train, examing the red dripping smear under the front wheels.

You will not throw up, Norman. Besides being un-dignified, it solves nothing. Just take a few deep breaths. Don't try to swallow. Now, one foot at a time, back up and get out of here.

I turned away from Albert Klein and walked slowly across the subway station to his widow.

Martha was curled in a shivering ball. She rased her head at my approach.

"You killed him! It was all your fault! You let him die!"

I let her cry, not answering.

Tears streamed down the wrinkled cheeks. "I did it all for him, you know. All the hiding and killing. I didn't care about it. I wanted to settle down. What would I do with the diamonds? I only wanted to be left in peace!"

Poor, poor Martha Klein. An old repentant soul, now all alone.

"You'll probably get your wish, Martha. All the time in the world to sift through those ancient sins."

I dug in my pocket and tossed one of the Boucheron stones to the floor. She watched my heel grind it into a fine pasty powder that glittered in the lamplight.

Once in Sonora I met a cornered rattlesnake caught, right after a recent kill, with empty venom bags. It was still baring its useless fangs as my friend smashed in its head with a walk-ing stick. At the time I felt a curiously tempered remorse, and I felt the same way now.

"Come on," I said. "Let's go."

Postscript 1

Our story appeared in *World*'s December 16, 1962, issue. To a planet that had flirted with World War III the previous October, our recounting of murder and kidnapping and antediluvian obsessions seemed refreshingly piquant. The magazine pulled out of the red for the first time in six years, and Janice and I found ourselves enduring the buttery good will of Geoffrey Proctor. We banked each bonus check as quickly as possible and tried not to look back.

Eva Ryker and her father shared our front seat on the media roller coaster. Paparazzis prowled her old hideouts in Madrid while she retreated to a rented cottage in Jamaica. I got one post card in January postmarked Kingston: "Greetings," it simply said. "Let me know when the war's over."

But the big guns of the press were really aimed at the Old Man. Columnists and politicos flapped their editorials and subpoenas in a feeding frenzy. Congressmen made lofty speeches on the "corrupting influence of American expatriates." Senate investigations would be made. Bureaucratic cogwheels would grind the Truth exceedingly fine.

William Ryker had been inflicted with the most terrible of all curses; his past transgressions had caught the public fancy.

He responded by putting a double guard at the château's entrance gate and unplugging the phones, while Mike Rogers squirted a squid-cloud of countersuits and indignant denials penned in "high lawyerese." The international courts would grow old and toothless trying to unravel the knots.

Two months after the publication of my story the Ryker Corporation withdrew its sponsorship of the *Titanic* salvage project. Jacques Cousteau, the National Geographic Society, and the Navy Department fell over each other, proclaiming their innocence of any diamond-recovery hoodwinks. The exploration of the sunken ship stumbled to a halt amid the flying of legal fur. One year after the project began the *Neptune* and *Marianas* ended up in moth balls at New Bedford, while the *Savonarola* was written off by Ryker as a tax-deductible donation to the Scripps Institute in La Jolla.

On May 7, 1963, Alfredo Petacchi was shot to death outside the porte-cochère of Miami's Fontainebleau Hotel by two men in a passing De Soto sedan. Neither the car nor the men were seen again. News clippings at the time stressed his long-standing affiliations with the Scalisi Family. Even so, I can't help remembering the quick frozen eyes of William Ryker when he learned of Petacchi's deceit. And the Old Man seemed to set great store in settling old grudges.

Martha Klein suffered a massive cerebral hemorrhage on June 12, 1963, ten days before her first scheduled court appearance in London. She regained consciousness but could no longer speak or walk. The doctors couldn't be sure how much of her mind was intact. Tom Bramel arranged a quiet transfer from prison to a state home in Pimlico. She spent her days sitting by a window overlooking a serene garden of forsythia and poplars. I once went to see her, but she gave no sign of noticing I was alive.

Her only other visitor was the recently widowed Mima Heinley. Fred had left her a tidy sum of money, and she chose to spend a summer holiday in England. Mima held a gentle but unshakable faith in her old neighbor. No one person, she would say, could be responsible for so much evil. The Kleins had been her best friends and she wasn't about to forget it.

So Mima came on visiting days, piloting Martha's wheelchair in the garden and softly chortling over old times.

Martha just smiled. Endlessly.

William Ryker died the day after Thanksgiving, 1963. He chose an unfortunate date of passing. I was still numb from the days of vigil by the television, listening to the endless funeral roll of drums down Pennsylvania Avenue, heralding the fall of Camelot.

The cause of death was listed as "acute pulmonary failure." Newspaper and television obituaries were halfhearted, perfunctory. For the moment, at least, people had lost their appetite for unhappy endings.

I was in Hollywood at the time, doing research on William Cameron Menzies for a forthcoming book about the making of *Gone With the Wind.* The telegram came to my room at the Beverly Wilshire.

"NO DOUBT YOU HAVE HEARD THE NEWS," Eva said. "PLEASE COME HALIFAX FAIRVIEW CEMETERY, NOVEMBER 30, 9 AM AND HELP ME COPE."

Ryker, I later learned, had purchased a plot untold years ago at the Fairview Cemetery, hoping that Clair was among the anonymous graves of *Titanic* victims. As time passed and he learned the truth in painful bits and snatches from Eva, his faith must have faded. But William Ryker did not easily cast aside an idea that had taken root.

* * *

I hate funerals. This isn't a recent conclusion. The Dallas shooting merely reenforced an old prejudice. A tribal rite cooked up to prolong human torment. I stood at the foot of the silver casket with snow in my socks and a white carnation in my lapel, feeling like a damn fool.

There weren't many others. The Old Man had been very specific on that point. No big fuss. An unmarked grave set in the middle of the cemetery, shoulder to shoulder with other faceless victims.

Mike Rogers, Fräulein Slote, and I were the pallbearers. Geoffrey Proctor had canceled at the last moment. Just we three, Eva, the Reverend Thomas Haggarty, and, oddly enough, Ruth and Harold Masterson.

The Reverend muttered his ritual words of consolation. I looked up at the sky. Slate gray, much the same as the first time I came to this place after my release from Victoria General nineteen months ago. A train moaned far down the neighboring tracks, threatening to compete with the Reverend for attention.

" . . . ashes to ashes, dust to dust . . . Amen." It was finished. Mike Rogers pushed a foot treadle and the casket began to sink beneath the surrounding ring of lilies, delphiniums, and tropicana roses.

I felt a hand grasp mine and hold tight. Eva's face was obscured by a huge veiled hat which made her look like a beekeeper in mourning. We stood together and watched the gleaming coffin disappear. Elegant letters were inscribed on the lid: WILLIAM ALFRED RYKER 1877–1963.

Our little group broke formation, leaving the funeral director and his men to finish their work.

"I'll get the car," she whispered, hurrying away.

I caught up with Mike Rogers, threading his way through the maze of headstones.

"Well, Norm . . . " he said, stuffily shaking my hand, "I appreciate your help." Mike kicked the snow into a little mound at his feet. "Even though I don't quite understand it. Why *did* you come?"

"A personal favor. Coupled with a little unwholesome curiosity."

"Whatever your reasons, Mr. Ryker would've been pleased. I think."

An awkward pause. His shoe added to the snow pile.

"So, Mike. What happens next?"

"How's that?"

"To you. And the big career."

He scratched his head. "Oh, I haven't thought about it much. There's enough unfinished business at the Ryker Corporation to tie me up for years."

" . . . if you let yourself be snarled. A bright young man like you must have better things to do besides cleaning out the Old Man's stable."

Mike smiled coldly. "Are you trying to be helpful, Norman? Or merely snotty?"

"A little of both. I have a natural writer's interest in hustlers. They're so much more colorful than the decent mediocre herd."

"Your interest is flattering. Are you going to give me some hallowed advice?"

"Not really. But I was struck by something, standing by the coffin." I pointed over his shoulder at the men with their flying shovels. "Sixty years ago he was just like you. Push and shove to the big time. You saw for yourself all the inner peace it brought him. And here he lies. All in all, not an enviable life."

A double-toned horn blasted in my ear. Looking beyond the cemetery gates, I saw Eva's black-gloved hand waving from the front seat of a red Maserati Ghibli.

"Got to go, Mike. Best of luck."

She was already at the wheel, revving as I slid in the seat. Burned rubber smoked behind us as we screeched around the indignant Cadillac hearse and limousine, speeding down Chishom Avenue.

Eva tore off her veil and tossed it in back. "I want to thank you for coming, Norman. I don't think I could have gotten through all the crap without you."

I smiled as we wheeled onto Connaught Avenue. "I won't say 'my pleasure' because I'd be lying. But I'm not sorry I came." I frowned as we stopped at a signal. "You know, in the end, he seemed so . . . alone."

"He wanted it that way, Norman. I'm not sure he'd approve of your gate-crashing."

"Did he hate me that much?"

"He blamed you for a lot of misery in his life."

"You expect an apology?"

"Hell no." She floored the Maserati through a yellow light. "All his precious schemes. Daddy reveled in his role of puppet-master. Where did it get him?"

"No diamonds, anyway."

"Well, at least there's some justice in the world." Her eyes bleakly surveyed the ice-slick asphalt flashing beneath us. "Some things should be laid to rest. Like the *Titanic*. All the hate and grief because of that ship. Bringing it to light was like indecent exposure."

I glanced at the scar above her right eye. "You kept it covered for fifty years, and it didn't do you much good."

"You're right, of course. Like always. Jesus, your head must ache from being so right all of the time!"

We sat in silence until Eva turned onto Quippool Road. "How's Jan?" she asked.

"Bedridden with a cold. Otherwise she'd have come."

"H'm."

"What does that mean?"

"What does *what* mean?" she replied innocently.

"The grunt of skepticism."

"Must you analyze every last twitch of the eyebrow?"

I didn't answer. She sighed lowly. "It's just that your wife puzzles me. After all, she must wonder about us."

"Maybe. But then, *I* wonder about us. Occasionally."

Eva neatly zipped around a double-parked Ford. "No angry confrontations? No bitchy tantrums of jealousy?"

"Hardly. I told her the truth."

"With a capital T?"

My head nodded.

"And did it Set You Free?"

"More of a long-term parole."

She laughed, spinning the wheel that turned us onto Robie Street.

"What about you, Eva?"

"What about me?"

"You still going to play games? The Rich Heiress dancing on Departed Daddy's grave? It'll get very stale very fast."

"What's this?" She raised an eyebrow my way. "Sermonette?"

"That's about it."

"God, what do you want? A Five Year Plan of my Golden Years?"

"No one's asking you to enter a convent, Eva. But you have to do something besides . . . drift."

"Norman, you really are getting increasingly pompous as the months wear on. Why don't you mind your own business?"

I leaned against the console as the car hooked a left onto South Street, grumbling on its snow tires. "You are my business. You have been since that night on the beach."

"How romantic! I'm swooning."

"Goddamit, Eva! Can't we scrape away the bullshit just this once?"

We braked at a red light. She closed her eyes. "Shut up. Please."

"You lived in a sewer and I threw it in your face. I acted selfishly and I try to shrug off any guilt. But how am I supposed to feel if nothing's changed for you?"

"Norman," she whispered, blinking furiously, "how do you manage to be so stupendously brilliant and idiotic at the same time?"

We looked at each other; it was one of those moments I'd rather not discuss.

The car in back of us honked in protest. Eva gulped at the green light and surged ahead.

We didn't speak until the Maserati turned into the driveway of the Lord Nelson Hotel. Shifting into neutral, Eva let the engine idle, both hands clamped on the wheel.

"Here's the place," she chirped in ghastly brightness.

I got out, then bent down through my open window. "Eva . . . "

"Norman, I know what you'd like me to say. That I'll start off scrubbed and untarnished in a brave new life. But, you know, I turned sixty-two this last birthday. Every time I'm feeling especially courageous, I see that forest of candles on the cake.

"Never too late to grow up, Eva. Just think of the first sixty years as a long, protracted puberty."

Against her will she returned my smile. "You're a bastard, Norman." She kissed my lips. "Don't let the world mellow you."

For a long time I stood and watched the red Maserati dwindle down Bell Road until it was lost in the confetti flurry of snowflakes.

I never saw her again.

Postscript 2
January 7, 1963

Twelve thousand four hundred eighty-two feet under the surface of the Atlantic Ocean the lights went out.

The quartz-halogen lamps stationed for ten months to illuminate the R.M.S. *Titanic* were uprooted by the *Marianas* and *Neptune*. Clenching onto the searchlights with their stainless steel claws, the two bathyscaphs began the slow ascent to the surface.

Their running lights twinkled above the wreckage; four red and green stars fading to blackness as the low vibrations from their propellers ceased to run through the water.

Thus the *Titanic* was left as it had been since the morning of April 15, 1912. Unwanted and abandoned.

The ship has new torch scars along its hull and superstructure, testifying to human meddling. Coins and cups and St. Christophers that had once rested below decks were now lying beneath plate glass in museums. But William Ryker began the exploration of the *Titanic* in search of one particular prize that after ten months remained elusive. The man and the machines at his command had at last given up. And the ship's previous tenants started returning home.

Some had never left. The prawns and lantern fish, among others, stayed with the wreckage during the long months of the salvage project. They scuttled among the passageways and broken funnels, snatching at plankton settling from the surface of the sea.

But many fish stayed away. Adapted to the blackness of the ocean floor, they were frightened by the glare of the lamps, which were, to them, brighter than the light of a thousand suns. Men had to leave before they returned and a normal pattern of life resumed aboard the *Titanic*.

It was in many ways a nightmare world. Generation upon generation hatched and grew and died in the dark bowels of the ship, where once huge men with great glistening torsos had stoked coal into the mouths of blazing boilers. Viper fish with luminescent tendrils for snaring prey prowled through the first-class corridors, only to be devoured by larger and craftier enemies.

One particularly successful predator was a six-year-old male of a type known to man as Melanocetus Johnsoni. His large belly was designed to expand upon swallowing an unusually large victim. The constant search for food had brought him to the *Titanic's* bow, where tiny remnants from the ship's cargo hold littered the silt below. Lurking among low rocks embedded in the sand, his belly scraped against sharp strands of baling wire.

The fish flailed in an instinctive evading maneuver and fled from the unexpected source of pain. He left behind a cloud of sand and silt which quickly resettled on the surface.

The baling wire now freshly covered from sight had once wrapped a crate labeled "Ryker Industries." The original wood had of course dissolved many years earlier, but some of the contents remained intact.

Lying several inches beneath the sand was a glass apothecary jar. A gum label, long since gone, had once designated the jar as containing three dozen of Mrs. Mannfred's Miracle Capsules.

The capsules survived, although seeping seawater had eaten the sugar coating. Each of the three dozen capsules was an uncut diamond. The stones were unperturbed by the elements. By nature, diamonds play a cold and patient game of hide-and-seek.

Two miles above the *Savonarola* was firing its diesels for the trip to Halifax. Those aboard the *Titanic* neither knew nor cared.

The ship and the diamonds sat in the dark and waited.

Forever.